TRUTH INSURRECTED

The Saint Mary Project

Daniel P. Douglas

ISBN: 0990737101
ISBN 13: 978-0990737100
eISBN: 9780990737117
Library of Congress Control Number: 2014914415
Geminid Press, LLC, Albuquerque, NM

ACKNOWLEDGEMENTS

Thank you, A. J. Galdamez, Tim and Lori Garver, Lynn Holland, Bryan Norman, and all of the other crowd-funding contributors, for your generous support in making the publication of *Truth Insurrected: The Saint Mary Project* possible. You've helped to make truth mighty and prevail!

"Magna est veritas et praevalebit"

"A time for truth against the lies...a time for faith, a time for science..."
—Paul Van Dyk, "Time of Our Lives"

ONE

Uncorrelated Observation

The star-filled sky over the northeast heights of Tucson, Arizona, stirred up both fond memories and awful pain within William Harrison. Viewing the *infinite horizons* above also provoked his sense of insignificance and rising uselessness.

As he sat inside his parked black Dodge Charger, he sighed, and looked through a pair of night-vision binoculars at a house down the street. The couple inside the house had drawn the curtains and turned out the lights an hour ago. This was the third illicit liaison Harrison had observed between this particular man and woman. Although both were married, neither one of their spouses were anywhere near this place.

Harrison had already gathered plenty of photographic evidence of their affair and looked forward to closing this case very soon. The husband, who had contracted him to investigate the rumored relationship, would be devastated for sure, but at least he would know the truth. Harrison could then move on to another case, *another boring case*. Life as a private investigator paid the bills, but offered little other reward.

After lowering the driver-side window and opening the sunroof, Harrison lit up a cigarette. The smoke floated skyward, carrying Harrison's gaze with it. As the smoke dissipated above him, he caught a glimpse of something out of the ordinary.

Out of confusion, and to clear his eyes of smoke, he blinked several times. More focused now, he saw the object again. His eyes had not played tricks on him. A radiant sphere high overhead darted back and forth, and then halted its erratic movement in a single abrupt stop. These maneuvers repeated several times. Harrison sat mesmerized, mouth agape, having never observed anything like this before.

The dangling cigarette in his hand scorched his middle finger. He cursed under his breath, and then dropped the cigarette onto the center console. It rolled off and lodged beyond his reach next to the leather seat.

"Damn it," Harrison said, pushing the door open. He exited the car and stood up, feeling his right thigh twinge with pain. The old injury still ached. After struggling to recover the smoldering cigarette between the seat and console, he tossed it onto the street and squished it under his boot.

Without hesitation, Harrison searched the sky for the object again. He found it right where he had observed it before, zigzagging back and forth. The sphere stopped for a few seconds, and then it flew in a straight line toward the northwest at an incalculable speed. The horizon consumed the object and it disappeared into the darkness.

While still standing in the street, Harrison tried to grasp what he had just witnessed. He searched for reasonable explanations, but they evaded him. None of them made sense.

After a few moments, headlights and a honking horn jerked his attention back to his terrestrial surroundings. When he stepped aside to allow the car to pass, embarrassment engulfed him. The vehicle's occupants were the adulterous couple from the house down the street.

Eighty miles or so north of Las Vegas, Nevada, endless sagebrush, stilled by daytime heat, rustled from the nocturnal movement of small creatures gathering, hunting, and exploring. Under a darkened sky, such rituals resumed as usual. Stealth, difficult in the revealing rays of a loitering sun, surrounded the area's inhabitants after the light faded, succumbing to Earth's ancient rhythms.

They moved, walking, crawling, slithering, hopping, flying, running. They mingled, roaming together among the endless acres of brush and sand. Occasionally, flash floods or tremors from live fire exercise at Yucca Flats disturbed these efforts. On July 7, however, the weather was clear, and the tremors did not come from underground. They rattled across the desert plain, scattering most critters to the safety of their dens.

Headlights cut through the heavy shroud, beams scanning erratically as the vehicles hobbled over rocky trails. Thick tires tore at the ground and sent plumes of gravel and dust through the air. Each truck appeared similar to a Chevrolet Suburban, but with an extra set of rear wheels and an extended roof. The vehicles sported dark-tinted windows, and their navy-blue exterior lacked markings or trim of any kind. A single dish antenna, about thirty inches in diameter, stood above the center of each cab.

One driver swerved his vehicle around a boulder that he spotted almost too late. He swore to himself, recovered, and then rejoined the formation of four other trucks just ahead of him. Preoccupied with the maneuver, he unknowingly steered into the path of an escaping jackrabbit. Confused, the animal froze in the sudden wash of light from the headlamps. Nothing in its experience or nature helped it to understand this bizarre intrusion into its environment. The light raced overhead and the rabbit vanished, trampled between the spinning heat of the tire tread and the coarse ground.

The caravan pressed onward, advancing with deliberate haste over familiar terrain. Then, as they approached their destination, a series of small hills and outcroppings, the tight formation slowed and methodically scattered. The lead vehicle stopped at the base of the first hill, and the others continued up the sandy slope. One parked at the crest, while the remaining trucks headed for positions on and around the adjoining hills. In unison, the headlights dimmed into darkness. Now motionless, the vehicles disappeared into the desert landscape.

Nearby, a restless coyote yelped at a million stars arched overhead in the black, cloudless sky, then trotted away to hunt mice. The distant glow of Las Vegas, some eighty miles to the southeast, appeared to be the only evidence of man.

Three men occupied the truck at the top of the first hill. One sat in the driver's seat, and the other two sat next to each other in front of a console full of monitors and humming electronic equipment. They were military, but their black jumpsuits bore no service insignia or ranks.

The driver, Airman Bresch, reached into a duffel bag and removed a pair of night-vision binoculars. From his vantage point, he possessed an unobstructed view to the south for twenty miles. He raised the binoculars and peered across the vacant stretch of desert. Seeing nothing unusual, he lowered the glasses and set them on the seat. A green digital display from the two-way radio in the dashboard illuminated the cab. In the thin light, he glanced at the M-16 rifle mounted next to the glove box.

Lethal force authorized, Bresch thought.

Bresch lifted the radio's microphone, paused for the end of another unit's broadcast, and said, "Tango Charlie twelve, status is Oscar." He set the microphone on the dashboard and settled back. *This will be interesting,* he thought. His right hand found the binoculars again. Slowly, methodically, he proceeded to do his job, surveying the sage and scrub brush for intruders.

In the passenger compartment behind the driver, two air traffic controllers worked over a panel of screens and indicator lights. Both perused the planned flight profile for the experimental aircraft under test tonight. They wore headsets, although only one of them responded to the radio traffic. "Confirm one target signal, quadrant zero, altitude zero. Standing by for resumption of countdown." They stopped their various movements and waited for the response.

"All stations, central control is go for countdown resumption at 2230 hours. This is not a scrub; we are in alpha hold only. Twelve minutes, mark, to countdown with T-minus eight and twenty. Commercial traffic is minimal. Restricted space is clear."

Hearing this, the two technicians removed their headsets. One of them, an air force lieutenant, clicked a brown knob to "cabin audio." He looked at his partner and said, "Sergeant Gonzales, when we acquire the target, keep a close eye on its downrange altitude. I'll monitor flight path deviation."

"Yes, sir."

"After reaching operational altitude, the experimental is not to fall below five thousand feet. Remember, its signal will be intermittent at times, so call out your figures early."

"Yes, sir," Sergeant Gonzales said.

The lieutenant read a checklist mounted on a panel above his position in the vehicle. Next to the panel, a six-inch computer screen displayed meteorological data transmitted from Nellis Air Force Base.

After several quiet minutes, Gonzales broke the silence. "Excuse me, Lieutenant? Sir, at the briefing earlier tonight, Colonel Stone said this would be our last field operation with the experimental."

The lieutenant nodded.

"So, I was wondering, will our unit help with the flight testing of the prototypes?"

Holding his breath, he hoped his question was not out of line. Discipline, his superiors informed him, represented the cornerstone of his unit's success. Sergeant Eric Filipe Gonzales had journeyed a long way from the barrios of East Los Angeles, and preferred not to compromise his standing in the air force, but there were some personal matters that bothered him.

"Our performance is excellent so far, but orders haven't been issued yet for the next cycle." The lieutenant ran a thumbnail along the underside of his narrowly trimmed mustache. His tone eased, sounding more conversational than official. "Frankly, I'd like to be rotated out, maybe to Wright-Pat, or even Edwards. This place is turning into a circus. We're eighty miles from Vegas, in the middle of the fucking desert, and people keep broadcasting their television shows on our front porch. It's getting to where even my dog knows what Area 51 is. I'm surprised the operations continue."

Unaccustomed to speaking so plainly, the lieutenant immediately wished to replace his comments with silence. His back stiffened, and he apologized to the sergeant for sounding overwrought. "I shouldn't let myself get so worked up; Colonel Stone's a good commander. He'll make sure things work out." He flicked his mustache again while finally answering the sergeant's question: "They tell me the prototypes won't be tested again until December. Scuttlebutt says it's due to power plant, or power cell, problems, something like that. Been an ongoing problem for years. Anyway, we'll probably have routine traffic-control assignments until then. My guess is they're concerned about curiosity seekers. Why do you ask?"

"My wife and I just had a baby, sir. Our first."

"Uh-huh."

"She doesn't say it, sir, but I know she'd like me to have a regular schedule. These late nights aren't too convenient."

"I see."

"Fortunately, Megan is very patient."

The lieutenant inspected the meteorological display. Light winds drifting across the test area were subsiding. "Good."

"Sometimes I wish I could talk to her about what I do, but when I think about it, it's not always that clear to me what work I'm involved in."

"I wonder myself sometimes. It's best that we don't know."

"Yes, sir. The military has its reasons."

"On that, Sergeant, there is no question."

Eighty miles away, cars and people packed the Las Vegas strip. The warm summer nights and allure of quick cash always invited untold numbers into the city to trade workaday customs for a roll of the dice, a draw of the cards, or the drop of a coin.

This night was no different from any other. Gamblers lost big. But the sound of jackpots, music, laughter, and the haphazard choreography of wheels, lights, and thousands of people overcame any hint of defeat.

Downtown, at the corner of Fremont and Clark, a motorcycle cop, Nick Ridley, watched some of those people walk and drive past him. For a Saturday night, the calls were unusually light, so he parked in a highly visible location to deter potential violators.

Ridley found the job interesting enough, and had earned a reputation as a reliable, if intellectual, cop. One of the few patrol officers who held a master's degree in psychology, Ridley understood how to talk to people, and by doing so, controlled situations better. To some of his law enforcement colleagues, he stood out as the "shrink" whose streetwise therapy sessions made him useful at times. Already a senior patrol officer, most assumed Ridley would earn his sergeant's stripes within one or two years more.

At the moment, he checked his watch. Ten forty-five. His shift ended at eleven, and his much-needed two-week Lake Havasu vacation started immediately afterward. Ridley turned on the motorcycle's ignition and drove to the station for debriefing. With no radio traffic, he proceeded to broadcast his status. "Mary-two-three."

"Mary-two-thr—"

Something interrupted the response.

Ridley waited for the dispatcher to continue, but nothing happened. "Mary-two-three," he said again.

This time, a burst of static and rapid clicking replied.

Weird, Ridley thought.

The interference ended after several seconds, followed by the dispatcher's voice. "Three, clear to transmit."

"Mary-two-three, ten-nineteen to yours."

"Ten-four."

Ridley made a note to report the motorcycle's radio malfunction to the watch commander. He proceeded along Clark Street and drove the eight blocks to the station. Similar to hundreds of times in the last three years, he entered the underground parking structure and cruised into one of the spaces reserved for patrol vehicles.

Removing his helmet, he heard familiar voices echoing around the gray cinder-block structure. He could not hear exactly what the other officers discussed, but something felt out of place. Instead of hearing the usual radio traffic from the dispatch speakers mounted along the walls of the parking structure, he heard no traffic at all. Although it was a slow night, during shift change, units regularly called in their on- or off-duty status.

But now, something else penetrated the air. The quiet speakers broadcasted clicking, rapid clicking, like earlier, except fainter, more distant.

Ridley approached the other officers and noticed that Lieutenant Walter Maxwell, the watch commander, stood with them. After flashing a cheerful, "I'm okay, you're okay" smile, Ridley said, "Lieutenant, I'd like to report a radio malfunction."

"Well, if you're reporting officially, then I'll need you to fill out the appropriate forms, in triplicate," Maxwell said, but without the typical firmness of his baritone voice.

"In that case, the report should come from someone with actual technical qualifications. I'm more of a people person."

Further radio interference produced a grimace on the watch commander's face. He rubbed his sun-scorched forehead. The motion caused flakes of dandruff to precipitate out of his stiff, black flattop, a hairstyle he had worn for thirty years or more, beginning with his service as a special agent with the Air Force Office of Special Investigations. The flakes landed on his wide shoulders and ever-thickening midriff. Some of it even fell the entire six feet, four inches from scalp to greasy cement floor. "Never heard anything like this before. The interference is on every channel, so we know it's not a cued microphone."

One of the officers tried a radio check, but dispatch still provided no response. Just rapid clicking interference permeated the parking structure.

Lieutenant Maxwell shrugged and yawned. "Well, it must be a system problem. They'll have to coordina—" A sharp jolt of static silenced his comments.

Ridley and the others winced at the harsh sound as it ricocheted throughout the parking structure. After several seconds, the static and clicking tapered off. A string of on-duty status reports came over the air in rapid succession. As the transmissions continued, the officers in the parking structure dispersed. Some entered the station, while others went to their waiting patrol vehicles, already forgetting about the odd interference. Ridley followed Lieutenant Maxwell to the building's entrance and held open the door.

"What do you think the problem was?" Ridley said.

"Don't know. Like you, I'm no technician. No biggie, though—seems to be working fine now."

"I thought it might have been my unit's radio, but since it's not, can I go ahead and take off now? I'm anxious to start my vacation."

"Just make sure your reports are done."

"They are. Dropped them off earlier."

"See you when you get back, then. Have a good one."

With that, Ridley stepped inside the police station and headed for the locker room.

What a slow night, he thought.

Inside the oversized navy-blue Chevrolet Suburban parked amidst the desert scrub, the controllers no longer engaged in idle conversation, but rather focused on their main display screens. Another ten-minute delay in the countdown had left them ample time to review the planned flight profile for the experimental aircraft and to triple-check their various electronic systems. The sergeant and lieutenant waited with practiced patience for resumption of the countdown, which held at T-minus forty-seven seconds.

On the radar panel in front of the sergeant, a flat, twenty-inch screen displayed white and blue lines crisscrossing a dark gray background. The white lines formed the perimeters of the test ranges adjacent to Nellis Air Force Base. The blue lines, which resembled the shape of an inverted pyramid with a narrow rectangle protruding from the bottom point, delineated the airspace assigned for this particular test of a flying saucer recovered in 1947. The craft, otherwise known as the "experimental," originated from beyond Earth. Its collision with another similar vehicle and their subsequent crashes in the desert near Roswell, New Mexico, had provided the US government decades' worth of reverse engineering and sporadic flight tests.

Words and numbers on the screen also denoted various mountain peaks and their elevations: "SHEEP PK/9750," "CHARLESTON PK/11918," and "MUDDY PK/5363." At the bottom of the screen, near the center, was, "LAS VEGAS/MCCARRAN." A similar screen on display in front of the lieutenant also included several dashed yellow lines within the borders of the assigned airspace. These marks indicated the planned flight path for the experimental, represented by a white dot on both screens and labeled as "XP/0." Radar data had the experimental positioned near the upper left corner of both screens. The dot flickered at irregular intervals, something the controllers had noticed during other tests and had been told would occur again.

As he watched the dot, the lieutenant lifted his headset back to his ears and nodded to the sergeant to do the same. He turned off the cabin audio switch and folded his arms. For a split second, he thought he heard his headset crackle with static, so he double-checked that its connector remained attached in the console jack. The interruption cleared, and both listened as the countdown resumed.

"T-minus forty-seven and counting. Med reports normal life signs. Thirty seconds, mark. Telemetry reports online. All systems normal—"

More static hissed through the controllers' headsets. The lieutenant tapped the earpiece with his index finger. He glanced at the sergeant and saw his subordinate's face change from a look of bored professionalism to utter confusion.

Sergeant Gonzales jerked forward. What he saw made no sense. Another white dot appeared near the "MUDDY PK" marker and moved in the direction of the experimental. *Report. Report as you've been trained to do,* he thought. His still boyish voice squeaked out the warning. "Target! Unknown target!"

The vehicle's onboard computer assigned the unknown target a designation, "UNK/7803." The dot tracked steadily, with its altitude indicator showing a rapid descent.

The lieutenant scanned the display. "What the hell?"

This time, the static blasted through the headphones at high volume, and both men instinctively ripped them off.

Anxious to call in his report, the lieutenant carefully raised the headphones to his ears. The static dissipated, but a strange clicking now emanated from the earpiece. With no radio transmissions, he attempted to broadcast an update. "Uncorrelated observation inbound at angels seven, rapid descent, entering quadrant four." He checked the screen. The experimental remained on the ground. "Can you hear anything, Sergeant?"

Preoccupied with the image on the display, the sergeant did not answer. The unknown target just performed an instantaneous ninety-degree turn and dropped to below two thousand feet.

"It's coming this way," Sergeant Gonzales said.

The lieutenant, despite the technical problem with the radio, kept sending the status reports. "Unknown now on course three-one-zero at sixteen hundred feet. Variable airspeed." He turned to Gonzales and said, "Get with the driver and do a visual check."

"Yes, sir." Gonzales stepped out of his seat and slid open the driver cab's access window. The driver leaned toward the radio console, checking different channels. "No time for that, Bresch; the radio's down. Get your binoculars and get out."

After grabbing his night-vision binoculars, Airman Bresch lifted the rifle from its dashboard mount and joined Sergeant Gonzales at the front of the vehicle.

"There's an unknown target, southeast, about five miles," Gonzales said.

Bresch searched the desert terrain for intruders.

"No," Gonzales said, pointing at the sky, "an unknown, *airborne* target."

"What altitude?"

"Under two thousand."

"Civilian or military?"

"Unknown!"

Gonzales's eyes darted back and forth, trying to find the object. He knew there must be a reasonable explanation for this situation. The briefing was clear enough: one flight, one target. *Must be a technical glitch,* he thought.

"There it is," Bresch said, confused. "It's low. I thought the experimental was restricted to five thousand or above?"

Looking toward the horizon, Sergeant Gonzales spotted a glowing ball of light. Alternating between glossy shades of green and blue, it moved steadily to the northwest.

Silently.

The luminous orb, orange now, instantaneously jumped skyward several hundred feet, and then danced ahead.

It stopped.

Red and silver strands, a flickering halo of plasma, encircled the sphere.

The rapid clicking now emanated, but not from the radio; it echoed through their heads. A chill shivered up Gonzales's spine, causing him to arch his shoulders and shake his head.

The unknown target hovered, emitting a radiant glow and obscuring the stars behind it.

With eyes fixed on the object, Airman Bresch stepped backward until the truck's bumper pressed against his trembling legs. "What's that clicking sound?" The binoculars dropped to the ground, and then so did he, onto his knees.

Out of the darkness, the air vibrated with another, more familiar noise. Sergeant Gonzales turned around and found a relieved expression on Bresch's face.

"Here they come!" Bresch said.

Two F-15 fighters raced in from the north. As dual intakes greedily consumed huge droughts of air, the hot turbofans propelled the planes toward the unknown. They approached, encountering their target in a matter of seconds.

It waited for them.

The fighters rushed in aggressively, closing the gap.

The object maneuvered, jumping again, two thousand feet straight up.

One of the F-15s fired its afterburners and accelerated into a steep climb. The second jet rolled through a right turn, heading west. It circled low, near the truck's location, and then ascended directly toward the target. The other F-15 also reversed direction, running parallel to the craft and slightly above it.

The fighters engaged.

A plume of white luminescence spiraled outward from the intruder, blanketing the hilltop in a brilliant flash, and then it collapsed as quickly as it had appeared.

And the fighters vanished.

Before Sergeant Gonzales comprehended what happened, the object disappeared in a white streak toward the northwest. "My God!"

"Where are they?" Bresch said.

Gonzales grabbed the binoculars from the ground and scanned the sky and terrain. "I don't see them."

"They can't just be gone. They must have crashed."

Gonzales ran back to the truck and spoke to the lieutenant. "Sir, we need search and rescue out here right away."

The lieutenant provided no response. His headphones lay on the console, and he held a cell phone next to his ear. He did not speak, except to say, "Yes, sir." After hanging up the phone, he said, "Sergeant, the test was scrubbed due to a communications malfunction. All other systems are normal. We're returning to base."

"But, sir—"

"The site is secure and all systems are normal! We are returning to base."

TWO

The Elusive Fifth Species

A mid-July morning in Washington, DC, formed into another oppressively hot and humid day. Beads of sweat joined easily into pesky rivulets on the brows of hurried commuters. They emerged, wet, from the many metro stations and headed for their nearby offices, silently cursing those who believed building such a city on a swamp was a good idea.

Meteorologists predicted rain for the afternoon. In anticipation of the inclement weather, some carried umbrellas concealed with other items in their bags or briefcases, or windbreakers tucked under their sticky arms. Most, squirming in their increasingly pasty garments, simply did not know what to expect.

At Reagan National Airport, lengthy rows of taxicabs inched forward, each approaching their turn to help transport the steady stream of travelers who exited the terminal. Tourists, soldiers, business executives, students, and other visitors waded into the muggy air that hung over the Potomac.

Among them stood a very purposeful figure, General Edward Taylor, US Air Force. After a brisk walk from the main terminal, he took his place behind several people waiting curbside for taxicabs. Instead of his uniform, the general wore an off-the-rack gray suit, which fit his trim six-foot frame well, but made him appear more like a warehouse supervisor unexpectedly promoted to management than a career military officer. Only the combination of Taylor's close-cropped gray hair and disciplined bearing suggested his real identity as he stood there, nearly at the position of attention, with a firm grip on the soft leather briefcase in his left hand. Polished black leather shoes stepped occasionally to move him forward. His green, motionless eyes stared directly ahead.

When Taylor reached the front of the line, an attendant asked him for his destination. He responded with Washington, DC, and the attendant directed him to the appropriate taxi. As others around him jostled and struggled with luggage, Taylor stepped immediately into the cab and shut the door. Glancing once at the driver, he informed him that his destination was the Naval Observatory.

The taxi wound its way onto the George Washington Parkway. This route, along the Potomac on the Virginia shore, offered a scenic view of Washington's distinctive and symbolic architecture. The monuments—Lincoln, Jefferson, and Washington—and the Capitol rose above the lush green of the mall and river foliage. Despite the summer heat and humidity, joggers filled the running trails. Although familiar sights to Taylor, they passed with little confirmation of their presence.

Instead, he focused his thoughts on the meeting due to commence, by his watch, in twenty-two minutes. He had attended dozens of these sessions in the last fourteen years. This one was different, however, as it was unscheduled and convened at a location other than Nellis or Wright-Patterson. As such, Taylor anticipated more-anxious-than-usual participants, especially when they learned of the latest developments.

He recognized why.

The walls of secrecy around the Saint Mary Project had weakened. Fear of a breach stalked his colleagues and threatened to expose the Circle. Time was running out for them.

And for Taylor.

Retirement was just under six months away. Thirty-five years had passed since he received his commission in the air force. As a fighter pilot in the 1970s, he thought he had reached the pinnacle of his aviation career. Work as a test pilot in the 1980s showed him otherwise.

Looking back, he would have preferred to remain assigned to an air wing after serving as a test pilot. But he chose, instead, what he thought would be the stable duty of air force intelligence.

For the most part the assignment was stable. In twenty years, he had served at two bases, Nellis and Wright-Patterson. This was ideal for his wife and son. They put down roots, and so did he.

Gradually, though, the duty came to dominate his life. The highly sensitive details and special burdens reshaped him. Once a model officer and family man, now an obedient sentinel guarding without distinction the gates of heaven and assassins of hell, Taylor felt his self-respect, like Saint Mary's secrecy, slipping away.

The taxi jerking to a stop on M Street in Georgetown interrupted his thoughts. Having just crossed the Key Bridge from Virginia, they ran into the remnants of heavy morning traffic. As the cab moved again, Taylor let his gaze drift out the window. Mist settled, casting the scene in a sullen, colorless hue.

"You don't have much luggage," the driver said, a tuneful Caribbean accent carrying the words toward his passenger.

Surprised by the comment, Taylor turned and said, "No."

"Your stay in Washington will be short?"

"Yes."

"Must be a business trip?"

"Yes."

"What business you in?"

"I sell computer systems. Hardware and such."

The cabby seemed impressed, and then mentioned something the general thought sounded like a question about his alleged profession.

Leaning forward, Taylor said, "I'm sorry, what did you say?" He did not want the driver to quiz him on this, but he was familiar the routine.

"Care for some music? I have a radio."

Taylor relaxed and sat back. "Yes. Fine. Perhaps a news station instead?"

The driver tuned the radio to one of the local news stations and nodded at his passenger. Taylor thanked him, and then watched the facades pass by as the taxi approached Wisconsin Avenue.

On the sidewalk, people scurried along, gaits hastened to avoid the intensifying drizzle.

Except for one person.

Clad in blue, this figure stood motionless, looking into a store window.

Was it a uniform? Taylor thought.

With cockpit-perfect vision, Taylor zeroed in on the individual's profile. A man with short brown hair. A young man, tilting his head to one side.

Looks like Drew, Taylor thought.

The stoplight turned red, but this did not prevent the cabby from getting them through the intersection. The acceleration brought Taylor's attention to the driver. Anger quickened his pulse. Grief, several years old but still fresh as the last breath of air filling his lungs, cranked his head back to the sidewalk.

The young man disappeared.

Taylor closed his eyes and tried to subdue the growing strain. As much as he missed his son, he had learned from previous instances that these encounters were the result of wishful thinking. Figments of his imagination, an imagination comfortably restrained by a precise mechanical mind.

Except when it came to Drew.

The facts were hard to accept, the explanation inadequate. By all accounts, official and otherwise, his son was dead, killed in a sortie over Baghdad during Operation Iraqi Freedom.

Naturally, he had been very proud the day his son graduated from the Air Force Academy. He told Drew time and again, "As long as you're in the air force, just fly. Don't do anything else. Just fly."

Drew had intended to do just that.

The military never found his remains. There was wreckage, but no body. At the time, no one at the Pentagon seemed interested in pursuing the case. As it turned out, the only information Taylor obtained was that his son's mission was classified.

"Edward, I am sorry," the air force chief had said. "Andrew was confirmed killed in action. How we know this, why we don't have the remains, and other mission details are classified. I'm sure you understand. You'll just have to trust me."

Taylor, turning to double shots of scotch, but mostly absorbed in his work, survived the uncertainty.

His marriage did not.

With diminished traffic on Wisconsin Avenue, the taxi hastened its pace to the Naval Observatory. After the driver pulled into the public entrance and parked, Taylor took two twenty-dollar bills out of his wallet. "Keep the change."

"Thanks, man, good luck to you," the driver said.

Once Taylor passed the guarded entrance, the air-conditioning cooled his skin and helped him to gather his thoughts. Just ahead, a wrinkled face smiled in his direction. Seeing the old man gave Taylor a sense of reassurance.

Professor Francis Moresby may have appeared as if he were there for a senior-center bridge tournament, but under the white flyaway hair and behind the creaky voice, there stood a genius. A genius who had participated in Saint Mary for nearly six decades, almost since the beginning.

"You are right on time, as usual, General Taylor," Moresby said, winking one of his cloudy eyes.

"Nice to see you again, Professor."

"Edward, I believe you know Colonel Randolph Stone," the professor said, presenting the air force officer standing next to him.

With his hand extended, Taylor said, "Of course. Our paths have crossed more than once. Glad to have you with us, Colonel." Reflexively, he inspected the subordinate officer's uniform. Nothing appeared out of order.

"Thank you, sir." Stone tolerated Taylor's gaze and returned the handshake. "I'm honored to be here."

Moresby leaned toward both officers and suggested they go to the conference room. "There is much to discuss, and the Circle is anxious to have their recommendations implemented."

He led the two officers down a corridor to an elevator, where Colonel Stone inserted a small key into the call switch. After several quiet seconds, the doors opened and the threesome stepped inside.

As the elevator descended, Taylor pondered Colonel Stone's presence at this meeting. He knew Stone had served for three years as the director of flight operations and security at Area 51. Still, the Circle strictly controlled membership in the working group. Attendees evaluated operations and conducted planning at these sessions. Although Stone held an important position, it was essentially a procedural one.

"You're wearing a suit today?" Moresby said.

Taylor's gears shifted. "Yes, sir. I did not want to draw any unnecessary attention to myself. Considering the observatory is not our usual meeting place, I wasn't comfortable with the idea of wearing a uniform."

After a long pause and probing stare, Moresby said, "I think maybe you are anxious to become a civilian."

"I really have not thought about it, sir."

The elevator doors opened, revealing another hallway, its tiled floor partially covered by thick Persian carpets. Following the sound of a nearby conversation, the three men exited the elevator and then entered a conference room. Colonel Stone closed the oak-paneled doors behind them and found a seat.

With ornate decorations, another Persian rug, and rows of bookshelves, the chamber felt more like a private library than conference room. Adding to its aristocratic atmosphere, handsome light sconces and framed paintings of various styles hung on the beige walls.

At the center of the room, a dozen men sat around a dark brown table. Most wore air force or navy uniforms; a few wore civilian attire. Colorful stacks of files, writing tablets, and notebooks sat arranged like tableware in front of them. No single conversation dominated the room. Rather, multiple discussions between two or three people occurred simultaneously.

Taylor and Moresby sat in the two remaining chairs. Across from them, one of the naval officers, Admiral Horner, fat and sweating, nodded at the general.

The loud, intervening voice of one of the civilians said, "Gentlemen, gentlemen, we all have very demanding and pressing needs that require attention. But let's begin with the incident of seven July."

The announcement resulted in silence, and brought the attention of the participants in Saint Mary's working group to the head of the table. There he sat, Dennis, the working group's chairman, arms folded, lips pursed, looking like an impatient teaching assistant from Harvard waiting for undergraduate term papers. The observatory was his choice for the meeting, a ploy to get the military types away from their turf. In many ways, he still struggled to earn their respect.

His youthfulness bothered many. When he flailed his arms while speaking, Taylor often thought Dennis resembled some sort of precocious composer conducting an orchestra. His bad breath, an odor similar to urine drying in an alleyway, certainly had not endeared him to anyone.

But, the Circle had chosen him.

This obscure program manager from the Pentagon fit their requirements better than others. Apparently, even better than Taylor.

Although he was relatively new, the chairman's grasp of Saint Mary's complex structure had helped guide the project through three very difficult years. The problems had originated mostly from increased pressure on the government, an unfortunate side effect of Saint Mary's socialization functions. As the public became more aware and accepting of the UFO phenomenon through a carefully orchestrated and subtle propaganda process undertaken by the project, they also grew more interested in the entire story, including the government's secrets.

Within recent months the chairman had gained the Circle's endorsement to curtail Saint Mary's activities, and developed plans for a renewed expansion of the project when their new base, known as North Range, would become operational. During the interim, the focus had shifted to limited flight tests and Professor Moresby's communication efforts with the four identified species already engaged in various stages of terrestrial contact. The professor's work, while valuable to him personally and facilitated by the possession of four live specimens, proved inconsequential.

Then the Dreamland encounter occurred, with the loss of two F-15 fighters.

"The details of the incident are in your briefing material," the chairman said. "I assume you've read it. If you have questions, Colonel Stone is here and will address those. Let us focus on the first issue, that being the one the Circle would like us to consider. How do we respond in terms of the Dreamland flights, the security protocols, and defense profiles?" The chairman rested his freckled arms on the table. "I guess those are really three issues, but they work together. Professor Moresby?"

Moresby's face took on a serious expression. He waited several seconds, until all eyes watched him. Bowing his head and clasping his hands, he said, "Our Father, who art in heaven..."

Taylor appreciated the gesture, but did not join with his colleagues in laughing aloud. He noticed Colonel Stone remained quiet. Clenching his jaw, the colonel narrowed his eyes, almost into slits.

"I am sorry, Dennis," Moresby said. "I hope you know that I do take this very seriously. I also know that I am the only one here with sufficient esteem and respect to dispense humor."

The chairman flicked his wrist, pointing an invisible baton at the professor.

Taking the cue, Moresby said, "First, let us dispense with the security aspect. I understand the standard protocols are in effect. The families of the missing pilots have been adequately informed. The witnesses? Colonel Stone, who were the witnesses?"

Without referring to his notes, Stone said, "Two personnel, both nonessential. An airman and a sergeant with traffic control." His voice, shaky and servile at first, grew firm, even contemptuous. "As you mentioned, the standard protocols are in place. The initial report from the security branch is that they anticipate a routine disposition. The exposure will be contained."

The old professor heard the words and mutated tone. "Thank you so much, Colonel. Your diligence has earned you yet another merit badge." He let his gaze drift around the room. "General Taylor's security branch will undoubtedly be of great help to you. However, the more pertinent question is the impact on flight operations."

"But wait," a soft-spoken voice said, emerging from the stillness left by Moresby's comments. The voice was that of Colonel Bennet, one of Taylor's colleagues at Nellis. "We've had more press attention with this one."

Subdued, oddly charming Bennet, Saint Mary's disinformation officer, was a tiny man, easily overlooked in a crowded room. Behind the military-issue, horn-rimmed eyeglasses, he had one brown eye and one green eye. Most people never noticed this though, as he rarely looked anyone squarely in the face. He sat a little farther back from the table than everyone else and contemplated a fraying seam on his blue pant leg.

Continuing, Bennet said, "The sighting was not confined to the test range. People spotted the object in Las Vegas. We even had reports from controllers at McCarran. This one has been more difficult to contain. The sightings coincided with extensive disruptions in radio communications." Bennet paused and aimed the top of his head at the chairman. He rolled his eyes upward until they were limited from moving any farther due to the physical design of the sockets and muscular tissue. "It's bringing a whole lot of attention down on us." Relaxing, he receded into his chair.

"Colonel Stone," the chairman said, "our test schedule is on hold, yes or no?"

"Yes." With attention from the group on him, Stone elaborated. "In fact, aside from site-specific runs for the prototypes, no large-scale tests are slated until December. Typical problems associated with the inadequate power cell preclude a more aggressive flight schedule. Also, our field agents from Dreamland will be engaged to suppress local evidence."

"Given the scaled-back test schedule, I anticipate that interest will wane rather quickly," the chairman said, his hands wafting his bad breath forward. “We will have the usual increase of sightseers around Nellis. But word will spread that nothing is going on. The standard denials and suppression should suffice.”

“What about that bitch, Senator Vaughn?” Sweat dripped from Admiral Horner as his question boomed across the table like a warning shot fired over the bow of an encroaching warship. “That woman’s got a real knack for stirring things up. She needs to find something other to do than nose in on our business. Needs to be home, raising kids, doing the laundry, servicing her husband, if you ask me. Can’t you do something about her, Taylor?”

“I am.” Taylor looked at the chairman and raised an eyebrow. A knowing expression from the chairman instructed the general to proceed with describing the latest information regarding the senator from New Mexico. “While her persistence about cattle mutilations continues to be a source of frustration for us, she is finding that navigating through our government’s dense bureaucracy can be a hopeless and confusing task.”

Thoughts of the mutilations made him pause. Their disinformation purpose seemed antiquated. To this day, he could not grasp why Saint Mary continued them. Such was the nature of the working group. They kept secrets from the public, of course, but they also kept them from each other. He did not always agree with this practice, but within the last few years, he’d found good reason to compartmentalize a few secrets of his own.

Resuming, Taylor said, “I am personally supervising every aspect of the senator’s inquiries. This is not a typical case, however. She has very close ties with the President. Their friendship goes back many years, to their days in law school.”

“I wonder if they ever had, you know, an affair,” General Lanham, an air force weapons specialist, said. “Wouldn’t that be something?”

“We could really sink her with a story like that,” Admiral Horner said.

“Yes, such a story could be damaging,” Taylor said. “It could also inadvertently expose us. Our fingerprints would be all over it. No, no, this is not a good time for such measures. As you know, we are not immune from outside politics. There is a chance, a very good chance, according to our sources, that Senator Vaughn will join the administration in a second term."

The working group hung on every word.

"To do what?" Admiral Horner said.

"The plan is for her to join the ticket. She will replace the current Vice President, who is having some medical problems that, for obvious reasons, haven't been made public yet." As Taylor looked around the table, he saw faces turn pale, more sweat drop from the admiral, and Stone's slits narrow even further. "We are not immune from politics."

Reaction to news of the senator's rising influence met his expectations. Professor Moresby sat serenely. Colonel Bennet's lips stirred. Admiral Horner, General Lanham, and the other officers chattered anxiously.

Then, fists thumped the table, shock waves sending file folders to the floor.

"Gentlemen, gentlemen," the chairman said, his arms cutting through the air. "Of course, anyone who meddles in our affairs, especially one with Vaughn's connections, is a danger. Eternal vigilance is the price we must pay for carrying the burden of secrecy. The Circle remains convinced, however, that our more relevant concerns relate to the defense profile." Poised like an expectant headmaster, he folded his arms and said, "Does anyone care to delineate for us the issues regarding this topic?"

"This is damn serious," Admiral Horner said. "The air force has been lucky so far, but naval assets have been lost, as you all should know, in incidents similar to this. This most recent Dreamland encounter swindled you out of two F-15s just like our loss of a P-3 and F-14 last year near Puerto Rico. Worse still, the Norfolk event. I don't think I need to remind anyone here about our losses in that incident. The pattern is the same."

"Could it be the elusive fifth species?" Professor Moresby said.

Silence.

Even the air seemed to disappear.

The officers sat frozen; fears of inadequacy compressed their innards. They hung there, suspended, as if dumped into the suffocating vacuum of space.

For once, the machinery in General Taylor's head powered down. Emotional batteries kicked in. *How will this ever end?*

Blood circulated again in his colleagues' arteries. Their cheeks blushed. Moresby twiddled his thumbs.

At first, the professor's movement unnerved Taylor. To remind the working group about the fifth species—the daunting, mysterious, unpredictable fifth species—would only encourage more self-destruction.

But watching the old man, Taylor realized the professor's simple act clarified everything.

"This group knows where I stand. The fifth species is obviously a dangerous threat," Admiral Horner said, confirming Taylor's concerns. "Could be the most dangerous. This is what Saint Mary is all about. I don't put much stock in such things as communications, the hybrids, disinformation, or other intangibles. We need to take a stand. Our day of infamy has come and gone, gentlemen, and I don't see us fighting back. Saint Mary may have grown out of fear, but I don't see us doing enough to conquer that fear."

"We have ELF," General Lanham said.

"Sure, we have ELF," Admiral Horner said. "But has it been deployed yet? Do we really know if these low-frequency sound waves will work in the field? Do you want to bet our safety on a multibillion-dollar erector set?"

"ELF will be up and running soon enough, and it has shown promise as a weapons platform," General Lanham said, his eyes moistening. "I don't suppose you have any solutions, specifically speaking?"

"All I'm saying is that we need to straighten out our priorities and quit wasting precious time. If I were running this show—"

"I appreciate your comments, Admiral," the chairman said, interrupting along with an upward hand slice. "But my inclination is to assert an element of diplomacy into this discussion. All functions of the project are supposed to work together. In a mission of this kind, the priorities can be difficult to assign. Everything is important. Security, technology, operations, disinformation. You cannot imagine the dependence we now have on our legal staff. Litigation over the tax status of our facilities has exploded. Apparently, some have found this to be a possible way to break open Saint Mary. In many ways, our front line is a group of lawyers huddled in the basement of Wright-Patterson. In the same sense, our frontier, our jurisdiction, extends virtually anywhere it has to. Remember when the Belgians showed everyone their secret files and photographic evidence? I have never seen the Circle so incensed. In that case, our security branch acted effectively. Their liaison work with NATO was invaluable. But your comments, I have to admit, do reflect the consensus of the Circle's members. In fact, their interpretation has led to a clarification of our priorities."

As Admiral Horner grunted his approval, General Taylor's mechanisms came back online, immediately trying to anticipate where the chairman was headed. Taylor glanced at Colonel Stone. He stared directly at him.

"Three years ago," the chairman said, "funding was obtained for what was described as a state-of-the-art plutonium storage facility, called North Range. The location of weapons-grade material is not seen by legitimate authorities as, shall we say, newsworthy. The budget submission was black. The secrecy was to our advantage. Not all of you know this, but North Range is actually a new air base, our new air base." The chairman thumped his chest, emphasizing the last three words. "It will be operational in January. Gentlemen, our primary mission will be weapons development. We are to pursue an aggressive policy of technology exploitation. Other functions will remain, but we will consolidate them. The Saint Mary Project must provide solutions, more so than ever before, to the defense question."

Attempting to hide his surprise and growing anguish, Taylor said, "As you know, my current duties are confined to the security branch and the hybrid programs. They have encompassed other areas in the past, but I am unclear about your use of the phrase, 'aggressive policy of technology exploitation.' What exactly does that mean?"

"Essentially, we will not simply rely on the recovered technology. Roswell and Norfolk provided us with great treasures, yes, but the Circle believes we should, and possibly can, intercept and capture these alien craft."

"You must remember," Professor Moresby said, "the fundamental reason for our secrecy is that upon the moment of disclosure, we must be able to reassure the public that we can defend ourselves." Most of the men around the table nodded. "Of course, once we declare war on the aliens, which is the implication of this policy, there probably won't be any public left to defend."

"Now wait, Professor—" the chairman said, but an uncharacteristic burst of noise from Colonel Bennet cut him off.

"Excuse me, excuse me, but with all due respect to my colleagues and the members of the Circle, I am concerned this policy was made in haste." Bennet paused. He slid off the horn-rims and folded them in his lap. "There is so much that we do not understand. I know that we have lost assets in the course of these encounters. The abduction phenomenon alone is reason enough to warrant serious concern. But think about where we are with the recovered technology. We've had the experimental for sixty-plus years, and we still haven't flown the damn thing more than a few miles. We don't even have the right power cell, or any clue how to fabricate one."

"What about Aurora? What about fiber optics? And the prototypes?" General Lanham said, leaning toward Colonel Bennet and throwing up his hands.

"Yes, yes, there have been significant adaptations," Bennet said. He looked at the chairman and twitched. "But remember who we are dealing with. These guys aren't from our neighborhood."

Returning the gaze, the chairman said, "What are you suggesting, Colonel?"

"Well, we can debate endlessly about the fifth species and the defense profile, but there is another very urgent problem."

The colonel's next words came haltingly. To General Taylor, Bennet sounded either very cautious, or very poorly rehearsed.

"There is an assumption that, at a certain point, disclosure will occur. This assumes we have control of the situation. We talk about the potential instability or disintegration of society that may happen when disclosure occurs. So we have pursued efforts that will prepare society for that moment. In other words, disinformation has changed the way society views the prospect of life elsewhere in the universe. This is the payoff for carrying the burden of secrecy. The problem now, however, is that secrecy has become the singular driving force behind Saint Mary. We have committed unimaginable crimes. Everything from funding to security is built upon unlawful and illegal means. Distrust is our greatest enemy, not a mysterious fifth species. Gentlemen, our mission, the Saint Mary Project, is complete. All that remains is the truth. And this belongs to the people we serve." Bennet reinstalled his glasses and then dropped his head.

The room grew quiet again.

The chairman waited. He looked around the table at all of the meeting's participants, searching for weakness and sympathy.

Then, he reacted.

"This is not an option, Colonel. Let me remind everyone that secrecy and the security branch are more important now than ever. The Circle's interpretation is that we face a hostile threat, against which we cannot defend. The need to protect this information is obvious. Our actions in Saint Mary must be commensurate with these circumstances. No weak links will be tolerated."

Following this warning, the chairman presented a brief lecture about revised disinformation tactics, the centralized command structure at North Range, weapons systems in development, and other changes necessitated by the new policy. General Taylor absorbed the information, becoming especially interested when the chairman mentioned the hybrid program.

"Currently under General Taylor, the hybrid program will be consolidated with the security and flight operations branches. When North Range is operational, these functions will move there permanently. General Taylor?"

"Sir?"

"The transfer procedures will begin at the end of this month. Transmit your summaries and status reports directly to Colonel Stone. The Nellis staff is at your disposal."

"To Colonel Stone?"

"Yes. Colonel Stone will be the officer in charge of the combined functions that I just mentioned. He will, of course, assume the rank of brigadier general on August first."

As General Taylor processed these new circumstances, begrudgingly impressed with the chairman's selection of an "outsider" to run the show, Colonel Stone rose from his chair and walked toward the chairman. Stone paused, making eye contact with each individual, including Colonel Bennet, whose head swiveled eagerly toward him.

"The Circle need not be concerned about my commitment to protect the project," Stone said. "My strong recommendation is that we not only reaffirm the security function, but attack the problem of residual evidence. Colonel Bennet mentioned the criminality of our many actions. This was necessary, absolutely necessary. But it has left, for lack of a better phrase, a 'paper trail.' Isolation of government records, documents, publications, and whatever else we may think of, is highly important. This flank must be protected."

Colonel Stone's scrutiny of the working group settled onto General Taylor.

"The government's credibility is at stake," Stone said. "The public's faith in its governing institutions is the fundamental mission. We will not fail, not on my watch."

"Thank you, Colonel," the chairman said. "Any questions? Does everyone know where we stand?"

None of the working group responded, except for Professor Moresby. "I can accept these changes, but I must insist on further communications efforts. I am certain the Circle would agree." Like Colonel Stone, he rose to his feet. The old man's limbs shook, so General Taylor braced him under the left elbow. He felt like it was the most useful thing he had done in a long time.

Finally, resting his hands on the table and taking a deep breath, Moresby continued, "If contact can be made in a more consistent way, perhaps this conflict we are preparing for can be avoided. I have seen too much war in my day. This is not something you should seek out. You said it yourself, Dennis, the functions work best together, despite the renewed importance of the defense profile."

"Do what you can, Professor," the chairman said. "Meeting adjourned." He pointed at General Taylor and said, "Not you, Edward. Stay for a moment."

While the others filed out, Taylor and the chairman remained seated. Facing the chairman across the wide table, the general tried to clear his mind.

"What do you think?" the chairman asked.

"Sir?"

"About Colonel Bennet?"

"Who is he trying to flush out?"

"Uh-huh, uh-huh. Was his performance that bad?"

"Let's just say I do my job."

"You do, and you do it well. In fact, I cannot say enough how much I appreciate all of your help."

The gratitude sounded outright banal, like something a neighbor might say to another neighbor after loading a U-Haul trailer with boxes and furniture. The compliment hardly befitted a career of deceit, fraud, and murder.

"Actually, Bennet's smoke screen is to help me out in case anyone's feathers were too ruffled by the restructuring. His comments may help to bring weaknesses to the surface."

"I see."

"Also, we haven't really had too much time to discuss these latest developments about Vaughn, not since you brought them to my attention last week. Work with Stone on it. Get him going in the right direction, will you?"

"Yes, sir."

The chairman's features grew thoughtful. The expression made him seem old, worn out. "Vaughn is after something which she will never obtain."

"What is that?"

"The truth, Edward. I'm surprised her political mind has not already realized that truth is the greatest mystery. It is like the concept of silence. Its existence is a matter of perspective. It eludes accountability. I understand that she suffers the ridicule of her colleagues?"

"Yes."

"Then why does she persist?"

"Faith."

"What, in the system? No one has faith in the system anymore. People don't even vote. Why should they? The system gave them Vietnam, Watergate, Iran-Contra, financial crises, useless government shutdowns, and an ocean of debt. It gave them apathy. It has stolen their future. Who in their right mind cares anymore? Tell me, General, do you think there is anyone out there who still has faith enough to make this system work?"

Sparks flickered off the cogs rotating in Taylor's skull. The question, an all too familiar one, triggered a stream of memories and his son's voice. "Dad, I want to fly. Dad, I got my pilot's license. Dad, I thought I'd join the air force." He wrestled against the rising floodwaters. Tactics and strategies wedged themselves forward. Lines connected distant places and objects. Bodies. And a name.

"I don't know, sir. Maybe."

"Hmm, then they are our greatest threat."

Restraining the anger was easy now.

Or our greatest hope, Taylor thought.

THREE

The Postcard

Steady.

Patient and relaxed.

The shooter's right hand gripped a stainless-steel Colt .45 semi-automatic handgun.

Easy breaths.

The thumb safety clicked, and the aim still held true. His right index finger smoothly squeezed the trigger. At last, the first round blasted down the barrel at its target.

A hit. The round penetrated center mass.

"Nice shot, Mr. Harrison."

William Harrison barely detected the compliment through his hearing protectors. Remaining focused on the black silhouette downrange, he nodded a polite acknowledgment to Norm, the range master standing behind him.

More bullets flew toward the target.

Two, three.

With each round, a distinct clap echoed off the surrounding cement walls.

Four, five.

The warm smell of gunpowder thickened in their nostrils and drifted through the other firing lanes, all empty, of Old Pueblo Guns and Range.

Six, seven.

Harrison raised his right hand a few degrees and gave Norm a thrill.

Eight.

"Right between the eyes," the range master said, chuckling. "Let me see your license to kill."

While Norm hee-hawed like an excited donkey, Harrison smiled and went about reloading and holstering the Colt. Slipping the hearing protectors from his head, he swiveled in the direction of the husky cowboy watching his performance.

"Thanks for letting me use the range, Norm."

"Not a problem, Mr. Harrison." The grin on the range master's face, asserting itself through the plump, reddish mounds of his cheeks, nose, chin, and lips, faded quickly. "You all right?"

Wincing, Harrison limped over to the firing lane's gun table and braced himself. "Yeah, just my leg." He rubbed his right thigh and said, "It hasn't felt like this for a while."

The pain did come and go, but his limp was always there and very noticeable. Walking was easy enough, but he was aware that the sight of him maneuvering through a room or crossing the street occasionally made some people nervous. Harrison was tall and solid, with long arms and legs. His broad shoulders and barrel chest, not the result of weight-training, but an endowment from distant Viking ancestors, made him appear top heavy. The limp gave the impression, at times, that he was in danger of losing balance altogether.

With Norm's help, Harrison placed his gear into a nylon gym bag. "Thanks. I guess I'll be in the same time next week."

"You have time for coffee?" The range master grinned again and fingered the turquoise clasp of his bolo tie. He wanted to hear another one of Harrison's war stories from his days working in the FBI. He especially liked accounts about the former special agent's counterintelligence work. For Norm, knowing Harrison was the next best thing to meeting James Bond. "You can have a smoke in the office if you want to."

"You just want to hear a story, don't you?"

"Well, it has been a while."

Norm was right. In fact, the stories were part of their deal, an exchange for the range master allowing him to come in early every Monday before the range opened for regular business. But lately, Harrison had not felt in the mood to relate past events. The tales reminded him of how bored he had become with his work as a private investigator in Tucson, Arizona.

"That's the truth. Can't argue with that," Harrison said, taking a step and straightening his posture. The pain had subsided. He ran a hand through his conservatively groomed brown hair and beard. "Is the aforementioned coffee brewed?"

"Huh? It's brewed, yeah."

"Okay, but I can't stay too long." Taking tentative steps, Harrison reached for his pack of menthol cigarettes and stuck one in the side of his mouth. "I've got an interview to conduct later this morning."

They went to the office with Norm leading the way. As usual, the range master's blue jeans squeaked with each step. Wrapped tightly around thick thighs and hips, the jeans seemed as though they could burst at any second. The sight amused Harrison, making him feel better, for the moment, about sharing another story.

Once inside the office, the rich, warm aroma of coffee immediately embraced the pair, and Harrison eagerly accepted a cup. After an appreciative sip, a snap from his lighter followed, and he relaxed, taking a long drag. "My apologies to the surgeon general," he said, smoke accompanying every syllable.

"What's that?" Years of firearms instruction had diminished Norm's hearing.

"Oh, nothing." Harrison found an empty chair in a corner of the cluttered office and settled into it. Trade magazines, stacks of invoices, NRA posters, two battered filing cabinets, and a scuffed wooden desk adorned the room. "So, Norm, how's business?"

"Good, good. Seems like we get more of the militia and sovereign-citizen types in all the time. Their unhappiness with the folks in Washington is good for me."

While Norm chuckled, Harrison raised an eyebrow and said, "Well, let's hope their shooting doesn't improve too much. They should be signing petitions instead of shooting bullets." He puffed on his cigarette and sipped some coffee. "But I suppose they find potentially holding democracy at gunpoint sexier than peaceful civil disobedience or electoral participation."

"Huh?" Norm removed a hearing aid from the desk and inserted it into his left ear.

Rolling his chair closer, Harrison said, "I really like your coffee. I think I'll switch to it." Pain quivered through his right thigh. "What's the brand?"

"Oh, I don't know. Something my wife picks out. Yuban, I think."

"It's good." Harrison set down the mug and rubbed his leg.

"Does it hurt much?"

"Once in a while, yeah."

"Do you mind?"

Harrison sipped more coffee, and then set the mug aside. "No, not at all. In fact, Norm, there's a really good story about it."

Intrigued, Norm moved forward in his chair, his jeans squeaking in response.

Looking at the cigarette dangling loosely between his fingers, Harrison lifted it dramatically to his mouth and inhaled. Out of respect for the range master's health, he expelled the smoke sideways, helping it along with a waft of his hand. "The government tells us that these things can kill a person. Well, in my case, that very nearly happened."

In college, during the late 1980s, Harrison had picked up smoking by chance. His roommate liked to smoke while drinking. Since Harrison often joined him in outings to bars or fraternity parties, an occasional cigarette found its way into his hands as well. After he graduated and made it through the FBI Academy, the habit grew, becoming a way to pass endless hours of surveillance.

"Anyway, I'm working in New York City five years ago, listening in on phone conversations between Russian mafia types, and I'm in need of tobacco. The wire taps were helpful, but we were hearing more about Sasha's wardrobe and Ivan's chess game than racketeering schemes."

"Were they talking in Russian?"

"You bet they were. Thick Crimean accents too, none of it clean Muscovite."

Sensing his fan's desire for more cinematic flair, Harrison continued, embellishing the details of the shooting incident that left him partially crippled.

"I embarked on a resupply foray, weaving a path through hookers and street hoodlums before reaching my destination. A seedy, foul-smelling liquor store. Once there, I found myself"—he took a long drag off his cigarette, and then extinguished it in an ashtray on the desk—"in the middle of an armed robbery in progress."

"No shit?"

"Let me tell you, a hundred scenarios about what to do flashed through my mind in an instant."

"I bet."

"Reflexes took over. All at once, I drew down on the bad guy and ordered him to drop his gun. The clerk behind the counter dove to the floor. The suspect hesitated and then made a fatal error in judgment."

The suspect had wheeled to his right and pointed his gun at Harrison, who then fired, striking the target center mass. The suspect tumbled backward and slammed to the ground. Harrison sensed what he thought was a strong recoil, only to realize that his balance was upset after taking a round in the right upper thigh.

"I kept my Colt pointed at the suspect though, unsure if the innocent bystanders were out of danger."

Increasingly dizzy, Harrison had collapsed, rapid blood loss rendering him unconscious.

"So that's how it happened?" Norm said, almost breathless.

A seasoned veteran, about to enter management, had nearly lost his life. Physical therapy helped, but his career was over. The FBI medically retired the forty-one-year-old special agent. On the advice of his doctors, Harrison relocated to the warm, mostly dry climate of Tucson.

"That's it," Harrison said.

"You still smoke."

"Yeah, and I still carry my forty-five in case I need to visit a liquor store."

Norm's body undulated. While his double chin and huge belly jiggled and his jeans cheeped, his large mouth released a barrage of laughter.

Swallowing the remaining contents of the coffee mug, Harrison looked at his watch. "Thanks for the java, but I should get a move on."

"Sure thing, Mr. Harrison." Norm settled back and wiped a tear droplet from his bright cheek. "Where you off to?"

To another dull, routine fraud case, Harrison thought. He stood, placing a hand on the corner of Norm's desk. "I've got to interview a guy about a bogus insurance claim."

"You going to put him under the lights?"

"Something like that." Harrison smiled. "He'll certainly wish he'd never heard of William Bernard Harrison."

In his black Dodge Charger, Harrison attached a red clip-on tie to his plain white shirt. He removed the Hopkins file from his briefcase, tucked a pen into the shirt's breast pocket, and clutched a digital recorder. As he stepped out of the Dodge, he set the file and digital recorder on the seat and put on a charcoal, wool-blend suit coat. He cleared his throat, checked the jacket's inner pocket, brushed dog hair off one sleeve, grabbed the file and digital recorder, and then shut the door.

Walking toward Hopkins's small, aging home, he tried to hide the limp. Even on this day, November 11, the midmorning air retained enough warmth to make his movement easy and smooth.

He knocked firmly on the wooden door. A few flakes of faded and cracked maroon paint dropped to the ground. On the right side of the front porch, a mustard-colored love seat, front legs broken, showed years of rot and decay.

A disheveled, middle-aged man answered Harrison's knocks. "Yes, what is it?" he said, yanking at the front of a dingy white bathrobe.

His thin, greasy black hair was compressed on the sides, but stood at attention on the crown of his head.

"Hello, my name is William Harrison. I'm calling on Jerry Hopkins regarding his insurance claim. I believe he's expecting me."

"Oh, that's me," Hopkins said, now smiling. "Please come in." Hopkins closed the door behind Harrison and then collected scattered newspapers and other household debris, clearing a spot on a brown vinyl sofa in the living room.

Instinctively, Harrison examined the unfamiliar surroundings. Within his view, he could see the kitchen, bathroom, and a hallway leading to the bedrooms. He focused more closely on the living room. It stood sparsely furnished with a sofa, brick-and-plywood coffee table, and several metal chairs. Its worn green carpeting, frayed and matted, had seen better days long ago. There was a television set on top of a bookcase filled with magazines and old newspapers. A "Perot for President" bumper sticker, placed diagonally across the side of the bookcase, was yellowing and beginning to peel off. Hopkins had the television tuned to *CNN Headline News*. A news anchor delivered report on increasing tensions between China and Taiwan.

"Have a seat."

"Thank you." Harrison stepped over a pair of work boots and sat down, the vinyl cushions slowly deflating underneath him. "You live alone, Mr. Hopkins?"

"Just me and my cat."

The fat, lazy creature sprawled itself in the middle of the hallway floor. It was mostly black, but with white fur on its stomach, paws, and face.

"Nice cat." Harrison sighed. "What's its name?"

"Sylvester. Don't you think he looks like Sylvester?"

"Yeah, like the cartoon."

"Exactly. 'Thufferin' thuccotash!'"

It was a good impersonation, even including spittle.

"Sylvester's about the best company I could ask for, outside of a good woman. Far less maintenance than a woman though, don't you think?"

The initial stage of these interviews was rarely interesting for Harrison. He wanted to make Hopkins twitch, not talk to him about Sylvester or his relationship experiences.

"Yes, well, there's a lot to be said for cats, but I need to discuss your insurance claim for the stolen computer."

"Aren't you here to pay me for it? You didn't bring a check?"

"I was asked by your adjuster, Susan Jacobs, to follow up on a few things because she's awfully busy right now. One of those things is to get another statement from you regarding the loss."

"Christ, you people are more difficult to deal with than I expected." Hopkins unfolded a metal chair and sat down. "Why do you need another statement when I've already told you everything? The police report should have everything you need for your adjusting, or paper pushing, or whatever you guys do. When will I get paid?"

Harrison fought back a yawn.

"I apologize, Mr. Hopkins. Believe me, I want nothing more than to see this claim come to a quick resolution. But please understand, when I take on a claim that I know nothing about, I like to make sure that I completely grasp the facts. That usually means interviewing the claimant myself. I know this may seem like the runaround to you, but the sooner I can get this interview done, the sooner this claim will be ready for settlement."

"Well, it seems like a lot of bull, but I want to get paid for my stolen computer."

"Thank you. And thanks for being patient." Harrison set his digital recorder on the coffee table. "Do you mind if I use this? It helps with accuracy and makes the interview go faster."

"If it will speed things up, sure."

After starting the recorder, Harrison proceeded to ask Hopkins a series of questions about the alleged loss. He did not expect to learn anything new. In fact, it was Hopkins whom Harrison planned to educate.

"So, if I understand correctly, you bought the computer for personal use, for financial record keeping, entertainment, and learning purposes?" As he finished the question, Harrison glanced around the room again.

"That's right. I figured it was time for me to catch up with the modern world. If people don't get computer literate, they lose out, don't you think? If I don't improve my computer skills, I'll never get promoted at the warehouse where I work."

"I agree with you. Tell me, since you didn't know much about computers, how did you go about buying the one that was later stolen from your home?"

"I pretty much relied on the salesman to help me pick one out. I told him why I wanted it, and he made a couple of suggestions."

"Did you shop around much, or did you just go to the one store, the Bits and Bytes on Craycroft?"

"Just to Bits and Bytes. I'm busy, the store was close, the salesman was helpful, so I decided to buy it from him."

"I see." Harrison's eyes scanned the living room, ceiling to floor, wall to wall. "Were there any signs of forced entry to the house that you or the police found?"

"No. I have a tendency to leave without locking the front door sometimes. It's a bad habit, but I grew up in different times. They must have just walked right in. Can't trust anyone these days. My neighbors never saw nothing either. They were all at work. I was at work myself. And Sylvester here isn't much of a watch cat. Hey, kitty, kitty."

Down the hallway, Harrison saw that Sylvester walked slowly into the bathroom. Then, turning his head back toward Hopkins, he noticed that CNN had a photograph of Harold Groom on the screen.

"Harold Groom, known more for his claims about government conspiracies than his crime, was found dead in his isolated cell today."

"Do you mind if we turn that up?" Harrison asked, pointing at the television.

"Are we done for the day?"

Harrison ignored the question and listened closely to the report.

"A prison spokesman said that determination of the cause of death will be pending an official inquiry, however, authorities suspect that Groom experienced a heart attack, as he was complaining of chest pains for several days. Awaiting execution on Florida's death row, a jury convicted Groom eighteen months ago for the triple murder of a computer software executive, his wife, and young daughter. In other news, Taiwanese shore guns fired on a Chinese navy patrol vessel."

"Do I get my money now?"

Hearing the news about Groom made Harrison wish he were back in his office. *Where did I put that postcard?*

"Huh? Oh, no, you don't," Harrison said.

"Well it better not take too much longer. I sure learned my lesson though. You can't trust anyone these days."

Harrison straightened his posture. "You're right, but I guess you would know that better than most people. This claim is fraudulent. You know it, I know it, and soon the police department will know it."

"What? What are you talking about?" Hopkins's face twitched.

Reaching into his inner coat pocket, Harrison withdrew and unfolded a document. "This is the receipt, and I use that term loosely, which you submitted in support of your claim. Please note that it is a photocopy. Do you have the original?"

"Not handy."

"I'm certain you don't. If you did, I know that I would find correction fluid all over it." After setting the receipt on the coffee table, Harrison opened the Hopkins file, revealing another document. "You see what that is?"

"Well, it looks like my receipt. I can expla—"

"No, let me. That is the store's copy of an estimate, your estimate, for a computer system which you had expressed an interest in purchasing. You altered the estimate, making it look like an actual receipt. The claim is fraudulent, Mr. Hopkins."

"I don't understand. Susan Jacobs handled the other ones." The perplexed expression on Hopkins's face suddenly brightened. "The claim can still be settled, can't it? Maybe you'd be willing to—"

"The recorder is still on, and I'd advise against further complicating your situation."

Hopkins sneered and shook his head. "The claim was only for a small amount. This can't be, it just can't."

"So, you thought it would be overlooked? It may very well have slipped through the system unnoticed, unsuspected, but you miscalculated. You've had multiple reported losses in recent months. Quite a paper trail. This made your last claim a red flag. Looks like your past has caught up with you."

"Go to hell!"

"Instead, I think I'll go see a detective I know in Tucson PD's fraud section. He enjoys it when I bring him cases that are all wrapped up. All he does is carry my documentation over to the DA's office, and they generally file a criminal complaint the same day. Oh, and by the way, cops hate it when they take bogus police reports. They'll want to charge you for that crime as well. You think it's hard to get a promotion at your job without computer skills? Well, just see how difficult it is when you have a criminal history."

"The cops will arrest me for this?"

"Oh yeah." Harrison collected the documents and closed the file. He leaned toward Hopkins, and then whispered, "Ever worn handcuffs?"

Quiet and sullen, Hopkins slumped in his seat. The front of his robe drooped open, exposing stained underwear. "What do you want from me?"

"Cover your crotch and I'll explain an alternative to you."

As Hopkins adjusted himself, Harrison opened the file again and removed an insurance company form, thick with multiple pages. He handed it, along with his pen, to Hopkins.

"Sign this form, and your claim and crimes will go quietly away."

"What is this?"

"It basically says that you want to withdraw your claim and that you would like to cancel your policy. Once you sign it, I'll give it to the insurance company."

With a quick flick of the wrist, Hopkins complied. "Goddamn, money-grubbing insurance companies."

Harrison turned off the recorder and took the paperwork from Hopkins. "Yes, yes. Their bottom line is all that matters. Your greed is all that matters to you. Frankly, all of you disgust me."

"Get out of my house before I throw you out!"

Collecting the file and tape recorder, Harrison was relieved to be finished, and did not mind that Hopkins still had his pen. He left without it. Outside, he heard the door slam. The noise did not bother him.

The news about Harold Groom did.

Zemdarsky and Associates.

Harrison and Associates.

Two private investigators shared a first-floor suite of an aging office building in downtown Tucson. The names of their firms were misleading, as no "associates" existed. But the use of the term provided prestige to their businesses, or so the owners believed. Their location, near the police station, courthouse, and central business district, lent itself to making contacts and attracting clients.

A new parking structure, just across the street, left only a short walk for Harrison. This was good for a man with a limp. He could park in a handicap space, but opted not do that.

Pushing open the glass and chrome door to his shared office suite, Harrison had only one thought on his mind. He wanted to find a postcard he had received last July. There had been a cryptic message on it, printed neatly, about Harold Groom.

"Yo no soy," a female voice said from behind the front counter.

Harrison stopped, confused, wondering if he had entered the wrong office. Pete Zemdarsky was nowhere in sight. A thin, worried-looking Hispanic male stood at the counter, and a very attractive woman spoke to him.

"Un momento, por favor." The woman looked at Harrison and said, "Can I help you, sir?" Her glowing face, blond hair, and bright blue eyes made him immediately think of a flight attendant he had once met on a long Lufthansa flight to Stockholm. Only the woman standing before him was much younger. Harrison guessed that she was probably in her mid- to late twenties.

Reluctantly, he drew his eyes away from her for a glance around the office. There was the small sofa and coffee table to his left. Along the wall directly ahead, there were bookshelves that he and Pete shared, although the space was mostly dedicated to Harrison's collection of American history and constitutional law books. Two gray filing cabinets and an aging green electric typewriter also occupied space in the familiar cramped alcove to his right, just beyond the yellow Formica counter.

There's that old globe Dad gave me, Harrison thought.

"Sir?" Her voice, professionally sensitive and youthfully seductive, invited his attention once more. "May I help you?"

For the moment, he forgot about Harold Groom.

"Can you help me? I don't know, can you? Who are you, and what have you done with the chubby, bearded fellow who sits over there?" Harrison pointed to the cluttered desk in Zemdarsky's office.

She responded with a warm smile, revealing perfectly aligned, white teeth. "You must be Mr. Harrison. Mr. Zemdarsky stepped out for a moment." Edging closer, the woman put out her hand.

"Yes, I'm William Harrison." He took her hand in his. "And you are?" *Working for us, I hope.*

Her cheeks blushed. "I'm Janice Evans, the new intern."

"New intern? We never had an old intern."

Janice tried to answer, but the sudden rattling and clanking from a heavy pastry cart entering the office overcame her words.

"Hey, Willy, my boy, scoot, scoot," Pete Zemdarsky said, pushing the cart. "You want a donut, or perhaps a bran muffin?"

Without turning around, Harrison said, "Pete, what are you doing with the whole damn cart?"

The racket ceased.

"Its attendant is in the restroom, not feeling well or something, and so I told her that I would keep an eye on her tasty commodities until she could fortify herself."

Turning around this time, Harrison saw Zemdarsky. He wore his usual brown three-piece, pinstriped suit and brushed some crumbs off his thick black beard.

"Scoot, scoot. I see you've met Janice." Zemdarsky's teeth and wide mouth fastened onto a fresh cheese Danish.

"Yes, I have, but, hey, you are going to pay for that and whatever else you've already consumed?"

Zemdarsky tilted right and looked at their new intern. "Oh, don't mind him; lately he's usually in a foul mood until noon or so. Would you like a bear claw?"

As Janice politely accepted, Harrison walked around the counter. "I haven't been in a foul mood." Harold Groom returned to his thoughts, and two stacks of case files on his desk came into view. "I just didn't expect...Are you even listening?"

Gazing at the pastry cart, Zemdarsky nodded. "You know, she still has Halloween napkins on here."

"Excuse me, gentlemen," Janice said with firmness and deference. "This is Alonzo, and he's concerned about his missing pet iguana, Huevos."

Harrison looked at Zemdarsky. Zemdarsky looked at Harrison. Both restrained smiles.

In Spanish, Janice asked Alonzo a quick question, then translated the answer. "He says that his cousin may have taken Huevos, and the police don't seem to be interested in investigating the situation."

"Why does he think his cousin would do that?" Harrison said.

Pete took another bite of Danish.

"Apparently, his cousin has made prior comments about turning Huevos into some form of clothing."

"I bet moe's wifey," Pete said, his mouth full.

Harrison cocked his head, not understanding that Pete had just tried to say, "A belt, most likely."

Also confused, Janice said, "He was wondering if one of you might be willing to look into it."

Pete swallowed hard. "Tell Alonzo that both our caseloads are quite full right now and we aren't taking on any more clients."

Before she translated, Janice looked at the other investigator. "Mr. Harrison?"

"I don't know." *The Huevos Caper. Is this the "infinite horizon," Dad?* Harrison thought. "Miss Evans, tell Alonzo that I respectfully decline. And tell him to try the Humane Society. Actually, take his name and phone number. I'll pass it along to Sergeant Verone at the PD. Maybe he can call Alonzo about the theft. I can't promise anything, but tell him that anyway."

Harrison walked into his office, listening to Janice translate the message. He saw that Alonzo seemed disappointed, but grateful. On his way out, Alonzo accepted a Danish from Pete, who then asked Janice to brew another pot of coffee.

After sitting, Harrison removed the Hopkins file from his briefcase and looked at the two tidy stacks of case files in the center of the blotter pad. The one on the left was for "active" cases, and the one on the right was for "completed" cases. He placed the Hopkins file on top of the completed stack, and then set his briefcase on the floor. Rather than preparing the final report for Susan Jacobs, the insurance company adjuster, he began opening the desk's various drawers, digging through forms, stationery, pens, and pencils. Everything had a proper place on or in Harrison's desk, but he was unable to recall exactly where he had put the postcard about Harold Groom.

"Poor Huevos. Maybe he got in a bite or two before Alonzo's cousin turned him into a clothing accessory," Pete said, shuffling into Harrison's office and sitting in a chair by the door. "You aren't serious about calling Verone, are you?"

"It's just a simple phone call. Verone owes me."

"But to cash in your chips for an iguana?"

Halting his search, Harrison leaned back into his chair. "When did we decide to hire Miss Evans?"

Pete exhaled, rounding out his husky frame. "This morning."

"This morning?"

"And she's not 'hired.' She's an intern. She won't cost us a dime."

"Shush."

Gracefully, Janice entered Harrison's office and handed him a cup of coffee. Her fair skin and Nordic features, along with the navy-blue suit and tartan scarf, summoned the memory of the flight attendant again. "I understand that you like it black."

"Yes, thanks." Harrison took the cup, looking at her ringless fingers.

"Mr. Zemdarsky, would you like some more?"

"No thanks, sweetie. Are you off now?"

"Yes."

"Off?" Harrison said.

"To school. I'll be back this afternoon, after my classes are over. I'm majoring in sociology at the university, with a minor in criminal justice. That's what this internship is for."

"I've already signed her curriculum form, Bill. She needs to complete an internship in order to graduate, don't you, Janice?"

"Yes. I'm afraid I missed the regular deadlines for the government positions. My counselor approved my request to intern with a private company."

"How did you happen to choose us?" Harrison asked.

"You're close to the campus. Plus, well, I kind of liked your ad. Your portraits made you seem very professional."

Harrison peered out the door. The pastry cart was still sitting in the middle of the office. "And you haven't changed your mind?"

Janice laughed. "Of course I haven't."

"I told her about your FBI background, Willy."

"Did you tell her about your background?"

"I also mentioned how you speak Russian, and that you studied law and American history at UCLA. She seemed very interested. I think you'll be of great help to her."

Harrison restrained the urge to roll his eyes. Instead, he stood and straightened his jacket. "Then let me formally welcome you aboard, Miss Evans."

"Thank you, and please, call me Janice," she said, shaking hands with Harrison.

"And Bill is fine with me."

"Gee," Pete said, "now that we have gotten most of the formalities out of the way, can anyone tell me where today's mail is?"

"I have it at the front desk," Janice said. "I sorted it into two piles, one for 'Zemdarsky' and one for 'Harrison.' I hope that was okay."

Pete grinned. "There, you see, Billy boy, things have already improved by having Janice here."

"Yeah," Harrison said, finding it difficult to look away from the new intern.

"Well, gentlemen, I really have to get going. Here is Alonzo's number." Janice handed Harrison a sticky note, which he took from her with a nod. "I'll see you this afternoon."

While Harrison's eyes escorted her out the door, his ears heard Pete chuckling.

"So, Willy, what do you think of her?"

"She seems bright. Her Spanish skills will be helpful." He returned to his seat and opened the desk's center drawer.

"Yes, and her pretty face will be nice to look at, as opposed to your sour mug. What's up, Bill? What's been bothering you?"

There it is, Harrison thought. Pulling the postcard from underneath an instruction manual for his computer, Harrison said, "Nothing. Just a little bored, I guess."

He glanced at the picture of Explorer 1 on the front, and then flipped it over. The postcard represented the first in a series printed by the National Air and Space Museum, commemorating the early years of space exploration.

"A little? I haven't seen you taking on many clients lately. I could not believe you were actually considering the case of the missing iguana."

"I was just trying to be helpful." Harrison gazed across the desk at Zemdarsky. He realized how, more and more, they were beginning to resemble each other. The beards, the suits, the large builds, the clientele. "Honestly," he continued, dropping his head, "helping Alonzo was probably the most useful thing I've done in a long time."

Harrison read the postmark: "July 24, Dayton, OH."

Zemdarsky got up and shuffled toward the door. “Training Janice to be a great investigator would make someone feel pretty useful as well, someone who has real expertise and is in need of a good challenge. You’re the right man for the job, wouldn’t you agree?”

Suddenly, Harrison was embarrassed. Not from the compliment, but because he had forgotten how perceptive Pete could be.

“Remember, your mail is out here, in the ‘Harrison’ pile.”

“Thanks.”

Harrison read the neatly printed words on the back of the postcard.

“Oh, look,” Zemdarsky said from the outer office, “the ‘Zemdarsky’ pile is bigger!”

But Harrison did not laugh. He winced and rubbed his injured leg. It had started to ache again.

FOUR

Systems Normal, Tell No One

In a private conversation during John and Anna Ridley's thirtieth wedding anniversary, Nick Ridley's sister, Megan, had arranged to meet with him to discuss her husband, an air force sergeant based at Nellis. Now sitting on a bar stool in his apartment's kitchen, Ridley sipped coffee, read a UNLV alumni newsletter, and waited for Megan. He yawned, brushing toast crumbs off his faded blue jeans and gray polo shirt.

Three years younger than Ridley, Megan always found her brother to be supportive and protective. She often came to him for advice, but this was the first time since her marriage that she sought him out for help. Ridley cared deeply for Megan, and he liked his brother-in-law, but with the strain from his job and difficulties with the police department's brass, he had enough of his own worries.

A light knock drew Ridley's attention from the newsletter. The door opened, and Megan's soft voice drifted tentatively from behind it. "You up, Nicky?"

"Come in, Megan. Just getting some coffee. Want some?"

Megan stepped inside and closed the door. She declined the coffee, and, sighing, she set her purse and sunglasses on the kitchen counter next to her brother.

"I hoped you would bring my little nephew with you," Ridley said, noticing Megan looked sad. "Is he okay?"

"He's great, Nick; he's with Mom and Pop for the day, and Eric is still up at the base."

"Did they ask what you were up to?"

"I'm Christmas shopping." Megan feigned a smile and winked. With her hand, she brushed long strawberry-blond locks away from her freckled forehead and cheeks.

"Well, you better pick something up after you leave. You know, supporting evidence."

"I'm not the one they'd blame for telling a fib."

Ridley chuckled, and then said, "Did you come here just to give me grief?"

"Don't be so silly." Then, sniffing the air, Megan said, "Did you have a date last night? She wears lovely perfume. Oh my gosh, Nicky, is she still here? Maybe she'd like to meet me?"

"You're too much. Yeah, I had a date. And no, she's not here. Are you here to spy on me for Mom and Dad, or to talk about Eric? What's going on with you guys? Is there a problem? You guys seemed fine at the anniversary party."

Megan's complexion noticeably whitened, almost matching the color of her long-sleeve blouse. The ache in her heart prompted tears to appear. Her next words came timidly. "Eric is in some kind of trouble at work. He won't talk about it. He tells me not to worry. But he just isn't the same."

"What kind of trouble?"

"He just says his work in air traffic control puts him under a lot of pressure. But he's been doing that kind of work since I met him. Until last summer, he never seemed stressed out."

"So that's when this started? Maybe it's the fact that he's a new father. Maybe it's not work at all, but the demands of being a parent."

"That's what I thought too. He's been so good with Owen. But he's been having nightmares, and walking in his sleep. Three or four times a month since about July, I'll find him standing next to the window in our bedroom, just staring. I don't dare wake him up. You know what they say, 'Never wake a sleepwalker.' The thing is he'll be talking to himself."

"What's he say?"

"It's gibberish. But sometimes it sounds like he's taking orders. He'll say things like 'yes, sir,' or 'no, sir.' It varies. But there's one phrase he always repeats." Megan paused to wipe away a tear from her cheek. "He says, 'Systems normal, tell no one.' At first, I wasn't sure, but I know that's it. I've heard him say it a dozen times. And then he will sometimes cry."

"Geez, Megan, I'm so sorry."

"Well,"—she attempted a smile—"other than some lost sleep and a bit of worrying, it hasn't been too difficult. He's going to need help, though. He's supposed to start on these weird shifts again next month, and I'm afraid he might get worse. He won't see anyone at the base, you know, a medical person."

"Why not?"

"He won't tell me. It upsets him when I ask about it. Look, he doesn't know that I'm asking you this, but would you be willing to talk to him?"

"I'd be willing, but if he won't talk to you, or a medical professional, what makes you think he'll talk to me?"

"I found this." Megan opened her purse and pulled out a wrinkled business card. "It fell out of his shirt pocket when I was sorting the laundry. Look on the back—it's Eric's writing."

Moving over to the sofa, Ridley knelt next to his sister and picked up the card. It was from a barbershop at the air base. On the back, a notation had Ridley's work phone number and the date, July 7. Ridley looked up from the card and noticed his sister's eyes were red and swollen. She pressed her arms tightly against her torso.

"See the date? That's right around the time when it started," Megan said, trembling.

"The sleep disturbances?"

"Yeah, like I said, the nightmares."

"Is he..." Ridley said, but he did not finish the question. The question was easy to ask in the field, on duty, out where the violence happened to others. "Sure, Megan." Each heartbeat carried a liberal dosage of anger. "How soon can I talk to him?"

FIVE

Echo Tango

Harrison's lungs expelled a gust of cigarette smoke, which blossomed into a wide plume before dissipating near the ceiling above his desk. After another puff, he looked again at the postcard, not at the photograph of US space satellite, Explorer 1, on the front, but at the odd message and signature on the back: "The truth about Harold Groom would give even healthy men coronaries. take Care, Echo Tango."

His reaction upon receiving the postcard last July was to dismiss it as an odd attempt at humor by one of his friends or former colleagues at the bureau. Harrison did, after all, have a reputation as an idealist, ever faithful in the wisdom of the governed. His respect for the virtues of democracy even earned him the nickname "TJ," short for Thomas Jefferson. Someone may have seen Groom's assertions about sinister deeds committed by the US government as a basis for poking fun at him.

But why sign it "Echo Tango"?

He had tried to contact his last partner, Art Holcomb, at FBI headquarters, but learned the special agent was on temporary duty elsewhere and unavailable. The secretary took a message, but Holcomb never returned the call.

Looking again at the postmark, Harrison wondered whom he knew in Dayton, Ohio.

Busy with his own work, Harrison probably would have forgotten about the matter entirely, except that Groom's name kept surfacing. For nearly a year, occasional stories had appeared in the press. Groom, the death row inmate, had made unspecified claims about political conspiracies and government assassins. An elderly, articulate, and vivacious man, the media saw Groom as an unlikely criminal, especially for someone convicted on multiple counts of murder.

But because of the overwhelming evidence against Groom, and his own admission of guilt, the angle was never about a possible miscarriage of justice, or even his claims. Rather, the Groom stories served another purpose. They focused attention on a disturbing new trend in capital crimes. Increasingly, felonious senior citizens were shooting, stabbing, bludgeoning, or poisoning their way into death rows across the country.

Harrison stared at the postcard's message, focusing on the words "take Care." *Why was that familiar?* he thought.

If it had been a joke, the announcement about Groom's death, apparently from a heart attack, eroded any intended humor. Extinguishing his cigarette, Harrison set the postcard aside and convinced himself that there was no reason to attach any significance to it. It was just a simple coincidence.

Swiveling right, he switched on his computer and angled the monitor downward, decreasing reflections of sunlight coming through the open window blinds. He grabbed the Hopkins file, opened it for reference, and began typing a summary for Susan Jacobs, the insurance company adjuster with whom he worked on the case. From the reception area, he heard the pastry attendant thanking Pete for tending to her cart.

"He owes you for a bear claw and at least two cheese Danishes," Harrison said.

"Really, Bill, must you disparage me so?"

The typing continued: "Subsequent to making a false burglary report to the Tucson Police DepArdment..." Spotting the misspelled word, he immediately corrected the mistake. "Department, Gerald

Hopkins submitted his fraudulent claim for stolen property, given to him by his father..."

"Wait," he said. "What the hell is that?"

The simple details of Hopkins's crime were suddenly difficult to recall. Harrison's eyelids fluttered, and his head began to ache. He felt like someone's fingers were pressing against his temples, harder and harder.

ARDCom's in Dayton, he thought.

He shook his head, moved the cursor, and then started typing again. "...stolen property, a personal computer described in an estimate from Bits and Bytes (See Appendix, Exhibit 1947). Amount of the purported loss was listed as a matter of national sec—"

"take Care that the Laws be faithfully executed..."

The tapping on the keyboard stopped. The format and language for these investigative summaries, so routine and familiar, vanished from his memory, collapsing into a mere pinpoint of light, surrounded by an endless black void. Harrison's expression became utterly vacant.

Fingers hovered over the keys.

Shallow breaths.

Pupils widened. Glassy spheres. A glimmering droplet receded below.

The volume on the cassette player was too low. Springsteen should be played loud. But studying came first. He reviewed laws of arrest and tried to translate them into Russian, just for practice.

Ochen khorosho, tovaresh.

The letter from his parents sat nearby. They were in Palm Springs, again. For a moment, he wished that he could be there too. A vacation would have been good.

He wanted to see them, but he knew they would come to Quantico for his graduation, to see their son become an FBI special agent. Would his dad find the time?

Aside from his books—more books than most people had—his possessions were minimal. Just the cassette player, some music, a few suits.

And an old globe.

A lonely heart too, but there was no time for dating.

When the phone rang, he saw that it was already 2:00 a.m. Who calls this late? *His roommate answered, guessing that it was his fiancée with another question about invitations or color schemes or the relatives in Poughkeepsie. The caller's voice was stern.*

"It's for you, Bill."

The caller did all the talking and offered condolences, assistance. He hung up the phone, closed his books, and packed a suitcase. In silence.

Harrison's parents were not coming to Quantico.

He flew to LAX and then drove to Pasadena, to their home. A neighbor was there.

"Hi, Mrs. Carr."

He went inside. Everything was the same, except for his room. The furniture was gone. It was a den now.

The time went slowly. He sorted things, sold items, and gave others away.

They went into the ground. Together.

Nothing was left, as far as he could tell.

A realtor and lawyer helped him.

He drove to LAX, but made a detour on his way. There were no tears during the stop. A few smiles. Even a laugh, to himself. At his stop, he admired the building's unique architecture and the view of the Los Angeles basin, but he did not go inside. Springsteen was on the radio as he drove away.

A pinpoint of light dilated. The darkness dissolved.

Quick taps on the keyboard resumed. He made a few corrections. Within minutes, two copies of the completed Hopkins investigative summary emerged from the printer on Harrison's credenza.

Although Harrison e-mailed a summary to Susan Jacobs, he also wanted to send her a hard copy, along with the signed disclaimer forms. After placing the materials in an envelope, he inserted the second copy into the Hopkins file. Normally, he would have prepared a billing statement, but he decided to wait until Janice Evans returned so that he could begin to explain administrative procedures to her.

With the envelope in one hand and his coffee cup in the other, Harrison walked to the outer office. The basket for outgoing mail was in an alcove next to the front counter. In this small room, the two private investigators had placed a photocopier, safe, metal cabinet, water cooler, and coffeemaker. The only sizable area within the alcove without clutter was in front of an emergency exit, which led to the building's lower-level fire corridor. There was also a drawer where Zemdarsky kept a flask of Jack Daniel's and other medicinal items.

"I thought you had some aspirin in here?"

Zemdarsky got up from his desk and followed the sound of Harrison's voice. Since there was room for only one person at a time in the alcove, he remained in the doorway. "Got a headache?"

"More like a migraine."

"I'm not surprised, what with how you were staring at that computer screen a few minutes ago. By the way, pizza's on its way."

"Double cheese? Found them."

"Yeah, the usual. You should use a typewriter, like I do. Does the job just as well, and you don't hurt your head."

Harrison swallowed the aspirin with a gulp of tepid coffee, and then refilled his mug. "Your flask is low. And it's only Monday. You just don't want to spend the money."

"I already bought the refill, just haven't transferred it."

"No, I mean for a computer. You're just cheap. They don't cost that much. How do you even manage to function these days without one? Having one will save you a lot of time. And time is money."

"Speaking of which, with tip the total is fourteen dollars and twenty-eight cents. A nice even figure."

Harrison laughed. "I've even got an estimate from Bits and Bytes. If you want, I'd be glad to give you a copy. We should try to save some pizza for Janice. What do you think?"

Closing one eye and furrowing his brow, Zemdarsky said, "Just a second." After a moment, his nose wrinkled and the other eye closed.

"Well?"

"Wait." Finally, the eyes reappeared, sweet and bright like maple syrup. "If we include Janice that makes it four dollars and seventy-six cents per person. Think she's good for it?"

"The question is whether you're good for it." Harrison massaged his forehead and limped from the alcove. He took seventeen dollars out of his wallet and laid it on a filing cabinet next to the globe. "It's my treat this time. Tell the delivery person that he, not you, can keep the change."

Pete swept by, mumbling something about rising cheese and dough prices, and grabbed the cash. Harrison gave the globe a gentle spin and grabbed his mail before returning to his desk.

One of his many marital infidelity cases involved a client whose husband allegedly had an affair with an attractive coworker. Since the case file was on top of the left stack on his desk, it was the first item he began to review. After unfolding it in his lap, he rotated the chair so that he could face the window and elevate his right leg on the credenza. The position helped to stretch his muscles and, with the help of the aspirin, to ease the pain in his thigh.

This particular case, initiated by an affluent and apparently unhappily married woman by the name of Elena Zinser, had been easy to investigate, and Harrison had more than enough photographs to implicate the husband.

There was also refuse. Receipts, notes, cards, and other innocuous pieces of litter, methodically collected for six weeks from restaurants, the Long Weekend Motor Lodge, A-1 Trips and Tours, and the other woman's garbage containers effectively documented Mr. Zinser's hidden agenda.

Harrison labeled or tagged each piece of evidence with a serial number that he cross-referenced to the log entries and field notes he had made during the investigation. These handwritten accounts of Zinser's comings and goings still needed to be typed, but there was one last document he wanted to include.

Harrison swiveled back to the desk and dialed a telephone number noted on one of Zinser's log sheets. "Hello, may I please speak to the office manager?"

After a moment, a man's gravelly voice answered, "I'm the manager."

"Hello, sir, my name is Wesley Hiatt. I hate to bother you, but one of our employees, Chuck Zinser, asked me to call. He stayed at your hotel last Wednesday night, and I'm trying to handle his reimbursement from the firm's expense account. The problem is that the date on the receipt is smudged and very illegible."

"Uh-huh."

"We've got kind of a strict accounting manager. She's insisting on seeing a copy of the registry form, where Chuck signed it. If it's not too much trouble?"

"What's the name?"

"Zinser. That's Z-I-N—"

"From last Wednesday?"

"Yes. It'll help me get him reimbursed."

"Yeah, here it is. You just want a copy of the page?"

"That's it. I really appreciate it. Just send it to my attention, Wes Hiatt." Harrison rattled off the address to a post office box he used for business purposes. "Thanks, and Chuck wanted me to tell you that he really likes your establishment."

"That's nice to hear."

"I'm sure if the need arises, he'll make it a point to come there again."

Harrison hung up the phone, smiling. He thumbed through his mail. Stopping abruptly, he went to the outer office and witnessed Zemdarsky, in one seamless movement, pay for, take, set down, open, and remove a slice of the pizza.

Harrison picked up one of the napkins left by the delivery person and then sat in the chair at the front counter. He examined the individual slices, finally selecting a piece that had the best overall combination of appealing characteristics, such as size, shape, amount of pepperoni, lean crust, and good cheese coverage. The first slice was always the most satisfying, and he wanted to make the right choice.

"Oh," Zemdarsky said, "I forgot to order the Coke."

"I guess we'll just have to drink coffee."

"Did Janice make it right? Strong, but not too strong?"

"Yep. She passed the first test with flying colors."

"Mmm, hat tree mimes me." Pete's mouth was full again.

"What? You should swallow first, then talk. I have to say, though, what you say with a full mouth is much more interesting than—"

"Let me try again. I said, 'That reminds me.'"

"About what?"

"I wanted to see if Janice sorted the mail correctly, you know, to check up on her work."

"Did she?"

"She did. Everything for me was in the 'Zemdarsky' pile, and everything for you was in the 'Harrison' pile. Nothing was mixed up."

"She does accurate work, and makes good coffee." Harrison eyed the tip of his carefully chosen slice, and then bit into it. A thick, sweaty pepperoni brushed against the roof of his mouth, moist crust collapsed under his teeth, and hot mozzarella cheese and sauce spilled across his tongue. He silently complimented himself for the excellent selection.

"Yeah, but I was curious about something, Bill."

"What?"

"Who's Echo Tango?"

Harrison looked at the mess. The underside of the pepperoni pizza slice, minus one bite, was staring up at him from the low-pile carpeting.

"What the hell do you mean, Pete?"

"In today's mail, there's a postcard from some 'Echo Tango' person. I thought it was rather mysterious, especially since that's the only thing on it."

Zemdarsky spoke to the back of Harrison's head, which grew smaller with each passing step.

Once inside his office, an attempt to halt his swift movement failed. The strain on the injury was too great, causing his right leg to stiffen, nearly pole-vaulting Harrison over the desk. He jammed an arm outward, a new axis, with counterclockwise rotation. The remaining journey to the floor gave him time enough for a wince, a chuckle, and a feeble grasp at something. Anything. Nothing.

Harrison's head thumped the wall. "Oh yeah, that'll hurt later. Isn't this day over yet?"

"In need of assistance?"

"No, no, I'm fine, thanks. Could you hand me my mail, please? It's next to the phone."

Stepping over Harrison's legs, Zemdarsky said, "I think, Billy boy, that you should practice your gymnastics at home. If not for your own safety, then for the preservation of our building's historic architecture." He shuffled through the envelopes. "Here it is."

Taking the postcard, Harrison immediately turned it over. "I don't get it—there's no message. It's just signed 'Echo Tango.'"

"That's what I was trying to tell you. It caught my attention."

Harrison stood slowly and squeezed past Pete, collapsing into his chair. "I have another one of these. Let's see, yes, here it is. Take a look."

While Zemdarsky examined Explorer 1 and read the message about Groom, Harrison flipped over the new postcard several times. On its front, an aerial photograph showed eight orderly rows of white and gray F-4 Phantom fighter jets partially surrounded by the desert terrain of Tucson. On the back, the postcard had a typewritten signature, "Echo Tango," Harrison's typewritten business address, the photograph's caption, and a Wichita postmark from October 31.

"Huh," Zemdarsky said, sitting. "So who's this Echo Tango?"

"I don't know." Harrison tapped a corner of the postcard on his lips. "That message about Groom is weird, but this one, frankly, is weirder."

"It's just a signature."

"The one about Groom was probably a joke, but this one—whoa!"

"What?"

Harrison sniffed again. "Take a whiff." He handed the postcard to Zemdarsky and smelled his fingertips. "What is that?"

"Kind of..." Zemdarsky snickered and then closed his eyes. "Kind of boozy, don't you think?"

"Yeah, but it...Here, let me smell it again." Harrison took the postcard and fanned it in front of his face. "It's sweet too. There's definitely an alcohol odor, sweet but clean."

"Rubbing alcohol?"

"It's sweeter, or cleaner, than that. Damn, I know I've smelled this before."

"Maybe the posty is nipping vodka on his rounds. Can't say that I would blame him, just as long as we get our mail on time. So, you don't know anybody with the initials ET?"

"You think someone's using the phonetic alphabet for their initials?"

"Why not? It makes sense. Law enforcement types use it, don't they? It's probably someone you worked with at the bureau. Either that or an extraterrestrial is trying to establish contact with you."

"Echo Tango. ET. Hmmm...No, no, none of the aliens I knew had those initials. Must be a former colleague."

"Well, obviously he has far too much time on his hands, whoever he is."

"I guess. Still, the pictures are nice." Reading the caption aloud, Harrison said, "These decommissioned F-4 Phantoms bask in the desert climate of southern Arizona. Tucson's low humidity make Davis-Monthan Air Force Base home to thousands of mothballed aircraft, stored for later use, deployment, or sale."

"It's the boneyard."

"Yeah, I've seen it from the road."

"They have tours. Maybe ET was in town and went for a visit?"

"But why mail it from Wichita? And why was the earlier one sent from Dayton?"

"I'm sure I wouldn't know. ET's your friend. Maybe he's a traveling salesman?"

"Wait, ARDCom's in Dayton."

"Huh?"

"ARDCom, it's the Air Research and Development Command, part of the air force. When I was at the bureau, I used to work with their liaisons, military types, air force officers who were assigned to assist us on counterintelligence cases. I wonder if our Echo Tango is one of them."

"An air force officer?"

"Maybe, although none of them were very humorous. They always seemed under siege. We bailed them out often enough; you'd think they would have taken a liking to us, but they didn't. There was this one that was just the absolute meanest son of a bitch."

"Mean to you?"

"To everyone. My last partner, Art Holcomb, stopped speaking to him. This guy was the worst."

"Doesn't sound like a promising lead."

"No, it doesn't. I doubt any of them would even remember me, let alone want to play some sort of postcard peekaboo, or whatever you'd call this. They're the kind of people who'd stamp the Bill of Rights 'top secret' and quietly file it away. I didn't make too many friends there."

"Then it's probably someone from the FBI."

"Yeah." Harrison fanned the postcard again, and then slid both cards into the desk.

Zemdarsky grunted and straightened his vest. "Let's eat."

Harrison's thumb found the "H" tab in the Rolodex on his desk. He started dialing Art Holcomb's phone number. "I'll be right out."

SIX

Las Cruces Alliances

Las Cruces, New Mexico, straddling the Rio Grande River roughly halfway between Truth or Consequences and Ciudad Juarez, could be a dreary and forlorn place without direct sunlight.

On this Saturday, November 16, billowy, rain-laden clouds converged just after sunrise, draining the color from adobe, plaster, and masonry. The city's rolling, scrubby, brown hills, dark against the gray sky, would soon struggle to absorb the heavy rainfall.

But the people gathered at the Ernesto A. Trujillo Community Partnership and Neighborhood Services Center were never happier. Some seventy strong, they stood close together, some arm in arm, in the parking lot or on the center's front walkway listening to hearty speeches.

Around the podium, the VIPs sat in folding chairs, waiting for their chance to speak. Behind them, an undulating breeze nudged a balloon arch anchored between two flagpoles. One pole flew the American flag, the other, the New Mexico flag. The arrangement wobbled occasionally, nudged by an increasing northerly breeze, which also wafted the wide, red ribbon draped across the front doors of the new community center.

With every congratulation made, or vision of success offered, the delighted families, dignitaries, business owners, and community members registered their approval. The vigorous applause and cheerful smiles spread easily through the crowd.

A few times, even Edward Taylor clapped his hands.

In the back row, which only he occupied, he saw Senator Vaughn after she stood and approached the podium. Plain in dress and looks, the second-term senator—a former journalist, lawyer, Chaves County executive, and college professor—struck her trademark pose: fists on hips, elbows out, hazel eyes centered on her audience.

The applause ended, Taylor's hands providing the final clap.

"I dare those clouds," Vaughn said, her voice loud and clear, "to rain on 'Nesto's parade. I just dare them." Cheering, some whistles, and then she continued, "I know that if Ernesto Trujillo has anything to do with it, he'll keep us dry."

Vaughn gazed skyward. Her little crow's feet deepened.

"He is still with us, and his inspiration is all around. His humble ways made his wisdom and imagination just that much more profound. His mere presence was enough to spur creativity in each of us. He was an example to us all, showing us that doubt and apprehension could be overcome through faithful commitment to such simple ideas as cooperation and mutual respect."

Her eyes met the crowd again. "I just know he is smiling at us, grateful, and wondering where we will go from here!"

The first tap on Taylor's right shoulder went unnoticed. His beige trench coat, covering his suit, V-neck sweater, and bulletproof vest, presented a formidable barrier for a polite fingertip.

A second tap, repetitive, culminated with a palm resting on the epaulet and a whispered, "I'm here, sir." The palm slid away.

"Just a moment," Taylor said.

Vaughn continued. "This community center not only honors the memory of a fine citizen, but forges a dynamic partnership between the university, chamber of commerce, local government, and the community as a whole to address the challenges we face in our homes and neighborhoods. This center and the services it will provide remind us that meaningful solutions do not just happen. They are nurtured by hard work and realized through the cooperation of many."

Taylor stepped away from the crowd and slowly walked out of the parking lot. He did not look back, though he knew the man who had tapped him on his shoulder was not far behind. Once behind the steering wheel of the rented Dodge Caravan, he checked the mirrors and started the engine. Taylor opened the sliding-panel door and gestured to the man to enter the van. "Please sit on the floor."

"Yes, sir."

As the door closed, Taylor eyed the rearview mirror. He was pleased with his passenger's choice of attire. The Colorado Rockies baseball cap, flannel shirt, Ray-Ban sunglasses, and bomber jacket made him look so ordinary, so American.

Pulling away from the curb, Taylor said, "What did you tell headquarters?"

The passenger's muffled voice emanated from behind the driver's seat. "White Sands is my next stop, so no explanation was necessary."

"Good. Stone is still in Ohio?"

"Yes. He has me working on the reclassifications and the online alert systems. Needless to say, I'm on the road a lot these days, like Jack Kerouac or Charles Kuralt."

"But that means you are out of touch."

The passenger took several seconds to respond.

"And what about yourself? You know, General, the border is only a short drive from here. What makes you so sure I won't just slip away for good?"

"That would only bring failure."

"For you."

"For me, yes. And for you."

More silence, except for a clicking turn signal and squeaky brakes.

After the van rounded a corner, Taylor said, "Besides, where would you go? Think about it. Your mission is the only thing you have left. History has seen to that."

"My point is that the more you rely on me, the more likely it is that we will get caught. And even if we succeed, where does that leave me?"

"This is not about you or me anymore. It is about everybody. I thought you understood that? Besides, I have to rely on you. Stone has managed to render me virtually irrelevant, while you are still very much on the inside. I cannot do this without you."

"So, I'm just supposed to trust you."

"Yes. I have protected you so far, have I not?"

The van crept over a shopping center speed bump. "What about the hybrids?"

"Hold on." Taylor parked and removed a cellular telephone from a pocket on his trench coat. He pretended to dial, and then held the phone next to his ear. "Avoid the male hybrid as much as possible. He has been transferred to Wright-Pat and reports directly to Stone now."

"And the female?"

"Still in Tucson and not scheduled for a medical exam until next month. I do not think she will be a factor."

"You're not sure then?"

"All you have to do is keep me posted on Stone's plans and run interference, if you have to."

"And the inventories?"

"Keep sending them. As a courtesy, I told Stone that I would review your retrieval lists and make recommendations."

"I've been getting your memos."

"Then you know that certain items are particularly sensitive."

"Yes, which makes it difficult to delay their containment."

"You will not have to wait much longer. I will keep you advised."

Taylor's passenger let out a loud sigh.

Taylor returned the phone to his pocket, and then drove toward the exit. Three blocks from the Trujillo Center, he had to turn on the windshield wipers.

"There's something else," Taylor said.

"Yes?"

"As you know, the most important document on your list remains missing and unaccounted for."

"Yes."

"It disappeared not long after you joined the ARDCom staff, did it not?"

Rhythmic windshield wipers set to high speed made the only discernible sound inside the van.

Taylor entered the vacant parking lot and stopped. A custodian detached two pieces of wide, red ribbon. He checked the van's mirrors, and then said, "I don't suppose you still have it?"

The van rocked slightly, and the passenger's door slid open. An abrupt slam from the shutting door prevented cold rain and wind from blowing inside.

SEVEN

Witch Hazel?

"I hope I look okay?" Janice said, placing a cup of coffee and her curriculum form on Harrison's desk.

He peered from behind the open briefcase on his lap. "Um, you look fine."

"I wasn't sure of the dress code, and since I go to school between shifts, I tried to find a good compromise."

Oh, your clothes? "No, you've been dressing just fine." Looking at her khaki slacks, olive blouse, trim waist, curved hips, and cerulean eyes, he was quite pleased. "I wouldn't change a thing." *Except my age.* "Have a seat."

As Janice sat, Harrison set the briefcase aside and sipped some coffee. He had just returned from another Monday-morning visit to Old Pueblo Guns and Range and found that Pete was out of the office, leaving Janice without any tasks other than taking phone messages.

"I'm sorry we haven't been more attentive during the past week, but we're not used to having an intern."

"I understand. I didn't exactly give you and Pete much warning."

"Still, we should try to be more organized about this. First, I don't know what feedback Pete has given you, but I really appreciate the fact you're on time, you've been courteous over the phone and at the counter with clients, and the clerical stuff has been accurate. I don't think you've made a single mistake. You've picked up things very quickly."

"Thank you, Bill."

"No, thank you. We're not all that busy, or at least I'm not, but it's been nice to have your help. Now, I've looked at your paperwork, and I don't think we'll have any problem covering the different areas. Of course, if there are other things you want to learn, just let me know."

"Well, now that you mention it, I am interested in learning more about field techniques."

"Sure, sure."

"I've also been reading some of your books out there, that is, when I've been in need of something to do."

"Oh really? Which ones?"

"Last week I read *The Federalist Papers*, and today I started *The Oxford History of the American People*."

"That one should take you a while. At least it won't collect dust. Wait, you've already finished *The Federalist Papers*?"

Janice smiled and said, "And I started *The Oxford History of the American People* today. Do you mind if I take it home until I've finished?"

"Home? No, no, not at all. It's a big book."

Silence accompanied mutual stares. She smiled. He coughed.

Harrison shifted in his seat and quickly scanned the curriculum form. "So, are you interested in maybe doing some essays? We could count those under 'research and report writing.'"

"That would be fine, but when do we get to do a stakeout?"

"Hah, I wish."

"Don't you do stakeouts?"

"Well, yeah, but they're not like what you see in the movies or on television. They can be very boring and unrewarding. Of course, that is part of the job."

"Right, and I want to see as much of it as I can."

"Your enthusiasm is certainly refreshing. What are your plans, anyway? Are you thinking about a career in law enforcement?"

"I don't know. My plans are kind of up in the air right now. I want to keep my options open."

Harrison hesitated, but then could not resist. "Have you ever thought about the FBI?"

"Actually, I have. You'd recommend it?"

"Well, I don't want you to neglect other options, but the FBI can be a great place to work. It's tough, but I sure enjoyed it."

"What made you choose them?"

"That's a good question. I guess..." Harrison swiveled left, toward the window. Two postcards were pinned to the bulletin board directly ahead, next to a memo from their building's security director about recent "prowler" sightings in the lower-level fire corridors. There was also a white, standard-sized envelope tacked below the memo. "I guess I wanted to serve my country," Harrison said. "Boy, that sure sounds naive."

"I don't think so."

He felt the comment more than he heard it. Twenty years was a long time to go without getting goose bumps. Harrison rubbed the back of his neck then folded his arms. "Yeah, well, those were different times, I guess. But I was also interested in law and couldn't see myself as an attorney stuck in some office all day long. I wanted to be out in the field to see things firsthand."

A portion of the standard-sized envelope hung below the bulletin board's wooden frame. White paper against white wall. As Harrison swiveled back toward Janice, his eyes met hers. She offered a perfect grin.

"Okay, so I guess your request to go on a stakeout isn't so unreasonable after all," Harrison said.

"When do we go?"

"I'll have to get back to you about that." He leaned back in the chair and raised his right leg, resting his calf on the corner of the desk. His eyes moved away from hers.

He saw light pine molding interrupted by white paper, again.

"Remember this first, Janice: There are three things that go together to make a good investigator, or special agent, or police officer, or lawyer, or just about any professional. Education, training, and experience. So, let's start with the basics, your education. Now, you are quite intelligent..." Pausing, Harrison massaged his temples and yawned. "Sorry, I haven't been sleeping too well lately."

"Maybe I shouldn't make the coffee so strong?"

"No, the coffee's fine. I probably just drink too much of it. Anyhow, using my little library out there, I want you to put together a short report for me."

Janice pointed to the notepad on his desk. "May I?"

"Help yourself. Need a pen?"

"Yes, please."

He pulled a pen from his shirt pocket. "Here you go."

"A report." Janice made a note, and then said, "On what?"

"Hmm...I know, why don't you surprise me? Use your own judgment and pick something that you're interested in that has some relevance to law, or legal history, or criminal justice. Maybe you can use it for one of your other classes. You know, kill two birds with one stone."

"Do you want me to start on it today?"

"Sure..." *Where did that envelope come from?* "And after you've finished it, then we'll move onto the next item, your training. It may sound too formal, but in law enforcement, credibility counts for a lot. If you don't have the right skills or knowledge, then you won't make good decisions. You won't be credible. It can make or break justice. Sometimes it can even mean the difference between life and death."

Harrison lowered his leg and stepped toward the bulletin board.

"Basically, people will come to rely on you, to trust you, only if they know you have the ability to get the job done. Instinct and intuition will only get you so far. What you know and how hard you work to fill in the blanks makes up the rest."

Typewritten on the front of the envelope was Harrison's name.

"In fact, as tough as the work may be, the toughest part is maintaining your commitment to it. If that falters, well, then you become useless, and the bad guys sleep easier."

"You know, I think you'd make a great teacher, Bill."

Harrison pulled out the pin holding the envelope to the bulletin board, reuniting the pine-molding border. The envelope had a sweet, clean smell.

"Why don't you go ahead and get started, okay, Janice?"

"I'm already on it."

As she slipped out the door, Harrison said, "Wait a second."

"Did you need something else?"

"Yeah." His deeply furrowed brow drew her closer. "What does this smell like?"

He held the envelope outward, looking down at her bright face. She was easily ten inches shorter than he was. Compact. Solid. But agile, athletic. *Even graceful.*

"Hold still." She steadied his hand with an embrace from her lean, smooth fingertips.

"Sorry, must be the caffeine."

Her warm breath brushed over his knuckles, dissipating near the white cuff around his wrist. "It's witch hazel."

Harrison's eyes stung. *Better blink now.* "Witch hazel?"

"Yes, I'm sure that's what it is." Janice slid her fingers away. "You know, it's like rubbing alcohol, but gentler. People use it for scrapes or abrasions. It's like a cleanser or disinfectant. Odd for a letter to smell that way."

Leaning on the edge of his desk, the injured leg dangling just above the floor, Harrison said, "Uh-huh."

"I've heard that some men use it after shaving. You know, for nicks on those sensitive spots."

"Uh-huh."

"Are you okay, Bill? You seem like you're a million miles away."

His response consisted of a few brief hand movements: pocket to mouth, pocket to mouth, a snap on his lighter. Minuscule flint fragments sparked and jettisoned from the flame. Two puffs. A third. He held the smoke inside. It emerged finally, when he raggedly said, "Probably just a coincidence."

"What?"

Harrison smiled and youthfully swung his leg back and forth. "Just thinking about something else. I should get to work. And you, young lady,"—he stood, tossing the envelope onto the stack of active case files—"have a report to do."

He did not let her see him wince. Once Janice was outside, poking through the bookshelves, Harrison quietly closed the door and limped back to his chair.

By the time he decided to open the envelope, Harrison had inhaled a second cigarette. Like the first, every shred of tobacco was scorched, turned to ash, the glowing ember sucked inexorably and completely to the butt. The coffee cup also ran dry.

"ATTN: WILLIAM B. HARRISON" was typed across the front of the envelope.

"Well," Harrison said aloud, "you've got my attention."

Transparent tape helped to form a tight seal on the back flap, leaving only a narrow lip on which to pull.

"Whoever you are."

His fingertips and thumb were too large, nails too closely trimmed, to make it work. He reached for his pen, and then remembered that Janice still had it. Taking the letter opener from the center drawer, he inserted the tip and made a clean incision.

The single folded sheet was thick. Something was inside it, attached with a paper clip. Slowly, Harrison unfolded the lower flap. The typewritten signature was there, way at the bottom. Above it, there were sentences. Long ones.

"At least ET has something to say this time."

Now, the upper flap.

"Damn."

A quick count of the cash totaled $3,000. After returning the money to the envelope, Harrison read the letter. When he finished, one more thing became clear.

No, this is not a joke.

He maneuvered patiently, keeping his thoughts in order and trying not to strain his leg. Easing the door open, Harrison saw Janice seated at the front counter, taking notes. Moving closer to her, he spoke calmly. A nice, pleasant Monday-morning office tone.

"Sorry to interrupt, Janice, but do you have today's paper? I think I see it under your book bag."

She lifted the bag. "Yes, here you go."

"Thanks." Harrison separated the sports and feature sections, folding them under his arm. "So, did you find something good yet?"

"Well, yes and no."

"I'm sure you'll do just fine."

His smile, wide at first, started to shrink on one side as he thumbed through the front section of the newspaper. He found the blurb buried on page six. The statement, issued by medical authorities in Florida, confirmed that Harold Groom had died from a heart attack.

"When did Pete say he'd be back?" Harrison said.

"After lunch. By two at the latest."

Reviving his grin, Harrison nodded and collated the paper, then politely handed it back to Janice. He returned to his office.

First pulling the suit jacket from the hook behind the door, and then shutting the door completely, Harrison checked and emptied his pockets. He dumped the coins, a cigarette pack, a lighter, a couple of throat lozenges, his key ring, and his wallet into a small heap on the desk. He put on the jacket.

He tapped the ashtray on the round rim of the trashcan beneath his desk. The ashtray went back onto the credenza. A wipe of his hands, then pictures of Explorer 1 and the aircraft boneyard came off the bulletin board. He inserted the postcards into a wide pocket on the briefcase's inner lid, along with Echo Tango's letter, envelope, and money. From the heap, his wallet, key ring, cigarettes, and lighter went inside too, into a floppy, zippered pocket. To those items he added a bottle of aspirin just in case his headaches returned.

Harrison looked at everything. Where things sat. The angle of each item. The position of the blinds. The twisted cord connecting the computer's keyboard to the terminal. He did not dwell very long.

Exiting his office, Harrison saw Janice at the front counter still reading. "Okay, I have a few errands to run," he said, trying to make the right, nonchalant inflection. "Just be sure to lock up. I guess I'll see you this afternoon."

Janice lifted her gaze, and then blinked a few times. "Yeah, about two o'clock."

"See you then."

To Harrison's surprise, the walk to his Dodge Charger was easy, without much, if any, limping. He figured this was due to the lighter-than-usual briefcase.

After driving away from the office, Harrison traveled only a few blocks to the Tucson Police Department's headquarters. From the briefcase, he took his wallet, a pen, and a notepad. Glancing at Echo Tango's letter, he wrote down the first of five reference numbers: "49-082705."

Although not confused by Harrison's request, the clerk in the Central Records Bureau showed mild interest.

"My client's a history buff, I guess. Who knows? I just do what they ask," Harrison said, a cheerful grin accompanying his response.

"I know what you mean," the clerk said. She was a buxom middle-aged Hispanic woman whose measured, ingratiating manner made Harrison's fingers sore—the ones clenching the notepad at his side. "Never a reason or explanation," she said. "Just 'I need it yesterday.'"

"Yep." Harrison's hand really hurt. "So, do you still have it on file?"

"Not in this office. A police report that old is kept on microfiche in the basement. I'm sure we can find it there. Just fill out this form. The fee is extra, of course, four instead of the usual three dollars." She leaned toward him. "It's to pay for the feather duster!"

"I can only imagine."

Another short drive and he arrived at the Sonora Travel Agency. The money accompanied Harrison this time, along with a list of four out-of-state destinations. He watched the lone agent, a young woman with curly black hair, tirelessly helping an elderly couple with Thanksgiving travel arrangements. They had many questions, mostly directed at each other and not the agent.

Under normal circumstances, Harrison made his own travel arrangements online. But with so many destinations involved, and the anonymity of a cash transaction, he opted for the assistance of a travel agent for this particular trip.

Harrison did not pass the time by gazing at the full-color posters advertising such exotic locales as Tahiti, Hawaii, and Cancun, nor by looking at the trifold brochures about European getaways. Magazines were also available, left untouched, their covers adorned with happy couples running on silky beaches, snowboarding in Colorado, windsurfing in Puerto Rico, dining in Rome. Even the lobby television, large, quiet, and unalterably tuned to the Travel Channel, eluded his attention.

After sitting, he briefly assessed the conversation under way between the agent and her customers. It would end soon enough.

So there was just the list. With legs crossed, it balanced on Harrison's left thigh. The yellow page, blue lines, and black ink, normally artless symbols, seemed to mock him and his circumstances.

Secrets did that to him. They insulted. They nauseated.

The residual scent on his fingertips, which spread across his lips and chin, only made matters worse.

He thought about leaving. The rush was wearing off.

Tucson, Seattle.

Escaping boredom was not a good enough reason for him to accept the case.

Albuquerque, Killeen.

But Echo Tango seemed to be right. Groom, apparently healthy, had died from a heart attack.

Los Angeles.

The five police reports in all of those cities would be worth collecting, and he had more than enough money.

Principles were at stake, and in Harrison's mind, next to an innocent life, nothing was more worthy of a fight.

Besides, his anonymous informant, the prowler who had gained access to his office, was someone he knew. And someone who knew him, his injury, his work history, his values, and the witch hazel.

Still chattering, the elderly couple completed their transaction and made their way past Harrison. He could tell the agent was relieved, so he immediately apologized when he approached her.

Twenty-one hundred and ninety-eight dollars later, he departed the travel agency.

Just after noon, Harrison entered the parking lot of Arroyo Verde, the townhouse complex where he lived. Set against the upward slopes of north Tucson, the residents of Arroyo Verde had a scenic view of the city below. Always freshly manicured, the grounds sympathetically combined indigenous flora with the amenities of suburban life. A swimming pool, tennis court, clubhouse, carports, and sandstone sidewalks sat among chubby saguaro and barrel cacti, mesquite, and ocotillo. Since yard space for each unit was minimal, the common-area landscaping was a charitable surrogate. Also helpful, the rocky skyline of the Catalina Mountains was not far away, a pleasant and rugged reminder of how close they really lived to the wilderness.

His unit, 2402 Padre Lane, was toward the back, next to where the crusty soil of Arroyo Verde dipped into a sandy creek bed that formed the western boundary of the complex. In the dry months, his neighbors were fond of walking their dogs along this natural trail. The dogs seemed to enjoy the ample variety of scents. The neighbors appreciated the open space and seclusion. While their eager pets sniffed for just the right spot, the owners knew that Fido would indeed go, gaining relief from the strict custodial rules of the complex and concerns about the sanctity of their carpeting.

Harrison also knew the routine well.

As he pulled into the assigned space in front of his townhouse, he saw her black snout poke through the curtains. She was on the sofa again. Within days of bringing her home, she had easily learned to distinguish the particular sounds of the Dodge—its engine, tires, transmission, and brakes. Two and a half years later, she never missed a single arrival. She always greeted him through the windowpane, smudging the glass while bracing herself on the sofa's cushions.

Harrison had heard the yelping and whining one night, about six months after he had moved in. It was very late. The dog, a puppy at the time, sat and scratched on the rim of the creek bed. When he approached, she crouched down, but still wagged her curled tail. After scooping her up, Harrison briefly looked around to see if her owner was also in the area. But no one was there. Between the wet licks, ecstatic barks, and an angry yell from a neighbor, he decided to take her in for the night.

She had been with him ever since. His "found dog" efforts—an ad in the paper, neighborly inquiries, a few flyers at the clubhouse, a listing in the monthly Arroyo Verde newsletter—never produced the owner. As it turned out, this was fine for Harrison. It only took him two days to decide on a name.

"Hi, Beano."

His hands were empty, except for the keys. The briefcase was in the car, along with five cans of Alpo, purchased at the grocery store just down the street. He intended to pack quickly.

"Want to stay with Uncle Pete?"

Through the office door they went, Beano darting around the front counter in search of Zemdarsky. She found him standing in the alcove next to the photocopier. His first reaction, from what Harrison could tell, was a response to Beano's peculiar gastrointestinal disorder.

"Holy Jesus," Zemdarsky said nasally. "Go away, you foul beast."

Dog and man emerged from the alcove, the man holding his nose.

"Come on, Beano," Harrison said, opening the door to his office. "Get in there."

The mutt, a black-and-tan shepherd-collie mix, obeyed.

"Oh, wait," Harrison said, remembering too late that he wanted to preserve the condition of his office.

Beano flew around the desk, sniffing, noisily and awkwardly climbing her way onto his chair. Her front paws came to rest, at first, squarely on his case files, then they slipped forward, sending the folders into a shuffling slide over the edge of the blotter pad, pushing his nameplate onto the floor.

"Stay," Harrison said. "Stay right there."

"What's up, Billy boy?"

Harrison hesitated until Beano made like a statue. Then, he turned around and saw Pete eyeing the leash and brown bag. Harrison cut right to the chase. "Can I ask you for a favor?"

"Does this have something to do with her?"

Beano barked.

"Well, yes, it does. I'm going out of town this afternoon, and I was hoping you wouldn't mind keeping her at your place."

"How long will you be gone?"

"Until Friday evening."

"I don't see why not. Mandy adores Beano, although I don't know why. She's a real stinkpot."

"You shouldn't say such things about your wife, Pete."

"As if you know anything about married life." He pointed to the leash and bag. "I assume those are for me."

"Remember, it's half a can in the morning and half a can at night."

"Please, William, I raised six children. I think I can tend to a dog for a few days."

"Whatever you do, do not give her any people food. You'll regret it."

"Well, if I do give her any, it'll be right before your return." Pete took the items from Harrison, momentarily inspecting the contents of the bag. "Speaking of which, if you're back early enough, why don't you join us for dinner. I'd love to fire up the grill. Weather's supposed to be divine this weekend."

"Sounds great."

"So, where are you headed?"

"Out of town."

"You don't say?" Pete rolled his eyes. "In regards to what?"

"A little break from the routine." Stepping into his office, Harrison lifted Beano off his desk and shooed her out. While he started collecting the scattered files and straightened up his office again, Beano trotted over to Zemdarsky and flung her front paws into his groin, panting.

"An attempt to rest and recreate? Right. Get down."

Beano sat briefly, and then sniffed her way into Zemdarsky's office.

Harrison mumbled a few unintelligible words as he continued to set things back as they were.

"What? I can't hear a word you're saying."

"A traveling client needs some security work. Bodyguard kind of stuff." Harrison knew it was a bad lie. Who would want a bodyguard with a limp? "Desperate for a replacement." He smiled, hoping the message elicited understanding from Zemdarsky.

"I guess so." Zemdarsky reciprocated, the wide grin stretching halfway to his portly earlobes. "Maybe we can discuss it another time?"

"Maybe. But that's what I'm doing, okay?" He emphasized it, repeating, "Okay?"

Zemdarsky nodded. "Yes, Mr. Harrison."

The abrupt noise was not loud. But it was prolonged and drawn out. A combination of scraping metal, rolling ceramic, rustling leaves, and sneezing dog. Pete stopped nodding. Harrison blinked heavily. Even without looking, they knew. There would be a mess to clean up in Pete's office. But after a bit of scooping, sweeping, and possibly some watering, Pete's plant, a recent gift from the pastry cart attendant, would be all right.

EIGHT

He Cop

Nick Ridley felt he would be more comfortable outside. Wednesday was his day off, and he normally spent such free time riding his Suzuki Intruder motorcycle in search of deserted roads. Sleek black and chrome, the fourteen-hundred cc's usually pushed him ever faster away from the city and closer to the sunset. In the solitude and twilight, he typically found what he was looking for.

But inside the Overton Valley Discount and Factory Outlet Mall, thirty miles northeast of Las Vegas on I-15, he felt like a runner who'd missed two weeks' worth of exercise. His limbs felt heavy, but every movement was quick as the energy tried to release itself.

The hands on his watch aligned. Six p.m. The banners of red and gold, wrapped in purple, faint streamers less than an hour ago, receded below the horizon. For him, all that remained was the cascade of meaningless fluorescent.

And then there was the guilt.

As deceptions go, it was mild, meant to help and not to harm. He and Megan agreed that they needed to do it.

Megan's husband, Eric, had eluded Ridley's efforts at direct contact. Ridley was unsure if Eric had purposefully done this, but mounting concern for his sister's welfare made Ridley suggest the scenario to Megan.

Resorting to the ruse was not the source of Ridley's anxiety, though. His private fears about her safety, and his difficulty confronting those fears, had shaken his self-confidence during the past ten days. He felt embarrassed that he had let his perceptions and comfortable assumptions about their lives prevent him from asking the hard questions. For a cop, for anyone, this was not good. There was no reason, he decided, that the facts should remain concealed, regardless of their impact on him or his family.

And so he waited and watched, resolute, concealed between the display racks and shelves of the Ascending Angels Bookstore. Sixty feet away, across the wide courtyard with its fountain and tiled planters, awaited the entrance to Ruby Tuesday Restaurant. Looking through a large glass case full of Jesus figurines and manger-scene snow domes, Ridley had a clear view of anyone who entered the restaurant. Behind him, an oil painting of giant, prayerful hands rested on an easel, while smaller vignettes of biblical stories hung on a nearby pegboard panel.

Within moments, Ridley saw them: Eric with his arm on Megan's shoulders, Owen comfortably asleep in the carrier Megan held.

Ridley's training took over, his eyes carefully assessing the scene. His sister and brother-in-law walked their way to dinner, a happily married couple, young and innocent, casual yet mindful of their child. Both dressed informally, she in a white blouse, sweater, and jeans; he wore jeans along with a green polo shirt and navy-blue windbreaker. It all appeared so normal, no hint of any problem.

Ridley let them move into the restaurant and continued to wait a few minutes more until he was certain that they had found a table, or better still, a quiet booth. Megan knew what he wanted.

Another couple entered the restaurant.

Slowly, Ridley stepped from behind the display case. Out of habit, he felt along the outside waistline of his leather jacket and ran a thumb inside the back pocket of his jeans. Gun and badge were there.

He strolled across the courtyard. People stirred all around, but apparently, none of them intended to eat at Ruby Tuesday.

One person, though, a late twenty-something blond man in a crimson sweater and squeaky brown loafers, sauntered past Ridley and turned toward the restaurant's entrance.

This was Ridley's chance, and he took it.

Just as he was about to enter the restaurant, however, his cover stopped suddenly. Ridley, a few paces behind, misjudged the duration of the pause and nearly collided with the blond man. Staring at the back of perfectly groomed blond hair, Ridley withdrew a step and leaned to his right, carefully trying to look beyond the obstruction. He saw Megan and Eric, seated as he had hoped at a booth near the rear of the restaurant.

"Excuse me, sir," Ridley said. The request went unacknowledged. Between the man, a potted plant on the left, and the vacant greeter's podium on the right, there was not enough room to pass. After a few seconds, though, the man moved ahead, rather casually, past the plant and toward the bar. Ridley sighed, a sigh of relief and frustration, and found his way to the booth, in full view of Megan, but not of Eric, who was facing the opposite direction.

"Hey, what a surprise this is," Ridley said. He noticed Owen was in his carrier on the seat with Megan. At five and a half months, the child already showed a remarkable resemblance to his father. Brown eyes, dark hair, olive skin.

Eric looked up, while Megan pleasantly said, "Nicky."

"Hope I'm not interrupting."

"Hi, Nick," Eric said. "Want to join us?"

Ridley believed his brother-in-law's invitation sounded genuine, without any trace of apprehension.

"You bet," Ridley said.

After Eric slid across the seat, opening a space, Ridley sat. Instinctively, he checked his subject's hands.

"So, how is the Gonzales family?" Ridley said, noticing that Eric was not wearing his wedding ring.

"We're doing just fine, Nicky," Megan said.

"That's good," Ridley said, gazing at Owen. The baby seemed excited by his uncle's arrival. For a moment, Ridley thought he saw the child wink at him. His parents apparently noticed this as well, as Eric and Megan laughed and voiced endearing "oohs" and "ahhhs."

"So, what's new with you?" Eric said, patting Ridley on the shoulder. "Megs says you have a new girlfriend."

Smiling was difficult, especially when he looked at Eric. His brother-in-law had dark circles under his bloodshot eyes. He remembered that this was how Megan had appeared when she met with him at his apartment.

"Let's not jump to any conclusions," Ridley said.

Withdrawing his hand, Eric said, "No pressure, no pressure. You'll know when the time is right."

"What, for marriage?"

"Yeah. I know I've never been—" Eric stopped midsentence. His eyelids fluttered. "Happier."

"That's good to hear," Ridley said, checking Megan for similar signs of weariness. There were no dark circles, but her eyes were red. Not a tired red, more of a crying red. "But, you know, cops generally make lousy husbands. Say, where's your wedding ring?"

Gripping the table, Eric slid toward Ridley. Water glasses and condiment containers fidgeted and rattled from the motion. "I...um... can you move?" Eric hunched his shoulders against his neck.

"Sure." As he stood, Ridley looked at Megan, confused.

She put her hands out, palms down, indicating to remain calm.

Eric mumbled something that Ridley could not understand, but it sounded like "He cop."

Ridley let his brother-in-law pass and watched him walk erratically toward the bathroom at the back of the restaurant.

"You can sit down now, Nicky."

Ridley returned to his seat. "What the hell was that all about?"

"I told you he was having problems."

"Has he been drinking?"

Megan cocked her head. "You know he doesn't drink."

"Drugs?"

"Of course not." She scowled at her brother. "Why don't you order something? We already have."

The suggestion made Ridley's stomach churn again. "I can't believe this." He took a deep breath, trying to quell the nausea, and stared at Megan. "Both of you look terrible, especially him."

Megan straightened the tableware that Eric's departure had jostled out of place. "He needs help. He's started having migraines."

"What about you?"

She continued her busywork, avoiding eye contact with her brother. "What do you mean?"

"You know what I mean."

"I'm tired, if that's what you mean, but only because of his sleep disturbances."

Slowly, Ridley reached out. He gently held his sister's hands. When she stopped moving and he had gained her attention, he let go, resting his arms on the table. "Megan, is he hurting you?"

"No." Her tone was reassuring, but an impatient riff blended in as well. "He thrashes about sometimes."

"In his sleep?"

"He used to, but not lately."

Ridley leaned closer and lowered his voice. "Did he ever hit you?"

Megan tried wiping a grease smudge on the table with her napkin, but Ridley stopped her. Megan exhaled, her dewy eyes floating upward before finally centering on Ridley. "Not on purpose."

"My God, Megan. Not on purpose? What the—" Ridley lowered his voice. "Have you talked to anyone?"

"Just you and base security."

"Then you reported it?"

She shook her head. "Not exactly. They came by a few weeks ago. They said the neighbors had reported fighting and arguing. I told them they were mistaken."

"So you've been protecting him?"

"He doesn't want them to know."

Through clenched teeth, Ridley said, "That's bullshit."

"It's not!" Megan glanced across the aisle, hoping their privacy was still intact. She lowered her voice. "Besides, we haven't been arguing or fighting."

"Then why would the police investigate?"

"They probably had the wrong address or something."

"So, he's not abusing you?"

"Absolutely not. You know Eric—he's the most loving, caring person I have ever met. But something just isn't right. He's losing control." And just then, Megan looked up and away from her brother, startled by what she saw. "Oh no!"

Dishes crashed to the ground, and a woman gasped. Another screamed. The commotion broke Ridley's concentration, and he quickly looked around. He saw Eric strolling up the aisle toward their booth. Shoulders hunched and brow furrowed, his brother-in-law's eyelids fluttered wildly. Despite the dim light, Ridley easily spotted the wedding ring. It hung attached to the chain of Eric's dog tags.

Metal glinted against smooth brown skin.

Eric was naked.

NINE

Stimulate the Nervous System

After Ridley's brother-in-law collapsed onto the floor in the restaurant, Ridley dragged the limp body into the restroom. A neat pile of folded clothes, shoes on top, awaited him in one of the stalls. The orderliness of the stall matched the restroom's pristine tiles, shiny doors, and an aroma of bleach and mountain pine, aerosol fresh. It felt clinical.

Only the squeak of Eric's bare heels rubbing on the tiled floor disturbed the quiet sterility. Ridley hurried, easily lifting him onto the toilet and propping him against the stainless-steel wall for support. Ridley eyed heavy waves of condensation, pitched out by Eric's deep breaths, rolling across the wall's cold surface. Reassured, he also pressed his fingers against Eric's neck, where he felt a steady pulse. Steady drool also flowed down Eric's cheek.

The presence of an angry and bewildered restaurant manager made dressing Eric difficult. The man contacted mall security, and as Ridley tied the last shoelace, security began taking a statement from Megan for their incident report.

"He hasn't been himself lately," Megan said, probably a dozen times.

Ridley showed the security guards his badge, gaining their full cooperation and an understanding that they did not need to contact the Clark County Sheriff's Department. When a packet of smelling salts failed to revive Eric, the security guards produced a wheelchair.

"We can have the paramedics come and check him out," one of the guards said, gravitating toward his newly found law-enforcement colleague.

"No thanks," Megan said, insistent.

Ridley struggled to understand, but deferred to his sister's decision. "Just help us out to the parking lot, and then we'll take it from there."

"Yes, sir."

The procession, with Eric at its head, plied through the mall's broad courtyards. Outside, they skimmed past green hedgerows on their way to the parking structure. What little sky Ridley saw was already black. The functional orange haze emanating from overhead lights, buzzing all around, filtered out any celestial details.

Once they made it to Nick and Megan's parents' house, John and Anna cooperated, helping to put Eric in Ridley's old room. Megan did all the talking, while Ridley borrowed a thermometer. Anna went downstairs to pray.

A nightlong rotation ensued.

By 6:00 a.m., Ridley was alone with his brother-in-law. Temperature, heart rate, respiration, and pupil dilation all seemed normal. Eric started snoring, but Ridley did not know whether that was a good sign. But it was something.

Downstairs, someone made coffee. The scent enlivened Ridley's alertness, but also made him realize how sore his muscles were from sitting on the hard Shaker chair, brought from the breakfast nook.

Ridley looked around the room. Not much had changed since he moved out after college. Simple furnishings, some pictures of the family, and a dusty Exercycle occupied the room. His eyes wandered to the closet, its mirrored doors reflecting an unflattering image. He stood, and then stretched, rolling his neck.

With blood flowing again and as Ridley's eyes settled back onto Eric, he realized something about his brother-in-law's condition.

Narcolepsy.

Aloud, Ridley said, “A neurological disorder in which a person suffers from irresistible sleep attacks and, and...Stimulate the nervous system.”

Ridley stopped speaking and headed straight for the kitchen. Once there, he mixed some fresh coffee grounds with those already brewed in the filter. As far as he knew, his brother-in-law never drank coffee, just juice, water, or milk. Eric was the healthiest person he'd ever met.

A few pats of coffee grounds should suffice, Ridley thought. For someone unacquainted with caffeine, Eric would not need much. Ridley felt confident about his rationale.

Ridley bounded up the stairs. By folding the pillows in half and pressing them against the pine headboard, he adjusted Eric into an upright position. He pinched some of the grounds, still warm and moist, between Eric's lower lip and gum, and then measured his pulse.

Sixty.

At around eighty-eight beats per minute, Eric spit out the coffee grounds and said his first words.

TEN

To Do List

Colonel Bennet, Saint Mary's disinformation officer, was already awake when the caller rang his office's phone number at Nellis Air Force Base. Bennet kept a cot in his office. Lying or sitting on it, he routinely made lists. "To do" lists. He never kept the lists, of course, just checked off the items, one by one, until he had fulfilled the tasks. Then, into the shredder they went, or sometimes, he burned them over an ashtray.

Strategy was for others. He just got things done.

That was why he did not mind complying with the caller's instructions and driving into Las Vegas for an unplanned Thursday-morning meeting at the Stratosphere Hotel.

Once inside the hotel room, Bennet's blond-haired host placed the "Do Not Disturb" placard on the doorknob, and then he said, "Take a load off, Colonel. This won't take long."

Unlike others, Bennet did not feel uneasy around this man. No anxiety. After all, he had nothing to hide.

"I assume there's a development?" Bennet said. He sat next to the window and took out his notepad.

The man started to put on his shoes, a new pair of brown loafers. "Yep. Stone decided to take Taylor's approach to, shall we say, the next level. No weak links."

“What are the details?” Poised to write, Bennet noticed his eyeglasses beginning to slip downward along the bridge of his nose. His skin was oily, as he had not yet showered.

“Both have been adequately discredited.” The man’s smile formed into a perfect grin. “But in about three hours, Airman Bresch will be found in his apartment. The girlfriend, from what I understand, is supposed to hook up with him there. She has been driving him to his counseling appointments.”

“Uh-huh. Did he leave a note?”

“Yep.”

“And the gun?”

The man shaped his right index finger and thumb into an imaginary pistol, pointing it at the colonel. “No problemo there. The airman liked to hunt.”

Bennet crossed his legs and cleared his throat. Protocol One measures never failed to arouse him. “What about the sergeant?”

“I’m on it. Had some fun with him last night in a restaurant. I am authorized to exercise my own discretion.”

“Will it be soon?”

“Given the renewed urgency, I don’t believe we need to wait very long. Can’t be too soon, though. People might get too curious if both of them croaked at the same time. We have to strike a balance.” He looked into the mirror and adjusted his turtleneck collar. “Sergeant Gonzales has been more difficult to manipulate than Airman Bresch, but the outcome will not change. Besides, I’ve grown impatient with this matter. It should have been wrapped up long ago.”

After a few more notations, Bennet said, “I’ll get to work on the press packets. The performance evaluations on Bresch should be enough.”

“They will have to be. Officially, we know zilch about his private counseling sessions.”

“I understand. And his family?”

“His thoughts were very clear on that subject. We won’t have anything to worry about. He’s been tight-lipped, just like Gonzales. But that's why we needed to act now instead of later. There's no telling what could happen down the road."

"Good. Then it seems to me that things will run their natural course."

"You betcha."

Bennet flipped to the top page of his notepad and targeted the first item on that day's list. *Meet with James Evans*. He checked it off.

ELEVEN

Just Normal Background Noise

"Where's Megan?" Eric said.

"She's in her room with Owen. They're both asleep," Ridley said. By Eric's expression, Ridley could tell some of the bitter coffee grounds remained in his mouth. He held the filter under Eric's chin and waited through several finger swipes before setting the mess aside on the dresser, next to his wallet, holster, and keys. And a business card.

"I need to talk to her."

"You will. But first, I need to talk to you. How do you feel?"

"Like I got a good night's sleep."

"Do you remember anything from last night?"

"Last night? Oh, you mean at the restaurant?"

"You remember being at the restaurant?"

"Sure I do. Why wouldn't I?"

"You passed out. You went to the bathroom, and, well, when you came back, you passed out. Do you know why that might've happened?"

"Allergies?" Eric folded his arms and nodded profusely. "Yeah, maybe I was allergic to something?"

"Nope." Impatience cut the single-syllable word short.

"It's possible. This guy I know told me about something like that happening to him. Couldn't do a thing about it."

Ridley clenched his jaw and said, "Did this guy's allergy cause him to completely disrobe and parade through a restaurant?"

"What? Why are you getting so angry?"

Ridley took a deep breath. "Look, Megan has told me about your recent problems."

"Nothing's wrong. It's just stress. She worries too much."

"No, Eric. Something is wrong, and you need to see a doctor. Your sleep disorder can be treated, if that's what it turns out to be. Frankly, I'm really surprised by your irresponsibility."

Eric's hands tightened into fists. "Don't lecture me about responsibility. You don't know what it's like. I'm trying to raise a family, to make a better future. Are you surprised by that? What would you know? I don't need some cop to tell me how to run my life."

"Oh no, that's not what this is about."

"Then what's it about?"

"You tell me." Ridley grabbed the business card. "Look at this."

Fists relaxed, Eric took the card, but did not look at it. His eyes rolled toward the ceiling. "Yeah, so?"

"I intended to show this to you last night. That is, before your 'allergies' kicked in. What did you want to talk to me about? And what does July seventh have to do with it?"

"That was nothing. I can't even remember now what it was about."

Ridley thought back to an earlier conversation he had with Megan, remembering the phrase she said Eric kept repeating. *Time for another ruse.* "That's not what you said last night. You were talking in your sleep again. You were responding to orders, weren't you? 'Yes, sir,' 'no, sir.'"

Eric closed his eyes.

"Systems normal, tell no one," Ridley said, suddenly coming to a realization. It hit him hard. Blurry intuition crystallized into something sharp. For some reason, autopsy photographs he and his fellow recruits saw in the academy came to mind. The pictures always had a keen focus and explicit colors. They also had white glare on the metal table where the camera's strobe reflected. There were pictures of belly wounds. He held his stomach. The outside, everything, pressed in. He never imagined that clarity could be so sickening. "Why the hell would they order you to tell no one if everything was normal?"

"There's nothing to tell."

"What happened on July seventh?"

Eric rolled onto his side, facing Ridley, and opened his eyes. They were clear. No darkness underneath. "You went on vacation the next day, you son of a bitch."

The Shaker chair underneath Ridley creaked as he leaned back.

"Did you have a good time in Havasu, Nick? A nice break from work? You know, from crooks, from the paperwork, from the routine?" Eric sounded as if he had just aged forty years.

"Yeah."

"Must have been nice. Did you take a radio with you?"

"Huh?"

"To listen to out on the lake."

"No."

"Oh well. You probably wouldn't have been able to pick up very much out there. Just static."

Ridley stood, feeling the need to pace. It helped him think. He paused by the window. Outside, he saw his father on the front lawn. John Ridley practiced chip shots. One trickled onto the driveway, coming to rest against the rear tire of Ridley's Suzuki.

"Yeah, static. Or maybe some kind of interference. Like clicking," Eric said.

When Ridley turned around, other images came to mind, memories of a slow Saturday night. "Rapid clicking?"

"Whatever. It doesn't mean anything though. Just normal background noise. Nothing to get upset about. You wouldn't want to turn it into something that it's not. People might get the wrong idea about you. So, you tell no one." Eric set the business card onto the dresser, next to Ridley's wallet, holster, and keys. "You leave it to others to figure out what really happened."

TWELVE

Weak Links

By 11:00 a.m. on Friday, Harrison collected the last police report. He was in Los Angeles, driving a rented Chevrolet Corsica along familiar streets, with nearly three hours until his flight to Tucson. Los Angeles had been his home before he entered the FBI, and it still felt like home. He'd left much behind at the time, but these days, there was nothing and no one to return to in Los Angeles.

Except for one place.

Harrison had what seemed like an easy choice to make. Either go to the airport for three hours of boredom, or, go to the hills just above the city, to Griffith Observatory. His parents would like that. They rested in Pasadena. Too far and too risky a trip to make given the incoherent impulses of LA traffic. Besides, he'd never liked cemeteries. Memories did not originate in cemeteries.

When Harrison arrived, empty school buses, rows of them, told him they had successfully delivered their hundreds of small occupants, sent to explore the lush hilltop grounds and discover, under the various Griffith Observatory domes, nothing less than the infinite horizons of their universe. He lit a cigarette and turned on KNX-News Radio for their regular traffic updates. As he rolled down the window to let out the smoke and to smell the air he had breathed growing up, Harrison wondered how many of the children he saw that day would eventually become astronomers or physicists. Or criminals.

"Damn."

He regretted the afterthought but knew it was unavoidable. Cynicism came easily for those who patrolled the streets, made arrests, or vowed that they would try to make a difference. Sometimes, over the years, the doubts tugged at his principles and his motivations. Bad guys were not supposed to win.

He had the sleepless nights. Dreams—nightmares—where he yelled, simply yelled, at the top of his huge lungs, in the faces of his coworkers and supervisors. Something was wrong. Bad guys were not supposed to win. Cynicism, embedded in doubt, could be enough to make anyone, even the most dedicated, also feel utterly useless.

But bad guys did win.

This had been a hard lesson for Harrison. Some would tell him—he knew whom—that he had not yet learned it, or even come close to learning it. But he had. What drove him to anger—to the nightmares—was that sometimes the bad guys won because they had so much help from the inside. From incompetence, politics, careerism, compartmentalization, distrust.

He let the cigarette dangle between his fingertips, holding it outside the driver's window. His briefcase sat on the front passenger's seat. He rested his right palm on it. The leather was cold, chilled by the car's air conditioner during the drive from downtown. Los Angeles was always warm or hot. Today it was warm, on its way to being hot. The radio said Santa Ana winds were kicking up again.

But the tree-shaded parking lot and breezy hilltop location gave enough relief. Only a small chunk of the Chevrolet's white hood poked out from under the tree and into the sun, depending on the wind. The familiarity of it all—comforting, like the effortless and faithful support of a corpulent recliner—helped Harrison relax. He needed to focus. Too much reflection on his bureau past strained his thoughts. Harrison, the private investigator, sought no reminders of what work Harrison, the FBI special agent, had done. He thought he had won the battle against remorse over lost opportunities. But feelings of uselessness due to an inadequate legacy still troubled him.

Harrison finished the cigarette and removed Echo Tango's most recent letter from his briefcase. His curiosity was not about its contents, although those did interest him. This anonymous client, sincere or not, tugged him in a direction he did not necessarily want to go.

Harrison needed to identify Echo Tango. His, *or her*, intentions and motivations may have sounded nice, and Harrison had worked with confidential informants on some of his FBI investigations, but he needed face-to-face contact to establish trust. The importance of this was perfectly obvious to Harrison. What was also obvious was that Echo Tango knew him.

One other thought surfaced again. It made him hold his breath this time. What if he did not know, or had not even met, Echo Tango? Eerie as this was, it remained a possibility. As he reread the latest letter, he hoped that this was not the case...

Mr. Harrison,
I apologize for intruding. There's much to do, little time, and great danger. My measures may disturb you, but please understand that I mean you no harm. Because of the sensitive nature of the matter at hand, and the secrecy surrounding it, I must go to great lengths to conceal my efforts and, hopefully, yours as well. Yes, I need your cooperation to accomplish a very important task. It's more important than any investigation you have ever conducted, including Silver Star or any of the other ARDCom assignments. The details will become clear as we proceed. Until I'm certain that you've joined me, I'll have to limit your direct knowledge. This is for your protection.

Here's what I can tell you: Harold Groom "died" of a heart attack. Medical authorities in Florida have confirmed this. The press has duly accepted the explanation, despite Groom's perfect health. The truth is, Mr. Harrison, agents of the US government eliminated Groom using sophisticated techniques developed under the pretense of "national security." Groom's assassination of the computer software executive wasn't directly related to the organization that he worked for many years ago, but Groom's ploy threatened this organization. They couldn't risk exposure, so, they eliminated him. But, these people need to be exposed. They have betrayed a sacred trust and violate, every day, the Constitution of the United States. Sadly, I've helped them to do this.

You might be skeptical. I understand. I need to establish credibility with you. Therefore, there's an assignment (funds included) that may help you accept the truth of which I speak. You must collect five traffic accident reports, all of which are around fifty years old. Do this in person. We don't have time to waste. You will not have difficulty retrieving them. I have seen to this. The police report numbers are Tucson/49-082705; LA/48-0114271; Albuquerque/51-112854T; Killeen/50-TA1214075; Seattle/47-1219035. The victims in these traffic accidents were military policemen assigned to Roswell Army Airfield when the crash of two UFOs occurred there in July, 1947. I assure you, these were no accidents, and a government entity responsible for covering up the Roswell incident killed them. The military policemen represented weak links in the chain of secrecy and were eliminated in the name of national security.

Keep these police reports with the postcards that I sent to you. The puzzle has many pieces. I cannot give all the pieces to you at once. To do so would place me in too much risk. I am fully aware of your experience and have confidence in your abilities, despite your unfortunate injury. Your values are our greatest weapon, TJ, and believe me, you're closer to the truth than you can possibly imagine. Upon your return to Tucson, immediately place a personal ad in the classifieds of the Tucson Sun Times. Have it read, "ET, back in town." I'll contact you after the ad appears.

Sincerely,
Echo Tango

The reference to ARDCom, Harrison concluded, had the most significance. While many were aware of his injury and the nickname, few knew about his classified work with the air force. In fact, "Silver Star" was so secret, it required him to work undercover throughout the investigation. He became "Wesley Hiatt," a greedy and loathsome security supervisor with McDonnell-Douglas who had "damaging" evidence on several engineers assigned to Department of Defense contracts. Hiatt's compromising information and photographs, in turn, attracted a bid through an ARDCom informant in the Soviet Union's consulate in San Francisco. The informant's superiors, Russian intelligence officers, planned to use Hiatt's materials in an effort to blackmail the engineers into providing technical details for a new air force reconnaissance satellite, the AMS-111, otherwise known as Silver Star.

Hiatt, AMS-111, the damaging information, and the engineers had been, of course, entirely and thoroughly fabricated. But the investigation did lead to the arrest and deportation of two consular officials, one a "grain agriculturist" and the other a "journalist." The informant entered the witness relocation program.

By Harrison's estimation, eight people officially knew these details. He had no way to know how information was shared, either formally or informally, among ARDCom officers, so it was possible that his anonymous client was not involved in Silver Star or, for that matter, any of the other cases. His last FBI partner, Art Holcomb, working primarily on surveillance, and Brian Holst, their supervisor, had direct knowledge. Holst was easy to eliminate, though, as a candidate for Echo Tango. Not long after the Silver Star case, Holst died from food poisoning contracted by eating a cheeseburger made from contaminated beef.

Holcomb, while a possibility, was not high on Harrison's list. Although odd and secretive at times, ET just was not his style. Echo Tango had to be someone closer to home.

Roswell also stood out in Harrison's mind. When he was a kid, he saw an old newspaper his father kept inside a desk at home. Old and faded, the paper's headline announced the US military had recovered a flying saucer.

Echo Tango's letter also reminded Harrison of that inexplicable, luminescent sphere he witnessed in the night sky over Tucson last July.

Silence interrupted the LA traffic broadcast. Mere seconds of dead air, but long enough to make Harrison pause. When an ad for Delta Airlines came on, it reminded him to check his watch.

He set the letter aside and removed the police reports. When he read them, he thought their historical features were noteworthy. They told as much about the time in which they were written as they did about the traffic accidents they recorded. At the very least, Harrison felt he was holding a bit of history in his hands, as if he were the scholar that all of his professors had hoped he would become. He turned over the details of the five articles again in his mind.

In 1949, Tucson motorist and tradesman Willis Jackson died after the car he was driving plunged over a cliff west of town. Investigators determined that the accident was due to brake failure in his '34 De Soto Airflow.

A year later, Howard Webster, truck driver, suffered fatal injuries when his vehicle lost control on a highway in Killeen, Texas. Webster's accident partially ejected his body through the windshield after a blown tire caused his truck to spin and roll into a cattle yard.

Gary McDonald, construction foreman, encountered a similar fate in 1951. Near Albuquerque, a tire blew out on his Pontiac, sending it into a roadside ditch. McDonald's severe head injury and internal bleeding did not cause his immediate death. An attachment to the original report indicated that, after lingering in unconsciousness for three days, his heart simply stopped beating.

Another victim, George Fairfield, drowned in 1947. Authorities listed inclement Seattle weather, high speed, and drunkenness as the reasons for the accident. Fairfield's new Studebaker careened off a waterfront pier, where he worked as a fisherman.

In the final case, Mike Pullman, actor, died in 1948 when he drove his agent's Lincoln Continental Cabriolet through a guardrail on the Pacific Coast Highway in Los Angeles. No skid marks. No evidence of mechanical failure. Investigators concluded that he simply must have fallen asleep at the wheel.

The sun reached through the driver's-side window into Harrison's rental car, just enough to cause uncomfortable glare on the white photocopied reports. He traded them for his sunglasses and another cigarette, which went unlit. Increasing the radio's volume came first.

"Yep."

Traffic, *Friday traffic,* slowed progress on the southbound lanes of the 405 Freeway. He needed to leave for LAX in a few minutes.

Harrison lit the cigarette and latched his seat belt. He tugged on it twice to make sure he had properly secured it. When he drove out of the parking lot, and the Griffith Observatory receded in the rear-view mirror, he double-checked the car's brakes. Good response. No squeaks. He gripped the steering wheel with both hands. The Chevrolet also had an airbag.

THIRTEEN

Too Late for Comfortable Ignorance

Mandy Zemdarsky foisted Harrison a beer and then opened one for herself. An amusing spout of carbonated suds erupted from her can. Some of it splattered onto her lime-green blouse and onto Harrison's sunglasses. Mandy gave Harrison her seal of approval, a giggle and slap on his shoulder. Her home was her playground. She always managed to make housework, raising children, taking care of her husband, and hosting friends a seamless act of joy. Forty-one years of marriage had made it nearly perfect.

"Pete's going to burn down the house," Mandy said.

Harrison smiled. "I'll see what I can do."

Mandy brushed aside a graying strand of brown forelock, suppressed a burp, and thanked Harrison. She wiped her sweaty brow. Ever frugal, her husband kept the air conditioning switched off most of the time.

"How was your work as a bodyguard?" Mandy said, winking. Her brown eyes, bright like her husband's, stood at equal height to Harrison's. She wore sandals, and he sported old sneakers.

"Just fine."

"Well, we're just glad you are back, safe and sound." One of Mandy's strong hands gripped Harrison's elbow as she escorted him through the house toward the backyard, while he sipped the beer. The Zemdarsky residence smelled like a home he once knew, except for the scent of barbecuing chicken and ribs. Their home cradled a scent similar to brown grocery bags and the inside of a recently run dishwasher, and it reminded Harrison of distant, quiet Saturday mornings.

As they passed through the walnut-paneled hallway from the foyer to the kitchen, Harrison pocketed his sunglasses and glanced at the twenty-something framed pictures hanging on the walls. One of them was new. Henry, the Zemdarskys' eldest son, stood next to a small business jet, his right thumb pointed up.

"What's this?" Harrison said. "Henry flying jets these days?"

"He's doing just that! We're so proud of him. He just started his own charter service out of Long Beach, and that's his one and only plane. He's promised to fly us anywhere we want to go. Hah!"

Harrison laughed, and Mandy slapped his shoulder again. They rounded the corner into the kitchen, where Harrison met an unanticipated guest.

In the kitchen, a perfect grin greeted him. "Hey, Bill, how are you?"

Harrison halted and sucked in his stomach. He had not worn a belt, so his khaki Dockers started to slip. As he relaxed his abdominal muscles, his expanding waist halted the slipping pants. Sweating now, Harrison suffered the frugality of his partner's decision-making about the air conditioner.

"Janice, what a nice surprise," Harrison said. "Have you finished your report?"

Tossing a salad, Janice said, "Last night. I brought it with me." Lettuce bounced delicately and competently up and down.

"Always so much business with you," Mandy said, shaking a finger at Harrison.

"It's okay, if Bill likes the report he's promised to keep training me. We may even go on a stakeout."

"Good, then the two of you can get better acquainted," Mandy said.

Harrison blushed. Beano barked from the backyard. "Pete's not cooking my dog, is he? I better get out there." He noticed the big toenail on Mandy's right foot needed trimming. Out of his peripheral vision, he saw Janice tossing the salad. Ahead, the sliding door leading to the backyard was already open. A dead fly and an orange peel shared space on the door's lower track. Harrison thought of mentioning this fact, but he was outside before he could say another word. A basketball waited for him on the patio table. His head started to ache.

Must be from the smoke?

The flames rose much too high, and the conflagration surrounded dinner. Zemdarsky, bedecked in a straw hat and checkered apron, stood too close to the inferno. Harrison shook his head and spotted Beano. Preoccupied, she sniffed along the wooden fence in the part of the yard that was farthest from grill.

After picking up the basketball, Harrison cautiously approached Zemdarsky. "They about done, don't you think?" He tried spinning the ball on his middle finger.

"Willy, my boy, about time. Apparently, everybody here likes them well done. Don't you?"

"I see you invited Janice," Harrison said, kneeling. Beano trotted over to him. "Hi, girl."

"She needs to eat."

"I gave you more than enough food."

"No, the Evans girl, not that girl. God, that's warm." Zemdarsky shuffled back from the flames. His eyes sparkled.

"She's young." Harrison lowered his voice. "I admit though, she seems pretty mature for her age."

"And she's very bright, Billy. I've read her report—hell, dissertation. 'Gubernaculum and Jurisdictio.' You will be impressed."

Harrison ran his hands over the basketball's surface and pressed it with his fingertips. "Can we just eat? Or, how about some free throws?"

"Okay, okay. But I think she likes you."

Fighting the urge to look over his shoulder, Harrison accepted a friendly lick on the cheek from Beano. "How was your week?"

"She's a dog, Bill. She doesn't have weeks. If you're interested, mine was fine. How was yours? Did your client pay well for such a last minute arrangement? All the necessary fees and expenses taken care of?"

"Yes, of course. It could lead to more work too."

Zemdarsky nodded and retrieved the chicken and ribs. "We can talk after dinner." Grease dripped into the charcoal. The flames hissed and flared.

Staring at the fire, at the rising flames, Harrison said, "Pete, this is going somewhere I'm not sure I want to go."

Smoke rose from the pile of meat and bones stacked on the plate.

"Would you rather eat outside?" Pete said.

Harrison stood, bouncing the basketball once on the cement patio. "No, I mean the case. It's taking me somewhere I'd rather not go. But, the thing is, I think it might already be too late."

"Too late for what?"

"To not get involved. To stay comfortably ignorant."

"Willy, in case you haven't noticed, there are people around who actually give a crap about you, and your smelly dog too." Zemdarsky lowered the grill's lid and looked Harrison square in the eyes. Smoke had darkened his cheeks and the hat's inner brim. "Whatever it is that you're facing, you don't have to face it alone. You don't have to carry these burdens alone." Zemdarsky removed the hat and tossed it onto the patio table. "Besides, no one person ever has all the answers. Got it?"

Harrison nodded.

"Now then," Zemdarsky said, helping himself to a rib, "dinnya ice surfed."

FOURTEEN

Who is Echo Tango?

Half asleep, Harrison stood on the edge of Arroyo Verde's sandy creek bed. Between light puffs on a cigarette and squinted glances at Beano down below, he wondered why he felt so tired. He'd slept through most of the weekend, drowsily lounging on the paw-scuffed sofa in the living room reading Janice's paper and, not so oddly, dreaming about her as well. His headaches had returned on Friday night and continued through Saturday. He bought more aspirin on Sunday, but found that he did not need it. By this Monday morning, his head was fine; he just felt tired. Back inside, he yawned and watched Beano scamper to the sliding glass door between the kitchen and staircase.

"Get the birds, get them."

Beano's ears instantly perked up. She liked watching the blackbirds land on the patio's railings. In Harrison's dream, the one with Janice, they had sat together on the patio.

But, a different patio.

Harrison walked into the kitchen, where a full pot of coffee awaited him. It had a twelve-cup capacity. He opened the cupboard, feeling like he had opened cupboards and drawers all weekend long.

Where were we?

"Let's see, shall it be the brown coffee mug or the other brown mug? Which one, Beano? Huh? Get them, Beano. Get the birds. Hmm..."

One of the two mugs sat near the back of the mostly empty cupboard, unused for several weeks, if not longer. Another cupboard on the other side of the stainless-steel sink contained more items. Two plates, two cereal bowls.

And why were we so sad?

A drawer near the sink contained his utensils. A fork, a spoon, a steak knife. Harrison took the mug closest to him and filled it with coffee, then returned to the living room to read the newspaper.

Except for the walls, sparse furnishings occupied his living room. As a student and even as an adult, Harrison collected and framed reproductions of famous newspaper headlines. They hung throughout the townhome. Above him, the front page of the *New York Times* announced the Hindenburg disaster. A pair next to the kitchen proclaimed war in Europe. By the front door, the Titanic sank.

Thumbing through the *Tucson Sun Times,* he came to the classified section and checked their procedures for placing an advertisement. From his open briefcase, which sat on the walnut coffee table, he retrieved a pen and circled the information. He put the pen in his mouth, separated the newspaper, and put the page with the circle into the briefcase. Harrison pondered yet again who waited for the advertisement to appear.

Harrison took out a notepad. *Holcomb?* Even though he felt this was the wrong answer, he wrote down his old partner's name nonetheless.

An old case code-named "Aurora" came to mind. He and Holcomb had worked hard to identify a leak, a man who passed information to the Russians about special materials used in the fuselage of Aurora, an air force reconnaissance aircraft.

Harrison sipped coffee, and then wrote, "The General," below Holcomb's name. Disgust crept through Harrison as he remembered this man's manipulative ways.

The stakeout had taken place at a dilapidated motel in Hemet, California. The FBI and military personnel watched as the Russian contact entered the suspect's room. Then, through the front door they went, Harrison leading the way. The suspects retreated into the bathroom, hoping to escape through the window. Outside, the general's security unit blocked their way. Gunfire erupted. Harrison, Holcomb, and other FBI agents dove for cover. Bullets from automatic weapons pierced the room's interior walls, knocking the bathroom door off its hinges. Screams came from outside.

Near the bodies lay two revolvers. Harrison always thought the guns looked out of place. "Case closed," the general said after the raid, his only comment.

Harrison's final report on the espionage investigation was almost as succinct: "Suspected source for the unlawful transfer of classified materials to Russia, and the source's contact, were both terminated after a brief exchange of gunfire at meeting site. All 'Project Aurora' files were recovered and returned to contractor's control."

The shooting incident left much distrust between the FBI and air force, but even Harrison's own agency seemed to brush the shooting incident under the carpet. Anger and bitterness still gripped Harrison whenever he recalled the episode. To this day, he remained suspicious of the *whole damn mess.*

Recalling his last name now, Harrison scratched out "The General," and wrote, "General Taylor."

Bastard.

Harrison tapped the pen on his lips, thinking of other, more likely prospects for ET. No one at ARDCom seemed likely of anything other than total obedience. Except for one man. He wrote down the name, nodding.

Sam Ritter.

Although Ritter's attitude appeared right, Harrison remained unconvinced he had sufficient rank and authority to have known about Silver Star details or other highly sensitive matters.

Harrison set the pad down and closed his briefcase.

After checking the time, he stepped over to the closet beneath the staircase and removed a black gun case containing a newer Colt .45. The older one was still at the office, locked in the safe. As it was Monday morning, the firing range would be Harrison's first stop, and then he would visit the offices of the *Tucson Sun Times.*

Maybe ask her out?

Aiming at the center of Titanic's third smokestack, Harrison's hand shook. He spit out the pen and relaxed, concentrating. *Easy breaths.*

"Get the birds, Beano."

The aim held true.

"Get 'em."

Both Janice and Zemdarsky stared at him as he entered the office and sprinted toward his desk.

"Morning all," Harrison said.

"Morning?" Zemdarsky said. "Why, it's half past noon."

"Stayed a bit longer at the range. Janice? Can I see you, please?"

By the time Janice caught up with him, Harrison had removed his coat, opened his briefcase, and sat in his office chair.

"You on your way out?" Harrison said.

"I was just leaving. I can stay if I have to," Janice said, wide-eyed.

"I just wanted you to know that your paper was excellent. Best explanation of gubernaculum and jurisdictio I've heard in a long time." He laughed hard enough to make his eyes water. "Sorry, I'm actually serious. I really enjoyed it, especially your historical examples. Would've chosen the same ones. It's like you read my mind. Want to write another one or move on to the training? Maybe we could have you do some legal research on the new fraud legis—"

"Wait! Let me write this down."

"Good, yes. Let's devise a plan. Ready? Sit down, by the way. No wait."

Midway between standing and sitting, Janice stopped moving and giggled.

"First things first," Harrison said.

"Would you like me to get you some coffee?"

"Nope, already had some. You should get to school. Your studies come first. We can talk about this later, or maybe, hmmm..." Harrison looked into his briefcase. "What about lunch?"

"I can't today."

"Actually, forget lunch. Bad idea. I guess this afternoon we could meet, or tomorrow morning."

"How about dinner?"

Harrison peered across the desk and watched Janice sit down and cross her legs. "Dinner?"

"I love to cook. I'm known for my gourmet cheeseburgers."

"You shouldn't have to go out of your way."

"It's really no problem."

Easy breaths. Patient and relaxed. "Let me buy you dinner."

"I can be an expensive date."

"Well, you, I guess...Why's that?"

"I eat like a pig!"

FIFTEEN

No Records Found

A trail of wet footprints, with long strides between steps, led from the police station's service elevator. A thunderous downpour had soaked an unprepared Ridley while he rode his motor to work. He passed the locker room, ignoring the wet uniform clinging to his skin, and hurried to the first cubicle area reserved for report writing. Swing-shift briefing started in forty minutes, which left him enough time to check records and transcripts for last July 7 and to change into a dry uniform.

Insistent chirps from one of the computer terminals in the report-writing cubicle area and a condescending "oops" greeted Ridley upon entering. Tom Ferris, another motor officer, fiddled with the keyboard. "Fuck this shit." Acoustic fibers lining the walls of the cubicle softened the deep sound of Ferris's voice, but not the bright chirps from the computer. Ferris kept pummeling the keys.

"Having a problem, Tom?" Ridley said.

"This fucker's constipated. And so am I."

Ridley sat at another terminal and brought up the main menu screen. Adjusting the mouse, Ridley clicked on the "Standard Reports" icon and selected the file containing dispatch records. He hoped to find an official explanation for the radio disruption attached to the transcript for July 7. Next to him, Ferris lifted the instruction template off the keyboard, bringing it within a few inches of his face.

"Are you working on a report?" Ridley asked.

"Yes, he is," Lieutenant Walter Maxwell said.

Officer Ferris bobbed his head back and forth, attempting to mock their watch commander's abrupt interruption. Ridley turned around, surprised he had not heard Lieutenant Maxwell approach them.

Continuing, Maxwell said, "Officer Ferris had a DUI arrest late last night."

Replacing the template, Ferris said, "And a traffic collision report, and a drive-by supplement, and two fucking burglaries, and the armed robbery at Pellegrino's."

"And what are you up to, Officer Ridley? Have a nice couple of days off?" Maxwell said.

A simple response became mired in Ridley's unexpected desire to answer the question seriously. Two days off—two days spent helping his sister, Megan, move back home. Her husband's "allergies" had flared up again. Eric was fine for a while, even managing to spend an enjoyable and uneventful Thanksgiving holiday with the family. But how to tell Maxwell, or anyone for that matter, the truth about Eric's mental health issues and the continuing disruption to his family ultimately eluded him.

"Yeah, it was a good weekend."

"Glad to hear it." Maxwell folded his burly arms and stared over Ridley's shoulder. "What are you working on?"

A list of questions on the screen awaited Ridley's answers: "USER? DATE OF TRANSCRIPT/RECORD? TIME INTERVAL?"

"Nothing really," Ridley said. "Just looking something up." Ridley wearied of Eric's insistent excuses for what had happened on July 7. His brother-in-law had protected someone, perhaps his superiors, or something else, all at the expense of his and his family's well-being.

More electronic protests erupted from Ferris's computer followed by the officer's clenched-tooth growl. "Does anyone care that I'm trying to concentrate here?"

"Of course we care, Tom." Maxwell said, swatting the back of Ferris's head. "I wanted to let both of you know that because of the storm, the motor officers will ride shotgun with the patrol units. Don't thank me, though. Thank the city's risk manager."

Lieutenant Maxwell smiled and closed his eyes. He pressed his folded arms tighter into himself. Ridley got the sensation that Maxwell, while a decent watch commander, enjoyed a warm embrace from some airy lover embodied in the form of memos, staff meetings, and policy decisions. Maxwell, the humble servant and beneficiary, basked in the smooth operation of perceived infallible grace and wisdom. He opened his eyes, and then said, "Tom, you finish up. I want that report by briefing. And Nick, for God's sake, change your uniform."

Maxwell exited the area, arms still wrapped around his chest.

Turning to the computer, Ridley entered the requested information. A very long minute passed, long enough to hear plenty more grunts and chirps come from the adjacent cubicle. While awaiting the computer's slow response to his query, coldness seeped into him from his wet uniform, and he could not find anywhere to wipe and warm his moist, chilled hands.

The computer finally returned a response to Ridley's query. He stared at the unhelpful information. "What, nothing found?"

Ridley ran the query again, double-checking the date and time frame.

Another long minute passed, giving frustration and doubt time to settle in with the cold. After all, what did Ridley know about radio communications? The brief disruption could have a very simple explanation. It could have been background noise for that matter. He once heard that solar flares caused radio interference. Given Eric's work as an air force air traffic controller, such a disruption could be stressful if it occurred on his watch.

The computer's response mocked his efforts again: "NO RECORDS FOUND." Ridley stood and smacked the side of the monitor. "Fucking computers."

"Oh, I hear you, brother, I hear you," Officer Ferris said, chuckling.

After changing uniforms, Ridley closed his locker and followed Officer Ferris to the briefing room. At the front, Lieutenant Maxwell waited for the remaining patrol officers to take their seats. Ridley took the chair next to Cliff Hamrick, one of the oldest patrol officers he had ever known, and then he took out a notepad.

Maxwell scanned the room, looking left to right, front to back. Satisfied that everyone was present, he quickly went through the routine beat assignments and general briefing information. As usual, his eyes panned along the floor, inspecting shoes, while he sauntered around the room.

"Now, day shift handled most of the early traffic collisions, but with the slick roads and our ever-growing population of idiots, expect more accidents during the evening commute," Maxwell said. After a drawn-out pause, he looked at Ridley and smiled. "Also, I'm one of the lucky ones to actually get a lengthy holiday vacation this month, which starts tomorrow, so try to get all reports done promptly by the end of shift. Let me rephrase that. All reports are due, without fail, at the end of shift. No dilly-dallying. Happy Hanukkah, merry Christmas, and happy New Year. Hit the road."

Ridley put away the notepad and stood. He chatted briefly with the old timer, Officer Hamrick, but an announcement from the building's public address system interrupted him. "Officer Ridley, phone call, line four."

Ridley walked to the back of the briefing room, next to several snack machines, where he picked up a wall-mounted telephone and punched the correct line. After answering, Ridley heard a muffled sob followed by a distinct click.

"Hello? This is Ridley."

The dial tone returned, and Ridley checked his watch. Hesitating, he hung up and noticed Officer Hamrick walking toward him, pointing at the snack machines.

"Maxwell says you'll be riding with me. Not enough cars for everybody. Want a cookie? I'll get you a cookie, and then you can do me a favor."

"What's that?"

"You drive."

With less than an hour remaining in their shift, Hamrick offered to drive, giving Ridley time to finish his reports. Things had slowed, allowing Ridley sufficient concentration to focus on writing. But as the end of his shift neared, an overwhelming sense of dread crept through him. He remembered the odd phone call just before the start of his shift. The memory raised questions about who had sobbed and hung up. *Had Eric called?*

"Okay, Chief," Hamrick said, interrupting Ridley's thoughts. "Let dispatch know we are en route to station. I need to poop, and by the time I'm done, our shift will be history."

Ridley shook his head and reached for the microphone. He halted his movement, however, because the dispatcher announced a pedestrian-involved accident. Other units responded to the call and headed in the direction of the scene.

"Hmmm...sounds messy," Hamrick said.

"Yeah."

"They'll be in late, which means their reports will be in late. Too bad for Maxwell."

After Ridley advised the dispatcher of their status, Hamrick headed toward the station. After a couple of minutes, he noticed his partner leaning forward on the steering wheel and peering upward through the top of the windshield.

"How's the weather?" Ridley said.

"Clearing up."

After a few more stoplights, Hamrick still leaned forward, gazing skyward. Hamrick drove cautiously, so Ridley was not worried they would have their own accident, but his curiosity got the best of him.

"What are you looking for?"

"Flying saucers. I've seen them before."

"Oh?" Ridley said, peering upward. Seeing Hamrick out of the corner of his eye made him chuckle. "Come on, Cliff, what are you really looking at?"

"I'm serious. I don't really know what they are, but I've seen some strange lights up there. They move real quick." Hamrick paused and smiled. "Maybe we'll see one tonight."

"Uh-huh. I guess I may have to cite them for speeding, then, if they move real quick, as you say.

"My trust in you is fading."

"Sorry, sorry, but they're probably just military aircraft."

The dispatcher interrupted their conversation, directing another unit to the pedestrian-involved accident. An officer already at the scene requested the coroner.

"Must be messy," Hamrick said, entering the police station's parking lot. "I can't stand traffic accidents."

Once inside the station, Hamrick headed for the nearest restroom, saying something about a burrito knocking at his back door, and Ridley walked to the dispatch office.

Nearing dispatch, Ridley put his reports on the center of Lieutenant Maxwell's vacant desk. He walked through the next doorway and entered the dispatch office. From there, he looked through a large window into an adjacent room where the dispatchers sat at their consoles. One of them, Judy Butler, noticed Ridley. She stood and walked toward an open doorway next to the window.

"You look like you need something," Butler said, leaning forward, accentuating her cleavage.

Butler had come on to Ridley in the past, and although he appreciated her interest, his attention focused on something else at the moment. "Where do we keep the dispatch records?"

"Stored on DVDs, right behind you, inside the cabinets. They are inside cardboard holders labeled by date." Butler said, stepping toward and then unlocking the cabinets. "Just tell me when you're done, so I can lock up." She sauntered away, heading toward the dispatch area.

Ridley waited until Butler returned to her seat before beginning a search. Looking inside the cabinet, he saw multiple rows of DVDs. Examining the labels, he ascertained a general area where he could find the chronologically ordered DVDs for last July. His eyes jumped several rows, and he spotted the white cardboard holder labeled "7 July." He pulled it from the cabinet. As he opened the lid, the hair on his neck stiffened.

Glancing at the dispatchers, Ridley saw that all appeared busy. He decided against interrupting them and checked the cabinet area for any loose DVDs.

He found none.

Seeing a clipboard hanging next to the cabinet, Ridley lifted it from its hook and recognized the pages attached to it as a check-out form. According to the form, no one had signed out the July 7 DVD.

Through the doorway just past the cabinet area, Ridley saw Maxwell return to his desk. He replaced the clipboard, got Butler's attention with a wave, and walked over to the watch commander, who listened to another officer on speaker phone. Over the speaker came "Pronounced dead at the scene. He's an air force sergeant; Ferris has the dog-tag information. We couldn't find his wallet. Just a minute, Lieutenant, let me go get the info."

"Go right ahead," Maxwell said, glancing at Ridley. "Got your reports? You and Hamrick lucked out on this one." He paused and pointed at the phone. "Pedestrian got himself run over in front of a bar. An air force sergeant. They're getting the identification info now, so we can track down a next of kin. Ferris will be out there for a while."

The officer's voice on the telephone returned. "Lieutenant, are you there?"

"Go ahead."

"The name's Eric Filipe Gonzales. Probably from Nellis. Let me give you his serial number."

Ridley's knees buckled and his voice shook. "Who...who did he say?" He leaned on the desk. Palms suddenly sweaty, his hands slipped, spreading a slick layer of moisture across the metal surface. The blood drained from his face.

"Hold on a second," Maxwell said. "Shit, what's wrong, Ridley?"

"Did he say Eric Filipe Gonzales?" His words struggled in their journey across the increasingly blurred space ahead of them.

"Yes. What's wrong?"

"Does he have a gold wedding band attached to his dog tags?"

"Yeah, it's right here with the tags," the officer at the scene said.

Collapsing into a chair next to the desk, Ridley fought hard to breathe. The room spun. Maxwell said something to him, but his voice seemed distant, distorted. Others gathered around, staring at him.

But all he could do was stare back.

SIXTEEN

Arthur Holcomb, FBI

"Thanks for dinner the other night. I really appreciated it, and all the time you've spent with me recently. The attention means a lot to me."

The voice registered with Harrison, but the words drifted around inside his head without any real direction. His eyes were fixed on the tip of a ballpoint pen, which he held about a foot in front of his face; it was about the most complex matter he could concentrate on at the moment.

"Earth to Bill, hello."

The remark jerked the pen away. There Janice stood, all smiles, blond hair pulled back from her face and tied with a pink ribbon. Her blue eyes looked at him from across his desk, patiently waiting.

"I'm sorry, I'm a little preoccupied, or tired, or something. I enjoyed dinner too. We should do it again soon."

"I agree."

Harrison took a moment to admire her beauty. He felt a connection with Janice that he could not explain, a sign he accepted that she was special. Unfortunately, resolution of another matter tugged him away from her.

"Is Pete in yet?" Harrison said.

"No, he's in Sierra Vista. He may stop in on his way home later this afternoon. Or he may just head home from there. He wasn't sure."

Harrison lifted the pen again, flipping it between his fingers, and then he guided it toward its previous position.

"Bill, finals are coming up, so I need the rest of the day off."

"Finals? Yeah, that's good. Go ahead. I'll see about some more training soon."

As Janice grabbed her backpack and headed for the front door, Harrison asked her to lock it. He did not want any interruptions for a while.

The pen hovered there for a while longer, floating across the myopic panorama like some sort of cigar-shaped vehicle drifting in a blurry atmosphere. He tossed it onto the desk and retrieved the phone number from his Rolodex again. This time he intended to get in touch with his former partner no matter what. Art Holcomb would be able to help, and Harrison needed an alternative source to ET. A trustworthy source who could corroborate information. Someone who had access to resources beyond what he or Zemdarsky could acquire.

Why the witch hazel? Why the reminder of—?

"Washington FBI, Special Agent Grier, may I help you?"

"Ah, yes, I apparently have the wrong number. I was trying to reach Special Agent Art Holcomb. I'm pretty sure he used to be at this number."

"Agent Holcomb, yes. Uh, is it something I might be able to help you with instead?"

"No, no, I appreciate that, but Art's the guy I need to talk to. We used to work together."

"I see, well, I'm sorry to hear that. He's in Baltimore these days. Try calling their main number. The receptionist should be able to put you in touch."

Harrison knew that Holcomb could rub people the wrong way, but he was nevertheless disappointed with Agent Grier's apparent disdain for him.

After a quick Internet search, Harrison found the Baltimore FBI's main number. A few transferred calls later, someone finally connected him with the right number. Apparently, Holcomb occupied space at a little-known location away from the Baltimore FBI's main office. In all the confusion, Harrison picked up that his former partner worked alone at the facility.

After several rings, a familiar loud and impatient voice answered Harrison's call. "Holcomb, go."

"The moon shines like a freshly unwrapped cheese ball at the holidays."

"Mongolian women eat Chinese food after cleaning their husbands' assault rifles," Holcomb said, laughing. "About time you called me, Bill."

"How'd you know it was me?"

"Duh. The only other person I know of, besides myself, who gets a kick out of using silly made-up code speak is that former special agent, now bum PI, Bill Harrison."

"Yeah, well it's good to talk to you too."

"Thanks for keeping in touch."

"Hell, I've tried a couple times lately and no one seemed to be able to put me in touch with you. I figured you were probably just blowing me off for one of your preoccupations. But then I remembered that you still had at least one hand typically available to dial the phone."

"I guess you didn't hear about the accident."

"No, sorry, what happened?"

"Lost both hands and all my fingers in a terrible masturbation mishap. The intense frictional heat led to spontaneous combustion."

"Wow, I thought that kind of thing only caused blindness."

"I'm wearing glasses nowadays too. I should have stopped while I was ahead. Actually, I've been shuffled around from here and there over the last couple of years or so. I don't think people like me very much. Right now, I'm working with Baltimore PD on gang and narcotics stuff." The first hint of genuine strain entered Holcomb's voice. "Nasty shit out there. I'm only a year shy of fifty, and then I will take my retirement and run for the hills. "

"I'm sure whatever assignment you have, you will carry it out in the utmost professional manner."

"Oh yeah, you know me. I'm surprised the bureau hasn't assigned my professional butt to Yemen or some other garden spot like it."

"They like to keep their best and brightest in the capital area. You know, as an example of what others should strive for in that city."

"We definitely have the best and brightest here in the greater DC area. They all work in that domed building or at some other Pennsylvania Avenue address."

"I'm glad to hear you haven't changed."

"God knows I've tried, but the bureau wouldn't approve my time off request for me to have that sex change operation in Sweden."

"Maybe when you retire you can take care of that."

Despite Holcomb's irreverent attitude, Harrison knew he was one of the best agents at the bureau. Hearing his voice made Harrison realize, more than ever, how lucky he had been to work with him.

"What are you working on these days?" Holcomb said.

"Lately, insurance fraud and marital infidelity stuff. It pays the bills and keeps me busy."

"Yawn."

"I know, not as exciting as chasing down gangbangers, but it's still a chance to beat the bad guys."

"There's the stalwart American hero I once knew. I think I'm going to be sick," Holcomb said, chuckling.

"Actually, I think it's the excessive amount of alcohol you drink that makes you feel sick."

"Could be. In fact, I could use a hit about now. Oh, that's right, my supervisor said I couldn't drink on duty anymore. He actually removed my vodka stash and poured it in the toilet."

"I'll send you a fresh bottle in the mail right away. Think of it as an early Christmas gift."

"Could you? That would be great. My gambling debt detracts from my discretionary income, so I haven't been able to buy much booze lately. So, what other cases are you working on?"

Holcomb would want to know—and deserved to know—details about this unique case if he were to assist with it. Harrison cleared his throat, and then said, "It's kind of difficult to accept if you don't have an open mind?"

"I'm listening."

Here it goes.

"The case involves extraterrestrials and a government conspiracy to prevent knowledge of their existence from becoming public."

Silence detonated in Harrison's ears. The shock waves razed his surroundings, sucked away the oxygen supply, and compressed his eardrums. He heard ringing too, a high-pitched whine that reverberated through his gray matter.

"I'm sorry, Bill, I thought you said something about aliens? Did you give up the menthols for marijuana? Or maybe they now have flavored joints as well?"

Harrison rubbed his temples. "I'm serious, Art. I'm speaking to you confidentially, by the way."

"Oh, you're right about that. I'm not going to say anything to anyone about aliens and a government conspiracy. They'll think I'm nuts for sure."

"I know it's difficult to accept. Hell, I haven't accepted it either. But the informant is paying me well, and I'm going to follow up on the leads he provides. I called because I know I can trust you and I hoped to get a little assistance."

"You don't call me for God knows how long, and when you do call me, you ask for my help proving that little green men from outer space exist?"

"More or less."

"What do you need me to do? Buy a telescope? Become an astronaut?"

"I need to have independent corroboration of what the informant provides me. I'm also trying to figure out his identity, so I want you to access some of our old aerospace cases and give me the names of the military liaison officers."

"You think this guy might be military?"

"That's my impression right now."

"Is that all?"

"For now it is. Can you help me out?"

Harrison only heard a quiet sigh. He hoped his request appealed to Holcomb's sense of adventure or, at least, that the bonds of their old partnership were strong enough to gain his assistance.

"Only because it's you and I need a break from reality," Holcomb said.

"You're the best."

"Most would disagree. Give me the names of the project cases. I'll need them to do a search."

Before he provided Holcomb with further details, Harrison realized he had just entered a new phase of the investigation. "This must remain confidential. The informant believes this assignment is dangerous."

"Do you feel that way?"

"I don't know for sure. He did inform me in a cryptic way of Harold Groom's demise before it happened."

"What does Groom have to do with this?"

"Nothing directly as far as I know, but according to the informant, Groom had been a government assassin since the 1960s, and he needed to be knocked off because he was going to start talking. I think the informant was using the Groom reference as a way of establishing credibility with me, along with some other details about traffic accidents from the late forties and early fifties."

"This is definitely spookish."

"Just like old times."

"Well, hell, your secrets are safe with me. What are the names of the project cases?"

"Aurora, Silver Star, and Black Hole."

"I remember working those with you now that you mention them. Of course, those were my heavy drinking days, so it's all a bit fuzzy."

"Can you also search FBI records for any unusual cases pertaining to Roswell, New Mexico, circa July, 1947?"

"Anything else?"

"I need verification of some air force discharge records."

"I'll need the names at least, but preferably both the names and service numbers."

"I have both." Harrison provided Holcomb with the names of the five traffic accident victims along with their service numbers.

"So what's important about these guys?"

"All of them died in traffic accidents."

"So?"

"My informant says they were military policemen assigned to Roswell Army Airfield when the crash of two UFOs occurred there in July, 1947."

"And who killed them? The aliens?"

"Right," Harrison said, laughing. "I'm glad to see you're keeping an open mind."

"I'm trying."

"I know this stuff is way out there, but we have got to deal with it professionally."

"Always keeping me in line, aren't you?"

"It makes me wonder how you've gotten by without me."

"I've been banished, exiled from the main office. No one comes around. That should tell you how well I've managed."

"Then it sounds like you could definitely use a break from the routine. So, to answer your question, the informant says these were no accidents and the men were killed by a government entity responsible for covering up the whole alien thing. The MPs were weak links in the chain of secrecy and were eliminated in the name of national security."

"I think I like my own answer better than that one."

"I know what you mean, pal."

A brief uncertainty crossed Harrison's mind when he hung up the phone. The anxiety caused his muscles to tighten, creating a noticeable ache in his right thigh. He rubbed it, helping the pain subside. He trusted Holcomb, but one lesson he had learned long ago was that sometimes, secrets eluded concealment.

SEVENTEEN

Thirty-Seven Fell to the Floor

Ninety-seven feet below Wright-Patterson Air Force Base in Dayton, Ohio, nobody's office, including the one assigned to General Randolph Stone, had windows. Stone's office occupied part of a larger cavern sunk beneath the rambling floors of Wright-Patterson's Air Research and Development Command Headquarters. Beyond his door, a web of circular tunnels connected him and others to the laboratories, meeting rooms, security stations, dormitories, communication posts, cold storage units, and the archives of the Saint Mary Project. A centrally placed cafeteria provided meals and refreshments.

The white walls and linoleum encircled Stone. White fluorescent lights buzzed from neat rectangles arranged in the low ceiling. Fixtures corseted by white acoustic tiles revealed gray only where pockmarked.

Blue squeezed him. The furnishings—desks, chairs, credenzas, telephones, dressers, cabinets—exactly alike throughout the complex and all pale blue like a midday sky, had multiplied over the years. They left less and less white.

"I miss you too," Stone said, trying to finish a conversation with his wife. He had been unable to visit her in Las Vegas for Thanksgiving, and now, with Christmas just over two weeks away, she wanted to know his plans.

"I'm not sure, honey. Yes, I know I shouldn't work so hard. I'll be fine."

Across from him, air force weapons specialist General Donald Lanham sat with one leg crossed over the other, the dangling foot impatiently shaking. Stone shared his colleague's excitement, but he diligently indulged his wife.

"You don't have to get me anything...That's right...For them? No fruitcake...Because, they never eat it...If we have to, sure...We can celebrate on our own after the holidays...Right, maybe even Paris...I thought you would."

General Lanham looked at the floor, his hands tapping the blue chair's armrests. His foot still bounced.

"I love you too...Bye."

Stone hung up the phone and looked at Lanham. "Well, Don, shall we take a walk?"

"You can walk—I think I'll run."

Simultaneously, they rose from their chairs, slowing only briefly to adjust their air force uniform jackets. They passed through an outer office, then steered themselves to a nearby stairwell. While whistling a few bars of "Little Drummer Boy," Stone slipped his identification badge through the electronic access lock and then held the door open for Lanham. They bounded ahead, their spit-polished black shoes tapping downward.

"Are you ready to deploy?" Stone asked.

"We can go in tonight if we have to."

"Including North Range?"

"Of course."

"And it won't overload?"

"No, the reactor has more than enough capacity. ELF will be ready."

After three flights of steps, they exited the stairwell and walked briskly through a corridor that curved to their left. They moved in tandem, as the tube was too narrow and its ceiling too low for humans to walk side by side.

They reached a security station attended by two air policemen. One of the guards, a sergeant, stood next to a podium with a computer console and checked IDs. The other guard, M-16 across his chest, positioned himself adjacent to a circular hatchway. The computer chirped an authorization, and the hatchway's double doors slid apart, revealing a dim compartment. Once both officers stepped inside, the entrance closed. Two firm clicks, and then a second hatch opened.

After walking twenty steps or so, they arrived at their destination, Arena Four. Dr. Schmidt, Saint Mary's chief exotics physician, waited for them. An elderly, beefy woman, Schmidt retained a dense Bavarian accent despite her decades of residence in the United States. Even in the low, almost nonexistent light of Arena Four, Stone easily spotted her, partially because of the white smock she wore, but mostly because of her face. Schmidt lived underground virtually year-round. Sunlight deprivation had taken a heavy toll on her complexion. Ghostly pale, wearing her medical garb, and stoically awaiting the two senior officers, Schmidt looked very much like a Doric column: heavy, white, and old.

An empty black box, Arena Four was about the size of a child's suburban bedroom. A sixty-inch surveillance monitor, telephone, and intercom panel adorned one of its walls. The panel hung next to where a one-way mirror once existed that allowed observation into an adjacent room, an empty white box known as Enclosure Four. Alien telepathic skills had made the mirror obsolete. The staff sealed it years ago and covered the void with interlaced metal plates to prevent the exotics in Enclosure Four from sensing the presence and thoughts of anyone observing them.

"Bring it in," Stone said.

Schmidt lifted the telephone receiver and said, "We are ready for you."

Arena Four's occupants gathered around the surveillance monitor. Digital lettering, an opaque horizontal message on the lower part of the screen, read, "Class 5[Restricted]: 7 DEC (SAT) < Auto\REC > E-4/16:22:02 (EST)."

A door slid open, the blue cushions of a gurney in the corridor behind it adding a momentary splash of color to the image on the screen. Then, more white. And gray.

An exotics technician, encased in an environment suit, entered the room, gazing downward through the clear faceplate at the specimen by her side.

"Which one is that, Doctor?" Stone asked, comparing the screen's time display with that of his Casio sport watch.

"Thirty-Seven."

"And Thirty-Eight?"

"Thirty-Eight is still in quarantine."

Enclosure Four's door closed. The technician took baby steps, leading her three-and-a-half-foot-tall companion to the center of the room. Kneeling, back to the camera, the technician's hood revealed her nodding head. Even in this position, she stood over the extraterrestrial, easily concealing from view its thin gray extremities and disproportionally large head.

"As you can see," Schmidt said, "the tech is responding to the EBE. From what we have learned, Thirty—Seven is a botanist. It is also exceptionally talkative. Its telepathy is profusely invasive, our highest category. Some of the staff describe their experiences with it as generally pleasant, but tiring. It asks many questions, 'why this,' 'why that,' and so on, or so Professor Moresby believes."

Lanham's shoulders tightened. "What precautions have been taken?"

"The technician has no knowledge about the nature of this test. I told her to escort Thirty-Seven into the enclosure, as the isolation cells were in need of some maintenance. In trying to simulate field conditions, we will only visually observe the effects of ELF. The use of electrodes would tip our hand, so to speak."

After this reassurance, Schmidt activated the intercom, instructing the technician to exit, which took approximately thirty seconds.

Alone, the creature stood with long, spindly arms at its sides, tilting its large head. Big black eyes stared at the camera recessed behind a glass plate.

"Go ahead, Don," General Stone said.

Phone fast in hand, Lanham said, "Control, you have omega clearance. Proceed with the program."

Its face filled the screen. Scrutiny of the equipment followed. Elongated fingers touched the transparent shield, leaving no smudge or prints. It moved away.

Stone's palms sweated.

It poked at the seam around the doorway. In an instant, it withdrew its hand and then moved away, stumbling toward the camera.

"Boy," Stone said, wiping his hands, "you can really feel it."

Extremely low-frequency sound waves resonated through the building's structure. As the sound waves grew in intensity, the volume from the associated vibration and hum also increased.

"Just like my son's stereo," Lanham said.

Its torso heaved. In, out. Black, almond-shaped pupils constricted. A milky film dripped from its slit of a mouth onto the floor. It moved erratically around the room, seeking escape. Its large face pressed against the shield over the camera, leaving an orange smudge. Its gangly legs failed. Thirty-Seven fell to the floor.

Arena Four's occupants coughed several times, swallowing phlegm that ELF's deep, pulsating tones loosened. The vibrations diminished. When they ended, Stone noticed his ears rang.

Its torso heaved again.

"It looks subdued to me," Lanham said.

"Let's make sure." Stone cleared his throat and picked up the telephone. "Send him in."

The door slid open, and a blond man, about thirty years old, entered, walking to the middle of the room.

In, out.

The blond man's black turtleneck, brown corduroy pants, crimson cardigan sweater, and brown suede loafers contrasted with the white walls of Enclosure Four. Beneath neat and trim blond hair, the man's blue eyes examined the lump that struggled to reach out at him. The man kicked away Thirty-Seven's hand. He stepped back, unbuttoned his sweater, and removed a Colt .380 pistol from a holster concealed in his waistline. Aiming center mass, the man said, "Aren't you going to stop me, Thirty—Seven?"

In.

"I'm waiting, and I'm not known for my patience."

Out.

The .380's sights aligned. Easy breaths. Two staccato blasts followed. A third round penetrated the target's head.

Activating the intercom, Stone said, "Thanks, James."

Inside Enclosure Four, James Evans looked at the camera and nodded.

Smiling, Stone walked to Arena Four's exit and opened the hatch. He turned to a grinning General Lanham and said, "After you, Don."

EIGHTEEN

Watch Where You Point That Thing

Harrison pulled into the parking lot of Old Pueblo Guns and Range and saw Janice waiting for him beside her car, a used Toyota Celica. She waved and smiled, excited about firearms training. Harrison had intended to provide her with training sometime, but figured her final exam schedule kept her too busy. But, she had brought up the topic in the midst of her tests and politely insisted she had plenty of time for it.

Hearing nothing from Holcomb, his former FBI partner, Harrison had plenty of time too.

He parked next to the Celica and grabbed a brown leather pancake-style holster from the passenger seat. Exiting the Dodge Charger, he said, "Did you wear a belt?"

Janice wore a red T-shirt, blue jeans, and a leather aviator's jacket. She lifted the jacket, exposing her slim waistline. "Why yes, I did."

Harrison handed her the holster, saying, "This will make it easier when you're not firing."

Janice took the holster and attached it to her belt.

After retrieving a stainless-steel Colt .45 from the trunk of his car, Harrison slid it into the holster on his belt. He reached into the trunk again and removed a blue steel Colt .45 from its carrying case. After confirming it was unloaded, Harrison gave it to Janice.

"It's a little older than the one I'll be using," Harrison said, "but I assure you, it still works as good as the day it was made, which was probably about fifty years ago."

"Always the history buff, aren't you?" Janice said, clasping the pistol, unsure of what to do next.

Harrison smiled and said, "No worries, it won't bite. Holster it."

Janice pulled back her jacket and slid the gun into the holster. Harrison shut the trunk and nodded in the direction of the range. As they walked, Harrison explained the gun's features.

"That's a Colt .45 semiautomatic handgun. It holds seven rounds in the magazine and one in the chamber. Eight rounds before firing. It's a big gun, Janice, but don't let it intimidate you. If you can handle it well, then you can handle just about any other handgun. If you ever need to defend yourself, the power of it will stop any bad guy, no matter how big. Even a shoulder or leg hit will knock him down."

"Won't that just make him angry?"

Harrison laughed. "You'll do just fine."

"I'm in your hands."

Harrison opened the door and followed Janice inside. Norm, the range master, looked up from behind the counter and stood to greet his familiar customer. Janice chuckled, but recovered and rubbed her nose. Harrison guessed that Norm's squeaking jeans amused her.

"Thanks for letting me bring a guest today," Harrison said.

"No problem. Who's this good-looking gunslinger?"

"This is Janice Evans, my investigative associate."

"Welcome, Ms. Evans," Norm said, shaking Janice's extended hand. "Well, she sure is prettier than that cheap old-school fellow you work with. You bring Ms. Evans in here anytime you want, Mr. Harrison."

"Thanks, Norm," Harrison said.

Janice smiled, and then giggled as Norm moved about while providing them with ammunition, hearing protectors, and paper targets. She and Harrison walked to the end of the indoor range and settled in at the last firing lane. Harrison reached for one of the black silhouette targets, clipped it to the metal wire over his head, and pushed the button on the wall next to him, sending the target downrange. When the target had traveled about ten yards, he released the button.

After removing four empty magazines from his trouser pockets, Harrison demonstrated how to load one with bullets. He handed Janice the others. Although an awkward task to complete at first, her proficiency improved after Harrison instructed her to load and unload the magazines several times.

Next, using the .45 he provided to Janice, Harrison demonstrated its various functions, safeties, the slide's back-and-forth movement, and proper sight alignment. Under his guidance, Janice took a firing stance with the gun in her right hand. Standing close and gently touching her, Harrison adjusted Janice's stiff and tense posture for better balance.

"Relax some," Harrison said. "Keep a firm grip, but not too tight, otherwise your hand will shake."

Janice settled down after dry firing the weapon several times.

"Breathing is important here. Calm your breathing, and just as you are about to fire, hold your breath. The firing should almost seem like a surprise."

When Harrison stood behind her and held her hands to explain a better grip, Janice leaned into him. He let her body relax against his while his hands caressed hers. Reluctantly, he stepped aside and showed her how to load the gun.

"You're a fast learner, Janice. Now the weapon is fully loaded and it's time to fire it. Remember the grip, the stance, the release of the thumb safety as you draw it. Relaxed breathing, align the sights, aim center mass at the target, gentle squeeze on the trigger. When you're out of bullets, the slide will lock to the rear. Drop the magazine and reload with a fresh one from your pocket. Keep your eyes and gun pointed downrange on the bad guy when you reload. Better take off that jacket first. Any questions?"

Janice holstered the gun, and removing her jacket, she said, "Only about what came after 'it's time to fire it.'"

"You'll do fine," Harrison said, handing her a pair of hearing protectors.

Returning her attention to the target, Janice said, "Here goes nothing." In a moment, she drew the Colt and carried out the steps she had just learned. "Holy cow!" she said, as the first round's recoil jarred her hands. Janice recovered and continued firing. Hot, empty casings flew over or by her right shoulder. She ignored them. After the eighth round, the slide locked in the rear position. She released the empty magazine, and it fell to the ground. And then, Janice made the mistake of looking down for the next magazine.

"Keep your eyes downrange," Harrison said, stepping up beside her.

Janice zeroed back in on the target and felt for the magazine inside her pants pocket. She pulled out the magazine and used her fingertips to feel for the roundness of the top bullet. "This end up," she said, sliding the magazine firmly into the Colt.

"Good," Harrison said, stepping back.

Janice released the slide, chambering the next round. With less hesitation than before, she emptied the gun and then holstered the .45. Removing the hearing protectors and turning around, Janice exposed her broad grin to Harrison. "I like it!"

"I've noticed."

Harrison pushed the target-return button, and the silhouette glided toward them. Janice looked at her returning target with wide eyes. She grimaced, however, when her aim revealed its results. "Ugh."

"Have you been to the eye doctor lately?"

"Is it really that bad?"

"Actually, for your first time handling such a big gun, you did fine." Harrison winked, and then said, "Your aim will naturally improve with more training."

"How many hits did I get?"

"It looks like four in the black, and as far as the others go, well, let's just say they would have made him duck. Reload the magazines and put your hearing protector back on."

Harrison grinned as he attached another target to the overhead wire and sent it fifteen yards downrange. He drew the stainless-steel Colt from his holster. Rapid firing ensued, one of the casings brushing his cheek, until the gun was empty. The returning target revealed eight holes concentrated in its center.

They removed their hearing protectors, and Harrison looked at Janice. "I never fired a gun until I was in the FBI. Before then, the mere sight of one gave me a sinking feeling in my gut. I know what you're thinking, but I assure you, if you apply what you learn, you will improve. And if you ever have to use it, heaven forbid, then you'll have the confidence you need to defend yourself and possibly others."

Janice nodded. "You got a little something there," she said, reaching up to his face. Harrison flinched a little at first, but relaxed and let her wipe away a little stain of gunpowder from his cheek where the empty casing had hit him.

The pair spent the next two hours on the range by themselves. Janice fired all the rounds Harrison purchased, and she demonstrated considerable improvement. He taught her more about the Colt, occasionally throwing in tidbits about its long history of service with the military, and how to use it more effectively by trying different firing techniques he had learned in the FBI. He stressed the need for firing discipline to encourage accuracy and to reduce the danger to bystanders. By the time they left the range, Harrison felt confident about Janice's new abilities, and so did she, thanking him again for the time and attention he gave her.

Lunch came afterward. Famished, both agreed that only a big meal of Mexican food would satisfy their hunger. There was laughter too, and political discussions about the situation in the Far East and whether or not it would improve. They solved problems, domestic and international, over tortillas and pinto beans.

Harrison made a guess. "Pennsylvania."

"Kind of all over, really," Janice said. "But much of my time has been spent in Ohio, so you're in the ballpark."

They engaged in more small talk, and then Harrison said, "And your parents?"

"Dad's a salesman, hardware and such, and Mom stays at home. How about yours?"

Harrison hesitated, and then said, “Dad was a salesman too. But, uh, my parents died shortly after I entered the FBI.”

“Bill, I’m so sorry.”

“I guess that’s why Pete’s family is important to me. They fill a void.”

“How’d you two meet?”

Harrison’s thoughts drifted to another place, another time. He smiled. “I met Pete probably twelve years ago or so. He was a PI back then, and I was working a fraud case that brought me through Tucson. He shared some information he had on the suspects with me, and I ended up getting a successful prosecution on that case, but I owed a lot of the credit to him. We stayed in touch over the years, and when I...when I retired and moved here, we struck up a partnership.”

The waiter interrupted, and Harrison paid the bill.

After a few moments more, they had to say good-bye. Studying for final exams tugged her away, so Harrison drove to the office.

“What’s this?” Zemdarsky said when his partner came through the front door. “Why, Willy, my boy, you have a positive glow about you. Are you feeling all right?”

“Shut it,” Harrison said, grinning and pushing Zemdarsky’s palms away from his face.

“So, how’s Janice?”

“Any messages?”

“Not talking, eh? Fine, be that way. I thought we were friends, pals, but I guess not.”

“Uh, messages?”

“Okay, okay, your buddy, Art Holcomb, called, but he didn’t seem too talkative.”

“Well, that’s just his way.”

“I didn’t know you’d been in touch with him.”

“Just gave him a buzz to rap about our Wild West days.”

“You going to get him to confess to that Echo Tango thing? Whatever that’s about.”

Harrison unlocked his office's door and stepped inside. Turning around, he said, "Oh, that. I don't know, maybe." He shut the door and sat down, listening until he was sure Zemdarsky went on about his business.

Then he picked up the phone.

NINETEEN

The Saint Mary Project

A dial tone and a few pressed buttons later, Harrison's call to Holcomb entered the fiber-optic stream toward the East Coast. After his fingers stopped the necessary inputs, he sat back and relaxed, but only for a moment. He lurched forward and hung up the phone. His eyes focused on the envelope tacked to the bulletin board in his office. Echo Tango's latest message waited for him.

"Damn."

No doubt the messenger had come in the night, long before the occupants arrived at the office. Harrison did not alert Zemdarsky. He wanted to avoid involving him any further, and in doing so, protect him and his family from any potential harm.

Harrison was not worried about Holcomb. He did not have a family and held a position from which he could corroborate certain information. Holcomb also carried a badge. And a gun.

Without taking it down, Harrison could tell the bulging envelope carried cash. He flinched, and stroked the smooth whiskers of his neatly trimmed beard. Harrison swore he could smell the witch hazel on the envelope all the way from his desk. The scent conjured up an image of his father shaving.

As unreal as this case came across, one bit of reality struck close to home. That single scrap of fact both pushed him away and pulled him closer. Staring at the envelope across the no-man's-land between his desk and the bulletin board, Harrison realized he stood entrenched in a battle that potentially crossed generations. Harrison cut a stretch of imaginary barbed wire and made his move. After reaching for and opening the envelope, he read the latest information Echo Tango provided...

The copy of the news article I've included discusses a UFO sighting over Las Vegas from last July. It is a piece of background information necessary to understand the other news articles I've enclosed about two recent deaths involving air force personnel. The suicide and accident victims witnessed the July UFO sighting. However, they were in closer proximity to the craft than any of the civilian witnesses in Las Vegas. The test of a rebuilt Roswell UFO vehicle was interrupted by another UFO described in the paper. The deceased airman and sergeant were the only eyewitnesses to the apparent destruction of two F-15 fighters that were sent to intercept the craft when it appeared over the test site. The status of the aircraft and their pilots, to my knowledge, is still unknown.

The test location is known as Area 51, which is part of a larger complex commonly referred to as Dreamland. Perhaps you have heard of it in the media. It is located approximately eighty miles northwest of Las Vegas. It is heavily guarded, and the military uses it for the research and development of new aircraft and weapons systems. Until recent years, it officially did not exist. This area was remote and isolated in 1947, and the military selected it as the test area for the recovered material and vehicles from Roswell. Dreamland has received much attention lately from the outside, making it much less suitable for secret tests. As a result, an entity in control of this matter made a decision to develop a new facility. This new facility will become operational by the end of the year. It is located in the basin and range area of northeastern Nevada. Development and testing of aircraft continues at Area 51 in the meantime, but at a much slower pace than in years past.

The air force personnel who witnessed the July incident at the test site were monitored for any unusual behavior that would indicate any weaknesses in their ability to remain silent. Unfortunately for them, both displayed strange behavior patterns following the incident, due probably more from the stress of secrecy than from the actual event. Nevertheless, the entity chose to take no chances, and a specially developed assassin eliminated them. I will reveal the methods used in these particular assassinations to you later, when the time is right.

The money I have included is for your next assignment. I need you to travel to Las Vegas and take a room at the Sundowner Inn. It is located on the southern end of the strip. Please be armed during this next assignment. I will reveal the details to you when I observe you in Las Vegas. Be there by December 20.

As he stood up, Harrison recalled the zigzagging luminescent sphere he witnessed last July. He held the letter and its attachments, and then exited his office. He walked to the alcove where they kept the photocopier. A quick glance into Zemdarsky's office assured Harrison that his partner remained preoccupied. Zemdarsky talked on the phone, laughing and wiping tears from the corners of his eyes.

Harrison made the necessary copies. He would separate them later, when he put them in a safe-deposit box he had rented. Back in his office, he closed and locked the door and then sat down at his desk to call Holcomb again. When Holcomb answered, Harrison said, "The snake charmer from India is Sigmund Freud's grandson."

"J. Edgar Hoover never wore white after Labor Day."

"Is that so?"

"Yeah, except for his favorite pair of pumps. You got a nosy partner."

"Did you find something?"

"More or less. Actually, it's sort of like finding out the whore—"

"What is it?"

"So, I ran a search of the projects you told me about. The aerospace cases have been sealed and transferred."

"Sealed and transferred?"

"There wasn't much information left in the computer at all. The cases are sealed. There is a class-five security clearance, with restrictions, indicated as necessary for access."

"What the hell kind of clearance is that?"

"Beats the hell out of me. I didn't ask around just in case it was some sort of clearance that only aliens have."

"Where were they transferred to?"

"The cases and all the associated evidence were transferred last August to the air force, to the Air Research and Development Command."

"To Dayton. Was any reason provided for their sealing and transfer?"

"Yeah, you'll love this. 'A matter of national security.'"

"Hmm...Anything on Roswell?"

"The bureau did have an open case under the heading of 'Aerospace Incident, Roswell, New Mexico,' and it was from July, 1947. The problem with this one, like the others, is that it's also been sealed and transferred."

"When was it transferred?"

"In 1947. A class fiver with restrictions on this one too. The transfer indicates it went to a project called 'Saint Mary.' Stated reason, 'A matter of national security.'"

"Saint Mary?"

"Yeah, but nothing came up under that name when I searched the computer records."

"Hmm..."

"One other thing came up in my research, and although not specific to Roswell, it did pertain to New Mexico."

"What's that?"

"Apparently, in 1950, the special agent in charge of the FBI's Washington Field Office wrote a memo to Hoover that concerned flying saucers recovered in New Mexico along with their occupants. It didn't specify a location or a date for the recovery, but the information the SAC reported apparently originated from an air force investigator."

"It gives the case a little more traction."

"Agreed. Just sorry I wasn't more helpful."

"Don't sell yourself short."

"You're too kind. I'm still working on the discharge records. You know how the bureaucracy can be. I'll probably give you a ring in a few more days."

"You may have to reach me in Vegas if it takes longer than that."

"You never struck me as the gambling type."

Harrison filled in Holcomb on the latest information from Echo Tango, including where he would stay in Las Vegas. Holcomb seemed to absorb the information more professionally this time. He, like Harrison, thought the sealing and transfers of the cases and their designation with a security clearance neither one of them had ever heard of was troubling.

"Watch your back," Holcomb said. "There just may be some truth to this craziness that ET has brought to you after all."

"You too, brother, you too."

TWENTY

Appropriate to the Region

With only a little over a week until Christmas, shoppers jammed the mall. But uncertainty also slowed Harrison's progress. He resisted help initially, but eventually gave in and sought out the jewelry store salesclerk who'd hovered around him earlier.

"She'll like it. It's simple, elegant, and tasteful," the clerk said, helping him pick out something for Janice. "And, it is appropriate to the region."

Although convinced the woman assisting him had other motivations for wanting to make the sale, Harrison nevertheless relied on her. He had not bought a gift for a woman in a long time.

He paid cash, paying extra for the clerk to gift wrap it for him.

Harrison expected to see Janice at the office and planned to give the gift to her there, where he could not make a big deal about it. The gift would be a combination Christmas and going-away gift. Low key. She would be leaving tonight, for home, for winter break from school. Her finals had ended this morning.

After exiting the store and making his way through the crowded mall, Harrison noticed Santa Claus sat surrounded by children and their parents. Elves did their best to keep everyone in line. Wish lists and candy canes blended with commercialism. Patiently, Harrison watched the scene as he waded through the crowds on his way out.

The Dodge Charger glinted in the late-morning sun, freshly washed for the drive to Las Vegas set for the day after next. The lube and oil change cost about thirty bucks. The car seemed to purr satisfyingly during the drive to the office.

Harrison had stepped barely inside the office door when Janice greeted him. Her outstretched arms grabbed him around his broad shoulders. Her body pressed against his, and he reached around her waist and returned the gesture.

"What's the hug for?" Harrison said.

"Because I'll miss you and Pete."

Releasing each other, Harrison stepped back and said, "I'll miss you too. But you'll be back sooner than you know it."

Her blue eyes looked away for just a moment, and then they returned to him. "I hope so."

They wandered into his office. She asked if he wanted coffee. He did, but said he could get it for himself. She got it for him anyway. The coffee was perfect, as always.

"What's this?" Janice said, seeing Harrison remove the small gift-wrapped box from his pocket.

"It's for you," Harrison replied, reaching to give it to her.

"Me?"

Harrison nodded and waited for her to take it from his steady palm.

"But I didn't get you—"

"No worries. I hope you like it."

She cradled the box in her hands and opened it. Smiling, she attached the sterling-silver roadrunner pin to her lapel. "It's perfect."

"And appropriate to the region."

"Very. I'll bring you back a surprise."

"What about me?" Zemdarsky said, interrupting.

Harrison and Janice turned around. Zemdarsky grinned at them and said, "What about me? What about my surprise? What about my gift?"

"How long have you been there?" Harrison said.

"Long enough," Zemdarsky said, winking. He settled for a hug from Janice, and Harrison told him he would have to wait until Christmas day.

"Promises, promises," Zemdarsky said, hurrying away. He fetched some sugar cookies from his office and returned to share. "Bounty from the pastry attendant."

Coffee, cookies, and conversation filled the next two hours. Harrison caught glimpses of Janice rubbing a finger over her gift from time to time. He assumed that meant she liked it. Memories of the first time he had met her brought a fond smile to his face. Janice's eyes met his, and she nodded. She mouthed the words "thank you" at him. Sadly, her next words announced that it was time for her to leave and pack.

Harrison walked her to the office's front door, held it open, and wished her a safe journey. Janice surprised him by kissing him on the cheek. She wished him a merry Christmas and then waved good-bye to Zemdarsky before she headed toward the building's lobby. Harrison watched her leave. Behind him, he heard his partner lamenting the fact that he had not received a kiss.

Harrison closed the door and turned around. "Actually, I can arrange that."

"Huh?"

"Beano needs a home for a few days, and she sure seems to like you."

TWENTY ONE

The Hybrids

Blue, pale blue. Everywhere around here, pale blue.

Under the interior lighting, the color did not register well on her hybridized retinas. She used care while walking. Sometimes the objects looked nearly invisible. And every time she reported in to ARDCom, more obstacles seemed to stand in her way.

Even the air policemen wore blue, ethereal figures under the dim fluorescent lights.

"I need Evans, Janice B., class fiver," the sergeant said.

The sergeant's subordinate opened a wall safe and removed a clip-on identification badge. The sergeant placed his log sheet on the blue countertop. "Please sign here, ma'am."

Signing the form, Janice did not need to convince herself that the white form rested on something solid. She had passed through this checkpoint often enough to know it did, but it seemed to float in mid-air. A side effect of her alien-human vision.

"Thank you, ma'am. Please hand me your book bag and step through the gate."

As she walked through the body scanner, the airman inspected the bag. Her luggage entered the facility elsewhere, no doubt by way of a process that also included thorough study.

Soon, it would be her turn.

With check-in completed, Janice clipped the badge to her coat and hoisted the book bag over her shoulder. A third sentry escorted her into a nearby elevator. The airman entered a passcode into the control panel and stepped back, nearly vanishing. Janice chuckled at the effect, until the doors closed, leaving her entirely alone. She placed her right palm onto a warm glass biometric pad above the control panel and listened for the soft, synthetic voice.

"Evans, Janice B., please state your priority access code."

After clearing her throat, Janice said, "Longitude."

"Match confirmed, entry authorized."

The elevator descended ninety-seven feet. Janice stared at the muddled reflection of herself in the dull aluminum doors. Waiting for them to open, she wondered if insanity could be a by-product of her construction. When they opened, she exited without any hesitation, not even bothering to acknowledge the two air policeman holding M-16 rifles who stood just past the doors. She turned left, taking a few steps to her temporary quarters, but a voice from behind halted her progress.

"I was about to come to Tucson and retrieve you myself."

Dr. Schmidt's choice of words never failed to insult.

Janice tightened her lips together and turned around. She offered a polite, practiced smile, and then said, "Sorry, this is the first chance I've had to get back here. It's nice to be home again and to see you."

"Come. Let's take you to exam room twelve."

The march down the hallway, in tandem, gave Janice a brief moment in which to sneer at the back of Dr. Schmidt's head. She was certain that none of the doctor's other specimens ever did that. Liberty was fleeting in Saint Mary. And it was always solitary. But, she hoped, that would change. It had to, or else she felt she would die.

Her suicidal thoughts were commonplace now, a silent debate that had started after General Stone's promotion to general last summer. Everyone with class-five clearance understood the implications of his new rank and the reorganization. Now it was just a question of when he would take absolute control of her life. The two hybrids represented trophies awarded to those within Saint Mary whose duties fit best with the Circle's priorities and good graces.

It had to stop.

Increasingly, dread and despair grew to be her closest companions. Except in Tucson, where they waited for her outside the city limits, lounging arrogantly at the fringes of her consciousness.

Once inside the examination room, which looked and smelled as ordinary as those on the outside, Janice and Dr. Schmidt settled into the routine.

"Remove your clothing."

Janice set the book bag and her flannel coat on the lower tier of a cart next to the metal door. While Janice disrobed, she neatly folded her garments into a tidy stack, placing them on the cart's upper tier, shoes laid on top.

"Stand here."

Dr. Schmidt, clipboard in hand, had the first checklist ready, the one with the androgynous outline of a human body.

"Turn."

As this was merely the beginning of a standard battery of examinations that normally lasted three days, dread and despair huddled up next to Janice.

"Sit."

The exam bench's disposable paper sheathing crimped, making a distinct crumpling noise so noticeable during the silence of a visit to the doctor. The paper adhered to her buttocks, an effective tactile constraint keeping her still, although she felt a slow slide off the table's edge was under way.

"Any illnesses since your last visit?"

"No."

"Are your cycles regular?"

"Yes."

"Any problems associated with your period at all?"

"No."

"Any sexual experiences?"

"That would violate standing orders, so no, absolutely not. Never."

More questions, more answers, more checks performed. Blood pressure, reflexes. A urine sample. Dr. Schmidt withdrew some red blood, with just the slightest tint of orange to it.

"And the exercises? Have you followed the regimen?"

"Yes."

"Both sensitivity and control aspects?"

"Yes."

Dr. Schmidt positioned the clipboard so Janice could not see it, then flipped to another form and stared at it. "Item A?"

Janice found relaxation difficult, but a few deep breaths helped. Item A's image appeared. "You are viewing a sequence of numbers."

Delving into Dr. Schmidt's thoughts, or anyone's for that matter, always put Janice at risk. Her brother's skills were stronger. A moment of uncertainty or sympathy while scanning Dr. Schmidt could induce reciprocity. Guarding against this prospect, she learned to slow the scanning process on her subjects. It gave her protection, but apparently caused severe headaches for those who experienced her invasive or prolonged scans. Just like Harrison.

"Eight hundred, two, seventeen," Janice said, continuing the test. "Oh, and the letter Z, then forty point two. And, yes."

"Yes what?"

"You wanted to know whether I knew what you had for breakfast."

"And it was?"

"A dry Denver omelet in the cafeteria. The eggs...hmmm...were a little dry. You liked the link sausage. You had five sausages. The eggs, hmmm—"

"That's enough. Release the scan. Fine. Get dressed and take these forms to General Stone. He is waiting for you in his office."

An air force colonel squinted at Janice's security badge. He sat at a desk in the outer office in front of General Randolph Stone's closed door. The colonel occupied the least space—stacks of folders filled most of it. Some folders seemed old, their various muted colors fading into a common shade of dirty yellow. There were also stacks of audio and video tapes, CDs, various other digital media devices, and what looked like jars of soil samples.

The officer, whom Janice did not recognize, appeared busy labeling and cataloging the diverse inventory. He looked approachable enough and showed no sign of irritation when she interrupted him.

"I'm Evans, Janice B. The general is expecting me."

"Just one moment, 'Evans, Janice B.'" The colonel picked up the phone, smiling. His unexpectedly approachable demeanor caught her dread and despair off guard, and they uncoiled some from Janice.

Continuing, the colonel said into the phone, "Janice Evans is here, sir. Yes, sir. Uh, much of it came this morning. Certainly. Lunch? No, I don't think I've met General Andrews. You name the time, sir. Very well. Unit zero? My recommendation is that we retain him. Thank you, sir." The colonel stood, saying, "He'll see you now, Janice. I'm sorry, may I call you Janice?"

"You may, thank you. And your name, Colonel?"

"Colonel Samuel Ritter, but please, call me Sam."

"Thank you, Sam."

"You're most welcome, Janice."

After opening the door to General Stone's office, Janice found him seated on the front corner of his desk, his sharp features pointed directly at her. She believed his informal posture was for effect and disingenuous. Feeling he would hug her, she backed away to avoid giving him the opportunity.

"Hello, sir. Dr. Schmidt wanted me to give these to you." Janice presented her medical forms and immediately took a seat, expressing exhaustion from the trip.

"How was your flight?"

"Fine."

"It's nice to have you home. Would you like some coffee or something?"

"No thanks."

Janice endured a stiff smile and pat on the head from General Stone, then watched him fill his Air Force Academy mug with old, burnt coffee, dark as cinder. He sat in the chair at his desk, took a long first gulp, and then reviewed the medical forms.

A black-and-white photograph above the coffeemaker caught Janice's attention. She recognized the woman in it as Senator Vaughn from New Mexico. Vaughn gave a speech on the Senate floor. Someone, probably General Stone, had taped a piece of paper in the shape of a cartoon bubble next to the senator's mouth. The quotation in the bubble read, "Well, if you honestly must know, I am the elusive fifth species. Now, please, take me to your leader."

"Very good," General Stone said, nodding. "According to this, initial tests indicate you are in perfect health. But, of course, more data to come on that."

"It's all in the genes, sir."

Stone's coarse laughter made Janice think he coughed.

"How is school?"

"Straight As."

"I know that. But are your studies beneficial to you?"

"You mean, in preparation for becoming an active Saint Mary operative?"

"Yes."

"There is a positive socialization factor, something I think my brother could benefit from. I've learned many practical skills, but mostly I'm learning how to fit in and interact with different people."

Stone stared at Janice over the rim of his mug as he took another long sip.

"There's also my internship."

"Ah, yes." Stone licked his lips. "Tell me about it."

"It's a requirement for the degree. It's part-time and pretty routine, but I'm learning some valuable lessons about civilian investigation practices."

Stone opened another file and clasped his hands together, resting them on the center of his desk. "What I mean is tell me about Peter Aaron Zemdarsky."

"He's a career PI. Mostly fraud cases, some missing person cases. He has some corporate security accounts. That's his most lucrative line of work. He has contacts everywhere in Tucson. Actually, throughout the Southwest. Politically, socially. Very connected. Although you wouldn't know it to see him or talk to him."

"We've noted contacts between Zemdarsky's office phone and Senator Vaughn's home phone."

"Yes, he and the senator's husband are longtime acquaintances going back to childhood. The two of them chat from time to time, but nothing more than discussions between old friends."

"And William Bernard Harrison?"

"That's a little different."

"You've checked him out then?"

"I did some background on my own, but General Taylor helped fill in the gaps. You should have a copy of my status reports. The transition instructions said to direct the correspondence to you. The Harrison matter is really just for practice. General Taylor thought it would be useful."

"So, Harrison is not a loose cannon?"

"No, and General Taylor didn't really think he would be. Harrison still maintains his liberal views about national security, but his concerns these days center on his work, his dog, and a desire to find a wife. General Taylor just wanted me to practice my infiltration skills, so to speak. It worked out well that this guy also happened to be in Tucson."

"You know, Harrison worked for the FBI."

"Right. In fact, he's helping to train me. My internship will extend to the next semester, because I started it late, so I'm looking forward to deepening my skills."

Closing the file, Stone said, "You really have come a long way, Janice. It's so fulfilling to see you making this progress."

Janice refrained from responding. A storm surge had suddenly engulfed her and dragged her under and away from solid ground. She squeezed blue padding on the chair's armrests. Her knuckles tightened, whitening from the pressure.

"That's why I don't believe there is any need for you to return to Tucson. You're ready for the real thing. We've got some exciting things coming up, and I want you involved. Your brother could use some help. We keep him busy. He never complains, though, but he shouldn't be expected to do all of the heavy lifting by himself. You need to contribute too."

"But what about my formal education?"

"Don't worry about it. We'll educate you here and, when the time comes, at North Range. You'll love the new base. It's in the mountains. Clean air, clear skies, quiet, and solitude. Everything is brand new. It has that fresh paint smell."

"I appreciate your confidence in me."

"That's the easy part. Believe me, if we had more people around like you, Saint Mary would be much better off. Now, I don't want to rush you out of here, but my adjutant out there and I have some important things to discuss over lunch. I'd ask you to join us, but you're scheduled to meet with Dr. Schmidt in about thirty minutes."

"I am?"

"Yes. And you don't want to keep that old fascist waiting."

"No. I better go."

General Stone interrupted Janice's exit with an awkward hug, saying, "I know how you need that now and again, Janice. Of course, I let James get his hugs from Frau Schmidt."

In the outer office, Janice shook off the creepy feeling. She saw Colonel Ritter squinting at a strip of old color photographic negatives. He stood up as Janice passed by.

"It was a pleasure, Janice."

His sentiment felt sincere. "Same here, Sam."

Breeding?

Silence filled the examination room, and the air inside vacated it. The vacuum surrounded and suffocated Janice.

"Did you hear me?" Dr. Schmidt said.

Janice blinked and sucked in what little oxygen seemed to exist in the room. "I heard you."

"Then report at eight a.m. tomorrow. We will retrieve the eggs first, and then continue the remaining exams. Get dressed now."

Fatigued and fearful, Janice lacked sufficient energy to fuel her anger at the disturbing news that Saint Mary planned to produce the next generation of hybrids. She used what little energy she had to resist the tears that wanted to fall.

After removing her hospital gown and changing into her comfortable navy-blue jumpsuit, she headed to the cafeteria, trying to clear her mind. A difficult journey, especially when she noticed some of the guards wore holsters that encased a familiar firearm. Not exactly like Harrison's Colt .45, but similarly constructed. How easy it would be to control its removal. How quickly the end would come.

No, they would blame the guard.

The route to the cafeteria took her through several checkpoints and up two flights of stairs. Interaction with sentries, identification scanners, and thoughts of Harrison helped repel notions of a final surrender. She hoped for change, for an escape, and for Harrison to remember what so many people needed him to remember. Assessing options was complicated and just plain hard. She was so hungry and tired.

And buried so deep in the ground.

"Sorry, ma'am, there's not much left." Along the food display, only scraps of white rice, mashed potatoes, gravy, baked chicken, and mixed vegetables remained. The young server looked confused.

"It is late," Janice said, noticing it was nearly seven o'clock. Some of the kitchen crew cleaned up the dinner mess.

"We still have some meatloaf in the oven. At least, I think we do, if they haven't already tossed it. Or, you're welcome to what's left of the chicken."

Neither sounded very appealing.

"She wants a cheeseburger, Airman," James Evans said, sauntering up to the counter next to his sister. "I'll eat the chicken. Add a slice of meatloaf, too." The airman's compliance with his orders began right away. "Whip her up some French fries while you're at it too. Hi, Janice, long time no see. The German bitch thought you might be here."

"James, I didn't know you were here. You look good." Janice exuded a pleasantly surprised tone, another practiced behavior.

"More than I can say for you. You look like shit. You'll perk up after dinner. You still like cheeseburgers, don't you?" He grabbed his plate from the server. "Bring it out to her when it's ready. And bring us some fruit, too. Oranges, preferably. And two Cokes."

"Yes, sir."

"Come on, Janice, let's sit and rap for a while. I would have hooked up with you earlier, but Schmidt wanted no interruptions. She's been in such a mood lately."

James took Janice by the arm and escorted her to a table in the corner of the cafeteria, well away from the service counter.

As they sat, James said, "Your burger will be right up."

Janice leaned toward her brother and whispered, "Thanks, but, do you think it was a good idea to use your control on him like that?"

James leaned forward too, mouth already full and chomping steadily. "I didn't. They just respect me so much it's ridiculous."

"I didn't get that impression."

"Respect comes in a variety of ways. It's a goddamn rainbow. A fucking spectrum."

"Uh-huh."

"Anyway, you know the rules. No unauthorized scans. Boy, if Randy Stone found out, there'd be hell to pay." Bits of food dropped at regular intervals from James's jabbering mouth. Scraps landed on the front of his black turtleneck and crimson cardigan sweater. He brushed away the loose particles. "We should have gone out to eat. The food sucks here. Oh well, into each life a little rain must fall, I suppose. Just ask Frau Schmidt."

"She seemed her usual self."

"Wait just a second."

The server approached the table. "Here you are, ma'am." Nervously, he set the items down, accidentally dropping an orange onto her lap. "Sorry, ma'am." He departed before she could accept his apology.

"That actually looks good," James said, staring at the cheeseburger.

And it was. Janice took three or four bites before saying another word. Cheeseburgers were her favorite. Eating one never failed to remind her of the first meal she ate on the outside, a trip to McDonald's on her sixteenth birthday.

"You know Thirty-Seven and Thirty-Eight?" James said.

Janice nodded, wiping a napkin across her mouth.

"Well, Thirty-Seven tested out, and Thirty-Eight must have had some sort of union with it, because it expired soon afterward. Just sort of slipped into a coma and expired."

"How'd Thirty-Seven test out?"

"I shot it. Hey, can I have some of your fries? So, Schmidt's bummed out because almost all she has now are more ice cubes. The freezer's loaded with them. Thirty-Nine and Forty are still kicking, though, and seem their usual annoying selves."

Janice pushed her plate closer to James. "Help yourself."

"Thanks. Schmidt just needs to get outside more often. She'd see things for what they are. She'd see what Saint Mary is up against. So many out there want us to fail. It's hard keeping tabs on all of them."

"So, is that what you've been doing lately, keeping tabs on people?"

"Yeah, no thanks to you, little miss schoolgirl. You're missing out on a lot."

"Not anymore. Stone's bringing me inside. My school days are over."

James's face lit up. Janice had to look away. His expression, circumstances aside, exuded such innocence and purity. It reminded her of their childhood, when things were still simple, when James read to his little sister, when they played music together, she on the flute, and he on the guitar. Skills mastered, skills tested. But they were too young to know otherwise. Everything was *so easy* for them.

"I know we'll make a great team. In fact, I could have used you in Vegas." James paused, staring into empty space. His chomping ceased. After a quiet moment, he said, "Yes, a female would have been less suspicious."

Janice did not need to sense her brother's thoughts. His arrogance thumped her. It was wavelike at first, then rapid pulses harmonized into steady pressure on her muscles. He was very strong, and he was not even trying.

His whispered, contemplative tone continued. "Yeah, that way if anyone saw you with the sergeant in the bar, it would have appeared like a couple out for drinks."

Disgusted, Janice asked the question anyway for appearance's sake. "How did you handle it?"

James glanced at Janice's class-five security badge, and then back at her. He winked and said, "I called him in advance and told him to meet me at a particular bar. I told him I had information concerning a friend of his that had died. Then, I got him drunk. Only, this guy never drank alcohol. Until he met me, of course. I manipulated him. I walked him out of the bar, and sent him into the street. Bam!" James smacked his palms together. "That was it, end of story."

"What about this friend of his?"

"I took care of that too." James's eyes appeared unfocused and glazed over. "Gunshot to the head. Just concentrated my thoughts and transmitted the image I wanted. No struggle, no resistance, no evidence. Except for the suicide note I had him write."

"They were security problems, weren't they?" She set her cheeseburger down.

"Yep. Are you going to finish that?"

"Help yourself."

"They were weak links." James shoved the remnants of her cheeseburger into his mouth. His cheeks bulged as he resumed speaking. "Nonessentials who witnessed things beyond the scope of their duties. Mmm, this is a good burger."

"What did they witness?"

"Bad guys from outer space. Real close up and personal with the incident. Mmm, shit, this is good." He swallowed the food along with some Coke.

Janice's facade weakened. Revulsion took control. She mustered what little remaining strength she had and said, "I can't wait to hear more about your work, but I'm worn out from the flight and the exams. I should get some rest." Janice stood, cupping her hand over her mouth.

"But you haven't told me about your life yet."

Janice faked a yawn. "How about tomorrow, big brother."

"Okay, but make sure it's tomorrow. I'm leaving on another assignment tomorrow night. We'll do lunch."

Hate and anger swelled within Janice on her way back to her quarters. The anger hit her hard, and she wanted to fight back any way she could. After reaching her quarters, retching and weakness overcame her. She clenched the toilet seat until her hands ached, a fitting end to the worst day ever. And tomorrow, Saint Mary planned to take her eggs. When she finished vomiting, Janice had no strength to stand. It did not matter. There was nowhere to go. No one to turn to here. She clutched the silver roadrunner pin in her hand. Hollow echoes from her sobs resonated off the solid white tiles that lined the bathroom walls and lulled her into sleep.

TWENTY TWO

He Kept Your Little Secrets

In Las Vegas, at the Sundowner Inn, Harrison made a point of being very visible, spending nearly two hours in the hotel's restaurant for breakfast, and walking to and from his car after his meal. Around ten o'clock, tired of merely waiting, he drove to the police station and requested copies of the reports for both incidents described in the newspaper articles Echo Tango had sent to him.

Now, Harrison drove to the end of a cul-de-sac in North Las Vegas trying to find an address listed on the police report about the death of air force sergeant Eric Gonzales. After finding the address and parking his car, he looked at himself in the rearview mirror. He should have trimmed his beard. Many stiff, gray whiskers, mostly around his chin, disrupted the smooth contours of the brown ones.

With a pen already in his shirt pocket, he retrieved a notepad and the police report from inside the briefcase. He took a deep breath. There were no headaches today, so Harrison felt good putting on his suit coat, determined not to be just an errand boy for Echo Tango.

The quiet, well-manicured neighborhood was void of cars parked on the street, with the exception of his black Dodge Charger. Bell- and holly-shaped frames adorned the street's light poles, each wrapped in garlands and Christmas lights. Most houses displayed decorations to one degree or another. A street sweeper must have driven through earlier, as a damp trail wound around the edge of the roadway. A gentle breeze carried the scent of freshly washed asphalt.

When he reached the door, the neighborhood's serenity made Harrison pause. He wished not to disturb it. Healing was under way behind the door. But, it was healing *without* the truth.

Harrison pushed the doorbell. A minute or so later, an elderly man, dressed in a blue sweatshirt and tan slacks, answered the door.

"Good morning, sir," Harrison said. "I'm Wesley Hiatt, with Insurance Underwriters. Is Megan Gonzales here?"

"Yes, my daughter, Megan, is here."

"I realize this is a difficult time, and I'm sorry to intrude, but I have a few questions regarding her husband's accident. It's just a routine follow-up for the air force and shouldn't take up much time."

"What was the name again?"

"Wes Hiatt."

"And you're with?"

"Insurance Underwriters," Harrison said. "We do some contract work with the Defense Department, in this instance, the air force."

Megan's father directed Harrison to a seat on the sofa in the living room. "Megan is upstairs with the baby. I'll go get her."

Out of habit, Harrison surveyed his surroundings. A Christmas tree, easily nine feet tall and densely decorated, dominated the room. Statuary, the style and characterization of which resembled that of lawn gnomes, shared space with the furniture. Three wise men stood next to Harrison where an end table might sit. Mary and Joseph, Christ in Mary's arms, sat between the tree and a corner fireplace. Greeting and sympathy cards hung throughout the room and on the mantle.

Just like when his parents died.

A woman descended the staircase. "Mr. Hiatt?"

Harrison stood and said, "Yes, ma'am, are you Mrs. Gonzales?"

"Yes."

"I'm so sorry for your loss and to intrude like this."

Megan sat in a rocking chair across from Harrison, while he returned to his seat next to the wise men.

"I promise this will be brief," Harrison said.

"Thank you."

"These are merely routine questions, ma'am."

"I understand, but I thought all of this was already taken care of? I've talked to so many people, so many."

"Understood, ma'am, which is why I intend to not take much more of your time." Harrison removed his pen and balanced the notepad on his leg. "Can you tell me, Mrs. Gonzales, did you and Eric live here?"

"We lived in base housing, but I moved in here shortly before the accident. I needed help with my son, and didn't want to be alone so much. Eric spent a lot of time at work."

"And his most recent assignment was in air traffic control?"

"Yes, it was."

Harrison took a deep breath and exhaled. "I know this is difficult, and I apologize for asking, but the police report stated your husband was intoxicated. Did he have a drinking problem to your knowledge?"

Megan blinked several times and sighed. "Actually, no. He never drank. I guess he was under more strain than I thought. This would have been the first time that I know of."

"What kind of strain?"

"Pressure from work. Odd schedules. I didn't think—" Megan clenched her jaw and held back tears. Her mouth formed into a deep frown, and her eyes closed.

"I'm sorry. We can do this later."

Megan held out her hand and regained her composure. "No. No, it's all right. I just keep thinking that I could have helped him more. He wanted to work through it on his own, though."

The sound of a motorcycle's engine approached the house. It seemed to be right outside in the driveway when it stopped. The sound drew Harrison's attention away from Megan briefly before he continued.

"To work through the strain?" Harrison said.

"He didn't want anyone to think he couldn't handle the stress. His air force career meant a lot to him."

Heavy footsteps approached the front door.

"Did he talk to you much about his work?"

"Not really." Megan paused, bowed her head, and then tightened her grasp on the rocking chair's arms.

The front door opened, then closed. A police officer turned the corner and entered the living room. Harrison rose from his seat and, confused, said, "Good morning."

The officer looked directly at Harrison, but did not acknowledge him. He stepped over to the rocking chair and knelt next to Megan, moving a lamb statue out of the way in the process. After the officer took Megan's hands into his, she nodded and said, "It's okay, thanks, Nicky."

The officer turned to Harrison and said, "You are?"

"Wes Hiatt. I'm with Insurance Underwriters."

"Nick Ridley. I'm Megan's brother." Ridley looked back at his sister. In a low voice, he said, "I thought I'd come by before my shift and see how you were doing."

"I'm okay, just answering some questions for Mr. Hiatt." She patted her brother's hand. "I'm sorry, you can continue, Mr. Hiatt."

"Umm." Harrison fumbled for his next question. "Do you know why your husband would have been in Vegas that evening?"

"That I don't know. It's unusual, but maybe he was there with a friend or two from the base."

Ridley released Megan's hands. "Are you investigating Eric's accident?"

"No, that's not what I'm here for. We're just trying to learn more about the nature of alcohol-related accidents. It's for prevention purposes, educational guidelines, and such."

"Oh," Ridley said, standing. He moved behind his sister, out of her view, and took a seat on the staircase.

"Do you think it warrants further investigation?" Harrison said.

Looking at Harrison through the vertical supports of the banister, Ridley said, "Nope."

Harrison looked back at Megan and said, "I know your husband didn't talk much about his work, and that his work was stressful, but was there anything in particular or specific you know of that may have made him feel under strain? Let me also mention that my inquiry is confidential."

"I've thought about that a lot, actually," Megan said, glancing left and right, trying to find her brother. She turned around. Ridley shrugged and shook his head. The rocking chair leaned forward as Megan faced Harrison again. "I think it was the combination of work and becoming a father. That happened last summer, and that's when he started having difficulties."

"Last summer?" Harrison said.

"Seemed like July, I think."

"Is it possible that he may have discussed these kinds of things with his friends?" Harrison said.

"You have to understand, Eric was a pretty quiet guy," Ridley said, interrupting. "His family was most important to him. He would have discussed these kinds of things, as you say, with us before anybody else. And he didn't. Whatever bothered Eric, he kept to himself. You can be certain of that."

After jotting down a few notes, mainly hunches about Ridley, Harrison said, "Would you say, Mrs. Gonzales, that your husband had a fairly average lifestyle?"

"Well, we attended church. In fact, that's how we met. He volunteered at a Catholic soup kitchen one Thanksgiving a number of years ago. I helped there too. Then, there was the air force. That was really a boost for him. He didn't have it easy growing up, and the military offered him a way to improve himself and his life. When he had time, he was a wonderful father. He was nervous about that, about being a father. I knew he'd be just fine, though. Eric really cared about others. He always put others ahead of himself. There are many good things to remember about him. Actually, you know, he wasn't average. He was better than average. He set an example for others. That's why this is so unfortunate, especially for our son. Owen will grow up not knowing his father. That's an awful price to pay for someone so young, don't you think? He'll want to know about his father, and I can tell him stories or show him pictures, but that is just so inadequate. It's fake in a way. He won't really know him. I can't imagine what that would be like."

Harrison found himself staring at the lamb statue next to the rocking chair. Its eyes seemed oddly human.

Megan broke the silence. "I'm sorry, I shouldn't go on like that. Do you have any more questions?"

"I don't think so. You've been most helpful. Thank you for your time. You have my deepest sympathies." Harrison stood and shook Megan's hand. He nodded at Ridley. "It was nice to meet you both."

Megan smiled and tilted her head toward Ridley, who whispered something in her ear. Megan looked up at Harrison and said, "Can you leave your business card? In case we think of anything else?"

"I'm sorry," Harrison said, patting the various pockets of his coat, shirt, and pants. "I must be out. If you have any questions, though, the personnel officer for Eric's unit will be able to help you further."

"Please, let me walk you to your car," Ridley said. He moved past Harrison and led him outside. When they reached the sidewalk, Harrison pulled the car keys from his pants pocket, but they dropped to the ground. He stooped and groaned.

"Are you all right?" Ridley said.

"Just old age." With the keys recovered and the car door opened, Harrison turned and said, "Thanks again. I know this is a difficult time."

"I'm glad you understand that. You don't need to worry though; Eric followed the rules."

Harrison tossed his paperwork onto the briefcase. Cops could be such clever, suspicious *bastards*. "Yes, he was a good guy."

"But not good enough to be trusted?"

"I'm afraid I don't follow you." In part, Harrison wanted to leave, but it was becoming clear that his hunches about Ridley were probably true. It also seemed that Ridley had a few hunches of his own.

"He kept your little secrets. That is why you're here, isn't it?"

"What?" Harrison's voice remained calm, but he also tried to sound virtuous.

Ridley assumed an interrogation stance, strong leg back, foot angled outward, knees bent, and torso forward. The position offered balance, strength, and flexibility. Cops used it to protect themselves while questioning suspects.

"Isn't it good enough that your rules killed him? Now you have to come here and make sure he didn't tell us anything he shouldn't."

"This is just a routine follow-up."

"Don't give me that, Mr. Hiatt, if that is your real name. I suppose if I ran your license plate, I'd find that out for myself. That's if I don't arrest you right now."

"You're making a big mistake."

"I don't think so."

"Listen to me for a second. If I were here, as you say, to find out whether Eric discussed anything with you, well, I'd have to say he did judging from your tone. In that case, you'd be in big trouble."

"What are you going to do? You can't order me around, or tell me to keep quiet."

"Calm down. Look, your instincts are sharp, but you're letting your emotions get the best of you. Obviously you have something to keep quiet about."

"At least I can talk about it. I don't have to keep it inside. Not that it would make any difference. So you don't have to worry. Whatever secret was so important to keep, it went to the grave with Eric. He should get a goddamn medal."

"You're right."

"Don't patronize me. He sacrificed his sanity keeping quiet for you guys. Well, you got what you wanted. Just leave us alone and stay out of other people's business."

"I can't."

"Bullshit."

"Okay, fine." Harrison walked over to Ridley's motor, hands out from his sides, in full view of the officer. "Let's stop this right now." He checked the motorcycle's rearview mirror. It was clean. "This will tell you who I am." He made perfect imprints of his thumbs and index fingers. "Check the license plate, too. Here's a pen. Write it down."

Ridley just stared at Harrison, and then he took the pen and wrote the information on the back of his left hand.

"My name is William Harrison, and I'm a private investigator. And believe me, I'm not trying to cause you or your sister any problems."

"Then why are you here?"

"I wanted to verify something an anonymous informant gave me regarding your brother-in-law's accident."

"What is it?"

"There was an article in the paper about the accident. Among other things, I wanted to get a better idea about what kind of person Eric was."

"Why did you have to lie about it?"

"For the same reasons Eric couldn't tell you the truth."

"What, you were under orders?"

"No, not exactly. But before I explain it to you, I have to know something."

"What?"

"What did he tell you? Believe me, it is important, and it can make a difference."

Ridley eased his position and gazed at his motorcycle. "Nothing."

Harrison shook his head. "Let's not play any more games."

"That is, I don't recall anything at the moment."

"I see. You know the Sundowner Inn?"

"Yep."

"Well, if you're able to recall anything, you can reach me there. I'll be there through Sunday. Maybe longer."

"Should I ask for Harrison or Hiatt?"

"Hiatt. Look, if you check hard enough, you'll also find out that I'm a former FBI agent."

"Uh-huh, and I'm Sigmund Freud."

"In that case, Herr Doctor, you can appreciate confidentiality. Whatever you do, whatever you believe, do yourself a favor. Don't discuss this with anyone. I'm not kidding. Keep it to yourself."

"I have so far."

"Good."

Harrison did not bother to continue the conversation. He got into his car and drove away, headed for the Sundowner Inn. Given the way this interview went, he decided not to embarrass himself any further by calling on the grieving relatives of suicide victim Airman Bresch.

TWENTY THREE

Maybe We'll Get Lucky

Colonel Samuel Ritter telephoned James Evans at his quarters and said, "General Stone will be too busy for his afternoon appointment with you. He needs to see you in his office now."

James waded through unusually crowded hallways full of people in a rush, pilots in flight suits, and triplets of the ones in black. Fifteen minutes later, James walked past Colonel Ritter—who also wore a flight suit—and stood before General Stone.

Seated at his desk, Stone flipped through the last few pages of a report, and then rubbed his face. He yawned, one that lasted long enough to redden his cheeks and forehead. "One of our Nevada sources updated the Protocol One report regarding Sergeant Gonzales."

James held little interest in the conversation. "What is there to update? Everything went better than could be expected."

"The source has acquired additional information, necessitating another visit."

"I'm going back to Vegas?"

"Gonzales has a brother-in-law who is a Las Vegas cop."

"I know that. The impression I got was that Gonzales didn't tell him or anyone about the Dreamland encounter. That was in my report."

"I understand, James, and probably nothing will come of it. But since then, the cop checked his department's records for radio transmissions surrounding last July's event. Maybe he's suspicious, I don't know. You may have missed something. I just don't want any loose ends. A cop is just the type of person we don't need taking a closer look at things." Stone leaned forward and handed the report over to James. "Review this on your flight to Nellis."

Colonel Ritter knocked on the door and stuck his head just inside the office. "Sorry to interrupt, sir—I just wanted to make sure you got these status reports before I leave for Nevada."

"Bring them here."

"The transfers and reclassifications are moving forward," Colonel Ritter said, handing several files to Stone. "But some of the research is a little time consuming. We're still having a problem bringing the computer access alerts online, but some of our tests are encouraging. All the pertinent updates are there."

"So, if I understand you correctly, Colonel, at some point in the very near future we will know when people go looking for these various government records?"

"Yes, sir, we will absolutely have that capability."

"How are things shaping up for tomorrow night?"

"We are in great shape, sir. General Lanham's team is excellent. And everything's a go with the experimental."

"Dare I ask about the weather forecast?"

"Only if you want more good news, sir."

"Excellent. Get out of here, Colonel. The ELF test is your top priority."

"Yes, sir."

After Colonel Ritter left, James said, "Is that what all the hullabaloo is about?"

Stone laughed. Or was it a cough? James was unsure.

"All I can say is that after tomorrow, Saint Mary won't be the same."

"I wish I could help."

"You are helping, but I can't have you in two places at once. Now, review the file on your flight. Simply put, I want you to find the cop, scan his thoughts, and find out what he knows or suspects, if anything. Don't initiate any resolutions until I say so. We can't afford any breaches or mistakes right now."

James stood and walked toward the door, his hand slipping off the knob when he reached for it. The scan was involuntary, reflexive. Stone felt anxious, uneasy, and James felt it with little effort. He shook it off and concentrated on leaving. Saint Mary maintained orders about unauthorized scans. James grabbed the knob and turned it. "I'll take care of this," he said, closing the door behind him.

"You want a hit?" the blond female blackjack dealer said, looking at Harrison.

Harrison peered at his cards. He held a ten and a four. "I'll stay."

The dealer also held fourteen. She drew her next card. A seven.

The players around the table grumbled, most of them obscured by cigarette smoke, primarily from Harrison.

"I'm out," Harrison said, departing the table. He had lost all of the imitation silver dollars provided to him compliments of the Sundowner Inn.

Stepping outside the Sundowner's small casino, Harrison found a bench in a small garden landscaped with desert rock and foliage. He sat, lit up his last cigarette, and watched the smoke trail off. The setting sun left a smooth blend of orange, blue, and purple across the sky. Muffled sounds of music and laughter came from inside the casino. The mild air, nudged by a dry breeze, filtered through the desert garden's walkways and open spaces.

The serenity simply stirred Harrison's frustration with Echo Tango. It welled momentarily into anger. *He could be watching me right now.* He felt useless waiting for an anonymous informant to make choices for him.

Harrison glanced once more at the sky, and then he stood up, looking around the area to see if anyone observed him. Approaching his room, he noted the cars parked in the lot next to his wing of the hotel, but only concluded that minivans seemed popular.

He unlocked the door and entered. Still, nothing.

Hating to do it, he grabbed the remote and planted himself at the end of his bed. During the third or fourth wave of semiattentive channel surfing, he finally settled on a local news station. Holiday shoppers stuffed the malls, according to the reporter. Only four shopping days left until Christmas. Retailers anxiously awaited sales comparisons with previous years. Harrison hoped Janice would have a nice Christmas.

The loud ring from the room's telephone startled Harrison and interrupted his unexpected but pleasant thoughts about Janice.

"Hello?"

No response.

"Hello?" Harrison said again.

Silence greeted him, and then the phone clicked and returned to a dial tone.

After hanging up, Harrison stepped over to the window and looked between the curtains.

Nothing unusual.

Harrison had stowed his briefcase under a writing desk next to the television stand. His Colt .45 was inside, wrapped in a nylon holster. He moved away from the window and removed the gun. After strapping it to his belt, he checked his watch. Nearly seven o'clock. Maybe he should leave the room? His thigh ached, so he leaned on the desk, relieving some of the pressure.

Before the quiet tapping on the motel room door finished, Harrison drew his gun and held it along the side of his leg.

Concentrate now!

Harrison crept to the door and pointed the .45's barrel at it from his side. He peered through the peephole and saw a man's face illuminated from the orange glow of the streetlights in the parking lot.

"Comrade, I've come for my vodka," the man said, with a cartoonish Russian accent.

The man's appearance differed from what Harrison remembered. He was thinner now, older of course, approaching the half-century mark. Baldness overtook his head almost completely now.

The chain lock kept Harrison from opening the door more than a few inches. But that's all he needed to see it, the permanent appearance of *baffled* consternation. A facade, a mantle, the look of a volcano on the verge of a long-overdue eruption. The expression kept most people away.

"Bill, it's me. Forty pounds lighter, but it's still me."

Holcomb's weight loss really made him look so much smaller than Harrison remembered. He had just one chin, instead of two. Yet, he seemed taller than before, nearly as tall as Harrison, standing up straight, shoulders back, chest out, instead of hunched over. Holcomb also stood with hands rolled into fists. That had not changed. Neither had the fidgeting, almost like he was warming up for a boxing match or a brawl.

"My God, Art, what the hell?"

Harrison's former FBI partner pointed to the small gap in the door's opening and said, "I know I've lost weight, but not enough for me to squeeze through this."

Harrison let him inside without any further delay.

"Did you just call me?" Harrison said, closing the door behind Holcomb.

"No." And then in a Russian accent, Holcomb said, "I thought I'd surprise you. Surprise!"

Harrison double-locked the door and said, "Pardon my gun."

"That's okay, I'm sure it doesn't get out much."

The two men laughed and hugged each other.

"I know this is unexpected, but I needed to meet with you," Holcomb said.

"I didn't recognize you. You look healthy for a change. I can't believe you're here. Have a seat." Harrison sat on the corner of the bed while Holcomb pulled up a chair from the desk. "What brings you to Vegas?"

"You."

"Me?"

"Well, you and this case of yours. I took the first flight out this afternoon. Call it a Christmas vacation. That's what I'm calling it."

"You must have something pretty important to talk about."

"That's what I like about you, Bill, your finely honed investigative instincts. Nothing gets past you."

"Just like old times, huh?"

"Yeah, just leave it to you to get us into a real fix." Holcomb paused and peeled off his tan trench coat. He tossed it onto the bed. Neither one of them was surprised that their gray suits, white shirts, and red ties were nearly identical. "I guess I should have called you first. Our matching wardrobe is kind of embarrassing."

Harrison smiled, and said, "Go on, go on."

"When I looked up those discharge records for the five dead military policemen from Roswell, they came up classified."

"Class fivers?"

"Yep, pretty strange. One of them, the earliest victim—I can't remember his name—the one killed in '47, well, his name was cross-referenced to an FBI case file. Can you guess which one?"

"The aerospace incident case in Roswell?"

"You got it. So I started thinking—"

"Oh no, now we're in trouble"

"I don't see the humor in that."

"I do."

"So, as I was saying, I don't know anything about aliens, but I do know a little about investigations. Your ET friend may be on to something. Anyway, not to be outdone by government spooks, I took a drive to the bureau's personnel section in DC. I have to say, I don't know if it was because of Hoover, or what, but we keep really good records. I looked up the agents assigned to the Albuquerque field office in '47. There were only a handful, and a young agent named Eugene Chamberlain handled the Roswell aerospace incident case. Guess where he's at now?"

"You know where we can find him?"

"Of course, what kind of investigator do you think I am?"

"Do you think he'd talk to us?"

"Given the situation, I doubt it. He's six feet under in the lovely Memorial Gardens of Springfield, Missouri."

"Shit," Harrison said, sighing.

"Bill, I wish I could say that Eugene lived to see the day when he could enjoy his pension, but the service file says that he died from a self-inflicted gunshot wound in January, 1948."

"They got him too."

"I don't know what kind of cover-up we're onto here, but these deaths are just too coincidental. Add that to the recent reclassification and transfers of our old cases. That's enough to make me suspicious."

"That's not all. I spoke today with the next of kin of an air force sergeant who died a few weeks ago. My informant says the sergeant witnessed an encounter between two fighters and an alien ship that interrupted a flight test of a rebuilt Roswell craft last July 7."

Holcomb rolled his eyes.

"Now, wait. ET says they knocked off this sergeant and another airman for security reasons, and made it look like an accident and suicide. Get this—the dead sergeant's brother-in-law is a Las Vegas cop. He didn't seem to think the sergeant's death was anything more than an accident, but was really concerned about why I was nosing around. It seems as though the sergeant was under orders not to talk about his work. Based on the cop's reaction to me, I think the sergeant may have told him something. We didn't get much further than that, but it would sure help to confirm ET's claims."

"Do you think it was just an accident?"

"It looks that way, but I think that's the point. There's a pattern that ET is trying to show me. Hmm, were the discharge records recently classified?"

Holcomb nodded and said, "In August, just like our old cases."

"All of this must be related in some way to the encounter of last July. Cases have been sealed and transferred, discharge records classified, witnesses eliminated in one way or another. It's like they're trying to cover their tracks, old and new."

"I'll say. There's something else I have to mention; it's why I decided to come see you right away."

"What is it?"

"Well, it's enough to make me start drinking heavily again. When I got back to my office yesterday afternoon, after my little visit to the personnel section, there was an e-mail message waiting for me from my supervisor, the little eunuch. The message read something like, 'Your errands are interfering with your caseload and are not consistent with current assignments. No more unauthorized visits to headquarters.' But what's interesting is that I hadn't told anyone where I went. Seems like either incredible insight on my boss's part, which I doubt, or someone told him. Again, it was just too coincidental. Someone must have gotten wind of my research."

"You think that's possible?"

"Hey, buddy, you haven't been out of the game that long. I think you know the answer to that question. But that's why I decided to come. You've got no one watching your back. And I assume you still don't know who this informant is?"

"Nope."

"That has to change."

"And that's what bothers me. Echo Tango seems to have all the answers. I can appreciate the safety factor, but I get the feeling he'd hang both of us out to dry for the sake of his own protection."

"Then it sounds like he definitely works for the government."

They both laughed, remembering the many times their so-called superiors seemed more interested in their own reputations than actual justice.

"Don't get me started," Holcomb said. "It's bad for my blood pressure."

"I won't, I won't. But I have to say, I'm really glad you're here. How long are you on vacation?"

"Eh, as long as I want, really. I'm sure the boss is glad I'm gone, the little invertebrate. And so am I."

"In that case, can I buy you a beverage? I've got nothing else to do until I hear from ET."

"Yeah, and maybe we'll get lucky and meet some lovely aliens. I hear the ones from Venus have big tits."

TWENTY FOUR

Protocol One

"I better see if I can get a room at this place," Holcomb said. "Even I'm not drunk enough to go to bed with you."

"The vacancy sign is still on, thank goodness," Harrison said, chuckling under the influence of too much alcohol. "I'll see you in the morning."

"Yeah, uh, which way?"

Harrison pointed to the Sundowner's office, but Holcomb wavered as he stood looking at the sidewalk beneath his feet. Gripping Holcomb by the shoulders, Harrison turned him in the direction of the office and said, "Just walk straight across the parking lot for about fifty feet—you'll run into it."

"Okay, buddy, I'm on my way," Holcomb said, belching and staggering ahead.

Harrison watched as his old partner arrived at the hotel's office without mishap. Once Holcomb stood safely inside the office, Harrison walked to his room. He turned on the light and saw nothing, not even envelopes with secret messages, waiting for him.

After moving over to the bed, he sat on it with a groan. He removed his suit coat, shoes, and tie, and unbuttoned his already untucked shirt. The Colt .45 went into the nightstand's top drawer. Leaning back onto the bed, Harrison sighed and let his eyelids fall shut, but only for a moment. He sat up and staggered over to the light switch, and then turned it off. The bed thumped and creaked when he collapsed onto it. He watched the room spin clockwise.

"I'm here," Harrison said. "Time for ET to phone home." Harrison laughed and rolled over. Not long after, the sound of low snoring filled the room.

At just past two o'clock on Saturday, December 21, General Edward Taylor watched the light go out in Harrison's room from the backseat of a rented minivan. He looked at the rucksack stowed on the floor next to his feet, and he readied himself for the delivery.

Nothing would be the same after this weekend.

His information was scant, pieced together from various sources: flight logs, a brief encounter with General Lanham, an oddly worded fax from ARDCom, a late-night delivery of fresh oranges to the VIP quarters at Nellis Air Force Base.

He could do this himself. Such an act could even be justified to General Stone. All of this, in fact, he could do alone, unnoticed. But he went over it a hundred times, and always arrived at the same conclusion: Without Harrison, they stood no chance of succeeding. Harrison must do the digging and see it all for himself. There was just no other way to convince him to help, or to help him recollect what so many needed him to remember.

After this dig, nothing would be the same.

General Taylor's feelings took him in another direction, and he thought about Janice. He'd known before asking for her help last summer that she would say yes. He possessed faith that she could protect herself, but he worried about her more now than ever. She was so completely involved in his final mission, and so vulnerable now while she underwent testing and observation at ARDCom.

Another barrel roll inside his heart and mind slid Taylor into memories about his son. *As long as you're in the air force, Drew, just fly. Don't do anything else. Just fly.* Tears came next, and then so did the small flask of Scotch from his coat. *"Edward, I am sorry, Andrew was confirmed killed in action."*

At 2:30 a.m., Taylor put the flask away and made his move. His face and throat were sore, and his nose ran. He had not cried like that in years.

Harrison awoke, his heart pounding. At first, he thought someone screamed. He held his breath and heard the shrill shriek again. Sitting up and focusing, he realized the *damn* telephone was ringing. He grabbed the receiver, accidentally yanking the rest of the phone onto the floor.

"Hello?"

"A package is on your doorstep."

"Wait, I have questions."

Just a click, and then the dial tone returned. Harrison dropped the phone and jumped out of bed.

"Christ!"

Unprepared for the sudden motion, Harrison halted and put a shaky hand on the nightstand to regain equilibrium. After bracing himself, Harrison reached down with his other hand and removed the Colt .45 from the nightstand's top drawer. Under better control and more stable now, Harrison stepped to the door. The peephole and alcohol in his system distorted everything, and it took him a moment to decode the outside imagery.

The sound of clicks, a chain's rattle, and creaking hinges greeted Harrison as he unlocked and opened the door. The night's cold temperature held a calm over the scene. Harrison sucked the refreshing air into his chest and lungs. The act awakened him, but he also started shivering.

He heard music not too far away, toward the flickering lights outside the entrance to the Sundowner's casino. Silhouettes approached the lights, momentarily losing their murkiness before going inside.

The music's volume fleetingly increased each time the doors to the casino opened.

Harrison felt some pressure on his feet. Gazing downward, he saw a tan canvas rucksack tilted on its side, with brown leather straps and brass buckles, waiting for him just outside the doorway. The rucksack's main pouch looked full. He picked up the heavy sack and set it on the bed. After sealing up the door, Harrison shielded his eyes and turned on the lights. After his pupils adjusted to the brightness, he turned his attention to the sack.

The canvas smelled wet, dirty, just like the army surplus tent he and his high school friends had used, *decades ago*, on summer camping trips to the mountains. According to Harrison's father, nothing smelled as bad, yet at the same time, as good, as wet, dirty canvas. Harrison nodded in agreement and unbuckled the top flap.

Inside, a manila folder sat on top of several other objects. The folder contained $2,000 in cash, a typed letter from Echo Tango, an air force aircraft accident report, a copy of a next-of-kin notification letter, a USGS map, and an ARDCom memorandum, classified as class five, regarding approval for "Protocol One" procedures.

Protocol One?

Harrison set the documents and cash aside and pulled out the sack's remaining objects: wire cutters, a collapsible shovel, a compass, a whiskbroom, a gardening trowel, scissors, a flashlight, night-vision goggles, and a GPS receiver.

Huh? What are we digging up?

The items, all arrayed neatly on the bed, made more sense once he read Echo Tango's letter. He looked at the other documents and pieces of equipment. "Wichita" appeared on the next-of-kin notification. "F-4 Phantom" appeared on the accident report. They were leads for Harrison to follow later.

The next step in the investigation would also wait, but not for very long. Just long enough that he and Holcomb could acquire a few other items necessary to complete the mission properly.

TWENTY FIVE

In Search of Major Jeffrey Blair

Colonel Samuel Ritter sipped hot coffee at his desk inside Dreamland's security control center. He and others, including James Evans, had arrived late last night, and the caffeine helped him begin what would likely be one of the longest days of his career.

Computer monitors and video screens scattered random bursts of color onto the walls of the dim control center and onto the faces of the figures working within. It reminded Ritter of the Vegas casinos where the lack of windows and absence of natural light defied anyone to guess what time it might be. Although cool air circulated throughout the room, Ritter felt warm. He had much on his mind and worried about anything going wrong. Taking deep, relaxing breaths, he focused on performing his tasks, monitoring radio traffic, taking phone calls, and sending and receiving e-mails regarding tonight's mission: a full-scale field test of Saint Mary's newest weapons system, a mammoth extremely low-frequency sound-wave projector, known simply as ELF.

Ritter knew much rode on tonight's field test. Saint Mary's working group had long believed ELF could become an effective weapon. Testing had shown that not only were aliens were vulnerable to high-powered focused ELF pulses, but their craft were also impaired by them. The craft's construction went beyond exotic metal and electronics; they also contained intelligent, bioelectronic and biomechanical components. Although shielded against the most intense forms of outer-space radiation, both a craft and its occupants succumbed to incapacitation when hit with ELF pulses.

"Sir?" a lieutenant in desert-camouflaged fatigues said, approaching Ritter.

Ritter looked at the lieutenant from behind a coffee mug. "Is this about the need for patrols in the vicinity of the Ranch Annex quad?"

"Yes, sir. Seems the perimeter coordinator is still concerned they won't have adequate technical coverage there due the maintenance shutdown on ground sensors."

Ritter took another sip of coffee and then said, "If he is requesting I change my mind, then tell him his request is denied. I need the majority of our air and ground patrols deployed in the test area." Ritter knew he did not need to explain further, but looked the lieutenant square in the eyes and said, "Trust me. We need them in the test area." He leaned forward and whispered, "They may be needed for crash-retrieval duties. Every single one of them. Do you understand?"

The lieutenant nodded.

Ritter leaned back. "The Ranch Annex is remote and could not be lower on our list of concerns. Please tell the perimeter coordinator to make do with the single patrol unit that I already approved."

"Yes, sir," the lieutenant said, and then he receded into the shadows of the control center.

Ritter took a deep breath, looked around the room, and wiped some sweat off his brow with the back of his hand. Sipping more coffee, he watched the dark figures move around the timeless room. Some sat silently, soft light from their computer screens dancing on their faces.

Shadows of the shadow government.

Ritter had never felt more alone within the Saint Mary Project than he did at that very moment. He shook his head, took another deep breath, and looked at the computer monitor, hoping everything would go as planned.

Harrison stared at Holcomb across their table in the Sundowner's coffee shop. Both tried eating breakfast, without much success. Queasiness dulled their appetites. Taking a break, his former partner reviewed Echo Tango's latest documents. Harrison watched a small bit of scrambled egg dangle from Holcomb's chin. He was sure Holcomb would have normally detected this irregularity, so he interpreted his continued attention on the documents as a sign of genuine interest.

After Holcomb finished reading and looked across the table, Harrison casually rubbed a finger across his own chin. Holcomb lowered and crossed his eyes. He glanced once more at Harrison, and then quickly flicked the egg away. The object spun and landed firmly on the table next to them, which a young mother and her toddler son occupied. Hidden behind a menu, the mother's eyes failed to notice the intrusion into her morning. But her observant child witnessed the projectile land inches from his elbows. He poked his finger into the egg.

"Eat it. It's good," Holcomb said, mouthing the words more than verbalizing them with his raspy, dehydrated voice. The boy put the egg in his mouth. Holcomb smiled and nodded at him. "Good boy." He turned back to Harrison. "Did you want some too?"

"Never a dull moment with you."

"No, that's your area of expertise."

"Speaking of which, we'll need to pick up a few things, like some water bottles, dark clothes, hiking boots, a digital camera, and tape measure."

"You want to handle it like a crime scene?"

"As much as possible. The only problem is, we'll be trespassing."

They both peered toward the next table. The mother still read the menu.

"We'll just have to make sure we don't get caught," Holcomb said.

"ET says that particular area is only subject to patrols, no sensors right now due to maintenance. With one of us on lookout, we should be able to see them coming."

"Assuming we actually find this guy's remains, how will we verify it? ET says the air force destroyed his dental and DNA records."

"Ah, the air force's records." Harrison paused and sipped his coffee. "There may be another source for these records, as well as a source for locating the F-4 that he allegedly piloted. But that comes later. What I need to know is who can do the forensic comparison? We need someone we can trust, someone discreet, someone good. You wouldn't happen to know anyone who might meet those qualifications?"

Holcomb hacked out a laugh and then said, "Yeah, Maggie will help us."

"You still on good enough terms with her?"

"Uh-huh, but mostly because I've been staying away. She's busy these days too, with extracurricular stuff. She paints."

"Paints? What, houses?"

"No. Geez, houses..." Holcomb shook his head. "What do you call it? Uh, still life, portraits. Hell, she's way out of my league."

"But she's still at Quantico?"

"Yep."

"Good, because I don't care how good ET's leads are; I need to know that the evidence can withstand scrutiny. I mean, he says this body is that of officially missing air force major Jeffrey Blair, and gives background on it, but for all I know, it could just as easily be Jimmy Hoffa."

Holcomb nodded and picked up the Protocol One memorandum. He looked it over and then glanced at Echo Tango's letter. "This is some crazy, scary shit, Bill. A fine mess you've landed us in. I mean, apparently they kill people who risk exposing them and their secrets."

Harrison took a bite of his cold omelet. He set the fork down, pursed his lips, and then said, "He says he's trying to establish credibility with me." Pausing, Harrison pointed at the documents. "I have to admit, if this body is there, and it is poor Major Blair's, then that would mean he's credible beyond any doubt for me."

"Have you asked why he's having you do this? You've said it yourself—Echo Tango already seems to have all the answers. He's obviously high on the food chain, high enough to get his hands on these different reports and documents, not to mention your alias identification. Why should he bother you with any of this? No offense, but you're not exactly in the loop these days."

None of these questions were new to Harrison. A logical, reasoned, or informed answer remained elusive. All he had was a hunch, a vague sense about his past.

"With any luck, we'll find that out," Harrison said.

Sears had everything they needed, and was the scene of a lengthy discussion about which would be best to purchase: dark or tan clothing.

Holcomb eventually won out, making authoritative references to his knowledge of such matters, based on his experience as a former soldier in the US Army.

"Tan is the color of the desert," Holcomb had insisted.

"Art, they don't have any tan sweat suits."

"Then gray will work."

"Great, we'll look like a couple of mutant squirrels."

"Better that than looking like a couple of Mummenschanz flunkies. Besides, infra-red will pick us up either way."

"Fabulous."

So, in their gray sweats and brown hiking boots, rucksack and gear in the trunk, they left old US Highway 93 at 10:00 p.m., eighty-five miles north of Las Vegas. They headed for the remains of Major Jeffrey Blair, officially missing former ARDCom test pilot.

Officially, the body rested somewhere on the bottom of the Pacific Ocean, twenty miles off the Oregon coast. The air force accident report stated that, on February 5, 1998, during a training flight, the major's aging F-4 Phantom, equipped with an experimental flight control system, inexplicably lost altitude and crashed. The air force listed Blair's failure to eject and his incoherent radio transmissions as indications that his oxygen supply malfunctioned. Suffering hypoxia, Blair became semiconscious and, presumably, lost control of his aircraft.

The next-of-kin notification regurgitated a cursory version of the accident report, but Echo Tango's letter and the memorandum with the unheard-of class-five classification about Protocol One procedures told a different story.

According to Echo Tango's information, ARDCom had assigned Major Jeffrey Blair, a test pilot at Dreamland, to fly the Roswell-originated experimental craft. ARDCom had other pilots, but none had ever developed into a weak link to the extent that Major Blair had. After dozens of flights, and one particularly unusual encounter with an unknown, the stress of secrecy became too burdensome, and Blair developed signs that he was psychologically unstable.

The unsigned Protocol One memorandum contained oblique language: "Major Blair's condition could pose the greatest risk to himself. Deterioration is likely. Authority stipulates Protocol One treatment at the earliest convenience."

According to Echo Tango, Protocol One meant termination of an individual in a manner that appeared consistent with suicide or accident. For Blair, an attempt to escape from his assassins resulted in a premature and messy death. Multiple gunshot wounds to the chest and back made a "suicide" cover impossible. Thus, the air force aircraft accident report became the new cover story. But what to do with the body? A newly acquired parcel of land—one of Dreamland's buffer zones known as the Ranch Annex—was hastily utilized, but precise coordinates were recorded so that future recovery and relocation, if necessary, could be undertaken. Surrounded by remote desert terrain and security systems, an obscure patch of land within the infamous Area 51 seemed the ideal burial ground. Besides, who would ever find out?

"How much farther?" Harrison said, driving his black Dodge Charger with its headlights off. Neither he nor Holcomb chose to wear the pair of night-vision goggles for very long while in the moving car. It made both of them dizzy. So progress was slow; even though the dirt road had straightened from its earlier course, now it was rockier. Gravel and stones scoured the Dodge's wheel wells. "Is that the ranch house?"

"Where?" Holcomb said from the front passenger seat.

"Over there, to the right."

Through the dusty windshield and passenger-side window, Holcomb could only see a dark mound. He held the flashlight close to the map, and then checked the GPS receiver.

"Art? Hello, pilot to navigator."

"Just a second, I don't think this is working right." Holcomb looked up and to the left. "Yep, there's the fence. I guess that was the ranch house. Not too much farther now."

The road angled left, then ran parallel and adjacent to Area 51's fence line. Harrison saw it clearly. High chain link, topped with barbed wire. White signs hung on it at regular intervals. He had a pretty good idea what the sign's warning message contained.

"Is that a hill up ahead?" Harrison said, squinting. "Or is it a cloud?"

"You know what?" Holcomb said, chuckling. "Yes, yes, I do believe it's the mother ship come to take us away."

"No, I think it's that hill. Check your equipment; ET said there is a lone hill near our stop."

Holcomb leaned forward and studied the map. He pressed the flashlight close, its beam a narrow sliver on the page.

"It's definitely a hill," Harrison said.

"Then it's our hill," Holcomb said, peering through the windshield. "Pull over and we'll cover the car with some brush."

Harrison parked, and while he removed the rucksack from the trunk, Holcomb set about collecting the camouflage. Harrison helped, but neither had thought to bring gloves of any kind. Their efforts produced meager results. They threw some dirt on the hood, trunk, and top as an additional measure. They concluded that, for their own benefit, leaving the Dodge partly exposed was acceptable. Holcomb also tagged its location in the GPS receiver as the "car" waypoint.

They approached the fence line and paused in front of a white sign posted on it at eye level. The "no trespassing" sign indicated violators were subject to the use of lethal force, search, seizure, arrest, detention, and/or punishment to the fullest extent of the law.

"Well, TJ?" Holcomb said.

Harrison waited. His new boots felt a little tight, but his leg and hip felt good, and so did the goose bumps. He looked to his right, squarely at the fidgeting Holcomb, and then said, "When in the course of human events..."

"I suppose that means you want the wire cutters?"

Nodding, Harrison reached into a side pocket of the rucksack and removed the cutters.

Harrison started snipping near the ground. With each clip, the metal made unruly retorts, too loud for the quiet surroundings. Harrison stayed focused, but quickened his work.

He bent the loosened part of the fence inward. "That should do it." He returned the wire cutters to the rucksack. "I sure hope ET was right about sensors, or else we'll be in jail soon."

"Or dead."

Holcomb and Harrison both sighed.

"Let's go," Harrison said.

They squeezed through. While Harrison pressed the fence back into place, Holcomb removed the rucksack and opened the top flap.

"Here," Holcomb said, handing the night-vision goggles to Harrison.

The goggles gave Harrison a clear view of the endless stretch of dirt and sand, patches of brush, rocky mounds, dry creek beds, and dark mountains in advance of them. He spotted no patrols. As Harrison looked skyward, the moon hung low over the mountains. Beyond it, an infinite horizon of stars twinkled overhead. He gazed past the constellations and saw the familiar shape. In the desert, he found it easy to see the Milky Way's thick waistline, so thick it was like a fogbank. "Fogbank" was the term the documentary narrator had used described it, a description he had heard dozens of times as a youth, father at his side, viewing the planetarium shows at Griffith Observatory in Los Angeles.

"That way," Holcomb said, whispering. "We go due west for about two miles. How does it look?"

Harrison concentrated on scanning the surrounding terrain. "Coast is clear."

They began their march, stopping occasionally for Holcomb to take a reading on the GPS receiver and to check its compass. Mostly, they proceeded in silence, both understanding that any sound, even that of their voices, could reveal their presence to a passing patrol.

Before long, Harrison started breathing heavily. Years of smoking had taken their toll and he took increasingly long pauses to search the area.

About a mile into their journey, Holcomb whispered into Harrison's ear, "Let's take five, buddy."

Harrison kept scanning.

Holcomb eased himself onto the ground, setting the rucksack and other gear to the side. He cupped his hands in front of his mouth and breathed into them.

Kneeling, Harrison said, "Maybe we should keep moving? We'll probably keep warmer that way."

Holcomb shook his head. "I was thinking, we need a little more of a plan. This could turn to shit at any time."

"I know. Look, we need to get dental records on Blair and documentation on the F-4 listed in the accident report. ET sent a postcard to me from Wichita with a picture of F-4s in the boneyard at Davis-Monthan Air Force Base in Tucson. Blair's next-of-kin letter shows a Wichita address. My plan was to check out both leads. I think the postcard was meant to point me that way."

"What about your other evidence?"

"It's in a safe-deposit box in Tucson under Wes Hiatt."

"What were you supposed to do with all of it?"

Harrison shrugged.

Holcomb put the equipment back into the rucksack, and the two headed off in the direction to Blair's grave.

After about half a mile, Harrison looked above the horizon and thought he saw a light. "Wait a second." They both stopped, and he continued to search the sky. *Nothing unusual.* "Did you see a light overhead a moment ago?"

"No."

"Must be my imagination. Let's keep going."

They continued to move through the quiet darkness, anxious to reach their destination, and anxious to avoid detection. After another half hour, they stopped to determine their location.

"We're close," Holcomb said. "How accurate is this thing?"

"According to ET, within a yard."

Holcomb pointed to their right. "That way, about another hundred yards or so."

After walking the distance, they stopped and rested. A slight breeze nudged the cool and silent desert landscape, refreshing them both. They drank from their water bottles, quenching their thirst and moistening their parched mouths.

Harrison rubbed his thigh and leg and anticipated three or four days of pain to follow. After a few minutes of rest, he said, "Can you check that gizmo and tell us if we're in the right spot?"

Holcomb stood and held the GPS receiver in front of him. He stepped to his right, and then forward, and then to his right some more. "Toss me the shovel."

From inside the rucksack, Harrison pulled out the shovel, unfolded it, and locked the tool into place. He tossed it to Holcomb, who had to walk a few steps to pick it up.

"Nice aim," Holcomb said, picking up the shovel. He returned to his starting point and said, "We dig here, and can expand the radius if needed."

"Let me get some photographs first." Harrison retrieved the camera out of the rucksack. He stood up and handed the night-vision goggles to Holcomb. "You keep watch, and I'll start on this."

"How's your leg?"

"It's felt better," Harrison said, taking his first picture of the scene.

Holcomb walked away and found a nearby hill. He perched there for sentry duty. He turned back to Harrison and was about to say something, but was suddenly blinded from the flash of the camera. "Jesus Christ." Holcomb put his hands over the front of the goggles and blinked his eyes several times. "I was just going to ask you to tell me when you were about to take a shot."

"Sorry, I'll let you know from now on."

"Thanks, but you better give me a minute until I can see again."

After a few more pictures, Harrison started digging for Blair's remains. At various points during the excavation, Harrison took additional photographs to ensure a proper record of the search. Holcomb continued to scan the horizon and their surroundings for any patrols. Occasionally, he looked skyward and amused himself with the thought of spotting a UFO.

Sixty minutes and two-and-a-half feet later, a weakened Harrison said, "I think I found something."

"What?"

"I don't know for sure. Let me take a few pictures first."

"Great," Holcomb said, covering his eyes.

Harrison photographed the object he had struck with the shovel, and then he dug with his hands around the object, finding more of it. He grabbed the flashlight and shined it down low on the area. "I think it's him." Harrison continued to photograph the scene and uncovered more of the earth surrounding the object. Twenty minutes later, he said, "It's a skeleton all right."

"Did you bring anything to carry it in?"

"I took a couple of trash bags from a maid's cart this morning."

"Well played."

Harrison stood and pulled the bags from the bottom of the rucksack. He noticed Holcomb looking at him. "Don't watch me. Watch the desert."

"Sorry, it's been a while since I've recovered a body in the desert on a secret military installation. Just grab the skull, if you've found it, and let's get out of here."

"Working on it, working on it."

Turning his attention back to the desert, Holcomb thought he saw a glint of light on the horizon ahead of him. "Hey, uh, did you just take another picture?"

"No, just digging like crazy over here, trying to free the man's skull."

"Uh, that's good, Bill, keep that up," Holcomb said, concerned they would not be alone for much longer.

"I've got most of it uncovered. Hide your eyes." Harrison pointed the camera at the ground, but Holcomb interrupted him.

"I wouldn't do that if I were you."

"We need the evidence."

"I realize that, but I don't think that patrol headed this way would find it difficult to spot us right now if that flash went off."

"Patrol?"

"I spotted some lights, pretty sure it is a vehicle."

"All right, I'll hurry. How far away do you figure?

"Not sure, maybe a couple of miles. There is some pretty rough terrain between us and them, though."

A few minutes passed, and Harrison could not free the skull. "Give me a hand with this and let's bug out."

Holcomb scrambled over to the exposed skull and joined Harrison in scratching away the dried earth surrounding it. Gently, once enough of the skull had revealed itself to them, Harrison peeled and lifted it away from the ground. Holcomb grabbed one of the garbage bags, and Harrison placed it inside. They double-wrapped their evidence with the other bag.

Harrison's digging had managed to reveal some of Blair's skeleton. He hated to do it, but he took one last photograph of the scene. "All right, let's get the hell out of here."

Hearts pounding, they collected their equipment and piled it into the rucksack. While Harrison put the rucksack on his back and grabbed the garbage bag, Holcomb laid some scrub brush over the grave and pushed some dirt into it. He checked their surroundings but found no sign of the patrol he had seen a short time ago.

"Which way out of here?" Harrison said.

Holcomb checked the GPS receiver's compass and got a general heading back to the "car" waypoint. "We go that way," Holcomb said.

Harrison handed his former partner the evidence, and they both headed toward the car, Holcomb leading the way.

They hurried together in silence, listening and watching for any sign of the patrol. Thirty minutes into their rushed escape, Holcomb stopped and turned to face the direction of Blair's grave. "Keep walking—I'll watch for a minute and catch up to you."

Harrison wheezed and coughed his way past Holcomb. Mumbling, he said, "I really have to quit smoking."

Holcomb watched the terrain but saw nothing. From where he sat, squatting behind a mound of rocks and dirt, the scene appeared clear. After a few minutes, he stood up and turned to run toward Harrison.

A bright flash across the sky knocked him off balance, and he fell down, clutching his face and the goggles. He removed the goggles and winced in pain. As he lay on the ground trying to recover from the flash, Holcomb heard a strange noise, something like low humming. Confused, he blinked, sat up, and looked around. He saw a faint light in the distance, in the direction of Major Blair's grave. It appeared to be on the ground.

The low humming continued, but Holcomb could not discern its origin. He spun around, searching for anything that would explain its source, but there was nothing. Wherever it came from, it was far away, and he felt it more than he heard it. It vibrated through him, wavelike.

Lights on the ground ahead of him flickered, so he put the night-vision goggles back on and looked in their direction. The lights moved methodically, side to side.

They're searching.

Holcomb jerked around and ran toward the barely visible lone hill in the distance. He ran as hard as he could across the desert floor and caught up with Harrison. "Old friend, we really have to get out of here."

Nearly out of breath, Harrison said, "What the hell is that noise?"

"I don't know."

"And that light. You see it? It moved so fast."

"Frankly, I'm more concerned about that patrol on its way."

Harrison continued to breathe heavily. “How far away?”

“I think near our grave robbing.” Holcomb felt himself tiring. His speech slowed, and he paused after each word or two. “Won’t take them long to pick up our trail.”

Harrison took the car keys out of his pants pocket and handed them to Holcomb.

At first, Holcomb refused to accept them.

“Take them,” Harrison insisted. “When we get close enough, I want you to run ahead and get the fence open and the car ready to go. You drive.”

“Understood,” Holcomb said, taking the keys. He looked at the lone hill ahead of them again. “Can you see our benchmark hill in the distance?”

Harrison squinted. He saw their destination and wished they were closer to it. “I got it, yeah.”

“Whatever happens, just keep heading for that hill.”

Harrison panted and coughed. “Roger that.”

A fast-moving, bright streak of light passed overhead.

“Shit!” Holcomb said, ripping off the goggles. “This has just got to stop.” He held his eyes and rocked back and forth. When Harrison reached down and put his hand on Holcomb’s shoulder, his former partner said, “Keep moving—I’ll catch up.”

Harrison said nothing and withdrew his hand. He continued moving toward the hill, baffled by the intense—yet vaguely familiar—light that passed overhead and the nonstop low humming vibrating through his body.

Holcomb rose to his knees and put the goggles back on. The humming abruptly subsided, growing fainter and more distant with every passing second. After standing, he searched for the patrol’s lights again. It did not take him long to spot it bouncing and hobbling their way. Opting not to ponder the distance to the patrol, he turned around and started to run.

After catching up to an exhausted Harrison again, Holcomb looked at the hill in the distance, and then back to his former partner. “Almost there—how you holding up?”

Harrison laughed and sucked air in and out as fast as he could. “Been better.”

“About a half mile or so to go.”

“You’ve got the skull and the keys, make a break for it now.”

“Not yet.”

“Just shut up and go.”

Holcomb looked back at the lights of the patrol vehicle he knew was closing the distance.

“Do it,” Harrison said.

Without saying anything, Holcomb stopped, put the skull down, and then grabbed Harrison by the shoulders. He snatched the rucksack from Harrison’s back and threw it onto his own, after which he retrieved the skull and started running.

Gaining some relief without the pack, Harrison felt a renewed sense of energy. He started a slow jog toward the lone hill, but soon lost sight of his partner.

Holcomb finally reached the fence line near the car. His chest heaved under deep breaths as he struggled to find the hole in the fence where Harrison had cut into it earlier. Less than a minute later, Holcomb found the hole. He dropped the rucksack from his shoulders and grabbed the wire cutters from inside it. Cutting the wire even more, he managed to expand the radius of the hole to the point where a car could drive through it. Smiling now, Holcomb retrieved the pack and skull and ran toward Harrison’s Dodge Charger. He put the gear and evidence in the trunk, slammed it shut, and turned around.

Then, he froze.

A man he did not recognize stood a few feet away and aimed a handgun at his chest. The man spoke, and his words nearly sent Holcomb into shock.

“Where’s Harrison?”

Harrison stumbled and fell. Not far away, he could see the lone hill glowing under the faint moonlight. He struggled to his feet, only to feel defeated once he stood. The sound of vehicles approached him, closing the gap. Ignoring the prospect of impending capture, he started running toward the hill again.

The sound of the engine from one of the vehicles seemed different from what he expected. This was no Humvee, which was the type of vehicle Harrison expected to drive right up behind and over him in due course. This other vehicle's engine noise was higher pitched, and it emanated from ahead of him, just behind the next dune.

Harrison stopped. Headlights approached him from two different directions now. Instinctively, he put his hand on the Colt .45 resting in the holster on his hip. The vehicle's sound that came from directly ahead finally registered with him. *A motorcycle?* He took his hand off the gun.

The Suzuki Intruder appeared out of the darkness. Its rider drove straight at him, sliding to a stop in the sand a few feet away. The rider ripped off his helmet and tossed it to Harrison. "Get on," he said.

Not choosing to argue, Harrison pulled the helmet on and then straddled the seat behind the driver—Nick Ridley.

"Hang on!" Ridley gunned the engine and sped toward the fence line.

Ridley and Harrison did not hear the staccato buzzing sound of bullets flying near their heads and bodies, but both soon realized the patrol vehicle behind them was firing on them. Puffs of sand and dirt erupted around and ahead of them, a sure sign of bullets coming at them. Harrison tightened his grip, and Ridley twisted the accelerator hard.

Harrison peered around Ridley's shoulders and discerned the fast-approaching fence line. The chain-link barrier grew ever closer, and Harrison expected, and hoped, Ridley would slow down. "Uh, uh..."

"Hang on and duck!" Ridley said.

Harrison barely had enough time to comply with Ridley's instructions. He closed his eyes and braced for a rough, high-speed impact with the fence.

The motorcycle shot through the larger opening Holcomb had cut earlier.

Instantly relieved and confused, Harrison opened his eyes. He and Ridley were through the fence and in a controlled slide onto the gravel and dirt road near the Dodge Charger.

As Ridley and Harrison shot past, Holcomb pressed down hard on the Dodge's accelerator. Metal tapping sounds from bullets striking the car made Holcomb hunch down. He swerved back and forth across the road, hoping for the best.

Harrison squeezed Ridley tighter. He never thought he would ever need a motorcycle cop for anything, but Ridley was a welcome surprise.

Behind them, Holcomb raced to keep up.

The speakers on a console inside Dreamland's security control center crackled with an update from a patrol unit. "Trespassers have now exited the property at high speed. What are your orders?"

Colonel Samuel Ritter heard the radio transmission and responded by asking the patrol to call him in the security control center. A few seconds later, Ritter picked up the receiver from the ringing telephone next to him. "Yes, I understand, confirm you are near the Ranch Annex." Ritter paused, and then nodded. "A dark sedan and a motorcycle, understood. Have all units return to base." He glanced around at the preoccupied staff. "Yes, return to base. We will pursue the matter through other means."

Ritter hung up the phone and reached for his coffee mug, but stopped. Instead, he grabbed the hat sitting on the corner of his desk. He put it on, and it felt good. The Colorado Rockies ball cap was one of his favorites. Looking around the control center, he pulled the brim down until it was tight and low across his forehead. Beneath it, a shadow covered his face. A brief smile emerged, and then he yawned, hoping he would get a good night's sleep very soon.

TWENTY SIX

The Truth Will Come Out

The sunrise over Las Vegas illuminated the city and loosened the night's frigid grip on Harrison and Ridley. As they approached the city limits, Ridley pulled over and stopped the Suzuki in a deserted parking lot at an office complex. After stopping, Harrison still clung to Ridley, too cold and too stiff to move.

Ridley leaned forward and put both of his feet on the ground. "You can let go of me now."

Harrison slowly and methodically relaxed his grasp and unseated himself from the motorcycle. His aching hip and chilled body made every step difficult. After managing to stand mostly upright, he removed the helmet and handed it back to Ridley, who took it from him with a jerk. Harrison and Ridley narrowed their eyes at each other until Holcomb interrupted their reproachful stares when he pulled the Dodge Charger in behind them and parked. After getting their attention, Holcomb waved and grinned at them from behind the steering wheel. He gave them two thumbs up.

Harrison flashed Holcomb a thumbs up and turned back to Ridley. "Thanks for saving my ass back there."

Ridley turned off the motorcycle's ignition, flipped the kickstand into place, got off the bike, and then proceeded to inspect it for damage.

Harrison shook his head and waddled with bowed legs toward Holcomb.

Holcomb finished lighting up one of Harrison's cigarettes and stepped out of the car. "Hey, guys—"

"Art, you got my car shot up," Harrison said, noticing two bullet holes in the right rear fender. He waddled farther around the car's rear end, where he saw more holes in the trunk. Holcomb and Ridley joined Harrison behind the car, where they saw the damage for themselves.

After a few seconds of silence, Holcomb said, "Well, this is awkward." He looked left, then right, and said, "I gotta pee."

Harrison said, "I take it you two have met?"

"Oh, yeah, I've met junior here," Holcomb said. "Seems nice enough, even though we got off to a rocky start." Holcomb paused and leaned toward Harrison like a tattler, and said, "He pointed his gun at me, Bill."

"I took your advice and checked you out. I followed you guys. From the Sundowner, to Sears, then out there," Ridley said, pointing into the distance. "I never imagined you'd be stupid enough to go on some hike into the desert, especially when that desert is government property."

In an even, matter-of-fact tone, Harrison said, "We had a lead to follow."

"Must be an incredibly important lead," Ridley said. "Does it have anything to do with what's in the trunk?"

Harrison glanced at Holcomb. "You put it in there?"

Holcomb nodded.

"Yes, it does," Harrison said, turning back to Ridley. "But my gut feeling at this point is that the less you know, the better."

"Better for whom?" Ridley said.

"For you," Harrison said. "For your own safety."

"I just saved your ass, Mr. Harrison. I think you owe me a little more than that."

"If we told you, you might run the risk of ending up as a bag of bones in the trunk of a car somewhere," Holcomb said, interrupting.

Harrison furrowed his brow at Holcomb, and then turned to Ridley. "Look, you saved my life out there. That's why it would be wrong for me to jeopardize your life by telling you more."

Ridley thought of his dead brother-in-law, Eric. Despite wanting to know more, he decided to trust Harrison. "We'll go with your instincts for now. But I'm a cop, so I just don't sit on the sidelines."

"Understood," Harrison said. He wanted to be honest with Ridley, but after finding the remains of a body where Echo Tango had specified, he grasped more than ever that a definite and serious threat existed. Harrison put his hand on Ridley's shoulder. "The truth will come out, and you've helped with that."

"I'm glad we have that all cleared up," Holcomb said. "But now we should consider the possibility the base authorities could identify us from that little incident back there." He peered up the road from where they had just traveled. "Seems odd, though, that we weren't intercepted on the highway. Maybe that's something you can check for us, Ridley?"

"I can see if the military has advised the department. I'll be discreet."

Harrison rubbed his leg and sighed heavily. "Art, we need to get back to Tucson and sort out the next steps in the investigation. But first, let's get checked out of the hotel."

"Good. I didn't like that dump anyway."

TWENTY SEVEN

More Tests

The loud knock on the door of Janice's quarters did not wake her. A sleepless night had left her sitting motionless on her bed for what seemed like hours. Now, she wished the interloper would simply go away.

"Evans, Janice B."

Why is she here?

Dr. Schmidt's rapping invaded Janice's only refuge, and chipped away her hope of having any solitude. There were no tests scheduled for today, Sunday, so confusion now contributed to her already anxious and depressed state of mind. Janice wanted nothing to do with any more poking or prodding; Saint Mary had jabbed her enough in the last few days.

"Janice!"

The sound of jangling keys made Janice drop her head. She spied an orange within reach on the foot of her bed. After lifting it, she dug a fingertip into the navel.

Dr. Schmidt turned the knob.

"I was just getting some breakfast."

"We have work to do," Dr. Schmidt said, making a swift entrance into the room. She halted after only a step or two. "No!" The door swung open farther, revealing the bright hallway behind it. The doctor had not arrived alone. "Give me that orange. You mustn't eat."

"Yes, ma'am." Janice took a deep breath. It helped her to form a kind smile. "Perhaps the nice airman would like it?" The guard merely continued to stare at the back of Schmidt's head. Janice realized that she could easily scan or control him. She could tell him things that would defy not only his security clearance, but also his entire understanding of life itself.

She could tell him *the truth*.

Tightening her grip on the orange, her soft fingers compressed it until she could feel it giving way to the pressure. Janice looked at Schmidt's outstretched pale hand. It was steady, so full of purpose, the pallid lifelessness of mechanized discipline. A slightly tighter grip could crush the orange. Its thin peel began to collapse.

"Now, Janice! Give it to me."

"Yes, ma'am." Janice relaxed and passed the orange to Schmidt. "I wasn't very hungry right now, anyway. Later though." Then, folding her arms, she said, "Has there been a change in schedule?"

Schmidt dropped the orange into a pocket of her white lab coat. She removed a pen and raised her clipboard. Instead of glancing between her notes and Janice, she took a small step forward and gestured for the airman to enter. He moved slowly into the room.

"You have more tests," Schmidt said, without looking up. "Now, come. There are people waiting. Any respiratory or nasal congestion this morning?"

Janice sighed, put on a robe, and followed Schmidt into the hallway. The guard trailed behind them. "No, clear as a whistle."

Dr. Schmidt made silent notations as they walked to this morning's destination.

"Any dizziness or nausea?"

"I feel fine."

"So, no dizziness or nausea?"

"No."

Schmidt refrained from further questions and accelerated her march. Entering a guarded stairwell, Janice felt tempted to scan the doctor. Schmidt seemed unusually tense. There were so many sentries present.

They headed downstairs, through a narrow hatch, and into a darkened corridor. A gurney, with orange-stained blue cushions, sat next to another sliding hatchway. Janice had never seen this area before. Focus eluded her. She thought she saw technicians in blue environment suits. Perhaps they were empty suits, just hanging on the white walls.

"Undress and change into this." Schmidt handed Janice a blue jumpsuit and slippers. "Hurry. Then join me inside."

"Yes, ma'am."

Janice edged herself to the end of the corridor and hastily disrobed. She glanced over her shoulder, but could not see inside the room well enough to determine what might be in store for her. The label above the hatch said "Enclosure 4."

Putting her slippers on at last, she still made time to fold her clothes into a neat pile. She entered the small room and noticed it was about the size of her apartment's bedroom in Tucson. Huge metal plates lined the far wall. Embedded into it, behind a thick glass panel, hung a video camera. Aside from that, and the black chair in the center of the room, everything else was white. Some details became clearer. The chair, like those in a dentist's office, sat bolted to the floor and had straps hanging from its sides. Across from it, the white wall looked like a movie screen. Beneath her slippers, the floor felt rough. She looked down and saw grooved white floor tiles made of rubber. A large orange stain splatter disturbed a portion of the floor near the chair.

"Sit down," Schmidt said.

Janice took a deep breath, stepped over the stain, and settled into the black chair.

"Now, tell me again," General Stone said, staring at Colonel Ritter. "I want to make sure I fully understand this."

"Yes, sir. We were set and online according to schedule. The experimental must have worked as a lure, because we didn't have to wait long before NORAD advised us of an unknown entering the area. When it was in range, we activated ELF immediately."

"Immediately?"

"Yes, sir. Once it entered restricted airspace. Our field units deployed to recover it as far as thirty miles out."

"And the object?"

"It had an erratic flight profile and never approached the experimental. It disappeared at t-plus seven and thirty."

Stone folded his hands and pursed his thin lips. "We need it in closer next time before we flip the switch. We need them close."

"Yes, sir."

"How did the experimental perform?"

Colonel Ritter dropped his head. "Performance was consistent with recent evaluations. It only hit 5 percent of its objectives."

"And had to be towed back to the hangar?"

"Yes, sir. The telepathic flight controls are difficult."

"I know. Of course, if we only had the right power cell too, maybe things would be different." Stone closed his eyes and breathed deeply. "Now, the other matter."

"Yes, sir." Ritter handed over a file. "This summarizes that issue. And, sir, I am sorry to say, I still have not been able to find General Taylor."

"Uh-huh. Does this include a map?" Stone's tone was low as he spoke through clenched teeth.

"Yes, sir. A few curiosity seekers penetrated the Ranch Annex. A patrol chased them off, but also found evidence of digging. The exact location is indicated on the map. Odd. I hoped General Taylor would be able to assist in explaining the reason—"

"Taylor is the reason," Stone said, setting the file down and opening it to the map.

"I don't understand, sir."

"It is very simple, Colonel. We are being betrayed." Stone's chest heaved. In, out. "Dismissed."

"Yes, sir." Ritter stood and walked out of the office. Behind him, the door slammed shut.

After Janice sat down, Dr. Schmidt personally strapped her into the black chair.

The chair's right armrest had attached to it a small black-and-silver box with several holes, each encircled by a different color. Drifting into view, two technicians approached. Schmidt receded into the darkness. Silently, the first technician reached around Janice's waist. He checked the straps, and then tightened them. Janice groaned.

From behind the chair, the other technician attached three electrodes to Janice's forehead and one to her neck. Each wire had a different color. He, *or she,* slid a fifth electrode just inside the jumpsuit's collar and affixed it to the center of Janice's chest. The technicians plugged the electrode wires into the small black-and-silver box, according to color.

When the technicians disappeared beyond the gurney in the hallway, Janice tested her freedom of movement. There was none. The door slid shut. She settled herself and stared at the white screen, then watched the dim light fade further.

Dr. Schmidt's voice rose from behind Janice. "You will see a series of images on the screen. Each image will have a number and three descriptive words next to it. You will tell me the number for each image, and state the word that best describes the image. Confine your statements to those two items. Do you understand?"

What is this?

Janice tried to nod, but stopped, feeling embarrassed by the movement of all those wires. "Yes, I understand."

"Keep your answers clear for as long as possible."

For as long as possible?

The first image slowly appeared. Children sat at desks in a room. Before them, a woman pointed at a map.

"One," Janice said, identifying the number on the display. Then, she said, "Learning," choosing from a list that also included "University" and "Conspiracy."

A quick dissolve, then, fire wrapped around tall pine trees and smoke filled the sky.

"Two." Janice looked at the three words, "Emergency," "Forest," and "Gothic." She chose and said, "Emergency."

Next, four people of various ages sat around a table with food on their plates. A large turkey rested on a serving tray in the center of the table.

"Three." The descriptive words in the upper right corner of the screen included "Rape," "Thanksgiving," and "Reunion." The choice distressed Janice, as she had never truly experienced the holiday. "Thanksgiving," she finally said.

Another image.

The number was out of sequence. Janice ignored this variation, and then correctly said, "Nineteen." A mushroom cloud billowed up from the desert floor. Soldiers marched toward it. "Concerto," "Discipline," "Technology." Janice believed "Discipline" was probably the expected answer. "Technology," she said, in defiance.

A shiver ran up Janice's neck, and she coughed. Her chest tingled. Vibrations undulated through her. She coughed again, but heavier and louder this time. Several seconds passed before the next image appeared. When it finally emerged, she could not make sense of it. "Thirty? No, thirty-four."

A man and woman walked along a beach. They held hands. The sun set behind them.

Janice started to provide a response, but realized she had not yet looked at the descriptive words. Her eyes floated upward, and "Arrangement," "Love," and "Friendship" slowly focused in her view. She stared at the choices, trying to breathe. In, out. In, out.

"Love," Janice said, her voice raspy.

The vibrations increased. Beads of sweat appeared on her temples. She closed her eyes, but this only made her dizzy.

In, out.

When Janice opened her eyes, she saw another image had appeared. A flicker. The screen faded to black. Another image appeared.

Or, was it the same as before?

Janice tugged and yanked her arms; the pulsations made her feel claustrophobic, and they pressed against her, all around her.

A city's crowded streets. Tall buildings rose into the sky. Countless people flooded the sidewalks.

In, out.

Janice examined the cityscape, trying to recognize anyone. A blurry number eighty-eight was all she could discern. Her ears rang, and she wanted to vomit.

"Eighty-eight," she said, yelling. Saliva dribbled from her mouth.

Another list, indecipherable words.

In, out.

Tears rolled down her cheeks. "Dr. Schmidt, please."

The humming, pulsating vibrations enveloped her. They squeezed her chest and strangled her throat. She gripped the arms of the chair. More coughs shook her harder and harder.

A planet, Earth, hung majestically in space. It drifted above the gray surface of the moon.

Janice dropped her head, and closed her eyes. She could not feel her body, could not feel the seat, nor the belt around her, anymore. A river of colors cut a swath through the blackness.

In, out.

The chair creaked as each of her arms fell lifelessly to her sides.

The humming ceased. General Stone coughed once then spat toward a dark corner of Arena Four. To his left, in another dim recess, an old man's nostrils, those of Professor Moresby, whistled with shallow inhalations. Stone watched the video screen. Technicians disconnected Janice and lifted her onto a gurney.

"Could she be faking this?" Stone said. "She was close to Taylor. His special project. His job was fakery."

He had faked Major Blair's accident. Why dig him up?

So many scenarios flashed through Stone's racing, paranoid mind. Continuing, he said, "Was Taylor involved in a special operation? Directed by Saint Mary? Wouldn't I know? Directed against Saint Mary? Very risky. Directed against me?"

"So many questions indeed," Professor Moresby said. "May I go now? This is very distressing."

The wall-mounted telephone buzzed. Stone answered, relieved it was only Dr. Schmidt calling as expected.

"Sir, the news is bad."

"Go on."

"Her condition deteriorated rapidly, similar to tests conducted on Evans, James A."

"This reconfirms our expectations. Why is this bad?"

Moresby's nostrils stopped whistling. Stone looked toward the corner of the room and noticed a subtle nod from the old man.

"The test has left Evans, Janice B., in serious condition, possibly comatose. I've never seen this before."

"Watch her," Stone said. "Are you certain of her condition?"

Dr. Schmidt did not address Stone's question right away. It sounded to him like she was busy speaking to someone else.

In German.

"Goddammit, Schmidt, are you listening to me? Is everyone around here out to scorn me?"

"No, sir. I have to go. The subject just went into respiratory arrest."

Stone slammed the phone back onto its hook.

"Sounds like ELF worked well, eh?" Professor Moresby said. He stepped closer to General Stone. "Perhaps too well."

"Then why did it fail in the desert?"

"Maybe there is something about proximity? Although vulnerable, the ship does afford some protection, to itself, to its occupants—"

"I am aware of this issue."

"Then it has to be close, or you need a great power supply."

"That was my predecessor's early assessment." Stone thought he detected a chuckle from Moresby.

"There are quite a few reminders of Taylor's work cropping up these days, eh, General?"

"Yes." A renewed surge of determination lifted Stone's spirits. "You included. And all that means is that there are plenty of clues to follow."

"I can see how this will be helpful," Moresby said, turning away from Stone. "As for me, Saint Mary knows the length, depth, and age of every wrinkle on my ass and on parts north and south. I have been followed since before you were born." He approached the exit hatchway. "I suggest you follow other leads."

"I am going to, Professor." Stone always found the title hard to utter. But in the vacant darkness, with Moresby half-obscured and opportunity nipping at Stone's pride, he chose to use it again. "Taylor's situation aside, Professor, I've come to believe the ELF operations can only succeed with your involvement."

"I gathered that."

"I know the hybrids are of interest to you."

"Don't you mean 'hybrid'?"

"She will recover. James always has."

"Assuming she does, what do you want from me?"

"Without your help, Professor, the Circle will not achieve its objectives. I need your cooperation. They need your cooperation. If Taylor's security breach is real, then progress is needed more so than ever before. You know better than anybody the consequences of failure." Stone stepped toward Moresby and put a hand on the old man's shoulder. "And just to be clear, I'm not talking about my own failure." He earnestly searched the professor's eyes for understanding. "I think you know what I'm talking about."

"Please, General, I've been with Saint Mary since nearly the beginning. Don't try to frighten me with suggestions or allusions to the Circle's contingency plans. Not even they are that crazy. Damage control against premature disclosure is fantasy. When the cat is finally out of the bag..." Moresby paused and squinted at Stone. Continuing, he said, "Yes, I know what you are talking about, but these plans are just figments of paranoid, self-destructive imaginations."

Stone stood speechless. He did not know whether Moresby was truly uninformed or merely lying to him about one of Saint Mary's most enigmatic functions, simply known as "the contingency." The old man's eyes offered no clear answer.

"If you want something, please be direct. Now, let's begin again," Moresby said.

Their conversation was lengthy, and the plans they discussed were complicated. Stone learned for the first time that the professor possessed specialized hardware that promised to increase their chances for success. In exchange, he offered Moresby complete access to and use of Janice.

"Pending her recovery," Moresby added.

"Yes, and pending an inquiry."

"Guilty until proven innocent, General?"

Stone straightened his tie and uniform, and then activated the exit's hatchway. "Uh-huh, beyond a reasonable doubt."

TWENTY EIGHT

The Boneyard

"God, I am pissed!"

These were Holcomb's first words in over an hour, and he expressed them within sight of Davis-Monthan Air Force Base's main gate. Harrison sat up in the passenger seat, winced, and looked over at Holcomb, who puffed on a cigarette.

"Did you say you had to pee again? It has been quite a long drive."

"I don't like it one bit, Bill."

"Being shot at?"

"Something ain't right. Sure, being shot at, but let's face it, I think you and I both know this F-4 is going to be sitting here."

"Credibility."

"Then what? Why? And who's going to get killed in the process?"

"The stakes do seem to be pretty high. Let's just keep focused on the work."

Holcomb pulled up to the gate and stopped the Dodge, which by now had bumper stickers glorifying Las Vegas on it that concealed multiple bullet holes.

"They better not give me any grief," Holcomb said.

"Just stick to the plan."

An air policeman stepped out of the guard shack and approached the car. Holcomb rolled down the window and said, "Good afternoon, officer."

"What is your destination, sir?"

"We are headed to the boneyard."

"Tours are provided only on Mondays, Wednesdays, and Fridays."

"I'm no tourist," Holcomb said, displaying his FBI credentials. "We are here on official business. A matter of national security."

From behind dark sunglasses, the sentry scrutinized the identification. "Hold on, sir." He turned around and walked to the guard shack.

"No grief," Holcomb said, sighing.

The air policeman returned to the car, carrying a clipboard and a small placard. He handed the clipboard to Holcomb and said, "Sign this please." After Holcomb signed his name, the guard asked him to set the placard on the dashboard, and then provided directions to their destination. "See Mr. Spencer in the admin facility at the site, building eight hundred."

"Will do. Have a certified copy of that page I just signed available for me upon my exit." Holcomb rolled up the window and drove toward the boneyard.

Harrison looked at his old partner and said, "A 'certified copy'?"

"Hopefully he is at the photocopier right now, wondering the same thing, but making the copy for me nevertheless."

Holcomb rounded a corner formed by large, gray warehouses. He slowed the vehicle, and Harrison's gaze joined Holcomb's on the neat rows of aircraft that seemed to go on forever. The car crept along. An entire history of American Cold War military aviation filled the expanse. Fighters, trainers, transports, and bombers, all gleaming monuments in their own right to duty, honor, and country, but for their surroundings. Now, they were merely sun-bleached bones of a mammoth skeleton interred in the desert for safekeeping.

Another gray building appeared, blemishing the uniformity of the boneyard. As they drew closer, it loomed larger from behind a short row of F-15 fighters.

"That's our admin building," Holcomb said, pointing.

Harrison grunted his agreement and dug out a digital camera from the rucksack at his feet. "Park as close as you can. I'm still pretty sore."

"Yeah, and you smell bad too." Holcomb maneuvered off the gravel roadway and parked in a handicapped space near the building's front door. "What if they are already here to greet us? It's possible they know what we'd be after, if the story is true, that is."

"I've been thinking about that."

"And?"

"They didn't pursue us in the desert. A little strange, don't you think?"

"A little, but they've had some time to piece it together."

"So, in that case, they'd eliminate the evidence, not take any chances, and be on alert for anyone who came looking for it."

"Exactly my point, Bill."

"You know what my gut feeling is? I think that plane is still out there. I think it will be gone by tomorrow at the latest. I think we are past the point of no return and that someone is giving us just enough of an edge, running interference for us, so that we stay ahead of the game for now."

"Okay, good."

"Good?"

"Yeah, good. Just as long as the Saint Mary folks, or whatever they may be called, aren't here now. That's good. Let's go, gimpy."

Entering the building behind Holcomb, Harrison immediately noticed a cluttered reception counter several feet away and began to scan the office. At first, no one appeared present, but the sound of rustling papers drew his attention. Ahead of Holcomb, behind the counter, a short man hunched over a gray metal filing cabinet. The man, whose back was turned, seemed preoccupied with his search.

While Harrison stayed back some, Holcomb approached the man and said, "Excuse me, sir, are you Mr. Spencer?"

Without halting his examination of the files inside the cabinet, the man said, "Yeah, that's me."

Holcomb waited briefly. Harrison expected that his partner would give Spencer at least five seconds of quiet patience. It ended up being less than three.

"Federal agents, sir," Holcomb said.

Spencer sighed, then reluctantly stood and approached Holcomb. Spencer stood at best five feet, five inches tall. He was deeply tanned, pudgy, and middle-aged with thin blond hair. In his beige overalls, he looked very much like a small sand dune. Squinting at the credentials in Holcomb's outstretched hand, he said, "What brings the bureau out here on a Sunday afternoon?"

"A matter of utmost urgency and discretion." Holcomb sauntered around the office, inspecting his surroundings. His gaze drifted between Spencer, the ceiling, the furnishings, and the floor. "We felt the weekend would be the best time to follow up on a lead we're working. You know, fewer people around and all." Holcomb nudged his way through the small gate attached to the counter and strolled over to the open filing cabinet that Spencer had been searching. He closed it. "We were told you could assist us." Holcomb then sat on the cabinet.

"I wasn't informed that you'd—"

"Good, very good," Holcomb said. "This is a highly classified case. Very few people know about it. I hope we can count on your confidentiality."

"Of course, I just assumed the military authorities would be involved."

"Ah, that's the sad part, Mr. Spencer." Holcomb stood and stepped closer to Spencer. He placed a hand on the man's low shoulder and leaned way forward. "You see, they are involved, but I'm afraid they are the ones who are the subject of this investigation." Whispering now, Holcomb said, "The FBI has recently received word from an informant that a particular terrorist group is operating in the United States with the assistance of certain military authorities."

Spencer gasped.

"I know, it is shocking," Holcomb said. "But all the more reason for us keeping it hush-hush. Apparently, the informant believes that some equipment may have been, well, stolen from this storage area."

"From the boneyard? What kind of equipment?"

Harrison swiveled his head away from Holcomb and Spencer and gazed out a window, hiding a smile.

"An aircraft, sir," Holcomb said.

Spencer's voice grew hoarse. "No, sir, not from this base. That's not possible."

"Well, let's hope so. Not that it would be your fault or anything like that. I'm sure you keep very good and accurate records of what's out there."

Harrison rolled his eyes.

"But you see, Mr. Spencer, we have to take these kinds of leads seriously. I think you'll agree."

The little dune migrated to a nearby computer terminal. "What kind of plane are you looking for?"

"An F-4 Phantom," Harrison said, stepping up to the counter and granting Holcomb a reprieve from his performance.

"We have a lot of those."

"I know, I've seen your postcards."

"Seven hundred and sixty-eight."

Harrison held out an open black notepad for Spencer to see. "Fortunately, we have very specific information. This is the serial number of the aircraft in question."

"Ah, uh-huh, hmm, yes, row A, section twenty-seven. If we have an F-4 with that serial number, it will be in row A, section twenty-seven. Follow me."

Harrison raised an eyebrow at Holcomb, and the two men followed Spencer outside.

"Row A, section twenty-seven," Spencer said, pointing. "Drive past that first group of planes, those F-104s, then turn right. After about half a mile you'll come to some of the F-4s. Look on the right side of the road and you'll see painted letters and numbers on the ground. Look for 'A twenty-seven.' If we have that plane, it'll be in that row. You go on out. I'll check the records some more, see what we have on it, if anything."

"Thanks, Mr. Spencer," Holcomb said. "Remember, hush-hush."

"Yes, sir."

They followed the directions, both anxiously checking the odometer after passing the F-104s. In just under half a mile, the familiar, heavy frames of the Phantoms appeared on the right.

Harrison watched the ground. The orderliness of the row numbers, painted in bright yellow, and the prospect of achieving a small victory brought a wry smile to his face. He grabbed the camera. "Okay, turn right here. A twenty-seven."

Holcomb turned, creeping by the fighters. There were easily thirty F-4s lined up ahead of them. Their serial numbers were roughly in sequence except for a few intermittent breaks.

"Nope," Holcomb said after passing each jet.

"Okay, ET, your credibility is on the line here," Harrison said.

"Maybe they already got to it. What do you think?"

"I think..." Harrison paused and cocked his head. The goose bumps came again. "I think you should stop the car."

For several seconds, neither Harrison nor Holcomb got out. Both stared at the F-4 sitting a few feet away.

"Doesn't look too bad for having crashed into the Pacific Ocean," Holcomb finally said.

"Yeah, let's go."

On foot, they circled the plane and reread the serial number on the fuselage and tail. "Keep an eye out, Art."

"Sure, just hurry it up a bit."

Twenty-four photographs later, Harrison had captured multiple views of the fighter. Close-ups of the serial number, long shots of the plane neatly aligned in its row, medium shots showing most of the plane with its serial number in view, two with Holcomb standing in front of the starboard intake, the plane's serial number and the special agent's credentials clearly in view.

After a hasty return to the boneyard's administration building, they found Spencer smiling in front of his computer screen. "Just found our records on the plane you were looking for."

"I knew you would," Harrison said. "We found that bird right where you said it would be."

“That’s a relief.”

“You said it.”

Holcomb leaned over the counter next to Spencer and said, “So, are these the records you were talking about?”

“Yes,” Spencer said, grabbing a file folder from the cluttered countertop. The file contained several pages of documents, one of which he removed. “This is a storage report we fill out whenever we get a new plane. As you can see, that F-4 has been here for a while and, obviously, still is.”

“How long has it been here?” Holcomb said.

Spencer looked at the document and said, “Oh, well, since 1989. Let’s see, uh-huh, transferred from Rhein Main in Germany, in April, 1989. Been here ever since, unless some terrorists borrowed it then returned it without us knowing about it.”

Holcomb laughed. “Right. Oh, say, Mr. Spencer, could I take this storage report for our case file? We’ll return it once this is all wrapped up.”

“Sure. It’s all on the computer anyway.”

“Thanks, you’ve been more than helpful,” Holcomb said. “The bureau appreciates your diligence. Your cooperation is truly commendable. You’re a good American.”

“Let’s go, Art,” Harrison said, holding the door open.

Holcomb thanked Spencer again, and then exited. Outside, he said, “So, what’s next?”

“The way I see it, it’s time to locate a dentist and, maybe if needed, get some saliva too. Ever been to Wichita this time of year?”

TWENTY NINE

The Greater Wichita Dental Association

Nick Ridley finished an uneventful and routine Sunday shift at 11:00 p.m. But given his experience in the desert with Harrison and Holcomb, he was unusually tired, more mentally than physically. Halfway up the steps to his apartment, he stopped and pulled the keys from his coat pocket. A sudden creeping of anxiety writhed its way through his mind and body, causing him to twist around and scan the area behind him.

He saw nothing unusual, but he felt like someone watched him.

Ridley returned his attention to entering the apartment and locking the door behind him. As tired as he felt, he found himself growing increasingly agitated. Stuck, with no clear direction to go, he pulled a business card out of his wallet. "First things first, I guess." He grabbed the phone and dialed.

The voice mail message from Harrison's cell phone greeted Ridley.

A faint noise outside, similar to footsteps, tugged Ridley's attention toward the door. A beep from inside his phone prompted him to speak. "Vegas PD not advised." He hung up the phone and then stepped toward the door.

A voice inside his head whispered to him. *"Relax, it's nothing."*

In response to the mental scan, Ridley's eyelids fluttered, and then he stopped in his tracks. "Relax it's nothing," he said, convincing himself nothing was wrong.

The internal voice came again. *"Relax, and sit."*

Ridley walked into the living room. With each step, he felt tiredness seep ever deeper into his extremities. He plopped into an easy chair feeling as if he had no strength left to hold himself up.

"Just relax. There's nothing you can do."

Mindlessly, he picked up the television remote and flipped through the channels. He leaned back and put his feet up on the coffee table.

"That's it."

With his mind cleared, he set the remote aside.

"Eric."

Ridley sighed, and his eyelids fluttered. "Eric, what did you want to tell me? I could have helped. Was it the communications failure? The incident Harrison talked about?"

"Wait, who is he?"

"Private investigator."

Other questions pulsated through Ridley's mind. He gave up the answers.

"Tucson. Anonymous informant. Military incident involving advanced hardware. Airman allegedly committed suicide. Don't know about it. Followed them. Harrison and Holcomb. No, FBI. Out to the desert. Yeah. Flying saucer? Area 51. Escaped. Bag of bones. Don't know. Back to Tucson. Vegas PD not advised. No. No one else."

"There's nothing you can do."

Ridley's eyelids stopped fluttering, and he closed his eyes.

At eight o'clock the next day, while driving to the Tucson International Airport, Harrison informed Holcomb of Ridley's phone message. Both felt a sense of relief while they went over last-minute details and security precautions. They discussed the case, devised a rudimentary code for telephone calls, and made plans to meet up after Holcomb returned from Wichita. Both agreed that Echo Tango intended the Wichita postmark on the boneyard postcard as a clue to where they may well locate Major Blair's nonmilitary dental records. They surmised that due to operational security reasons, Echo Tango opted not to broadcast that fact and risk losing the records to Saint Mary's representatives. The next-of-kin notification, which Echo Tango had also provided, indicated that Blair's parents lived there, and Harrison hoped they could assist Holcomb.

"Be tactful," Harrison said to his former partner when he dropped him curbside. "And be careful."

On the drive to the office, Harrison stopped and rented a storage unit. Inside, he left the rucksack and other equipment from their dig. After arriving at the office, he made photocopies of Echo Tango's latest documents, the F-4 storage report, and the gate sign-in sheet. He deposited them, along with a thumb drive of digital images, in his safe-deposit box at the bank. A personal advertisement in the Tucson Sun Times came next. The simple and concise message read: "ET, got it."

After these errands, Harrison's cell phone vibrated, alerting him to an incoming call.

"Good morning, Willy, my boy," Zemdarsky said.

"Pete, sorry for not calling you sooner."

"I'll bet. Hey, look, I still have your dog. He's halfway to California right now."

"Huh?"

"Seeing as how I hadn't heard from you, Mandy and I decided to take Beano with us on a trip to see the boys out in California."

"That's very generous. I owe you, buddy."

"No worries. But whatever you're up to, Billy, just remember to get paid in full."

"Payment seems to be the easy part on this one."

"Good to hear. Well, if you get lonely, you know where to find us."

"Thanks, Pete."

"Happy, happy! Bye now."

Harrison chuckled and hung up the phone.

Less than five minutes later, the phone buzzed again. Thinking it was Zemdarsky calling back, Harrison answered, saying, "She farted one too many times and you've decided to leave her at the side of the road."

"Merry Christmas, Mr. Harrison. It's time for us to meet. Three p.m. today, Agua Caliente Park. Make sure you aren't followed."

"What?"

Silence.

Harrison checked his watch. Less than two hours remained before the requested meeting.

From a phone booth in Wichita's airport terminal, Holcomb dialed the number for Robert and Noreen Blair. The next-of-kin notification only listed their names and address, but he easily found their number in the phone book. He had completely ruled out using his own name or any reference to an FBI investigation. Although he preferred a direct approach, he did not want to arouse suspicion or, worse, renew painful memories for the family. As the phone rang, he thought of the questions he would ask, and hoped his chosen strategy would work.

"Hello?" an older woman's voice said.

In his most sincere and polite manner, Holcomb said, "Good afternoon, may I please speak with Robert or Noreen Blair?"

"This is Noreen."

"Please let me introduce myself. My name is Alan, and I'm calling on behalf of the Greater Wichita Dental Association."

"Oh, thanks, but I don't think I'm interested."

"I understand, but I'm not selling anything. In fact, I have been authorized to send you a complimentary coupon book, a twenty-dollar value, good toward the purchase of dental care supplies, just for answering a few quick survey questions." Holcomb tightened his grip around the phone.

"Well, I guess maybe. Will this take long?"

"Hardly two or three minutes of your valuable time, Noreen. May I call you Noreen?"

"Yes, go ahead, Alan. I have a few minutes. That's all it will take, won't it? Just a few minutes?"

"Less than that," Holcomb said, feeling a twinge of guilt. Noreen sounded like his own mother. "First, could you please tell me what brand of toothpaste you use?"

"Well, my husband uses Polident Dentu-Creme, and I use Colgate."

"Okay. And the next question, about how many times a year do you visit your dentist?"

"Oh, my, my, do I have to be honest about that?" Noreen shared a laugh with Holcomb, and then said, "At least once a year."

"Do you have a family dentist?"

"Yes."

"And how many years have you been seeing your current dentist?"

"Let's see now. Bob and I were married in 1965 and moved here when Jeffrey was a teenager. I guess it's about twenty-five, going on thirty years."

"Oh my, ma'am, that's very loyal of you. Your dentist must be very, very good."

"He is, he definitely is. We wouldn't think of going to anybody else. Dr. Crenshaw is wonderful. I don't know what we'll do when he retires."

"Dr. Crenshaw? Why, many of our respondents have said just the same thing about him, Mrs. Blair."

"I'm not surprised. We've been quite happy with him. He's a good neighborhood dentist. Goes to our church, too."

"I want to thank you, Mrs. Blair, on behalf of the Greater Dentists, uh, Greater Wichita Dentistry Committee for your time answering our survey. We'll be sure to get those coupons out to you right away."

"Okay, well, thank you. Have a merry Christmas."

Holcomb hung up the phone and wiped a thin layer of sweat from his forehead. He grabbed his smartphone and entered a search. He quickly found the listing for Dr. Crenshaw—"Your Neighborhood Dentist since 1981"—and he wrote down the address.

After renting a Ford Taurus with GPS, he drove to Crenshaw's office. Inside, he found the office trimmed with Christmas decorations, and stereo speakers emitted an instrumental version of "Silent Night." Noticing no patients in the waiting room, Holcomb approached the young blond receptionist who sat behind a large Formica counter.

"Hello, I'm here to see Dr. Crenshaw."

The receptionist smiled, and in a soft, light voice, she said, "Did you have an appointment? We are about to close for the holiday."

"I got here just in time then. Actually, I'm here on official government business," Holcomb said, watching the receptionist's reaction.

"Oh, very good, we've been expecting you. I'll get the doctor right away for you, sir."

Holcomb nodded and watched the receptionist disappear down an adjacent hallway, where she started an inaudible conversation with someone.

Expecting me?

Uneasy now, Holcomb hummed along to the music. He stopped when he thought he heard the words, "air force." He gripped the counter and stared toward the now silent hallway. A thin, elderly man in a blue smock emerged, followed by the still-smiling receptionist.

"You must be here about the dental records," the man said.

Holcomb looked over his shoulder, then to the man standing behind the counter. He stopped breathing and put out his hand. "Yes, and you must be Dr. Crenshaw, so nice to meet you."

"I am," the man said, shaking Holcomb's hand. "I pulled Jeffrey's records out of storage. Under normal circumstances, I would have destroyed these old records years ago, but I've held onto them just in case Jeffrey's remains were found."

"Thank you for doing that, sir."

"Quite frankly, though, I was under the impression that someone from the air force would be out to pick them up." Crenshaw looked Holcomb up and down through smudged glasses.

The hair on Holcomb's neck stiffened.

"I don't think I caught your name?" Crenshaw said. "Are you the person who called earlier?"

"No, sir, I'm with the Federal Bureau of Investigation. The name's Sheraton, Ronald Sheraton. You see, Dr. Crenshaw, the FBI routinely assists the air force in these matters. The bureau has the best forensic specialists in the world, thank goodness." Holcomb felt warm. "My, these are festive decorations you have in your office."

A broad grin crossed Crenshaw's face. "Well, I honestly can't take credit." He paused and pointed at the receptionist. "Maxine, here, was in charge of the decorations."

Holcomb saw Maxine smiling at him. He smiled back. Crenshaw smiled at both of them. The longest-running rendition of "Silent Night" Holcomb had ever heard continued playing in the background. The only movement in the room consisted of the gentle wafting of garland strands near the heater vents.

Holcomb finally chimed in and said, "Well, Doctor, Maxine here says that you're about to close. I can imagine you must be anxious to start your holiday, so if you'd like, I'll be happy to go ahead and take those records now and get out of your hair."

Waving his hand at Holcomb, Crenshaw said, "Come on back." Crenshaw led him down the hallway to an office. "I have the file in here. So, is it true the air force may have found Jeffrey's remains?"

"Uh, the records should be able to help us determine that. I really don't know much about the case. I was just asked to stop by here."

"Oh, I understand. Still, it was such a tragedy for the Blairs, not being able to lay their son to rest. I was surprised to hear the air force couldn't find their own dental records." Crenshaw opened the center drawer of his desk.

"It's a very rare occurrence, but it happens from time to time."

"Here you are." Crenshaw retrieved a folder from the drawer and handed it to Holcomb. "I hope it helps you out."

"I'm sure it will. Say, Doc, when was the last time Jeffrey came for a visit?"

"As I remember, it was about six months before the accident. He so hated air force dentists. Anyway, he was home on leave and just wanted a simple checkup. Yep, that was the last time I saw him."

"Well, thank you so much for your help. We can only hope for the best." Holcomb turned to leave, easy breaths returning to him.

From his desk, Crenshaw smiled and wished Holcomb a merry Christmas and happy New Year.

Over his shoulder, Holcomb said, "You too, Doc." He walked toward the exit, exchanging brief holiday wishes with Maxine.

Stepping outside and heading for the Ford Taurus, Holcomb tightened his grip on the folder. Shallow breaths returned, and his blood pressure shot up. He fought the urge to run, and to swear. Instead, as he reached the sidewalk, he politely nodded at the two air force officers going in the opposite direction on their way to Crenshaw's office. The officers passed him silently, except for the rhythmic tapping of their shoes on the sidewalk.

A few more steps and Holcomb peered over his shoulder. Through the front window of Crenshaw's office, he could see Maxine smiling and pointing at him. Holcomb turned back around and said, "Aw, shit!"

He dashed to the Ford, pressing the unlock button on the key fob repeatedly before he got there. In slick movement, Holcomb yanked the door open, jumped in, started the car, and pulled into the street. The abrupt forward momentum of the car swung the driver door closed, but the sound of screeching brakes made him slam the car to a sudden stop. A white delivery van blocked his way. Holcomb waved to the driver to move forward, indicating his vehicle was clear. An angry stare from the van's driver returned his gesture. The white van crept forward, inching out of his way.

Holcomb floored the accelerator, cornering around the delivery van. The Ford spun sideways and stopped, facing back toward Crenshaw's office. The two air force officers sprinted to a dark-blue sedan.

"Damn," Holcomb said. He cranked the steering wheel and gunned the engine.

THIRTY

On the Run

Harrison drove his black Dodge Charger through light eastbound traffic in Tucson, making his way toward Agua Caliente Park. Mostly cloudy skies dropped random rays of afternoon sunlight onto the city's streets. Tired, almost sleepy at times, Harrison struggled to stay alert, especially to detect anyone who might be following him. Backtracking once, he shook his head and wished he could just drive straight to the park. However, security concerns and instinct kept him from doing just that. Instead, he stopped at a Starbucks and purchased a venti-sized Pike Place Roast. Sipping his drink, he sat inside the cafe for about ten minutes and watched his surroundings inside and out. He got back into his car and headed toward the park, but not before backtracking on occasion to identify any potential tails.

Confident no one followed him, Harrison pulled into Agua Caliente's gravel parking lot. Two unoccupied coupes, one red and one silver, parked side by side, sat at the far end of the lot to his right. With no one visible in the area, Harrison guessed that any visitors had likely strolled to the lake a short distance from the parking lot.

He backed the Dodge into a space near the park's entrance and turned off the ignition. Harrison sipped the Pike Place Roast and rubbed his thigh, but he did not have to wait long for an interruption.

A late-model maroon Lincoln Town Car with tinted windows approached and crept its way to the far end of the parking lot. After making a wide U-turn near the parked coupes, the vehicle returned to the end of the lot near Harrison, eventually stopping adjacent to his car.

Mild waves of anxiety fluttered through Harrison's gut. He knew Echo Tango sought secrecy, and the privacy of the park, with its out-of-the-way location and quiet surroundings, facilitated that purpose. The flutter suggested that, perhaps, they would have been better off meeting somewhere not so secluded. He shook off the feeling, took a deep breath, and waited.

The Town Car's door opened, and the driver stepped out. Harrison could only see the man's back. He had brown hair, graying slightly on the sides, and a medium build. He wore casual civilian clothing. The man closed the door and turned around. Harrison had no trouble recognizing the man.

Sam Ritter.

Seeing an old acquaintance from his FBI days, Harrison calmed down some, but one thing still nagged him. He watched Ritter sit at a nearby bench and fold his arms.

After getting out of the Dodge, Harrison paused to look around. A couple strolled hand in hand from the direction of the lake along a footpath, heading toward the far end of the parking lot. Taking note of the couple, Harrison limped in Ritter's direction. So many questions pushed their way to be the first in line.

"You look tired. Please, take a load off," Ritter said, pointing at the bench.

A wintry breeze swirled around them.

Harrison buttoned his coat and coughed. "How long has it been, Sam?"

"Well, I'm a colonel now. Guess it's going on six years or so. Bet you never thought you'd see me again, huh?"

"I didn't know who to expect today, let alone you."

Ritter nodded. "Fate has a way of influencing our circumstances."

"I have many questions about those circumstances. Particularly, why you've chosen to meet with me now."

"I was anxious for an update on what evidence you've managed to gather, and how strong a case we may have."

That nagging feeling tweaked Harrison again. He looked at Ritter and said, "I have done some additional checking, but mainly followed up your leads."

"Good, good. And Major Blair?"

"He's in a safe place."

Holcomb slammed the brakes on the Ford Taurus.

The backpack containing Blair's skull flew off the front seat and onto the floorboard. The dental records shot against the dashboard and emptied their contents across his knees and the front seat. An X-ray flipped and hung for a moment against the windshield before tumbling onto the seat.

Holcomb accelerated again but had no clue where he should drive to escape his Air Force officer pursuers. He had never been to Wichita before.

As the Ford bounced and shuffled over a set of railroad tracks, he found himself in a decaying industrial section of the city. Within seconds, the dark-blue sedan behind him hit the tracks and became airborne. It landed with a sharp jolt on the wet ground and slid sideways into a thick cement loading dock, where it came to an abrupt stop.

"Yes!" Holcomb said, believing his escape was now possible.

But the collision only temporarily halted the chase car's pursuit, and it accelerated away from the loading dock.

Gaining some distance, Holcomb turned left down a narrow street that ran between long rows of warehouses. The metal-sided buildings blurred past him as an intersection drew nearer.

A glance rearward revealed no sign of his pursuers. Holcomb swung the car left, through the intersection, but hurriedly swerved right. The blue-sedan screamed by him, barely avoiding a head-on collision.

Scraping against a line of trash Dumpsters, Holcomb struggled to keep the car from careening out of control. Recovering, he saw his pursuers turning back in his direction. They passed from view as the street Holcomb followed curved to the right. The road curved back to the left and then straightened out, paralleling a fence along the railroad tracks.

"Damn!" Holcomb said.

A train moved toward him, not far from a crossing he spotted and quickly judged to be a possible escape route. Buildings and the lack of side roads channeled him relentlessly forward. He looked in the rearview mirror. The other vehicle emerged from the curve. Holcomb looked ahead again. The timing would be close.

As the train's loud horn pierced the air, Holcomb gunned the Ford's engine, and then backed off. He tapped the brakes twice. Just ahead, the crossing came ever closer. Flooring the accelerator again, Holcomb winced at the pummeling from the train horn's deafening sound waves.

Now or never.

Holcomb tightened his grip on the steering wheel and cranked it to the right. The car swerved, and then straightened when he counter steered. He pressed down hard on the accelerator, and with solid forward momentum again, the Ford Taurus bounced with violent jolts across the railroad tracks.

The train's front coupler connected with the car's left rear panel and tore into it. The force of the impact tossed the car sideways, knocking it clear of the crossing and into a metal railing that gave way under the pressure and weight from the tumbling car.

Holcomb jerked against his seat belt in multiple directions. His smartphone tumbled out of its case on his hip. Unable to focus on anything, he was tugged and shoved, then felt an airborne sensation followed by an intense flash of white light all around him. He exhaled involuntarily as airbags pressed against him in a life-saving embrace.

Gathering his wits, Holcomb smelled an odor, like tree sap. Over his right shoulder, where the right rear passenger's door used to be, he saw a brown, oily telephone pole. The car sounded like it sizzled.

Shaking his head, he realized the train decelerated but pressed onward, blocking his pursuers from crossing the tracks.

He reached down, fumbling for a moment, and unbuckled his seat belt. The pressure around his midsection eased, and he leaned over to the passenger side of the car. He collected Blair's dental records and grabbed the backpack with the dead aviator's skull inside. After squeezing out of the car, Holcomb fled, not realizing his smartphone remained in the car and feeling certain his freedom would be short-lived.

Ritter rested his arms on his thighs. "And the other evidence?"

"Secure," Harrison said. "I took some time earlier today to write an initial summary, but I hoped to get further details from you. I'm also interested in your plans for resolution of the case."

"Before we proceed, I need to make absolutely sure all of the evidence is secure. What measures have you taken?"

"Safe-deposit box and a storage unit."

Ritter sat up straight. "And other than Holcomb, who have you told about the operation?"

Harrison hesitated. Ritter knew Holcomb too, and mentioning him confirmed that he must have observed the two of them at the Sundowner Inn. Harrison struggled with an honest answer to Ritter's question, but was concerned about protecting Ridley. "Sam." Harrison paused and picked his next words carefully. "I have not given anyone else any details of the case."

"Does this include Nick Ridley?"

Harrison glanced at Ritter, and saw him staring straight ahead. "Yes. He's involved, but I haven't given him any details. You know, of course, his brother-in-law died in one of the recent accidents."

Ritter nodded slowly. "Can he be trusted?"

"I believe so, yes. He saved my life."

Ritter looked at the couple walking toward them, and then said, "Are those the only ones who are involved?"

"Yes. There are lives at stake here, Sam. So, what about you? Who have you involved in all this? And more importantly, why are you doing this, Sam?"

"I have my reasons," Ritter said, fidgeting. He crossed his arms.

To Harrison, Ritter's body language telegraphed obvious deceit. Harrison's leg ached and irritation crept into his voice. "I've been honest with you. I've stuck my neck out for you and so have others, and all you can say is, 'I have my reasons'? I want the whole story." He rubbed his eyes and face, fighting back exhaustion and frustration. "What's with the witch hazel?"

Ritter looked lost. He pursed his lips, widened his eyes, and looked away. "Witch hazel? What's that got to do with it? It's just time for the truth to come out."

Wrong answer.

"Okay, but why me, and why in this manner? Why not come forward yourself with the information instead of sending me in pursuit of things you already know about?"

"Simply because it is safer that way," Ritter said, shifting again.

The strolling couple drew closer, no more than within fifty yards away now.

"Safer for whom?" Harrison said, his concerns mounting.

"Safer for us all, of course. Now then, about the evidence."

Harrison stood.

"Where are you going?" Ritter said.

"Nowhere, just stretching my leg."

"Oh yes, that's right. How is the injury?"

"Just aches now and then." *Two cars, far end of lot. Young couple.*

Harrison looked at Ritter and said, "Tell me, Sam, what did you think of the new personal ad I left for you?"

Ritter twitched, and then nodded. "Quite informative."

Harrison smiled and said, "Thanks, Sam." He pointed at the Dodge Charger and said, "I have something else for you in my car."

Ritter looked away from Harrison toward the car and never saw the impending attack launched at him.

Harrison raised his good leg and struck Ritter with a firm kick in the chest. The impact sent a rush of air out of Ritter's lungs and mouth. The strength of the blow knocked the bench rearward, and Ritter tumbled backward onto the ground, clutching his chest and heaving in and out.

Harrison almost lost his balance, but he regained control by grabbing onto Ritter's feet. Harrison pushed away and hobbled back to his car.

As he feared, the young couple sprinted toward him. They changed direction, though, and headed for one of the coupes parked at the end of the lot. The silver coupe came to life, spinning its rear wheels as its previously hidden driver accelerated across the gravel surface.

Pulling the car keys from his coat pocket, Harrison heard the commotion while he struggled to reach his car. Heart pounding, Harrison flung open the driver's side door.

Easy breaths.

The coupe continued its collision course toward Harrison.

The Colt slid easily from its holster. Harrison leaned over the hood and aligned the sights with the driver's chest. Exhaling, Harrison flipped off the thumb safety.

One, two.

The two rounds struck the coupe's windshield in front of the driver. The car swerved left and skidded to a stop. Gravel flew through the air and pelted Harrison and his car.

Three, four.

Twice more he fired into the coupe's front-seat area.

Harrison jumped into the Dodge and started the engine. At the far end of the lot, the young couple entered the red coupe.

Harrison slammed the transmission lever into drive and stomped down hard on the accelerator.

THIRTY ONE

Fight or Flight?

General Stone, furious, sat at his underground desk, deep below the ARDCom surface buildings. The Saint Mary Project was within days of conducting the most important mission in its history, and failure surrounded him. Failure was unacceptable. He struggled to maintain his composure.

Professor Moresby sat across from him, a smug expression on his face. The professor portrayed no hint of strain, no weakness.

When an irritating knock came at Stone's office door, interrupting his meeting, the general gave a firm, but calm response. "Enter."

James Evans walked in and stood next to Professor Moresby.

"Well?" General Stone said.

"Janice is in no condition right now to be scanned," James said. "Schmidt believes one more day, perhaps longer."

"So you have nothing to report?"

"Nope, nada."

Stone sighed and looked again at an e-mail on his computer screen. The message relayed some sketchy details about an FBI agent named Sheraton who absconded with Major Blair's dental records in Wichita. After he read the final portion of the message about an accident with the train, Stone typed a quick reply ordering a check of local hospitals and the airport for an FBI agent named either Holcomb or Sheraton.

"Problems, General?" Professor Moresby said, his sarcastic tone failing to escape General Stone.

"Nothing that we won't have wrapped up soon enough. But you know what might help? Why don't you meet with Dr. Schmidt? Two heads will certainly be better than one when helping Janice recover sufficiently for our use."

"I couldn't agree more," Moresby said, rising from his chair. He looked at James and then said, "Maybe we can talk later? Hmm?"

James nodded politely and then sat in the empty chair. "What now, sir?"

Stone rubbed his face. His features softened. They firmed up again when he spoke. "I am finding it hard to know who to trust anymore. Take Moresby, for example. He's been here forever, he's neck deep in the upcoming operation, and he's going around as if nothing is wrong. His closest ally, General Taylor, has vanished at the same time a major security breach is threatening to swallow us whole."

Stone paused and leaned back. Staring somewhere just below the hybrid's neck, he spoke again. "I don't mean to unburden myself on you or cause you to doubt my ability in any way. On the contrary, I just want you to know how much I appreciate your hard work. I'm finding a true sense of resolve and loyalty in you that many of my other colleagues seem to lack. And in one particular case, those deficiencies have brought about a major crisis. We all thought he was loyal. Just demonstrates that even the most trusted aren't, or shouldn't be, above suspicion." Stone shook his head. "And to think, less than a week before his official retirement, too." His head kept shaking. When it stopped, Stone had stood and moved over to the corner of his desk, where he sat and looked James squarely in the eyes. "Find General Taylor and find out what he's done and what his plans are."

"Yes, sir."

"I don't care how you do it."

"Yes, sir."

"Meet again with our source in Las Vegas. He and a security team are arranging to bring in this police officer, Ridley. I want him isolated and under our positive control until we obtain Protocol One authorization. Scan him again. I don't care if you send him into seizures—get more from him. We must find and stop Taylor at all costs."

"I'm on my way."

As James exited, the telephone on Stone's desk rang. Hearing the news from Colonel Ritter in Tucson, Stone clenched his fists. Through gritted teeth he said, "You lost him? Inexcusable, Colonel!"

Stone kicked his blue leather office chair, slamming it into a metal filing cabinet.

"What do you mean he became suspicious?"

Eyeing another target, Stone picked up a pencil from his desk and snapped it in half.

"Return here now, Colonel...Gunfire?...Then bring the body and car back here with you. We'll dispose of it...Yes, surveillance on Harrison's apartment and office."

Stone gripped a desk lamp. He wanted to yank it from its power outlet and throw it against the wall, but refrained.

"Just get the fuck back here!"

The windows of the Travelodge's rooms vibrated as an airliner clamored into the night sky from nearby Tucson International Airport. From inside one of the second-floor rooms, Harrison listened to the noise move farther away until it became imperceptible. Lights out and curtains drawn, a pale glow from the street and parking lot lights below crept in from behind the curtains. Harrison sat on the bed, angry, wondering what went wrong.

During the escape from the park, he had concentrated on evasion. Harrison had ditched the Dodge at the Tucson Mall, and he'd reached the motel by taxi.

Now, a rush of anger engulfed him. Mostly, he was mad at himself, but betrayal fueled his growing rage.

Ritter.

Harrison recalled what little Ritter had told him.

It became obvious to Harrison that his adversaries knew Holcomb was involved. Merely by Ritter's presence, it was clear they also knew an anonymous informant was Harrison's contact.

How did they find out?

Another plane's ascent disrupted his concentration. As the sound dissipated, he felt the immediate need to contact Ridley. He reached for the telephone on the nightstand. Reluctantly, he switched on the table lamp and then dialed the information operator for Las Vegas. The operator connected him to the Las Vegas Metropolitan Police Department. After a few transfers, Harrison finally spoke with a dispatcher who could pass a message to Ridley.

"Just tell him that Wes Hiatt called, and it's very urgent that I speak with him. It's regarding his late brother-in-law. He can reach me on my cell."

Harrison hung up the phone. Next, he called Holcomb's cell phone, but it went to voice mail. He provided a previously agreed on duress signal: "Hey, buddy, we need to check out that new club soon. Call me, Bubba."

Uselessness seeped into Harrison's consciousness, making him feel heavy, unable to move. Guilt approached him next, guilt about endangering his friends.

Harrison lay back onto the bed. His whole body ached. He lay there for several seconds until another realization came to him. Sitting up, he wondered if Saint Mary had captured Echo Tango.

Whoever he was.

His capture could explain how Ritter knew Harrison relied on an anonymous informant and about Holcomb's participation. Harrison presumed his adversaries had likely acquired these details through interrogation.

ET's probably dead by now.

With his informant eliminated, resolution of the case was entirely up to him.

I'm a weak link.

Saint Mary existed. Harrison no longer doubted this. They had eliminated others: FBI agent Eugene Chamberlain, five Roswell MPs, the airman from Nellis, Eric Gonzales, Major Blair, and...

God knows who else since 1947.

Harrison's stomach sank. The list could easily include Ridley, Holcomb, and himself. He believed they would kill anyone.

Shit!

And all he could do was wait.

Exiting the service elevator soon after eleven o'clock, Ridley walked through the police station and made his way to the front desk area. Once there, he saw Officer Ferris waving at him from the watch commander's office.

"What did you need?" Ridley said.

"You got a phone message," Ferris said, handing Ridley a pink message pad.

Ridley took the note and read it.

"By the way, Nick, some of us are getting together at Mobley's for a little celebrating. You interested? I could give you a lift if you need one."

Ridley stared at Ferris. Memories of the missing audio records came to mind. "No thanks, I've got some family responsibilities to attend to."

"Sure, I understand. Maybe some other time then, huh?" Ferris patted Ridley on the shoulder and walked out of the room.

Ridley watched him leave. Once Ferris was out of view, he headed for the locker room to change. Although he wanted to call Harrison from the station, he decided to wait until he reached the safety of his apartment.

After changing clothes, Ridley drove home on his own motorcycle. An unusual rattling noise had been emanating from his Suzuki Intruder ever since he'd helped Harrison escape in the desert. Unlike the persistent impression that he could do little to nothing about Eric's death—an enigmatic notion that infiltrated his normal sense of duty from somewhere behind the shadow of his subconscious—he knew exactly how to address the bike's rattle. A good mechanic he knew would be available after Christmas. At the very least, he could get *that* fixed.

In the meantime, his family needed him.

Ridley pulled into the parking area at his apartment complex and cruised into a space. He tapped his back pocket. His badge was there. Running a hand along his waistline assured him his gun rested in a holster there.

From the bottom of the stairs, he noticed that someone was waiting for him just outside of his apartment. Moving closer, hand on gun, Ridley realized who stood before him. Recognizing the man, he managed a smile and laugh.

"Ho, ho, ho, merrrrry Christmaaaassss," Lieutenant Walter Maxwell said.

Ridley laughed again. "Lieutenant, what are you doing here?"

"Aren't you going to wish me a merrrrry Christmaaaassss, Nick?" Maxwell wobbled, and then sat down, leaning against Ridley's front door. Maxwell wore a Santa Claus hat. Askew, the hat looked as if it was ready to fall off at any moment. Maxwell also gripped a carton of eggnog in one hand and half-full bottle of rum in the other.

"Of course. Merry Christmas, sir."

"Oh please, Nick, Nick, Nick..." Maxwell paused for a belch to pass. "You can call me Walter."

Noticing Maxwell trying to stand, Ridley moved forward, saying, "Okay, let me help you, Walter."

"Oops," Maxwell said upon seeing the Santa hat fall to the ground. He frowned.

"I'll get it." Ridley grabbed the hat. He struggled to replace it on Maxwell's swaying head, but managed to do so after a couple of attempts.

"There you go, Santa, but shouldn't you be home getting ready for the big day? It's almost Christmas Eve, you know."

"Nuts to that, home is where Mrs. Claus is."

"And how is your wife?"

"She kicked me out. Don't ever, ever get married, Nick."

Ridley had never heard that Maxwell's marriage was troubled, but was not surprised. Many cops made for lousy husbands. "I'm really sorry to hear that."

"This vacation sucks. Wanted to go to Florida, but noooo...Want a drink?"

Looking at his apartment's front door, Ridley thought about calling Harrison, and then realized how much Maxwell needed assistance. "How did you end up here? You didn't drive, did you?"

After vaporous laughter, Maxwell said in a low voice, "I had to. Santa can't fly without his reindeer. Shhh...You won't give me a ticky, Nicky?"

"Nope, but you're lucky you didn't have an accident. Come in, Walter."

"Thanks, Nick. You're a real saint. I really hoped I could talk to you about this."

Ridley guided him through the front door, saying, "I hope I can help."

Once inside, Maxwell looked around. "Where's the pisser?"

"Not far. Straight through there." Ridley pointed to an alcove next to the bedroom door.

While Maxwell carefully set the rum and eggnog on the coffee table and then went into the bathroom, Ridley walked into the kitchen. He pulled a phone book out from a cabinet and thumbed through it until he found the section for taxi service. He paused.

Why would Harrison call?

He looked at the front door.

No, "Hiatt" called. That's a signal.

Ridley had left the door unlocked. Shaking his head, Ridley set the phone book aside and then walked to the front door, locking it. Turning around, he saw Maxwell reappear and zip up his fly.

Dropping onto the couch, Maxwell said, "Care for that drink now, Nick?"

Ridley glanced at the rum and started to shake his head.

"Oh come on, join your boss in a toast to the holidays."

"Well, maybe some eggnog." Ridley grabbed two clean glasses from the dishwasher, and then joined Maxwell in the living room.

"It's all yours. I've had too much of it already. Getting too fat. Like my wife."

"I'll pour." Ridley filled one glass with eggnog, but was unable to serve the rum.

Maxwell swiped the bottle away and raised it in a toast. "Here's to a long life, without a nagging wife."

Ridley raised his glass and sipped the eggnog. Its taste and smell provided him with the first tangible reminder that Christmas was at hand. He accepted it, letting the reminder stir fond memories of a holiday he always enjoyed.

"Here, have some more before it spoils," Maxwell said, topping off Ridley's glass with more eggnog. After filling Ridley's glass, Maxwell took a swig of rum, and then said, "Wouldn't want it to spoil. Just because I work a lot, doesn't mean I've spoiled anything."

"Is that the problem? Because if it is, we can talk more about that, Walter."

His head bowed, Maxwell suckled the bottle.

Ridley repeated his inquiry. "You want to talk about it?"

"Talk about what?"

"Your wife, she kicked you out."

"Oh yeah, what a bitch. Don't you ever get married, kid."

"So you've said." Ridley took another pleasant drink of eggnog, and then said, "But this isn't about me. How long have you been married?"

"Just shortly before we started fighting," Maxwell said, smiling. He leaned back into the couch and placed his feet on the coffee table. Balancing his drink on his chest, he said, "She doesn't understand what it's like to be a cop. You know how it is. We bring it home with us. Ain't right, but it just is. Says I talk to her like I'm interrogating a suspect."

"And having seen you do that, I can see why she'd be pissed."

"So emotional too. Everything's a melodrama. Damn cat's ear mites."

"You have a cat?"

"She has a cat. Can I help it if the cat's ear mites don't upset me like they do her?"

Ridley suppressed a yawn. "Uh-huh."

"We deal with so much shit. Can she really expect me to get upset over ear mites? Didn't want the cat in the first place. Now it's breaking up our damn marriage. Nick, you getting any of this?"

Opening his eyes, Ridley said, "Sorry, I guess I'm more tired than I thought. Walter, a cat can't break up a marriage."

"Well, this cat is."

"No, no, no." Ridley scratched the back of his head.

"I just don't see why she gets so emotional all the time."

"See, that's the paradox that most cops have to deal with in their personal relationships. Here's how I see it..." Feeling warm, Ridley paused and removed his coat. "She gets upset because she feels like you don't care about her."

"I care. I care a lot."

"I know you do, but chances are you don't show it." Ridley yawned and felt dizzy. "Uh, it's not something you do on purpose. You are right, cops do deal with a lot of shit. We shield ourselves from it by desensitizing our emotions." Ridley closed his eyes.

"What do I have to do to make this work? I mean, there's been a lot of water under the bridge. I don't want to give up, but sometimes I feel like, maybe, there's no choice."

As Ridley breathed heavier now, his next words came in spurts. "You have to, have to, not all that water under the bridge." Weakening, Ridley mustered what strength he could. "Not all of it was bad. Rebuild on the good." He opened his eyes.

Maxwell stood next to the front door, unlocking it.

"Don't do that, Walter."

"It's okay, Nick. How do you feel?"

"Dizzy. Whoa."

The front door opened.

Fight or flight?

In an instant, Ridley's heart raced. He tried turning on the seat, but lost his balance and fell to the floor.

Carpet fibers tickled his nose hairs. Cold air swept across his face along with the smell of leather and shoe polish. He opened his eyes and saw black boots. Through feelings of nauseated sickness, he heard the front door close. Male voices came next. Catching muffled fragments of their calm utterances, Ridley heard "All clear...He's armed... Nobody else...Headquarters...Isolation."

Then, a black gloved hand, *or boot,* pushed him onto his side.

"Here, Nick, let me give you a hand with that."

Fight or flight?

He smelled rum, felt a warm exhalation on his cheek. Maxwell knelt beside him. His large frame obscured the others.

Fight!

Ridley's rage exploded. His fist hit Maxwell squarely in his crotch, sending him bowling over into the coffee table. Ridley rolled, drawing his gun from the holster.

"No guns!" It sounded like Maxwell. "No!"

Confusion. A muffled kick sent Ridley onto his back. His gun was gone, thrown from his hand. A red puddle formed on the carpet next to him. "Oh, God, no."

The voice again. "It's not authorized. Oh, damn."

Ridley panted and heard ringing in his ears. He tried to speak, but could not. He saw men, in black, holstering their weapons. One had a silencer.

The voice came again. "Find the casing and the bullet if it came out. We got work to do."

Ridley's lungs heaved. The blackness spread. He pressed his arms against his stomach, tightening himself ever further into a panting, bleeding ball.

THIRTY TWO

Death Warrants

Professor Moresby looked at his watch. At nearly three in the morning on Christmas Eve, he remained alert. After decades with Saint Mary, his routine had been a fog of late nights, odd hours, and little sleep, so this night was no different from the thousands that had come before.

General Stone, on the other hand, faced utter exhaustion. Red, glazed eyes hovered above stark black circles. His pupils seemed fixed on a single point.

Moresby noticed Stone reacted solely to audible stimuli and maneuvered with stiff mechanical movements as they walked through Saint Mary's underground complex at Wright-Patterson Air Force Base.

Stone led Moresby to a secluded communications office, a compartment reserved for class-five security clearance conversations with project members located elsewhere. Once inside the secure office, Stone activated a video conferencing console. Both men placed their right hands on biometric panels next to a keyboard. The panel scanned their hands, and then General Stone punched several buttons on the keyboard. They waited for a response. The monitor glowed, and a blue screen appeared that displayed the emblem of the US Department of Defense.

"Pentagon communications control, how may I direct?" a computer-simulated voice said over the speakers in the room.

"ARDCom. Class-five link to project office, flash multi," Stone said.

"Clearance and access codes?"

"From General Randolph Stone and Professor Francis Moresby, to the chairman. Priority access codes, 'Drum Roll' and 'Skywriter.'"

"Thank you. I will connect your call."

The image on the monitor's screen faded, and the face of Saint Mary's working-group chairman replaced the DOD emblem and blue screen. The chairman nodded at the two men.

"Good morning, Dennis," Moresby said.

"Hello, gentlemen," the chairman said. "Let's get right to it. The Circle expects a briefing from me very soon so they can enjoy some of the Christmas holiday with their families. General Stone, what's the status on the security situation?"

Stone cleared his throat and then said, "Our security team in Las Vegas is moving in to take the police officer into custody. Thus far, our effort to find and bring in Special Agent Arthur Holcomb has met with negative results. He is in possession of Major Blair's civilian dental records. We've contacted the FBI through official channels notifying them of our concerns that Holcomb has essentially gone rogue and is interfering with classified DOD matters. Fortunately for us, Holcomb's reputation at the FBI isn't good and perceptions are that he is unstable. These factors should aid our cover story and his retrieval. We've relocated the F-4 from Tucson and purged all records. We will destroy the plane and turn it into scrap metal. This is something that Taylor should have done a fucking long time ago."

Moresby shifted in his chair and sat upright.

"Very good, General," the chairman said. "What about other loose ends?"

"Ensuring effective security protocols to preserve our national security is a monumental task, but we are moving as fast as possible."

"More specifically, General, what about Blair's remains?" the chairman said.

"What the private investigator, William Harrison, and Holcomb left behind in the desert no longer exists. Again, something left unattended to by my fucking predecessor. As far as Blair's skull goes, we are operating under the assumption that it is with Holcomb. We hoped to determine this specifically from Harrison, but he eluded immediate capture. We believe he is hiding out in Tucson. We've sent in a security team to watch his apartment, office, and the residence of his partner, Peter Zemdarsky."

"I see," the chairman said. He fixated solely on Stone through the screen and leaned forward. "The female hybrid worked for Harrison." His voice grew impatient and harsh. "For me this confirms it. General Taylor is guilty of treason, and by implication so is the bitch hybrid."

"We continue to research the issue as it pertains to the female hybrid. Right now, our focus is to apprehend Harrison and Holcomb, and recover any evidence they may have acquired. As for Taylor, I have already dispatched James Evans to focus on locating and capturing him."

"Yes, yes, I know, and I think you need to bring him back now," the chairman said.

"Sir?" Stone said.

Moresby faced away from the monitor and General Stone to conceal his smirk.

"General, our resources in the hybrid area are perhaps a little too meager these days to risk the male hybrid on such an assignment. He needs to return and have his skills put to use on the female hybrid. She needs to be scanned immediately."

Grunting, Moresby turned and focused on the chairman. "Janice can't be successfully scanned. Have you read the latest status reports, Dennis? Dr. Schmidt says Janice continues to suffer from nonaligned synaptic closure. In other words, her mind is scrambled."

Belying his tiredness, Stone interrupted. "The male hybrid has always recovered from these tests and has never been adversely damaged. In fact, he's stronger today than he's ever been. I can recall him. That's not a problem, sir. As for the female hybrid's condition, well, isn't her condition the result we seek for the alien threat?" As Stone's words trailed off, he peered at Moresby through narrowed eye slits.

"Then why did the ELF operation fail during the last encounter? Were the systems performing properly?"

Stone edged his folded arms along the table, closer to the screen. "The system functioned within parameters, but we engaged prematurely. Follow-up tests on the experimental suggest the ship's antigravity field partially shields it against the ELF waves at a distance."

"Then where are we with ELF?"

"Sir, I have instructed Professor Moresby to design an adjunct action to supplement the ELF operation."

"Good. Professor?"

Moresby stared at the side of Stone's head and said, "Well, at the general's request I took some time to consider his predicament. I have come to the conclusion that a hybrid-assisted communication attempt will be necessary."

"We've tried hybrid communications," the chairman said, irritated.

Moresby nodded, and then said, "Yes, yes, but in those attempts we lacked an adequate understanding of the symbols from the legitimate crop circles. The aliens have also imprinted these same symbolic messages on the subconscious minds of abductees, recalled through hypnosis. The Dreamland encounter last July brought us further evidence revealed through the rapid clicking transmissions during the radio interference. Now, we have correlated the database to such a degree that the mathematical relationships in the less complex symbols are clearer. These symbols seem to be universal among the other species, and our hope is that the fifth species will also comprehend them. We can engage in a basic dialogue, using the hybrid to transmit the message and draw the ship, or ships, closer so that ELF can be effectively engaged."

"But doesn't the hybrid also have to be in close proximity to successfully transmit?" the chairman said.

“Normally, yes,” Moresby said. “Recently, however, I have acquired a piece of equipment that should not only alleviate that problem, but also enhance the focus of telepathically transmitted messages.”

The chairman looked down at a file on the desk in front of him. Without looking up, he said, “Are you referring to the ‘psychotronic generator’? I take it, then, that you have figured out how it works?”

“Oh yes, Dennis. As you recall, Dr. Semyonov from the Bulgarian Institute of Technology was instrumental not only in extricating it from Sofia, but in explaining how it functioned. Sad that he’s not still with us to see it put to good use. I never knew he had heart trouble.”

The chairman gazed at Moresby. “I am with you so far.”

“You see, the generator will allow the hybrid to project certain symbols. The specific statement has yet to be formulated. We want to encourage the unknown to land, possibly allowing us to make direct contact with its occupants. From what General Stone tells me, we would initiate ELF at the moment the gravitational field is disengaged. They would be especially vulnerable at that point.”

The chairman nodded, repeatedly, excited by what he just heard. “I’ll brief the Circle. When have you scheduled the operation?”

Stone perked up again. “A date has not been set, but we expect that it will occur within the next thirty days. In the meantime, use of the hybrids is limited pending the resolution of the security matter.”

“Uh-huh. Just one word of advice, General Stone,” the chairman said, pointing. “Handle the protocols smoothly. There may be undue scrutiny if done in haste.” He wafted his hands and then held them out toward the screen, as if he held a brick. “Our responsibility is clear. This is a crucial moment for Saint Mary. We must not disappoint the Circle. In any event, gentlemen, treat this with the highest level of secrecy, as always. Nonessentials must be strictly controlled and monitored. Even some essential personnel should be led to believe something other than the truth. Understood?”

Stone muttered an affirmative response, while Moresby sat silently. The chairman looked down at the desk in front of him and spent several seconds typing a message on the computer. A memo rolled out of the printer next to Stone, who immediately read it as it emerged from the machine. He pulled it out and set it on the table.

"Yes, sir," Stone said.

The video screen faded into a blank, blue field.

Moresby peered across the table. The memo authorizing Protocol One measures included four names: William Harrison, Arthur Holcomb, Nicholas Ridley, and his old colleague, General Edward Taylor.

God help us all.

THIRTY THREE

Welcome Back

A light from the hallway outside the infirmary was Janice's only clue that she was finally awake. Staring at the soft glow, she grew more alert. Her body reclined on a stiff bed. She tried to sit, but soon gave up. Her temples throbbed, and any movement triggered pain throughout her body. It made her queasy. Janice lay flat on the bed and took deep breaths.

What have they done?

Despite the physical pain, she sensed an unfamiliar inner strength. She felt powerful. Her mind flashed through a frenzied series of images and memories: the first time she met Harrison; her first day in college; the color red; the face of her mentor; human bones; the desert; a silver roadrunner pin; her desk at work; a bright flash in the night sky; Colonel Sam; her brother, James...

Relax, relax.

Janice closed her eyes and inhaled. Exhaling slowly, she opened her eyes. The throbbing stopped.

The room stood empty and quiet. Janice looked around and wondered how much time had passed since her brutal treatment. She turned and saw her watch on the table next to the bed, out of reach. Leaning toward the table, she tried to grab the watch. Before she could reach it, the watch flew off the table and into her waiting hand.

Four in the morning.

Janice tilted her head and raised an eyebrow. She peered around the room and saw no one.

Was it me?

A small vial on a desk near the doorway caught her attention. She looked at it and held out her hand, making an effort to visualize it in her grasp. After a couple of seconds, the vial took flight from across the room and landed in her palm. She looked at the vial in her left hand and the watch in her right hand, and then she smiled.

Janice relaxed her grip on the vial and pictured it back on the desk. After a gentle flutter, the vial departed her hand. It glided back to the desk but landed off balance and tumbled over. The vial rolled back and forth for a few seconds before its swaying ceased.

Close enough.

Janice's growling stomach interrupted her delight over her new telekinetic prowess. Feeling better, she stood, but several wires connected to her neck, chest, and forehead impeded any further progress. She also realized that only a thin, flimsy hospital gown covered her body.

She easily detached the wires, and after a brief search, Janice found her clothes in a closet and changed into them. Running her hands through her hair, she decided that, if she were fortunate enough to find something to eat in the dining facility, a shower was next on her to-do list.

Outside the infirmary, Janice walked through numerous deserted hallways before she reached the dining facility, also deserted. In the kitchen, she opened several refrigerators and storage cabinets. Inside one of the cabinets, next to several trays of butter and oversized condiment containers, sat boxes of apples and oranges. She reached into the boxes and grabbed two of each.

Janice bit into an apple and dabbed some of the juice, which ran from the corner of her mouth, with the sleeve of her sweatshirt. She took two more bites and wandered into the dining room. In the dimness, she found a seat at one of the tables. After laying the fruit out in front of her, she peeled an orange. At first, Janice found it difficult to do, but as she examined the piece of fruit further, she found a small notch in its rind. She pushed her index finger into the surface of the orange and pulled a large portion of the peel away. The inside of the orange felt dry and rough on her fingertips. Janice paused, and then set the orange aside.

More rapid thoughts and images emerged in her consciousness, each racing to reveal themselves. Janice steadied herself and concentrated, hoping to make sense of them: sunrise, dental X-rays, Las Vegas, airplanes, teddy bear, gunfire...

"Wait, concentrate," Janice said aloud.

A steady flow of scenes returned: gravel, a black car, a man firing a handgun, pain...

Janice reached down and rubbed her right leg. She focused on the man firing the gun, and she felt...betrayed.

"Where are you now?" Janice said, now recognizing the man was Harrison.

Janice searched for an answer, tried to imagine Harrison's voice reassuring her, but no clear images appeared. After a deep breath, she tried again. This attempt also revealed nothing, just darkness.

Janice returned to her regular quarters, winding through empty hallways illuminated by occasional exit signs. After rounding the corner of the final hallway, she stopped in her tracks. At the far end of the hallway, past her room, a lone guard stood watch. The soft light from an exit sign illuminated the rifle on his shoulder. Janice waited for several seconds, watching him. She got the impression the guard was numb with boredom, and was, for all practical purposes, "zoned out" while he stood watch.

Convinced the guard had not detected her presence, she visualized him sitting down and resting his head. After a few seconds, the guard took two or three steps and sat down at a nearby desk. He set the rifle aside, folded his arms on top of the desk, and then laid his head down.

Janice smiled and then strolled toward her quarters. After stepping inside, she closed and locked the door behind her. After allowing her eyes to adjust to the dim light inside her room, she noticed her unmade bed and the outline of a desk next to it. Janice stepped forward and reached for the desk lamp, fumbling a bit before turning it on. She aimed the light toward her bed, and then pulled out a suitcase from underneath it.

Most of the clothes from the suitcase landed on the bed, making just enough room for her to reach in and grasp the roadrunner pin Harrison had given her. She had felt the need to hide it inside her suitcase after her first day back underground.

Putting her fingers around the gift, she realized something was different about it. For a moment, she believed she had grabbed the wrong item. Pulling her hand out of the suitcase, she saw a single sheet of notepaper wrapped around the pin. She unwrapped it, revealing the pin, which she clasped with her right hand. After further unfolding the paper, she found a brief handwritten note scribbled on it that said, "Janice, Harrison is on the run. Orders are to keep you from leaving. Situation under control, but may turn to shit fast. I will help you and Harrison if I can. Stay focused."

"What?"

Janice reread the note, not understanding who inside Saint Mary would want to help. Regardless, the note bolstered her sense that she was not alone.

But it could also be a trap.

Standing, she ripped up the note and then walked into the bathroom. Flushing the toilet, she dropped the bits of paper into the swirling water, watching them disappear.

But it doesn't feel like one.

THIRTY FOUR

Room 117

Harrison paced and cursed inside his room at the Travelodge. He managed to track down Ridley's home telephone number through an obscure, two-year-old Internet posting for a ten-kilometer charity run. A point of contact for the run, Ridley helped organize some of the event's activities. But after repeated unanswered calls and no return calls from Ridley, Harrison feared for the young officer and struggled to contain his feelings of regret and guilt for involving him.

All day long, hour by excruciating hour, he ran different scenarios though his head.

Why hasn't Art called?

The keys to the safe-deposit box and storage unit alternated between sitting on the hotel room's dresser, where they sat now, and resting in his sweaty palm.

Risk getting the evidence?

Harrison needed help, someone to turn to. By sunset, Christmas Eve, he had called directory assistance for the number. Although fairly certain he had the right number, he hesitated dialing it. Harrison sought to avoid endangering others.

He stood, and staring at himself in the mirror, he realized that he had on the same clothes he put on yesterday morning before taking Holcomb to the airport. His wrinkled white dress shirt remained tucked into gray slacks. The suit coat, along with the tie, lay on the chair next to him. The holstered Colt .45 stayed strapped to his black dress belt. Next to it, his cell phone hung inside a clip-on case.

Unexpectedly, the thought of reaching out to Zemdarsky for help led Harrison to recall holiday memories. The thoughts gave him a welcome distraction from his current circumstances.

Harrison's memories of past Christmases *without* his own family usually made him feel sorrow. But over the years, the generous and kind Zemdarsky family eased those sufferings by including Harrison in all of their holiday celebrations and get-togethers. Now, Harrison pictured Pete and Mandy in their son's living room in California. Three generations of Zemdarskys surrounding a Christmas tree. He could almost hear the wrapping paper ripping and tearing, flying every direction, with Beano right in the middle of all the action. His sentimentality surprised him, but he embraced it, and what little embarrassment he felt faded without much effort. In the dim, quiet sanctuary of his motel room, Harrison contemplated these and other pleasant thoughts, culminating with reflections on Janice's smiling face, beautiful intelligence, and warm personality.

But somewhere in the sliver of time between hearing the postcard slip under the door and the release of the Colt's thumb safety, his fleeting reprieve disappeared. He rotated and knelt, pointing the .45 at the door. Dropping in behind a wood dresser, Harrison strained to listen for sounds outside.

The rush of blood slamming through his arteries with the full force of his huge heart hammered away at his head and chest. But the hand holding the gun remained steady. Eyes locked on the door, the anticipation of a final firefight surged his respiration and inflamed his nostrils. Rising heat from inside wetted his clothes and brow with salty sweat.

He waited.

Nothing. No battering ram, not so much as a knock, either. No sounds, no voices.

And yet there he crouched, cowering in a corner of his motel room. He felt more manipulated than ever and *so goddamn, motherfucking useless!*

Standing, gun still pointing at the door, Harrison moved forward. A quick retrieval of the postcard with his free hand preceded a hasty glance at the image on the front of it.

Jesus fuckin' Christ!

He shoved the card with the Jefferson Memorial on it into his pocket.

He unlocked the door next, then knelt. The door's knob twisted under his sweaty grip as he opened it to peer outside. He looked right at the second-floor landing, down at the parking lot below, and then left at the remainder of the second-floor landing and more of the parking lot below.

No one.

He closed the door and locked it.

Harrison backed into the room until he reached an area between the corner of a wall by the bathroom and the still unmade king-sized bed, and then he pulled out the postcard. Once settled into his cover, Harrison looked at the card and a saw a handwritten message. This time, however, the name that followed the message was not "Echo Tango." Reading the name several times, Harrison's consciousness flashed to an incident many years ago, to the Aurora case, to the time when an air force general and his security team in Hemet California nearly shot and killed him, Holcomb, and other FBI personnel.

The memory and the name, Edward Taylor, forced Harrison's teeth together into a gritty, angry clench. "Fucking asshole."

The scent of witch hazel coming from the card made Harrison even more angry and frustrated.

"How would he know about that?"

Harrison shook his head and read the short message on the card: "One more errand. Come to room 117 and I'll explain. No harm will come to you."

Harrison knew what the underlined "you" meant. Taylor had demonstrated all too well on the Aurora case a willingness to use violence as a primary enforcement option.

But the postcard also raised another obvious question for Harrison.

"How the hell did he find me?"

Harrison held no clear reason to trust Taylor. No rationale could get him to put on his coat, collect his keys and wallet, and walk downstairs. Anger did not do it either. Curiosity was an afterthought.

The lump in his throat could have been from sadness.

But, as he stood there in front of room 117, ready to turn the knob and meet his informant, Harrison knew that sadness was just a thin layer, a tiny core wrapped inside a thick mantle of regret. He had missed so much, and like it or not, behind Taylor's manipulation, some very important answers waited for him.

He swallowed hard, hoping for clarity, and for purpose.

Just before stepping into the unlocked room, Harrison drew the Colt and held it at his side. He nudged inward and saw Taylor, a vulnerable, unarmed target sitting in a padded cloth chair facing the door about midway through the room. He too looked forlorn, his hands resting in clear view on the chair's arms.

Harrison closed the door behind him and then raised his gun. "You don't mind if I look around, do you?"

Taylor nodded. "Please do, Mr. Harrison. But I assure you, I am alone and you are safe for the moment. And we have much to discuss."

"And for the moment, just shut the fuck up."

THIRTY FIVE

Margaret O'Donnell, FBI

For the fifth time in less than an hour, Maggie O'Donnell checked her watch. The Christmas Eve party in Old Town Alexandria, Virginia, was crowded, noisy, and just plain dull. She wanted little to do with this particular crowd. Everyone tried so hard to promote their connections, real or fabricated, to the Washington, DC, scene.

"What they're really after is good parking," she said to herself, looking at the morass.

She was under no obligation to attend the party in the first place. But, as it was with most of these get-togethers, Maggie attended out of hope, and, like it or not, she was connected to the Washington scene. An FBI forensic scientist by trade, she also taught, wrote columns, advocated for environmental causes, and, most notably, painted artwork whose creations had found their way into some of the most prominent of Washington, DC, homes. Maggie also served as a board member for several regional arts organizations.

Maggie searched for substance, and managed to thrive on what little came her way or what she found by *hoping* for it. In her early forties, Maggie O'Donnell was involved, active, still single, and optimistic about people but impatient with those who carried *no soul.*

Maggie's sofa mate interrupted her meandering thoughts. "No, seriously, Dr. O'Donnell, Georgetown University most definitely has many professional opportunities that you should consider. Most definitely."

At the moment, Maggie preferred career advice from the potted plant sitting next to her. At the very least, she had known the plant about ten minutes longer than she had known this Georgetown dean.

"So you've told me," Maggie said.

"Most definitely. You're in the prime of your life, after all." The dean's subtle and clever caress of her kneecap with the back side of his fingertips accompanied the sultry tone in his voice.

Maggie set her wine glass on the end table next to the sofa, bid a silent adieu to her plant friend, and stood up. She saw the dean begin to rise, but she cut him off. "No, don't get up. I am late for an appointment."

"Really?" The dean said, looking confused.

"Most definitely."

Following the path she had charted after her arrival at the party, Maggie maneuvered toward the exit. Patience exhausted, she grabbed her coat from the rack next to the door and reached for the knob.

"Oh! Oh, Maggie! You're not leaving so soon?"

The pleasant, cheerful voice from behind reminded her of the opening pitch from a solicitous telemarketer, and it was just too loud to ignore. Maggie could not pretend that she had not heard the woman's voice, so she turned around, smiling.

"Ah, Gretchen, the party looks like a hit, as always," Maggie said. "But it is Christmas Eve, and I have so many gifts yet to wrap and a house full of relatives in Richmond I have to face tomorrow." Maggie put her hand on the doorknob and turned it.

"But this won't take long. You haven't spoken a word to Alfredo tonight. I wanted so much for you two to get acquainted. He's a real success story. An inspiration."

Maggie looked at her hostess, a development director for an arts coalition that promoted artists-in-residence programs. Alfredo was their latest shooting star. She opened the door just enough to feel the cold outside air press through the opening. "It will have to wait, sorry. Thanks for having me over."

"All right, dear, have a merry Christmas, and plan on attending my New Year's Eve celebration. But I can't guarantee Alfredo will still be available." Gretchen winked and chortled.

"Barring anything unforeseen, I'll be here. Well, Merry Christmas." Maggie waved and stepped outside.

A steady northwesterly wind scoured the frozen surface of the Potomac River, and a fresh blanket of snow covered the streets and sidewalks in Old Town Alexandria. Maggie walked two blocks along the waterfront to her parked car, a red MINI Cooper, located on a cul-de-sac next to a row of fashionable townhomes. From the trunk, she pulled out a scraper and started with the roof. An imaginary line bisected the surface. She brushed fore and aft. Next came the rear and front windows, followed by trunk, hood, and bumpers. After the side windows, she cleared the mirrors, lights, and turn signals. Afterward, she paused to examine her work.

"You always were thorough," a male voice commented from behind her.

At first startled, Maggie then returned to her work after recognizing the voice belonged to Art Holcomb. She put the scraper in the trunk. Holcomb moved from behind a sidewalk-buckling oak tree and onto the curb next to her car. He held a muddy backpack.

"Let me guess, Maggie, you have a house full of relatives to deal with and gifts to wrap?"

"You know me too well."

"Scary, huh? How's milady Gretchen? Still trying to fix you up good and proper?"

"You don't scare me, you just annoy me. Sometimes, anyway. Not now, but sometimes." Maggie paused and inspected Holcomb's clothes and appearance. "You look dirty. You probably stink. Somebody beat you up?"

"A freight train ran into me." Holcomb pointed at Maggie's car. "I don't mean to be forward, but can you help me to your car, such as it is, and let me stay at your place tonight?"

Maggie stepped forward. In addition to Holcomb's tattered, torn, and dirty clothes, he also endured multiple scratches, scrapes, and bruises. His lips were pale and chapped.

And yet, he's smiling.

Maggie helped Holcomb into her MINI, saying, "Don't make fun of my car." Once seated herself, Maggie set the heat, checked her mirrors, switched on the headlamps, and headed for the Beltway. She glanced at her passenger. "You asleep already?"

"Huh? No, no, just resting my eyes," Holcomb said, yawning.

"Judging from your appearance, I'd say the scuttlebutt is true."

Holcomb lifted his head from the passenger-side window. "What scuttlebutt?"

"That you're in trouble with the brass."

"As if that's anything new."

"I think it's serious this time. The orders are to detain you on sight. Any reason why I shouldn't do just that?"

Holcomb gazed at her with his best impression of a sad puppy-dog face he could muster. "Because you love me?"

"Huh, you wish. You're going to have to do much better than that, Art."

Holcomb smiled; even his teeth looked dingy. "All right, all right, Maggie, let me ask you, have you ever been to Wichita this time of year?"

THIRTY SIX

I Enjoy History, Keep Going

Taylor remained quiet while Harrison finished the search of the room and of him. After checking the door one last time to ensure it remained locked and chained, Harrison holstered the .45 and sat on the edge of the bed near Taylor. He exhaled a cleansing, relaxing breath.

"Have you seen today's paper?" Taylor said.

"Fuck you, General. I've been too busy to keep up on the latest headlines."

"Take a look." Taylor pointed to a newspaper on the table next to them. "It's an interesting story. It includes your friend, Officer Ridley."

"Hand it to me, and then sit in the chair next to the window. I'd rather you get shot at than me."

Taylor complied.

Harrison looked at the front page of the *Tucson Sun Times.* An air force file photo of Taylor accompanied a headline that read, "Top Officer Missing, Linked to Drug Probe."

"There's no mention of you or Agent Holcomb in that story yet, but they do allude to you two. Go ahead, read it," Taylor said.

Intermittent glances at Taylor interrupted Harrison's review of the article, but he noticed right away that a secondary headline related to the story read, "Also Implicated in Disappearance of Las Vegas Police Officer."

"Ridley's missing?" Harrison said.

"That's what the newspaper says."

Harrison read on and learned that between statements from air force investigators, police detectives, and descriptions of seized evidence, the story presented a remarkably plausible account of a drug trafficking scheme orchestrated by General Edward Taylor, a former pilot, squadron commander, and, most recently, intelligence officer. Portions of the story indicated air force authorities had Taylor under scrutiny for some time and suspected he had connections to both civilian and government trafficking associates. Las Vegas police officials reported the case of the missing police officer to the air force after they found an empty bottle of scotch with Taylor's fingerprints inside Officer Ridley's bloodstained apartment.

"Christ, is he dead?" Harrison said.

"Judging from the story, I'm guessing he put up a struggle. But I don't know if he is dead or not, Mr. Harrison. Now I'm the cover story. Just like Major Blair had a cover story. They must have found the scotch bottle in my house. They would have plenty to pick from."

"So they know you betrayed them."

"Most certainly. Whether you like me or not, we are in this together."

Harrison tossed the newspaper on the bed and paced a few steps away from the general.

"You have every reason to be upset," Taylor said. "But there are important matters that still need tending."

"You bet there are," Harrison said, turning to face Taylor.

"Then let's discuss our situation."

Harrison pulled up a chair near Taylor and sat down. "How did you know I would be here?"

"I've had audio surveillance on your apartment and office for quite some time."

"You're a bastard. For how long?"

"Long enough to know that your client Elena Zinser and her husband, Chuck, are getting divorced. But more importantly, I overheard you and Holcomb discuss plans before he left for Wichita. You both agreed this motel would be your fallback point if something went wrong on your end. By the way, has he contacted you?

"No." Harrison's patience wore thin. "How am I supposed to know this isn't some elaborate scheme to reel in me and Art? But instead of using Ritter this time they're using you?"

"Colonel Ritter?" Taylor smiled and said, "Hmm, interesting choice on their part."

"I wouldn't describe it that way. Look, I don't know about you, but I don't like being stabbed in the back by people I thought I could trust—"

"You escaped, didn't you? You escaped from Dreamland and from the park."

The comments caught Harrison off guard, and he hesitated before continuing.

"I guess I was lucky."

"Luck had some small part in it, yes."

"Look, how the fuck did they know I had an anonymous informant? Huh? How? And while we're at it, maybe you can tell me a little about what I saw in the desert, and I'm not just talking about Blair's dried-up remains and skull. And—" Harrison stopped, knowing what he really wanted to ask, but he threw his hands up and said, "First things first. How'd they know?"

Taylor sat up straight. His green eyes with their cockpit-perfect vison focused on Harrison. "They learned it from you."

"From me?"

"Yes, but not directly, though. I blame myself for that. I should have revealed certain information about their intelligence-gathering methods to you sooner. Probably happened in Vegas; Ridley must have been scanned."

"Scanned?"

"Yes. What did you tell Ridley?"

"Not much, I—" Harrison's stomach dropped. He remembered the conversation he had with Ridley at his father's home in which he disclosed his work with an anonymous informant.

"You must have told him. It's unfortunate, but, like I said, I blame myself."

"When you say, 'scanned,' what do you mean?"

Taylor put his right palm on his forehead and rubbed the front of his short, cropped hair. "Perhaps I should start at the beginning?"

To Harrison, the general's request seemed genuinely respectful, as if he were still trying to sort out all the details himself, while at the same time trying to convey his sensitivity toward Harrison's rapidly diminishing patience. "Go ahead," Harrison said, leaning back into his chair. "Don't leave anything out."

Relieved, Taylor folded his hands on his lap and said, "I have spent the last fifteen years assigned to the Saint Mary Project. Officially, Saint Mary does not exist. But concealed within the Air Research and Development Command at Wright-Patterson Air Base, it has a reach that extends around the world, and into history."

"I enjoy history—keep going."

"As I have explained, the Roswell incident was indeed the result of an accident involving two alien craft. The exact reason for this accident is still unknown, at least by me. The Army Air Corps managed the recovery, survey, and research operations, but the Department of Defense took over those responsibilities following the passage of the National Security Act of 1947.

"A secret unit within DOD that combined military and civilian specialists was assigned the task of analyzing the wreckage and the alien life forms. A special security group was assembled and assigned to protect, with extreme prejudice, the new project, code-named Saint Mary. Financing channeled through accounts fronted and maintained by the newly created Central Intelligence Agency. Information was, and still is, highly compartmentalized. Only a small group of people known as the Circle are aware of the complete details."

"The Circle? Who are the members?"

Taylor sighed and shook his head. "I do not know."

"Bullshit."

"It's the truth. My project assignment was to a working group that serves the Circle. The chairman of the working group acts as a liaison with the Circle. He knows the identity of that body's members. I do not."

"What's the chairman's name?"

"Dennis."

"And does Dennis have a last name?"

"I'm sure he does, but I have not been made aware of it."

Harrison waved his hand. "Go on."

"Ordered by President Truman, the Saint Mary Project was implemented with a twofold mission: one, total secrecy maintained at any cost, and two, the exploitation and understanding of alien technology and biology. This second part of the mission was oriented toward the enhancement of US national security. No deviations from these particulars were allowed under any circumstances. Complete responsibility for control of the project, including applications of alien technology, rests permanently with the Circle. This unusual protocol has been maintained due to the overriding perception by those responsible that if the knowledge of such a discovery were made public, national and worldwide institutions would collapse."

"What about the Presidents since Truman? Certainly, if all of this is true, they would have—"

"Kennedy was the last to know. Harold Groom resolved that."

"Groom? His claims were true?"

"He was one of a handful of specialists over the years, yes. Groom also helped with Major Blair, and others." Taylor paused, and then said, "I thought Agent Holcomb was to contact you once he was in possession of Blair's dental records?"

"He was, but I don't even know if he has records."

"He has them."

"How would you know that?"

"The same way I knew that Colonel Ritter tried to reel you in, as you say."

"I told you that."

"The same way I know that you abandoned your car at the Tucson Mall, and that's as far as the search for you progressed, other than surveillance on your home and office."

"All right, fine, you have someone on the inside. Why the hell do you need me, anyway? You seem to have all the answers." Harrison held his breath, but anxiety found an outlet. His right leg bounced up and down.

"Let me ask you something. Were you completely forthcoming with Officer Ridley?" Harrison drew back, but before he could reply, Taylor continued. "You weren't. If you had been, things may be much worse."

"I thought I could protect him that way."

"Right. You thought you could protect him. He may be dead, but we are not. Therefore, our mission can continue. Your discretion offered us a measure of protection." Taylor leaned forward. He put a hand on Harrison's bouncing knee. Harrison looked away from the green eyes staring at him. The nervousness subsided.

Taylor continued, saying "The same methods they used against him could easily be employed against you. You wouldn't even know it was happening. While you know enough to be a weak link, keeping certain facts from you will help to protect the investigation. As to your involvement, I could just say that I was impressed with your skill as an investigator, with your devotion and instincts. Certainly, this was part of the decision, but there is a larger purpose. In time, you will find out."

The lump formed again in Harrison's throat. In a low, almost quivering voice, he said, "And this is for my protection?" He turned back to Taylor, forced himself to look directly at him. The cool, green eyes had reddened and moistened. Harrison never imagined that he could ever feel sympathy for Taylor.

With a strained voice, Taylor said, "You never had any children, did you?"

Harrison shook his head.

"Parenthood is a special experience. How we raise our children means so much in terms of our relationships with each other and the future." Taylor blinked a few times and cleared his throat. "Saint Mary has produced offspring. Like any children, their potential, their bearing, is greatly influenced by the parents. Saint Mary used the life-seed from a recovered, dying alien to create a line of alien-human hybrids. Third-generation hybrids display superior intellect, learning abilities, and telepathic and telekinetic skills. The hybrids are intended as a unique security function for the Saint Mary Project. Their physical attributes allow them to blend in, and their mental attributes allow them to scan others, such as what likely happened to Officer Ridley."

"Mind readers?"

"Yes, but much more than that. These hybrids look very human. They are also capable of mind control." Taylor emphasized his next words. "They can make people do things against their will."

"Like Eric Gonzales getting drunk and walking into traffic," Harrison said.

"And like Airman Bresch committing suicide. Would you like to see what they look like?"

Harrison nodded, and then watched Taylor retrieve a laptop computer from underneath the bed. Taylor set the computer on the bed next to them, booted it up, and then opened a video file.

The gray figure had a humanoid body, but it was far from looking human. Enclosed inside some sort of white chamber, it flailed its fragile arms and body from side to side. A humming sound, like the one Harrison had heard in the desert, buzzed at an ever-increasing volume. The louder it became, the more the creature seemed to be in agony. Eventually, it collapsed into a heap on the floor and the humming sound subsided. Soon after, a hatch opened and a blond-haired man in casual clothes entered the chamber.

"This is the third-generation male hybrid," Taylor said.

"He looks like an average Joe. Does he have a name?"

"He does. He goes by James."

This man, this hybrid named James, kicked away the gray figure's outstretched hand. He stepped back, unbuttoned his sweater, and removed a pistol from his waistline. Aiming the pistol at the figure, he said, "Aren't you going to stop me, Thirty—Seven?"

"Why?" Harrison said. "It's not a threat, it's injured, and it looks like it is dying for crying out loud."

The hybrid, James, said, "I'm waiting, and I'm not known for my patience."

Harrison watched James shoot the gray humanoid three times, two to the chest and one to the head, and then the video faded to black.

Harrison turned to Taylor. The general shook his head and pointed at the computer. "There's more."

The black screen gave way to another episode in the same white chamber as before. This time, medical technicians surrounded a woman strapped into an oversized black chair.

"The female hybrid is strapped in the chair," Taylor said.

Harrison nodded. An old woman in a white smock holding a clipboard stood next to the hybrid.

"What's her name?"

"The woman with the clipboard is Dr. Schmidt," Taylor said.

"No, I mean the—" After a sudden adjustment to the camera's lens filter and angle, the video provided Harrison with an answer. He found himself staring at Janice Evans. The filtered image was a mottled blend of hazy green, white, and black patches. It made her look so pale. Her voice was strong, though.

The revelation about Janice caused Harrison to reach for the video's stop button on the computer. But the humming sound came again, and he halted his movement. And in horror, he watched as Janice thrashed in pain until she went limp. The lights came up, and he saw technicians racing to her side with a gurney. The video faded to black and stopped.

Taylor started to speak, but Harrison put up his hands, preventing the general from saying anything.

After several seconds, Harrison said, "Is she dead too?"

"No."

"Thank God."

"She is recuperating."

Harrison lowered his head and stared at the floor.

"Janice is not at all like the male hybrid. Although brother and sister, she is most definitely on our side. On your side, William. You will see her again."

"Right now I find it hard to fucking believe I'll ever see anyone or anything outside of this motel ever again." He stood, stretching and rubbing his leg. Limping as he paced, he said, "Ritter knows about the safe-deposit box and storage unit. Although not much in the way of evidence so far, Saint Mary could have already seized everything I've put inside those."

Taylor smiled and said, "Why did you trust Ritter during your ARDCom days?"

"I don't know, he just seemed different than the rest of you. He seemed...unpretentious and friendly. Likable."

"Different from the rest of us?"

"Very much so."

"Your stored evidence, although limited, is safe for now. Let me unburden you from that worry. I do have something else I need to show you, though." Taylor retrieved a briefcase from under the bed and set it next to the laptop computer. "Holcomb, on the other hand, faces a serious a problem."

"How immediate is the threat?"

"If he reports back to duty, it will result in his death. A simple escort to headquarters to discuss procedural violations will unwittingly deliver him into the hands of the enemy. He'll disappear for a while, and then somewhere, perhaps in his own home, perhaps on the street, an accident will occur. We both know how his death will be portrayed. When he contacts you, make sure he understands that."

"I will."

"Saint Mary has yet to track him down, but they do have some leads they're going to follow. It won't take them long to look up Dr. O'Donnell. She was the one you intended to use to verify the skull was that of Major Blair, correct?"

"If that's what you heard, then she must be the one."

Taylor opened the briefcase and removed a folder. "This contains a complete dossier on James Evans, including photographs and biological data. Study his face well. If you ever see him, kill him without any hesitation and with as little forethought as possible. He must not sense what is coming. He would do the same to you."

"Is he the danger you spoke of in your first letter to me?"

"James is an afterthought when compared to the overall danger." The general's voice grew grave, somber. "Not all aspects of Saint Mary have been negative. There has been a genuine research effort aimed at understanding and communicating with the alien species. Some of the people working in this area have made great strides..."

Taylor paused, sighing; he seemed restless, agitated. He cleared his throat before continuing.

"For decades, the United States was protected from foreign invasion because of our geography. The great oceans separated us from hostile powers. When the enemy equipped itself with ICBMs, our frontier became the open sky above our heads. It was a border over which an attack could cross at any time. All of this, our entire world, could have vanished in barely an hour if men acted without reason, without regard for our posterity.

"So much fear, so much waste, comes when we abandon our more civilized qualities and values in favor of reckless pursuits. We let our lack of understanding back us into a corner. The unknown becomes our enemy. And we will destroy all that we cherish before we would admit that we were wrong.

"One of the theories that exemplifies the mind-set at Saint Mary is something that you would be very interested in. Some believe that the extraterrestrials are systematically overhauling human genetics, returning us to a more primal level. They see evidence of the aliens' success in the worldwide increase of violence, aggression, crime, racism, social stratification."

Now it was Harrison's turn to feel agitated. "What do you believe?"

"I believe there are no excuses for bad behavior. I have also come to believe that if a real extraterrestrial threat existed, we would already be dead, enslaved, or suffering in some other manner envisioned by the paranoid delusions of the Circle's members. Unfortunately, they have made a decision that could change all of that. The Circle intends to take aggressive action against the perceived threat. They are desperate, and have subordinated all functions of Saint Mary to this effort."

"What kind of action?"

"The specifics of the operation have not been made clear to me yet. What I do know is that it involves the use of ELF waves."

"ELF waves?"

"Extremely low-frequency sound waves—it's the humming sound you heard in the desert and on the video. In the desert, it was a live test against an alien ship. And as you saw on the video, their effects can be debilitating to them, making them vulnerable to more lethal, and more prosaic, weapons."

"This is how they are going to defend us? It didn't seem to work in the desert."

"Their folly has yet to fully blossom. When it does, it could very well lead to war, a war that could devastate humankind."

"But you don't know that for sure."

"In the past, our military has lost aircraft during encounters with these objects. One can reasonably presume these losses were the result of self-defense measures. Imagine what could happen if we began to succeed in disabling these craft or their occupants. If we miscalculate their intentions, as I believe we have, the repercussions could be irrevocable. We should not make this mistake. And you are an integral part of the effort to stop them."

"So I've gathered. Why are you doing this? You never struck me as the traitorous type."

"I'm not. They are the traitors."

"But you've helped them. Why stop now?"

"When you make up lies for a living, you tend to gradually forget any truth in your life. Trouble is, when you look back on such a life, as I've been doing, there are no tangible reminders that you've accomplished anything useful or constructive. I depended on my family to give me a sense of that. But I don't have a family anymore. It's like my work, all just an illusion. Nothing real. All I have is the chance to create a little truth for a change. If I can do that, I will feel as though I've helped in some small way. You may not understand."

Harrison understood. He knew exactly how Taylor felt. "What more can I do to help?"

Taylor nodded and then pulled another folder from inside the briefcase. He handed it to Harrison and said, "This will take you out of the country for a while, so you probably won't have to look over your back so much. Your flight leaves San Diego tomorrow night. You'll have to shave your beard and mustache. The fabricated visa and passport have an old FBI photo of you, before you grew the beard."

Harrison opened the folder and read the information. "Seems straightforward—why can't you just do this yourself?"

Taylor grabbed the newspaper from the bed and held it up so Harrison could see the headline and his photograph next to his face.

"Right, sorry," Harrison said. "Hard to keep it all straight."

"Besides, your undercover experience and language skills will serve us well in this matter."

"We'll see. It's been a while since I had to use them." Harrison continued to review the information in the folder and then said, "This document we're after, the one mentioned here, is it the only one that exists?"

"The only original that exists, yes."

"How did you find out it was over there?"

"I did my job."

"Are you sure it's still there? And what about the code phrases listed here? You're sure they're correct?"

"I have every reason to believe the document is still there and that the codes are correct. I am assured it will go smoothly."

Harrison flipped through the pages. "This will take three, maybe four days. Do we have that kind of time? I mean, if Holcomb can hold out for that long, and the remains are identified as Blair's—"

"They're Blair's."

"Then this next piece of evidence should give us enough to build a strong case. What do you plan to do with it?"

"We will evaluate that when we meet again. But let's just say that there are high-level political figures who will make for strong allies for us at the appropriate time."

"High-level political allies?" Harrison said, rolling his eyes.

Taylor smiled and said, "Come on, TJ, you haven't lost all faith, have you?"

Harrison shrugged and said, "No, I haven't. I guess. Where should we meet upon my return?"

"I recommend your hometown, Los Angeles. This will be convenient for another step we must take, and I would also recommend in your next communication with Holcomb that you suggest this to him."

"Any particular place?"

"Remember where you two stayed during the Rockwell audit?"

"How could I forget—we were there for a month and half."

"I will be there next Monday afternoon." From inside the briefcase, Taylor removed a DVD, another folder, and a set of keys. He set them on the table. "It's a copy of my service record and a video I made of myself. On it, I make a full and complete confession about Saint Mary, my work, and all of my lies."

"And the keys?"

"A car is parked out back for you. A blue Chevy Caprice, Nevada plates. Just park it at the airport in San Diego and use it for the drive to LA upon your return. Obviously, your firearm will have to stay behind as well, but you should be safe while out of the country. Any questions before I leave?"

"About a million of them. But here's one for you..." Harrison stepped toward the drawn curtains and tugged them open. He pointed at the sky and said, "Where do they come from?"

"The truth has finally hit you, huh? It takes a while to accept it, I know. As to where they're from, well, the more compelling question is, where did we come from?"

THIRTY SEVEN

Travels, Tactics, and Recollections

After returning to his motel room with more questions than he had before leaving it, Harrison decided to focus on the first major stage in his current assignment: getting to Russia. Although Harrison remained worried about Holcomb and Ridley, Taylor had provided him sufficient information to convince him that the best thing he could do for them and for this case was to take this next step.

When Harrison finished shaving after a long, cleansing shower, he looked at the face staring back at him from the mirror. It appeared ten years younger, surprising him. Getting dressed, just past midnight on Christmas morning, he felt reassured, refreshed, and anxious to start his journey.

As he took one last look around the room before leaving, the BlackBerry smartphone clipped to his hip vibrated. Harrison snatched the phone off his hip and read the incoming text message: "Clipping Colgate coupons, a twenty-dollar value, to send to helpful friends. Mrs. Claus working hard, as expected."

"Thank God," Harrison said, realizing Holcomb sent the message. Without hesitating, Harrison placed a call to the message's originating phone number.

After one ring, Holcomb answered the call, saying, "The bald eagle has landed."

"It's been a while since we last talked, you okay?"

“What’s past is past. Why brood about it? But I lost my phone in the process. You owe me for a new one I bought.”

“By the way, you work too hard, so stay on vacation.”

“Agreed.”

“Also, Mrs. Claus will likely become well known.”

“She can handle it.”

“Good.”

“What’s next?”

“Remember the Rockwell audit from about ten years ago?”

“Uh...yeah.”

“Now, don’t swear, I know you don’t like it out there, but I need you there a few days from now.”

“Fuck, I don’t like that place.”

“Bring your swim trunks—a float in a pool or soak in a hot tub would do you some good. You could use a little color too.”

The stale air in the rarely used conference room modified, taking on a musky blend of Aqua Velva, number-two pencil lead, and sweat. General Stone’s blue uniform coat, bearing a silver star on each epaulet, lay on top of overwrought cardboard boxes stacked on the floor. Other boxes sat on the blue metal table that occupied space in the center of the room.

A silent gaze at Colonel Ritter from Stone brought a pause to their conversation.

Although standing at attention, head still, Ritter averted the scrutiny, looking instead for cracks in the fading white wall paint. The Colonel’s chest ached from Harrison’s kick, and he assumed Stone intended to bring his time at Saint Mary to a close. The general’s next words appeared to confirm his distress.

“Your meeting with Harrison confirms my suspicions,” Stone said, his voice weary.

Ritter blinked and looked at his superior. Stone looked unkempt. Stubble covered half of the hard edges on his face, and ever-increasing wrinkles created abrupt ridges on his shirt. But he also appeared calm.

"Harrison is the key to Taylor's operation." Stone sighed, and then said, "At ease, Colonel."

"Yes, sir," Ritter said, fresh air filling his respiratory system again. "Are we certain Taylor is the anonymous informant?"

Stone nibbled on the broken tip of a new pencil. "Actual confirmation, we don't have. But the connection is obvious. He's still missing." His face reddened, but his voice remained poised. "Yes, Taylor's been planning this for some time. He sent the female hybrid to school in Tucson—Harrison is employed there—and Taylor and Harrison worked together to suppress the Aurora breach. Yes, Harrison is the key."

"What about Zemdarsky's tie to Senator Vaughn?"

"Secondary. No, no, Harrison's the key."

"Have we interrogated or scanned the female hybrid to get at the truth?"

"That's about to get under way. But I'm more concerned about finding Harrison."

"Shouldn't we be looking for Taylor?"

Stone pushed a folder across the table. "This will explain why Harrison is the priority."

Ritter picked up the folder but did not open it.

"Let's face facts. If Taylor wanted to go public about Saint Mary, he wouldn't need an outsider's assistance, unless he needed something from him. Something pretty important. Something indisputable. Something tangible. You know the kind of evidence I'm referring to?"

"Hardware."

"Harrison is involved for a reason. If we find him, if we concentrate on him, we can eliminate the whole problem. The others are just loose ends."

Ritter nodded and opened the folder. Inside, he read an old memorandum on dried-out paper with faded type. Despite the many years working inside Saint Mary, Ritter never grew accustomed to the remarkable knowledge that revealed itself on a regular basis. This moment was no different from many others, except that, in addition to aching, his chest now felt tight.

He finally understood why William Bernard Harrison was involved.

"The Protocol One resolution in that particular matter was likely premature," Stone said. "If Taylor's hunch about Harrison is right, and they go public, then we have a major, major problem on our hands."

"Yes, sir. We must find Harrison immediately. Maybe Colonel Bennet should add him to the drug-ring conspiracy. Put his face on every front page in the country."

"But wait for a moment, Colonel. Think tactically. I believe Taylor is right about Harrison, so bringing him in right away would be a mistake. We do need to find him, but before we haul him, he needs to help us find our missing property. Including him in our disinformation now will not help us at this point."

"What can I do, sir?"

"Holcomb uses an alias, Ronald Sheraton, and Harrison uses Wesley Hiatt. Use this information to track down the FBI agent and to locate Harrison's evidence that he has concealed in the safety-deposit box and storage unit." Stone rose from his chair and put on his coat. "Taylor will turn up. It's only a matter of time. Besides, Holcomb may lead us right to Harrison, assuming we can track him down. And as for Harrison, I just hope his memory is good."

At Security Post Alpha, near Saint Mary's underground entrance, the guard personnel recognized the personable and casual Colonel Ritter, acknowledging him with smiles and nods. Ritter entered a private control booth adjacent to the security station and booted up one of several desktop computers inside the room. While it processed his access code and presented the security menu, he took a seat and used his left foot to close the booth's soundproof door, shutting himself off from the rest of the staff outside. He unlocked a drawer in the desk at which he sat and withdrew a Beretta 9 mm. After verifying it contained a loaded magazine, he slipped the weapon into his waistline.

A chirp from the computer signaled it was ready. Ritter scanned the security camera images on the monitor of laboratories, offices, and various other rooms within the Saint Mary complex and then found the one of interest to him. He clicked on the image for that room, and the computer chirped at him again.

"Shunt code override? No problem," Ritter said, typing the additional access commands. The text on the screen faded to black. A brief flicker transitioned into a video image. He tapped the arrow keys, adjusting the angle of the camera he now controlled.

Another drawer contained the headset he needed. After plugging it in and putting it on, Ritter pressed the *A* key. Static hissed through the headset for a second or two, and then it dissipated. He guessed at the correct volume level for now, and then regulated it as needed as the activity progressed inside the room under his observation.

Three minutes and nineteen seconds later, he leaned forward and put his right index finger on the computer's power button, ready to depress it in an instant. Sitting there with his thumb on the button, sweating now, he hoped his standing with Saint Mary was not about to change.

James Evans ran a finger along the dusty base of a one-way mirror. A mistake. There was nowhere to wipe his finger. So, with regret, he thought about wiping it on his unsullied clothes. But just then, a smile formed on his pallid face. A guard's camouflaged fatigues hid the dirt well as James gave him a friendly pat on his back and shoulder.

"You're dismissed, Sergeant," General Stone said to the guard as he joined James Evans in the observation room adjacent to Janice's detention cell.

Stone pushed the top button on a gray panel near the room's exit. A steel door rumbled out from the wall's interior and crept along its track. A muffled, baritone click signaled the door had sealed them off and they were ready to begin.

"Are you certain you can find out?" Stone asked.

James straightened his new dark-blue cardigan sweater, unsure if he liked the color. Noticing a loose thread dangling from one of the sweater's buttons, he furrowed his brow. "If my sister has hooked up with Harrison and Taylor, well then, gotcha! We'll know yesterday."

"She looks asleep."

James stepped up to the mirror again. Janice lay on a cot, wrapped in a tight green wool blanket. Her white tennis shoes sat perfectly aligned on the floor at the foot of her cot.

"She is," James said. "It will be to our advantage. My scan shouldn't tip her off. Her subconscious will accept me as if I'm part of a dream, a visitor in need of a guided tour. All aboard."

"And what if she awakes?"

"No problemo. I'll still get what we need. It'll just take a little longer."

Stone took a couple of steps back, and then said, "Do it."

James took deep, relaxing breaths while he aimed and focused his blue eyes on his target. The target lay there, unaware, well within range. The glass partition and thick cement walls presented no barrier to his weapon.

James's eyelids fluttered, and then they opened wide. He made a slow turn, looking up and behind, into one of the corners of the room.

"Something wrong?" Stone said.

James continued his gaze. The outline of the camera, recessed and shielded by a plate of glass, hung there in the corner, barely discernible, just a hidden, amorphous shape of black and gray.

"It's deactivated for this session," Stone said.

"Certain?"

"Yes, James, it's off. Do what you must, there will be no record."

James's focus returned to his target. "Sister, tell me about your life...tell me..."

Janice sat inside a classroom, one of the ceiling lights, near a corner, flickered and died. Other students also occupied the room. A woman, the professor, stood before the audience and lectured. She searched for chalk—just a nub would do. Scribbling on the blackboard came next. "Legislative" topped the list, then "Executive," and lastly, "Judicial."

With the chalk and the lecture over, the group talked about less formal topics—club meetings and campus events. The bulletin board, the one with all the beautiful, bright colors, had further information posted on it.

In, out.

Inside another classroom, Janice sat in the front row, center. Her notations were quick and thorough. Someone passed her a note, not meant for her, but for another. She passed the note along without reading it, but wondered if it concerned the test.

In.

The professor erased the blackboard.

Out.

The students stood and exited. Janice slid her notebook and textbook into her backpack and zipped it up. "What about the test?"

"Don't worry about it," the professor said.

"I was concerned about the test."

"Precisely what concerns you?"

"I just feel like I don't know anything, and that I'll fail. I can't fail."

"Just answer truthfully and you'll do fine."

In, out.

Brick buildings surrounded a sprawling lawn crowded with students. A tall bearded man, wearing a sullied white tunic, stood in the center of the crowd. He shouted, "I will not be kicked around like some Judean dog! After all I have done for you and your dad by not revealing you to David. Is this my reward? To find fault with me because of some wench?"

Another man, also bearded, but well dressed in a suit-and-tie ensemble, ignored the shouting. He handed out voter registration forms.

Janice took one. A warm breeze blew hair across her face. She pulled it aside. "Are you a teacher?"

"I'm an older student," he said. "Be sure to register and vote."

The man in the white tunic approached, interrupting, grabbing the forms. "Blasphemer!"

"Are you a registered voter, sir?" the suited man said.

A roadrunner scooted up to them, stopping by the man in the suit. It sat. Janice watched the bird, admiring its colorful, mascara-like eyeliner. The bird clicked its tongue, and then trotted away, vanishing into the crowd.

In, out.

Another classroom. The professor called on Janice to answer a question. She fumbled through her notes, back and forth through the pages. Silence, giggles, stares. Someone blew his or her nose. The professor cleared his throat.

"The answer, Miss Evans."

Janice picked up a textbook. She opened it and scanned highlighted passages. Some were yellow. Some were pink. Despite her embarrassment, the colors made her smile. Looking up, she said, "I was afraid this would happen. I don't have the answer, sir. I don't know how or why they did that. That makes no sense to me. Was this covered?"

Someone sneezed.

The professor walked toward her. "This was on the midterm. You got an A. Certainly you remember. The truth is simple to remember."

"I don't recall, sir. Sorry, I don't have an answer for you." Janice's eyes moistened as the professor drew nearer. She looked away.

"Why are you crying, little girl?"

"I'm not, sir." Janice wiped her eyes, sniffling, and then she met the professor's stare. "Are you a substitute?"

Another voice, this time from the back of the room, said, "Sir, I checked my notes too; Harrison and the others weren't covered before. Must be some new material."

Heads swiveled to the back, to a chubby red-haired girl.

"My mistake," the professor said.

In, out.

White walls. The scent of ammonia. Metallic surfaces.

Janice, about twelve years old, squeezed a fuzzy teddy bear. Brown. Not dark brown, but light, almost tan. Beige, perhaps. And it looked brand new. It had a pink bow tied around its neck.

General Taylor stood beside her.

She tugged at his coat.

He hugged her.

In, out.

Men and women, technicians in blue smocks with plastic shields covering their facial features, gathered around Janice, who still held the fuzzy bear. One aimed a test tube at her and jiggled it. She squealed, looked away, and covered the teddy bear's eyes.

Taylor distracted her. "What do you want to be when you grow up?"

"I don't want to look."

The technician moved closer.

Taylor held her hand and helped cover the bear's eyes.

Janice, whispering, said, "I...I...want to be good."

Taylor stood and patted her head.

Braver now, Janice peered at the technician and the test tube. "That's where babies come from, don't they?"

"We all come from these," the technician said. "Will you be a good girl and do as you're told?"

"But what if—"

"Will you follow orders?" the technician said, jiggling the test tube at her.

In, out.

White walls. The scent of ammonia. Metallic surfaces.

Janice put the bear inside a box; she no longer needed it. Turning to Taylor and the technician, she said, "Lawful orders."

The technician put his hand on Taylor's chest, pressing him away until he disappeared.

"Why only lawful orders?" the technician said.

No response from Janice.

Shouting now, the technician repeated his question. "Why only lawful orders?"

"You know whose laws, don't you?"

"What do you mean?"

In, out.

White walls. The scent of ammonia. Metallic surfaces. Janice and the technician. Alone.

"Saint Mary's laws, of course," Janice said.

"You're lying." He repeated, whispering, "You're lying."

Overhead, a light flickered and died.

"Saint Mary's laws."

"Rest, Janice. I will be back to check on your health later. Don't leave me."

"I'll be here, waiting. We are alone, James. So alone."

"Don't lie to me."

"I haven't. Trust me."

"Don't leave me all alone."

"I haven't, James. Trust me."

In, out.

Empty blackness. A deep, dark cave.

James felt the pressure and opened his eyes. His forehead and torso pressed against the one-way mirror. He stepped back and stretched, rolling his neck and shoulders. As he squinted at the mirror, his focus returned. A line of dust had creased the bottom front of his new cardigan. "Damn."

"What is it?" Stone said.

Brushing himself off, James said, "She's clean, sir."

"Are you certain?"

"Taylor and Harrison don't mean anything to her. Taylor was a father figure to her at one time, but not for a while. Only Saint Mary holds any meaning. Just like me. We are both alike."

"That has yet to be seen. Perhaps Taylor intended to use her, but didn't get that far."

James watched his sleeping sister. "That's possible." Janice appeared delicate, fragile, and so easily breakable. "She would never join him. It would mean throwing everything away. She'd be alone. She knows where she belongs."

Stone sighed. Although still uncertain for the moment, he accepted James's analysis. He turned to him and said, "In that case, I have a new assignment for you."

"Harrison?"

"Yes."

"How?"

"Not here, I'll brief you in my office."

THIRTY EIGHT

A Big Chalkboard

Professor Moresby snared a thicket of folders under his left arm. Sheaths of papers and photos crept out from his precarious grip. The documents dangled in danger of falling out, in total, onto the floor. Their condition went unnoticed by the MIT-educated physicist and astronomer, who shuffled along a narrow and deserted tube in the aging bowels of the Saint Mary complex. The fluorescent lighting cast an uncomfortable glare on his fading retinas, but this did not stop him from accomplishing his mission: finding a big chalkboard.

The professor paused in front of a door, squinting, trying to read the blue sign mounted across it. He attempted to adjust his eyeglasses, but then realized he had not worn them. Chuckling, Moresby reached into his lab coat and felt for the spectacles.

"There we are."

Sliding on the eyeglasses, he read the sign—Section R/R Trng—and decided the room held promise. Finding it locked, however, he pressed on.

Five doors later, he found an unsecured, unlit room and stepped inside, nearly smacking into a row of filing cabinets in the process.

"Such a storage problem. Ha, too many secrets, heh, heh."

"Halt," someone said from behind.

"Oh my," Moresby said, turning and clutching his chest. Papers, photos—aerial views of crop circles—tumbled to the floor.

The barrel of a handgun pressed against his forehead.

The voice came again, "Were you messing with my doorknob?"

"Up the corridor?"

"Roger that."

"Eh, yes. I...I have ID."

Moresby felt a tug on his coat as the gunman yanked away his badge. Anger rattled his heart. He knew this one was being rude, a bully, for no good purpose. His kind was like that.

The gun lowered, revealing the man. Dark all over, he wore a black jumpsuit, black beret, and black boots. He even had a deep tan. Black eyes stared at Moresby. After shoving the ID back into the professor's coat, the man holstered his gun. Leather creaked and snapped. Leaning close to his prey revealed his sharp features. His black clothes and sharp facial features made him look like a big black bird. The bird exhaled fresh breath, as if he had just sucked down a mint.

Moresby pressed his stiff back against the door, waiting, just waiting for him to leave, so he could be alone. He hated the men in black. He hadn't originally, but now he did; after all the years, he finally felt hate for something. At first, this had bothered him, but no longer. He prayed they would someday suffer for their blind, sickening, and well-paid-for obedience. His aging, decaying retinas stared into the blackness.

"You need a haircut, old man."

"Young man, pick up the mess you made."

The blackbird grinned and tapped one of his jump boots near a crop circle photo on the floor. "Scotland. Been to that one. Have you, old man?"

"Back up," Moresby said, motioning with his wrinkled hands. The movement concealed their shaking. "I'll take care of it myself. Just move along. I have important work to do." He crouched to the floor and scooped the debris into a single pile.

Heels struck the floor. The blackness diminished and then disappeared. Seconds later, a man in blue approached from the other direction. Looking up, Moresby saw the man had a friendly face.

"Professor, is there something I can help you find?" the air policeman said, helping Moresby up. The old man wheezed.

"I was looking for a place to work."

"Was the comm office inadequate? Are you all right, sir?"

Moresby cupped a hand over his mouth, nodded, and coughed twice. The wheezing subsided. "Yes, the computer limited my progress."

"If there's a problem with your computer, I'm sure we can set you up with another one. Why don't you follow me back?"

"It's not the computer, my son. I need a chalkboard, a big chalkboard. I was trying to find a room with a big chalkboard."

The air policeman hesitated, and his head jerked back. "A chalkboard?"

"A big chalkboard. Do you know where I can find one? The format is more familiar to me than a computer terminal. The future of humanity depends upon it."

The guard smiled and pointed a thumb down the corridor. "The old briefing room. I'll unlock it for you."

"Thank you. You are too kind. Been in the air force long, young man?" Moresby said, following the air policeman the short distance to the room. His first glance inside the room brought a cheery expression to the old man's face. "Yes, yes, this will do nicely."

"Do you have chalk?"

The professor removed a carton of chalk from the back pocket of his trousers and held it up. "But around here, an eraser would be more important," he said, winking.

"Yes, sir" the air policeman said, exiting and closing the door behind him.

Moresby stepped toward the front of the room, laid the disorganized folders on top of a large counter, and started sorting. Equations went in one stack, photos another, and transcripts from abductee interviews into a third. Once done with that task, he arrayed the photos chronologically, in a line on the counter. The symbols had changed over the years. Moresby believed the "alphabet" had become more complex, as if the aliens assumed we had learned it all along.

So mysterious, these little guys.

While still examining the photos, Moresby slid a piece of chalk from the carton. He rubbed it between his fingers. Feeling its grittiness, the professor finally relaxed. The encounter with the man in black faded from his consciousness, and his thoughts flowed again. The boundaries dissolved. He overlooked nothing and became connected to all of it. Before long, he walked, happily, in a wheat field in Scotland. A steady, cool wind carried the sounds of sheep. Tips of a swaying wheat crop tickled his palms.

Soon thereafter, he drew a series of circles—linked, adjacent, stacked side-by-side—on the chalkboard. Lines, dash marks, and symbols took shape. Labeling them came next: Earth, Ship, Hemisphere, Union, One.

Moresby paused and compared his work to a chart he'd prepared earlier. "Check the math," he said, mumbling.

Nearly an hour later, calculus equations filled every inch of open space on the chalkboard. With reluctance, Moresby resorted to writing inside the circles as well. He set down what remained of his third piece of chalk and brushed his hands on his trousers. Arms folded, he stepped back and inspected his work.

"Is this our little greeting?" General Stone said from behind.

Moresby's heart jumped.

"Is this the message?" Stone said.

Moresby turned around and saw Stone standing by the door wearing an olive-drab flight suit. "It's *a* message. There are several more combinations that I still need to check. Going somewhere, General?"

"Professor Moresby, the Circle has directed the chairman to accelerate our joint operation. I just received the instructions, and I am en route to Nellis. The experimental is being loaded onto a C-5, and I will accompany it to its new base, North Range."

"Did Dennis say why the Circle insists on the new timetable?"

"I didn't ask."

Moresby did not believe him. He knew that Stone and the chairman were tightening their grips.

"You are to finish here," Stone said. "Afterward, you are to proceed with the female hybrid to the new base. I will meet you there tomorrow evening. General Lanham has seen to the logistics personally and assures me that ELF is installed and operational."

"What about arrangements for the psychotronic generator?"

"Couriers have retrieved it from your lab at the university. It will be at North Range when you arrive."

Moresby summoned a look of acceptance. "General, I can be ready to go immediately. However, I am concerned that Janice is not fully recovered from the test. Has Dr. Schmidt released her yet?"

"She has," Stone said, clenching his teeth.

"This is a crucial operation. I just wanted to make sure our assets are in proper order."

Stone's jaw relaxed. "You needn't worry. But you are right, this is a crucial operation, crucial for Saint Mary. And this time next week our country will be better defended because of it. We are lucky men, Professor. Our years of work are about to pay off. The North Range operation..."

Stone's words drifted past Moresby unheard. The thick scent of chalk dust hovered under his nostrils. He remembered the first lecture he gave after earning his degree in astrophysics.

How much we've learned.

But he had long since discarded many, perhaps all, of the concepts he had once believed as a student and teacher. His studies as a scientist for Saint Mary effectively discredited them.

How much we don't know.

Moresby had learned a difficult lesson. He had to stretch his imagination beyond the curiosity usually characteristic of scientists. Facts were hard to distill from the endless cascade of data, observations, and encounters. Except for one fact.

How little we understand.

He managed a nod when Stone finished speaking. After the general left, Moresby turned to the chalkboard and sighed. "I better erase this."

THIRTY NINE

Russia

A pale face—that of a young border guard—with no discernible expression, peered out from behind a panel of glass. Inside the booth, the dim overhead light barely illuminated his dark clothing and dark hair. Even his hands hid within tattered gray winter gloves.

He made a request of William Bernard Harrison, who stood before him. Harrison handed over his phony passport and visa, too tired for nervousness about scrutiny of the items. His weighty eyelids closed without a fight. Only the sound of shuffling shoes, quiet conversations, and chattering teeth blended with occasional erratic movements kept him from falling asleep.

The guard was slow, methodical, and preoccupied with fine-tuning a transistor radio.

Harrison shifted his stance and looked about. The armed guards searched minimal luggage. He read unfamiliar signs, heard strange languages, and felt bitterly cold. His face, mainly his chin and cheeks, ached from the trauma of the below-freezing temperature. He wondered if he would ever accomplish his task.

Ahead of him, the border guard's eyes darted between the forged documents and Harrison. The movement seemed artificial, practiced, without any real concern for proper procedure. The officer reached unenthusiastically for a stamp, but stopped short of putting rubber and ink to paper. His reddish-brown eyes narrowed, focusing on Harrison's puzzled expression.

"U vas ruchka?"

"Huh?"

"U vas ruchka?" the guard said again, lowering his gaze to Harrison's chest.

Harrison looked down.

"Ruchka? A pen?"

"Uh, yeah," Harrison said, unzipping his jacket. He pulled a ballpoint pen from the inside pocket. He pushed it through the slot under the pane of glass. "Pozhalesta."

"Oi, spacebo vam, Mister Khiet." The guard tucked away the pen and stamped Harrison's passport and visa. With a grin and thick accent the young man said, "Welcome to Moscow, Mister Hiatt."

"Spacebo," Harrison said, grateful and relieved. The loss of the pen was a small price to pay. The guard obviously needed it more than he did.

Stepping ahead, Harrison spotted the large avocado-green suitcase he had purchased at a thrift shop in San Diego. The suitcase sat randomly among the luggage of other travelers. As he picked it up, he looked around and found the next, and final, line in which he had to wait. Except for a carton of Marlboro Menthol Light cigarettes, he knew the customs officials would not be terribly interested in the items he carried: secondhand clothes, also purchased at the thrift shop, and some toiletries.

The customs officer said a few barely audible phrases, then without explanation, left his post and exited through a doorway. Harrison watched the travelers ahead of him and searched their faces for an understanding of the disruption. But they stood there, looking disinterested in their circumstances, except for a woman, sneezing and coughing, at the front of the line. A man next to her whispered. She shrugged and furrowed her brow.

Weariness embraced Harrison again, and the disorder troubled him. He had never been to the former enemy's land before, and he expected more diligence. He knew the Russians had problems, but the shabby conditions and inefficiency thus far surprised him.

Checking his watch, he saw that it was nearly five o'clock. He tried to calculate what time it would be in Tucson, but realized it did not matter. He had barely slept since boarding the plane in San Diego, and his stamina rapidly diminished. Long-distance air travel always wore him out, and getting to the hotel was all that mattered.

Moments later, a different customs clerk, a short obese man, approached and hastily checked through the line of travelers. "Dobrie dehn," Harrison said, offering a cordial greeting when it was his turn.

The clerk ignored him and studied the declaration form. He scratched his nose and mumbled, "American?"

"Da."

"Cigarettes?"

"No thanks, I don't smoke."

"Nu, vikhoditeh!"

Harrison recognized the order to exit and complied despite the dark, frozen air outside. Ice and snow hugged the ground and wrapped their way up the sides of buildings, light posts, and ashen tree trunks. A dingy yellow tour bus with a raspy engine sent a puffy column of exhaust and condensation into the air.

After a brief search, Harrison found a battered Lada parked at a taxi stand and hoped its heater functioned properly. He moved toward it, nearly slipping on a patch of ice. Organizing his thoughts in Russian, he reached the Lada and opened its rear passenger-side door. "Gostinitsa Rossiya, pozhalesta."

"Khorosho," the driver said. He was an adolescent with a shaved head and wearing a black leather jacket.

Harrison tossed his suitcase into the backseat and followed it in. He barely finished closing the door before the Lada jumped forward into traffic. Horns and fists protested as the teenager drove him to the center of Moscow. As the car bounced and swerved, swayed and vibrated, he could not resist the urge to close his eyes and rest.

Fleeting images, places, and people punctuated his subconscious journey. Soon, the renderings slowed and became more cohesive.

Between consciousness and sleep, he met Holcomb in a long gray corridor.

A figure, blue and familiar, beckoned them.

"I have someone I want you to meet," Holcomb kept repeating.

"Again? But we've already met. He's one of Mary's angels."

Their footsteps echoed. The blue figure stood in front of them now, rubbing his chest. "We have met," he said. "And droog, droog! Oi! Teper ti znaesh."

"You see," Holcomb said. "Now you know. You're his friend, and he is yours."

"Droog, droog!" the figure said, insistent, rubbing his chest.

Another voice floated through the corridor. Harrison stopped and listened. "Do you hear that, Art?"

"No. Only you can hear it."

Harrison lowered his head.

"What's wrong?" Holcomb said.

"Art, the voice sounds the same. I knew it, but never—"

A squeal, a skid, and Harrison slid forward.

"Ha ha ha. Mi zdece. Eta Gostinitsa Rossiya. Khey! Khey!"

His eyelids opened, barely, but enough for Harrison to see that he was face to face with the Lada driver. The bald youngster pointed out the window. "Mi zdece. Eta Gostinitsa Rossiya. We khere."

Harrison paid the kid and then got out of the taxi and back into the cold. Snow fell, but he restrained the urge to rush inside. Not far away, the red brick walls of the Kremlin rose above the snowdrifts. The intricate colors and patterns of Saint Basil's Cathedral clung to spiraling towers and onion-shaped domes. Countless silhouettes moved in and out of Red Square. Chimes from the clock above Spassky Gate signaled 6:00 p.m.

Harrison never imagined that he would ever set eyes on such a beautiful scene. Half a world away from home, he felt both excitement and anxiety. And cold, very cold. Shivering, he brushed snowflakes from his dampening hair and tromped through heavy, gray slush toward the hotel.

FORTY

Hands Gripped the Truth

After a sound sleep through the night, a shower, and no shave, Harrison dressed. He tried to recall, then realized exactly, the last time he had stood inside a house of God.

According to the information Taylor provided, Harrison was to proceed to Krasniya Sobor, a church in the Sparrow Hills section of Moscow. His contact was Father Petrov.

As he looked out his hotel room window at the dim, gray sky, he wondered how Petrov had come into possession of such an important document. He also wished that he had purchased gloves.

Taylor's file lacked specific details, but it was clear that the loss to the Russians of a comprehensive Roswell UFO–crash engineering report seriously compromised Saint Mary's security. Apparently, Father Petrov awaited the arrival of a courier to retrieve the item, which had been in his possession for several years.

But the courier never arrived.

Harrison made his way to the hotel's main floor. He needed coffee, at least, and wanted to find a shop where he could purchase gloves. A cafe tucked into a tiny room near the hotel's entrance offered him the opportunity to order breakfast. The only waitress was an older woman who went about her work with solid disinterest. When she brought the cup of coffee, he gave her several dollars and insisted that she keep the change. At first, she refused, but he gently complimented her service. This brought a smile and her acceptance of the excessive tip.

Harrison took a slow sip of the hot and strong coffee, a ritual that made him think of Janice. He felt angry that she faced harm and that he could not protect her. Sadness about her life, the loneliness and strangeness of it, also stung his consciousness. Disappointment that the government, his government, would so readily betray her rights as an individual, and treat her as nothing more than a lab specimen, throttled his heart rate. More than anything, he simply wanted to talk to her. To tell her that he accepted and loved her. He could admit that to himself now, and he was comfortable and secure with his feelings.

Harrison stood and set down the half-full coffee cup. In a hurry, he asked the waitress where he could find the subway. In very basic Russian, she gave him directions, using her hands to point the way to the nearest station.

He thanked her and shoved his bare hands into his pockets.

The route led him through Red Square to an intersection at Tverskaya Prospekt. As he passed Saint Basil's Cathedral, he looked across the square and easily recognized Lenin's Tomb. Mushy brown snow and dozens of people covered the square. Two very old women, bundled in tattered winter coats and heavy boots, stepped foot into his path. Halting, Harrison realized they were asking him something. Their wrinkled faces concealed endless memories, and their words struck at his heart.

"Mi odni. Kakiye u vas? Mi khoteli bie syest," they both said, crying.

Without hesitating, Harrison gave each of them ten dollars and politely told them to find a warm place and to buy themselves something to eat. Tears rolled down their cheeks, and sobs churned white puffs of air from their mouths. He continued onward, feeling a twinge of embarrassment and guilt.

As he approached the Lenin Library, he saw the sign for the subway. An arrow pointed to a descending staircase. A map at the bottom of the steps allowed him to determine which train to take and which stop he needed. Once he identified the correct train, he walked to an escalator that drew him farther below ground. Most of the people gliding on the escalator around him stood silently, and those few who spoke discussed mundane topics. The scene reminded him of the many times he'd ridden the metro in Washington, DC, and out of reflex, Harrison stood to the right, out of the way of others trotting downward on the left.

At the bottom, he stepped off the escalator and admired the platform area. Works of art, statues, and colorful mosaics made Harrison believe he stood inside a museum instead of a subway station. He did not expect to make such a discovery, and he nearly missed his train.

Squeezing through the closing doors, Harrison found the car had plenty of empty seats. Everyone inside, though, had something to read, and most squinted at the pages of their newspapers, books, or magazines. One man, arms folded, slept and snored.

The ride to Moscow State University lasted just long enough for Harrison to feel warm and ready to handle the wintry chill outside. He exited the train and, again, found himself among beautifully sculptured figures and brightly decorated hallways. The crowd at this station was livelier than the one in downtown, mainly due to a boisterous group of children waiting for a train.

Outside, mustard-colored buildings stood among dull gray structures with dark windows. The streets, a mix of cobblestone and cracked asphalt, held few pedestrians and offered no indications of any taxis. Harrison realized that the church could be anywhere within several blocks of the station. A block away, Harrison saw a few people standing in line at a booth. He walked their way, hoping to get directions. Drawing closer, he noticed there were several of these booths. Each one a mini shop, selling various goods from sunglasses and wallets, to beer and vodka.

None appeared to have gloves.

The shop with the least number of customers sold sausages and rye bread. He got in line and placed an order. The server worked fast and provided helpful directions to Krasny Sobor, just four blocks away.

Harrison wrapped the sausage in the rye bread and ate it while walking. Although satisfying, the meal left him hungrier than before. He took a final bite, and then turned a corner onto Mechtatelnaya Ulitsa. The church waited for him at the end of this street, in a courtyard between two old dormitories.

Puzzled by what he saw, Harrison stood there in front of the building where he expected to find Krasny Sobor, wondering why it did not look at all like a church. He saw the two dormitories, but noticed the building between them had a rather plain appearance, and did not have any domes or other features common to Russian churches. Its facade split and crumbled in places, and he could not see any identifiable entrance.

Walking across the courtyard, Harrison approached the far side of the building and managed to find a stone stairwell that led below street level. He descended the icy steps and tugged on a thick, solid wood door. The door let out a loud creak when opened. Inside, Harrison felt a wave of warm, scented air embrace him. The aroma, richly blended incense, candle wax, and burning wood, filled his lungs.

Dark wood floors buckled under his shoes. As his eyes adjusted to the low light, he found another staircase to his right that appeared to lead up to the main hall. He ascended the steps and entered a wide room. Round alabaster pillars rose from the floor in several rows. Hundreds of flickering candles spiraled around each pillar. Icons and more candles lined an altar at the front. Faded biblical murals adorned the walls. An old woman sat next to a young boy on one of the two benches inside the room. The child watched her pray, his patience waning. Harrison could not see any others in the church, so he waited respectfully for the old woman to finish before continuing his search.

The boy noticed Harrison looking in his direction, and immediately bowed his head. The woman patted him on the knee.

A door closed in a corner of the room hidden by one of the pillars. An old man with a long, uneven beard and garbed in beige-and-white robes walked into view. The man read a book and looked deep in thought. As the man approached Harrison, he prepared himself to make contact.

"Excuse me," Harrison said in Russian. "Unhappily, I was told Father Petrov is deceased?"

The man stopped. His head remained motionless, but his eyes gazed over the top of the book. After blinking a few times, he closed the book and raised his head. "Your news is premature. My travels are extensive, but I have yet to make that journey," Father Petrov said, his voice clear and strong. He also seemed to make an effort to speak slowly.

"You must have many interesting souvenirs."

Father Petrov looked at the ceiling and around the room. "A priest has but meager possessions. Having possessions does not make one happy, but perhaps I can share with you a small gift?"

"If you wish. Maybe something literary and unique?"

Petrov nodded, and then motioned for Harrison to follow him. They walked toward the door where the priest had entered the room. In silence, Petrov opened the door and led his visitor into a short hallway. A few steps more and they crammed into a small storage room. Flimsy shelves surrounded them and buckled under the weight from candles, matchboxes, and English-language Bibles. Several large baskets, filled with jars of pickled tomatoes and cucumbers, sat on the floor.

After placing his book onto a shelf, Petrov knelt beside a basket next to one of the walls. He slid the basket away and lifted a wood plank from the floor. A latch clicked. Behind him, another floorboard released. He reached around and pulled it out of the way. The motion sent a plume of dust into the air. Inserting his hands into the hole in the floor, he recovered a black nylon gym bag.

"I will make a donation in your name to the Orthodox Church," Harrison said.

"Take it. It belongs to you now."

Harrison leaned forward and withdrew the bag from Petrov's trembling hands. He cradled it against his chest.

Petrov led him back into the church's main hall. A youth choir had formed and gathered near the altar. Harmonious voices rose, sweet and unsullied, filling every inch of the room.

"Prekrassny, da?" Petrov said.

Harrison nodded. *Yes, beautiful.*

"You know, for an American you speak Russian very well," Petrov said in impeccable English.

Harrison held still. He had anticipated the priest would realize he was a foreigner, but hoped the subject would not come up for discussion.

"It is all right; I will understand if you do not wish to speak." The priest bent close and said, whispering, "It is just that I did not expect the courier to be an American."

"Allies can be found in unexpected places."

"Yes. This is God's will. I am sure he will guide you safely." Petrov's eyes exuded genuine kindness and reassurance.

"I must be going." In Russian, Harrison wished the priest good health and a happy New Year. As the choir continued to sing, he drifted toward the exit. Nearing the door, he paused again, closed his eyes, and inhaled a deep breath of the warm, scented air of the church. Outside, the frosty wind shoved him toward the subway. The hotel and strong coffee broke the physical chill. In the privacy of his room, he felt his sovereignty returning. The document contained so many secrets. But they were in his hands now.

Hands that gripped the truth.

What is the larger purpose?

He searched the pages. The document had so many names.

My purpose?

The document could answer so many questions. When he finally found an answer, and accepted it, his hands trembled.

And so did his heart.

FORTY ONE

That Fresh Paint Smell

The scent of new paint and carpeting floated through the corridors of North Range's command building. General Stone and Colonel Ritter found odd comfort in the freshness of the place. That comfort did not prevent their hurried steps. After exiting an elevator, both men nearly collided with Janice and Professor Moresby as they, accompanied by two armed guards, headed topside for a break in the fresh air. The foursome scooted aside, offering up some extra space for the two officers to pass them in the hallway.

But General Stone stepped in their path, saying, "How are we feeling?

The professor ignored Stone. He flipped through a notebook and scratched his gray head. Colonel Ritter walked on with a quickened pace, leaving the group behind.

Janice watched the colonel for a moment before looking at Stone. "Fine, sir. Still a little shaky, but doing a lot better. It is kind of you to ask."

"Let Schmidt know right away if you feel sick or something."

"I will, thank you."

Stone aimed his sharp features at the professor. "Are we on schedule?"

"Yes, General," Moresby said without making eye contact. He mumbled something derogatory, barely audible, about the need for an armed escort.

"Very well, Professor. Keep up the good work." Stone excused himself and joined Ritter inside the general's sparsely furnished office.

The movement of equipment and furniture from Ohio to Nevada remained an ongoing process. The general settled into his temporary seating arrangements, a white-and-black folding director's chair, and rubbed his face. Tiredness, like floodwaters breaking through a disintegrating barrier, swept over him. He wanted sleep, but too many activities required his direct supervision. Stone took his time, perhaps too much time, to sandbag the crumbling walls that kept the tiredness at bay.

"What you'll need to do next, Colonel, is proceed to Tucson and seize the contents."

"Sir, as I mentioned earlier, there are a dozen safe-deposit boxes registered to individuals under the name William Harrison, or under his known alias. How will I justify all of the seizures?

Stone unlocked his desk's top drawer and withdrew a crisp piece of paper. While reaching for the document, he realized how much lower than normal he sat. A momentary awkwardness encouraged him to straighten up. It did not help. The worn-out director's chair failed to elevate him to a more comfortable level. The idea of finding a cushion or pillow to place under his backside occurred to him, but a still-alert cell of gray matter sparked, fueling his self-respect. He reached up and stretched his arm across the desk. "The federal courts believe in fighting espionage as much as we do."

Ritter took hold of the paper and read it over. The document, a court order, authorized the Department of the Air Force, in conjunction with the Department of Justice, to seize any necessary bank records and holdings of William Harrison, a.k.a. Wesley Hiatt.

"We can't afford to overlook any of them. We won't retain the property of any innocents," Stone said.

Ritter nodded and read further. A half smile crinkled his features. "This says that Harrison is a Russian spy."

"Suspected Russian spy. Apparently, he made too many friends with the other side when he worked counterespionage in the FBI. They seduced him with money, women, so forth. The shooting that ended his career apparently didn't end his real work. A former partner at the FBI is involved too. We're uncertain exactly how far up their network goes—could be linked to Taylor. Arms traders, drug dealers. It's all the same. And they must be stopped, because although the former enemy is gone, the world is still a dangerous place. Got it?"

Ritter folded the paper and slid it inside his jacket. "Yes, sir. Shall I use the security team already in Tucson to assist me?"

"That will be fine. Just leave a couple agents on surveillance in case Harrison shows up at his home or office."

"Yes, sir, but you don't think he'll show?"

"If I'm right, he'll turn up in Los Angeles, but the male hybrid is handling that. Now, about Holcomb?"

"There was one credit card charge, in his real name, for an airline ticket to Houston, but that turned out to be a dead end. One encouraging lead comes from the Atlanta FBI office. An agent assigned to a railroad liaison task force thinks he may have seen Holcomb at the Amtrak station there."

"Anything else?"

"No, sir."

The sandbags loosened. Stone steadied himself before speaking. "Aside from the fact he could be anywhere, it's important to remember that we don't approach. We want him to lead the way."

"Yes, sir. I've contacted Quantico, just on the off chance he attempts to use their facilities. There's a forensic scientist there whom some of his colleagues say he's friendly with."

"Follow it up. Chances are he won't go through Quantico, though, given the reception he received in Wichita."

"Yes, sir."

Stone leaned back, sinking, rubbing his face again. "Any other ideas, Colonel?"

"If Harrison turns up in Los Angeles, then Holcomb will probably be there as well, like you say. But sir, if I may be honest, all of them could be on the other side of the planet for all we know. Who knows what their plans are?"

A sandbag or two fell completely away. Stone yawned, and then said, "I don't mind your honesty, Colonel." The tone remained polite, but Stone's cheeks and forehead grew warm. He wrapped his palm around the partially drained coffee mug sitting on his desk. "It's better than 'yes, sir' all the time." Stone's other hand found an aspirin bottle in the desk's center drawer. "But my gut feeling is that Taylor brought Harrison in so they could recover property stolen from the project, property that disappeared many years ago, when Harrison's family still lived in California." His face cooled, and he stared, expressionless, at Ritter before flipping the lid off the aspirin bottle. "Yeah, Los Angeles is where we need to focus the search for them all." He tapped four of the pills into his coffee mug and swirled it around. "But there's work to be done in Tucson as well." Stone nodded at the door. "Get on it. And, Colonel..." Stone paused to loosen his shirt collar and gulp down the lukewarm brew.

"Sir?"

"Hurry back." The bitterness made Stone's lips curl. "We are very rapidly running out of time."

FORTY TWO

Infinite Horizons

The setting sun's rays diffused through the hazy late-Monday-afternoon sky over Los Angeles. Soon, the cityscape would glisten in a false twilight, masking the grime it had collected daily for decades. A wide horizon of twinkling, glowing points of light fooled the eyes. Each shining at the center of an orbit, they flickered on, beginning their deception for another night.

Sitting on the bed next to a table lamp inside room 509 of the Metropolitan Suites on Los Feliz Boulevard, Harrison stared at some of the pages in the thick classified document he had recovered in Moscow. A multitude of thoughts and emotions clamored for his attention, but all he could grasp in full was the brewing noisy agitation on the crowded lanes of the nearby Hollywood Freeway.

Harrison checked the door, ensuring it remained locked, just as it had been for the last four hours. He edged toward the window, pulling one of the drawn drapes aside. Peering through the gap, he recognized no one.

He chose the armchair next to a glass coffee table and tried to sit again, forcing himself to stay put. Raising his right leg onto the table elicited a subtle groan before he stared at the crashed Roswell craft's engineering document again.

W. Von Kreuzen, chief metallurgist, had filed a seven-page report in January, 1948. It summarized the results of an examination of a metallic plate he'd conducted for the air force. The conclusion, simple and concise, read as follows: "Nothing in our nature or science could be responsible for its creation."

There were other such summaries, filed from July, 1947, through the early 1970s. Technical drawings, chemical formulas, and countless frustrations. But they'd had some success regarding the analysis of the saucer-shaped craft and its components.

One name, near the bottom of the table of contents, stood out next to the "Propulsion Dynamics" section. The researcher's remarks for this section appeared on pages 89 through 97. Harrison read portions of them again:

> *The translucent plate is definitely utilized in conjunction with the propulsion system. Reconstruction of the experimental showed this to be the case...Analysis of the components is difficult due to the exotic materials used in their construction...Identification of the external and internal objects was completed through lengthy modeling of existing natural elements combining with heavier elements yet undiscovered...Our guesswork has revealed a significant finding...The power cell will bring* infinite horizons *within our reach.*

A diagram showed the power cell measured eight inches in length and width, and a half an inch thick. Its gross weight barely reached two ounces.

Infinite horizons, Dad?

A month before his *accident*, Harrison's father had telephoned him at the FBI Academy. He was planning to retire soon, worn out from years of travel *as a salesman*, and wanted to relax with *Mom*.

They were together in Palm Springs, one of their favorite getaways. A day of golf, shopping, drinks with friends—the Carrs. Then, later, their dreams ended. A gas leak in their hotel room ignited. The explosion and fire left only charred remains, collapsed between the twisted bed frame and fused to the mattress coils.

Harrison never doubted the explanation.

Until now.

Protocol One.

Such a benign expression for terminal malignancy.

Almost always gone or away on business, Harrison's father seemed distant on the rare occasions when he rejoined the family at home. He was a quiet man who never angered except occasionally during the evening news or when he nicked himself shaving.

"Damn it! Where is the goddamn witch hazel?"

Harrison's occasional trips to Griffith Observatory with his father when he was a youngster were the only clear memories of closeness to him. And now, seeing his father's name on the Roswell documents, he treasured the memories of those trips even more than the extraordinary knowledge at his fingertips.

The man, fascinated with the exhibitions, would talk endlessly about the untouchable, infinite horizons beyond Earth that observatories around the globe reached for with telescopes. The adolescent Harrison thought his father odd for saying such things, dismissing the words as an attempt to help him develop an interest in science. At that tumultuous age, Harrison's only persistent curiosity concerned the girls who sat next to him in class.

The visits ended in Harrison's junior year in high school. His father traveled on a more frequent basis, and so the trips together to the hills above Los Angeles faded. Soon, college studies came, consuming Harrison's time, widening their times apart even more.

College graduation brought the family together, and in a private moment, the proud father gave his son a gift.

"Always remember, Bill, infinite horizons are within your reach."

Harrison still had the gift, an old globe. Woefully out-of-date, it remained one of his most valuable possessions. It sat inside his office. He wondered if he would ever see it again.

Harrison understood the sometimes-painful burden of secrecy. People outside the circle of government trust often did not understand this hardship. Some people with secrets found it easier to shut themselves off and suffer the burden in silence.

You were trying to tell me.

Closing the document, Harrison stood and wandered over to the suitcase lying on the well-made bed. He dug out a pack of cigarettes, smoking two of them in a row while pacing. Angry flicks from his wrist tossed ashes onto the carpeted floor. As he was about to light a third, the telephone rang. His hand, jittery from the sudden intake of nicotine, lifted the receiver.

"Yes?"

"Mr. Hiatt, this is Karen from the front desk."

"Uh-huh."

"There is a Ronald Sheraton waiting for you."

"Can you describe him?"

"Uh, about, well, average height, light colored hair, but it's..." The front desk clerk paused, lowering her voice. "It's kind of only on the sides and very thin on top. He has a scraggly beard. He looks very intense, sir."

"Send him up."

A blond male, wearing khaki chinos, brown loafers, a red cardigan sweater, and a white T-shirt flashed a devious smile. The brunette who sat at the sidewalk cafe noticed him and returned the expression. He knew he could have her, but for now, this sensation was enough.

James Evans had other prey to hunt.

Exhaust fumes from a loud MTA bus encircled him. The bothersome vapors made James think of rancid microscopic particles sullying his new clothes. He groaned and wondered anew if an alleged earlier Holcomb sighting at Union Station by FBI personnel was yet another dead end.

A car honked its horn. James looked around, peering over the top of his Perry Ellis sunglasses, but he did not see the two FBI agents who had contacted him earlier about Holcomb and their plans to tail him. Tiny blond follicles on the nape of his neck came to life. The sensation deepened. He pocketed his sunglasses, smiled again, and then dialed his cellular phone.

"I'm here," James said. His smile grew wider as he stepped along the sidewalk. "On Los Feliz, just as you asked...Yes, I'm heading that way now...I think I'll walk instead...Yes...Yes, this time it just feels right..."

James left his blue sedan behind, the one he drove from Griffith Observatory, and approached on foot two FBI agents who'd parked three blocks away.

"Yeah, I see you now." James paused and rubbed the back of his neck. "And just to let you know, I think we've hit the jackpot."

"Nice beard, Art."

"I see you shaved yours."

"Yep."

"And developed a new fashion sense."

Harrison glanced down at his thrift-store ensemble, and then said, "Get in here."

Holcomb entered the room and closed the door behind him. He slumped his exhausted body into the nearest chair. His bloodshot eyes shifted to the bed, looking like they were trying to convince the rest of his body to move there.

Walking back to his seat next to the coffee table, Harrison said, "I just got back from Moscow."

"You sure took the long way around."

Harrison gazed at the thick document; hazy light draped across the aging blue binder containing the Roswell craft data. "It's been an eventful week. I'm just glad you're alive."

"Same here." Holcomb stretched his arms and closed his eyes.

"How'd you get out here?"

"Amtrak. Capitol Limited, Texas Eagle, Sunset Limited." A smirk emerged on Holcomb's face. "Speaking of trains, I had a little problem with one in Wichita."

"I'm sorry to hear that, buddy, but the records and skull are still ours, correct?"

"Yep."

"And what does Maggie say?"

"She's working with a colleague, Sherman Teague, in Richmond and is waiting for us to contact her. The code phrase is 'Rock around the clock.'"

"'Fangs and Gums'?" The guy who always dressed as Dracula at the Halloween parties?"

"The one and only."

Harrison grew somber and he lit another cigarette. Smoke drifted and swirled into a cloud near the ceiling. "Nick Ridley is likely dead."

Holcomb tilted his head back and closed his eyes. A few seconds passed, and then he opened his eyes and jerked forward. "Dead?"

Harrison flicked ashes from his cigarette again. "A weak link, just like the rest of us."

The FBI agents remained in their sedan, not even offering to roll down their window and exchange a friendly greeting. James knew why; their feelings were so obvious to him. He repulsed them. One of them kept thinking how *creeped out* James made him feel. That did not stop James from flipping open the back door and jumping in.

"Howdy guys," James said, watching the driver eye him in the rearview mirror. James held up his hands and said, "No, don't say it. I know what happened. You've lost him again, didn't you?"

The driver averted his gaze. The agent in the front passenger seat spoke without turning around. "We followed Holcomb's taxi from Union Station, but lost him after he got out near here."

"Yes?" James said.

This time, the driver, an older man with white hair and a white moustache, said, "I know Art. We've trained together. He is one of the best agents in the bureau. I find it hard to believe he's a traitor."

James looked at the driver again in the rearview mirror. "Well, amigo, take comfort in your beliefs all you want. In the meantime, Comrade Holcomb is out there somewhere selling secrets to the

Russians. Don't you know why this country is going down the tubes? Because you can't trust anyone anymore."

James stared at the back of the driver's head.

Oh really? You think I'm a faggot? Hmmm, guess you've never told anyone about your own experiments in that area. Shall I mention it now?

The driver coughed, and then said, "He could have left the area entirely."

"That's possible, but so is staying at one of the area hotels," James said. "He's been homeless and needs a home, at least for the night."

"We'll need additional help if you want us to cover all of them in the area," the driver said. He typed a quick search into his smartphone. "There are at least three around here."

"Call for back up, but in the meantime, you two get set up on the one just down the block," James said, opening the door.

"Where are you going?" the driver said.

"For a walk."

A knock at the door startled Holcomb. He sat up, while Harrison moved across the room. "Are you expecting someone?" Holcomb said, standing and gripping the concealed 9 mm pistol inside his waistline.

Harrison peered through the door's peephole. When he allowed General Edward Taylor to enter, Holcomb drew his 9 mm and aimed it at Taylor's chest.

Taylor stood still, quiet. His face was sunburned, and he wore clothes that suggested he had just finished playing a round of golf: navy-blue slacks, a white knit shirt with pale blue stripes, and a green windbreaker.

Harrison double-locked the door and said, "It's okay, Art, this is Echo Tango."

Holcomb held his aim on Taylor. "What? Are you sure?"

"I am. Besides, I need him alive for just a little while longer." Harrison walked between the two men, waving off Holcomb's intensity. The agent holstered the pistol and returned to sitting in the nearest chair.

Harrison turned around. The general's clear green eyes looked rested, perhaps signaling relief that enough of the secrets contained behind them had finally seeped through. Harrison's muscles tightened. He put his strong leg back, angled his foot, and faced his hips forward. "I ran your errand," Harrison said, waiting for the right moment to present itself.

"Yes. And you made it back safely."

The moment came. The green eyes blinked.

Harrison's fist made a firm connection with the side of Taylor's mouth. The solid impact against soft lips and hard teeth filled the room with a quick, fleshy snap. As Taylor floundered, colliding into the wall behind him and then collapsing to the floor, Harrison saw the blood on his knuckles and felt...no better for his actions.

"And you're sure he is ET?" Holcomb said.

"He's the son of a bitch all right."

Taylor slipped a white handkerchief from a back pocket of his golf pants and wiped away some of the blood before pulling himself up. He balled up the moist rag and held it under his lower lip. "I take it you retrieved the item."

"I retrieved it all right. You've got a lot more explaining to do."

"Item? What item?" Holcomb said.

"The reason I was in Moscow, Art."

Taylor looked like he just swallowed a mouthful of salt water. "It was important to take this one step at a time."

"Maybe that's how you'd describe it. I'd call it manipulation. I don't like to be manipulated."

"Can someone please tell me what's going on?" Holcomb said.

"Yeah, that's a good idea," Harrison said. He lifted Taylor up and then pushed him into a chair next to the coffee table. "General, it's time for you to tell your story again. Start from the beginning, and don't leave anything out. Frankly, I wouldn't mind hearing it again, and I know Art would enjoy it as well."

Taylor dabbed at his chin. He winced, but soon, the words came. Roswell, the cover-up, Saint Mary, the hybrids, the whole *damn* story again.

"Which brings us to that," Harrison said, pointing at the thick blue folder. He instructed Taylor to give it to Holcomb. "Look toward the bottom of the first page."

Holcomb's left middle finger followed the list of names. It stopped, then tapped a few times. He looked up. "Your father?"

"Apparently so," Harrison said, standing over Taylor. He did not want to hit the general again. He just wanted the truth. "And the witch hazel?"

Taylor set the handkerchief aside. "Saint Mary knows many things about its employees. It was just a method to bolster your interest in the case, and jog your memory."

Harrison restrained his desire to shout. He clenched his teeth. "Did they kill my parents?"

Taylor sat still and answered the question in a calm voice. "Yes. As for those in the report who are still alive, there's a reason for that. They are not weak links. Saint Mary determined otherwise for Bernard Harrison."

In the silence that followed, Taylor picked up the handkerchief and wiped the last trickle of blood from his face. He tossed the once-white rag into a trash can. "The CIA recruited your father in graduate school. The agency needed to fill scientific positions with well-educated and loyal individuals. Your father accepted the job. He was a patriot and believed he could make a difference. It was an incredible opportunity for young and old scientists alike. It was a chance to serve the American government, to have access to advanced equipment and technology. Seemingly unlimited resources poured into research and development in the name of national security. Many scientists believed they were the front line of defense against tyranny and injustice from abroad. It was an idealistic time, and your father fell right into their trap."

"Then my mother didn't meet him until after he started work for the CIA."

"She knew him as you did. At least, the scrutiny your father was under never determined that he told any nonessentials about his work. Of course, it didn't appear like he would continue to do so near the end."

"So, my father wanted out? And by the way, like all mothers, mine was essential."

"Some of Saint Mary's security branch records indicated that he not only wanted out, but threatened to go public if they didn't let him out. The pressure of secrecy had become an overwhelming burden. They considered him unstable and a weak link, and so, they killed him."

"Along with my mother."

"It was a Protocol One ordered by the Circle. They reasoned an accident, such as what occurred, would be the least suspicious. Your parents took vacations to Palm Springs?"

Harrison nodded.

"This kind of knowledge was routine. Where people took vacations, where they shopped, who their friends were."

"What they used to cleanse shaving nicks?" Harrison said, clenching his fists.

"And whether their sons became FBI agents or insurance agents. It all goes in their files."

"What else is in my dad's file?"

Taylor hurried his speech. He seemed anxious to answer the question. Even his hands shook, so, he clasped them together and rested them on his lap. "Your father was a member of a team of scientists that researched the propulsion systems of the crashed Roswell craft. His team examined a component that gave the ship, and its systems, power."

"I read that in the report," Harrison said.

"Now, there were two of these power cells. One was intact, and the other was damaged. In the early 1980s, Saint Mary scheduled flight tests of the repaired, rebuilt craft for the first time. All of the studies and reconstruction had reached a point that allowed this to occur. But then, a problem arose."

"A problem?" Harrison and Holcomb said, in unison.

"Yes, a problem. One of the propulsion scientists defected to the Soviet Union. When he left, the intact power cell also disappeared."

"So, the Russians have it?" Harrison said.

"Initially, that's what we believed. But Saint Mary didn't take any chances. All of the project's scientists were put under tight surveillance, including your father. This scrutiny revealed nothing. The findings seemed to suggest that our defector was the one responsible."

"I'm sure Saint Mary had the means to determine this for certain, even if the guy was behind the Iron Curtain," Holcomb said.

"It took time. After a few years, we confirmed that he had taken some things with him."

Taylor's smoldering nervousness sparked a fuse in Harrison. The faint, flickering light burned past a tight corner of his mind, where instinct and knowledge intersected. "But not the power cell."

"He took his research notes, a few documents, but not much else of consequence. This brought relief and disappointment to Saint Mary all at the same time. It was a relief because we knew the enemy did not have the power cell. But it was a disappointment because the project didn't know where to look for it next. The defection prompted the Soviets to begin an intensive espionage effort to find out more about our UFO technology, but thanks to some of your work on sensitive aerospace cases while in the FBI, they were never able to get enough of what they really wanted."

Harrison pointed at the thick folder. "They managed to get that to Father Petrov. That's pretty damn close. Must have someone inside Saint Mary itself to get their hands on that."

Taylor remained silent, staring at Harrison, apparently not ready or willing to admit that he had been harboring a spy.

The fuse hissed onward. "The cell has never been recovered?" Harrison said.

"It's still out there." Years of suppressed hope surfaced in Taylor's expression. His features softened. Eyes grew round. He tilted his head to one side and looked up, his calm voice lifting his words toward Harrison. "But I think we can find it."

Harrison scowled at Taylor, impatient for an explanation. "How?"

Taylor paused while he straightened himself in the chair and grasped the armrests. "By the time Saint Mary determined the defector had not taken the cell with him, your father had already been killed. It is my belief that the defector and your father worked together."

Harrison shook his head. "That doesn't make sense. If they had collaborated, the investigation would have revealed it."

"But not if your father wasn't involved until later, when the aggressive scrutiny had been lifted from the scientists, and before our findings in the Soviet Union."

"You mean he was duped by the Soviets?" Holcomb said.

"No, not at all. I am not saying your father was a traitor, willing or otherwise. I think he had his own plans, but collaborating with the enemy was not part of them."

The fuse split and accelerated. "Then what are you suggesting?" One fuse burned a trail to the past, while the other went forward, into a realm where the future was formed.

"Since the Soviet collapse, thousands of KGB documents continue to filter their way into American intelligence organizations, including Saint Mary's network. One of those documents crossed my desk. It was a letter written in 1988 and addressed to Marshal Akhromeyev, who was Gorbachev's military advisor. In the letter, which Akhromeyev soon forwarded to Interior Minister Pugo, the writer—our propulsion scientist—described remorse over his decision to defect. He said that his plans to retrieve a special component did not succeed because the assistance he hoped to get was never forthcoming. The assistance was to come from 'a good man on the inside' whom he tried to contact through cryptic measures."

"Cryptic measures?" Holcomb said.

"He didn't elaborate. I can only assume it was some sort of trail that the insider would be able to find and follow on his own."

"And you think this man was my father?"

"Yes. You see, the scientist's letter indicates the KGB helped determine for him that this man had died in an accident, and that the component was not where the defector had left it. It's my belief that your father discovered the cryptic trail, followed it, and found the component."

"But wait," Holcomb said. "If the defector had the power cell in the first place, why didn't he just take it with him and give it to the Russkies?"

Taylor shook his head and shrugged. "Perhaps he felt it was too much of a risk at the time, or maybe he wanted to use it as some sort of bargaining chip with the Soviets. In any case, he obviously left it behind, and Bernard Harrison was the only propulsion scientist to die in an 'accident.' He knew its value, where it could take us, what it could prove." Taylor's nervous energy wore out. His voice now sounded tired. "And he would have seen to it that it was protected."

His eyes off Taylor and on the Roswell document, Harrison felt the fuse to the past detonate its charges. Bright flashes sheared away dark mounds of deceit. Like new, the colors sparkled. The memories of *graduation day*, and those leading toward it, felt real for the first time. At last, their true meaning was his to know and understand.

"This was the 'larger purpose,' wasn't it, Taylor? You think my father gave it to me?"

"Yes, I do."

"Wait, Bill," Holcomb said, trying to caution his old partner.

"It's okay, Art," Harrison said, giving Holcomb a reassuring nod. He looked back at Taylor. "How do I know this isn't some insane plot by Saint Mary to use me to recover the missing power cell?"

Harrison expected a flinch, a twitch, something that pegged the general to a fraudulent scheme. All he got was an urgent, desperate stare and more of the tired voice.

"This Roswell document is for you. Protect it, along with the other evidence. I'm prepared to turn myself in now if you would like. But I think we need the power cell. The naysayers won't believe us unless we bring them a piece of it, some hardware, a goddamn tailpipe or a power cell, that can bring infinite horizons within our reach. And that's the way it's always been."

Harrison sighed and folded his arms. Holcomb slumped farther into his chair.

"You should also know that Saint Mary has James Evans in Los Angeles now. We can probably assume your family's former residence and Griffith Observatory are being watched."

Harrison furrowed his brow. "Well, I think I understand why my old home in Pasadena would be under surveillance, but I don't quite follow about the observatory."

"At various times during your father's career with Saint Mary, he maintained an office there. Of course, if we visited these places, we would be exposed, but it might also present us with a chance to eliminate the male hybrid."

"Doesn't sound like you like this guy very much," Holcomb said. "Uh, what's a hybrid?"

"He's our most immediate threat," Taylor said.

Harrison shook his head and said, "But if he had time to scan us, it would put Janice and your contact in danger. We won't go to either place and risk that happening."

In the Metropolitan Suites' lobby, James Evans sat, legs crossed, in a puffy, brown leather chair. Intuition had tugged him into the building. The sensation was fresh, stronger inside the hotel than outside. The air vibrated with a blend of hatred, fear, and grief. Notions about justice and atonement cut a wake through the pedestrian preoccupations of approaching New Year's Eve celebrations.

James stared at the female desk clerk, waiting until she finished her telephone conversation. Her name was Karen, and she was very pretty.

She can give me what I want.

FORTY THREE

The Tailpipe Solution

"I was concerned all along that you may not recall anything about the power cell, even when presented with this evidence about your father," Taylor said. "The witch hazel was also meant to spur memories of your father, memories that could be scanned. He used it every day after shaving."

"Janice?" Harrison said.

"She was there to help you remember. Her scans were necessary to help stimulate faded memories, anything that might assist us in our search."

"And what did she find?"

"Hope."

Harrison averted his blurring eyes, blinking them dry. He cleared his throat and said, "I guess you had some sort of plan for resolving this case?"

Taylor nodded and said, "I had two goals in mind. First, we must halt the operation at the new base. It's scheduled for Wednesday night. They plan to coordinate several functions of the project in order to intercept an alien craft and capture its occupants. Second, we must expose Saint Mary. To do both, we must present the evidence to Senator Vaughn from New Mexico."

"Senator Vaughn?" Harrison said.

"She has actively pressured our government for assistance in investigating cattle mutilations, a phenomenon for which Saint Mary is also responsible. Publically and privately, she has never accepted the air force's explanations of the Roswell event, and continues to demand the release of all government records on the subject. She is also a close friend of the President. Unfortunately, Saint Mary has effectively stalled her through well-managed disinformation. My plan was meant to overcome that, with the power cell as the best evidence."

"The tailpipe solution," Holcomb said.

"Wouldn't she have the same fears that motivate Saint Mary?" Harrison said.

"At what cost though?" Taylor said. "The continued deterioration of legitimate government? Her values and integrity are beyond reproach. She will see the truth and know we are better served by it than fear, murder, and deceit. If we are to face a new world, then we should face it with a clean slate. We have to force those who have destroyed so much to be accountable for their crimes."

"A senator, no matter how well intentioned or well connected, can't possibly make the kind of difference you're talking about," Holcomb said.

Taylor's sunburnt face reddened. "Your cynicism is counterproductive. Our government can never recover its credibility unless the resolution of the Saint Mary crisis comes from the institutions you so readily dismiss. And a strong government will be needed to lead us into the unknown."

"General, I'm afraid I don't share your faith in Washington."

"Wait," Harrison said. "The general's right." He stepped toward the window and peered outside. Turning around, he said. "Art, you wouldn't work as hard as you do if you didn't care. And you care because somewhere deep inside, you know Americans need people like you and organizations like the FBI. They depend on the protection you provide, protection of their rights against forces that can overwhelm them. If they don't believe our government can still do that, then Saint Mary will forever sweep aside our history, our traditions. Can the government reign in Saint Mary? It can if we help. After all, the government is not some sort of enemy or abstract entity. It can be if we relinquish our control of it. It belongs to all of us, and people deserve to have it work. We get out of it what we put into it."

"That's all well and good, buddy," Holcomb said. "But won't the government still be expected to protect us against the aliens? They will, and that's why I say we can't expect much to change."

"Art, threat or not, the government, our government, has no right to deny us from such a profound truth. It certainly has no right or power to violate the law. Besides, maybe the threat is only something we imagine out of fear and isn't real at all."

"Bill, that sounds noble, but how will it play with the bureaucrats and good old boys on the Hill, let alone the public? The status quo is the only truth that seems to matter. Civics may not have been my best subject, but politics is something I know all too well."

"What makes you think the public is less capable than you to deal with the truth, Agent Holcomb?" Taylor said. "It is exactly that kind of arrogance which has driven Saint Mary and keeps the cover-up in place. Honestly, I expected more from you."

Holcomb rubbed his bald head and glared at the general. "Look, ET, I want us to succeed as much as you, but I'm just trying to point out the obstacles. We need to be realistic here."

"Assuming we proceed with your plan," Harrison said, attempting to intervene. "How did you intend to make contact with Senator Vaughn?"

"Following my signal, a message will be sent to the senator through discreet channels to expect a visit. I've laid some prior groundwork for this with her. But first, I have to ask, do you have any ideas at all about where your father may have hidden the power cell?"

Harrison heard the general's question, but did not reply. His eyelids fluttered, and he felt pressure on his temples increase, and then give way. As his mind moved him down a path of memories, he felt like someone watched him.

Drifting back, years now, into his past, Harrison began to recall a long ceremony. It ended, and his mother hugged him. Dad gave him a gift and insisted that infinite horizons were within his reach.

This is my secret! My truth!

Harrison held the gift, smiling, thanking his father.

For a torturous moment, Harrison regained control, nearly forcing away the intruder from his mind. *You will not know this!*

But the trespasser fought back, unrelenting; it had so many questions.

More memories blended with images, images that encroached from outside, from *the intruder*. Harrison gave Janice a silver roadrunner pin. As she lay on a blue gurney in a blank, white room, he told her that he would come for her. He assured her that he could help, just as she tried to help him. Soon, her lonely existence in Saint Mary would end.

And then the intruder took control of his thoughts. Memories twisted into revelations. His mind ached as the intruder solved the deep, unknown riddle that Harrison's father had concocted.

Harrison jogged up a long set of white steps. Slowing, and then setting down the briefcase, he looked across the National Mall, through the falling snow. Behind him, the Capitol dome rose into the low cloud cover. He searched the horizon and spotted the Jefferson Memorial. Smiling and raising his hands above his head, he slammed the old globe his Dad gave him against the cold, hard steps. It split evenly down the middle, revealing its secret, an alien power cell capable of bringing infinite horizons within reach. The cell tumbled downward, out of reach. As Harrison stared at the piece of exotic metal and mesh, the intruder told Harrison to open his briefcase. He complied.

"Bill, you okay?" Holcomb said.

Harrison stepped away from the hotel-room window, feeling arrogant, decisive, and headed to the hotel room's door.

More muted questions emanated from behind him, but he needed to unlock the door.

Harrison drew his Colt, unlatched the door, and turned around, holding Taylor and Holcomb at gunpoint. He clicked off the gun's thumb safety and applied light pressure to its trigger.

FORTY FOUR

The Old Globe

Taylor and Holcomb dropped their guns to the floor and raised their hands. Harrison ordered them to back up, toward the window.

The *intruder* told Harrison to shoot them; *they* did not need them any longer.

Gasping for air, Harrison fought the wrongful urge to shoot.

"Fine!" the intruder said.

Harrison took a slow, deep breath. His eyes, wide and clear, saw nothing as he lowered the Colt. He felt, somehow, it would not enter the room until he put the gun down. His hand shook.

"Put the gun on the nightstand."

The clear voice emanated from behind him. He listened, but fought back.

"Seems like infinite horizons are within your reach," the intruder said.

Harrison felt so grateful for the gift. But then, a sharper noise interrupted.

"Hey, buddy, take it easy, okay?"

Harrison fought to focus. His eyelids fluttered again, sucking stinging sweat into his eyes.

Holcomb stood before him. "Just do what he says, Bill."

"Just put the gun on the nightstand and no one will get hurt."

Then, he heard another voice from behind him. *"You should do what he says."* The voice belonged to Janice. *"Bill, he knows what he's doing. Trust me."*

Harrison took a step, and then stopped. He fought for control. "Where are you?"

"Trust me, Bill."

"I can't."

It hollered at him to lower the gun. *"Now, just drop it!"*

"I can't."

"Why not?"

"Because..." Harrison said, twisting toward the door.

It ordered him to turn back. *"Besides, Janice did not want anything to do with you. She loved Saint Mary, not you."*

Harrison fought the lies. Images of a distant memory appeared at the end of a dark tunnel. The vision tugged his consciousness down the shadowy passageway into the light. He and Janice embraced, they told each other good-bye, and they felt unconditional love for each other.

"Liar!" Harrison shouted at the intruder.

The pressure evaporated, and in that same instant, Harrison felt a rush of fear. But he was not the one who felt afraid. He pulled the trigger. At the end of what seemed like an eternity, the Colt fired, sending a single round through the door.

A muffled cry erupted from the hallway.

Harrison collapsed onto the floor. He clutched his head and lurched toward the door.

"Throw it open!" Holcomb said.

Harrison's left hand tugged at the door, yanking it open, but he fell to the floor again.

Holcomb recovered his 9 mm and then jumped past Harrison, kneeling in the doorframe. He looked left, then right. "He ducked into the stairwell."

James Evans stumbled down the first flight of stairs and landed hard against a concrete wall. The pain in his right arm intensified with each hysterical breath. He had never experienced panic, except when he sensed it in others. Dizziness dimmed his surroundings, and distress gripped him. General Stone would never forgive him for rushing in without help.

The pain and panic pushed James onward, trying to distance himself from his pursuers. He needed time to use his phone. Not much use to him, his right arm dangled at his side drenched in blood. The right side of his sweater was saturated, and he clutched the seeping wound with his left hand. Descending the stairs, he could feel the shattered bone in his arm swing loosely by its tendons.

At ground level, shock sieged his consciousness. A sensation of drowning threatened to suffocate him. He could feel nothing in his right arm and shoulder. With his left hand smeared with blood, he tightened his grasp on the wound and stopped to rest.

His chest heaved.

In, out.

From above, the sound drew closer—metallic tapping, like that heard in the stairwells of the underground Saint Mary complex.

James had never felt so alone, and he fought hard not to cry. He summoned all of his courage and what remained of his strength. Then, he cleared his mind.

Holcomb aimed the 9 mm through the railing on the stairs. His quick movements carried him downward. He did not wait for Harrison to recover before beginning the chase; he believed his friend would be there soon enough to back him up.

With sweat dripping from his forehead and with heavy breath, Holcomb descended the stairs. A fleeting, floating sensation trifled with his concentration. He jerked back, pressing against the wall, next to a reddish-orange smear. Thick drops of it splattered the steps in places. Above, he heard a door slam and hoped Harrison was on his way. The sensation tugged him again, and Holcomb worried he had made a mistake.

But a possible solution revealed itself.

Another tug.

Holcomb performed the necessary functions on the 9 mm, and then let *the thing* tug him down the stairs.

Harrison preferred not to kill James Evans, but he resolved himself to stop the hybrid from communicating the knowledge he'd stolen from him. And if that meant killing him, then he would do it without hesitation to protect Janice and the truth.

Descending the stairs, limping, hurrying despite the pain throbbing in his thigh and head, he hoped Holcomb would take care of himself should his friend encounter the hybrid alone.

And at the bottom of the stairs, Harrison ran into both of them. Holcomb, poised to shoot, aimed the 9 mm at Harrison.

Taylor collected the Roswell engineering document and his snub-nosed .357 magnum revolver. He patted his chest and confirmed that he carried his cell phone. A quick check of Harrison's suitcase revealed no other items of importance.

Entering the hallway, he offered a few official-sounding words to the handful of people who had gathered following the disturbance. He announced the police were already on their way and that everyone should remain calm and return to their rooms to await their arrival.

Then, he headed for the elevator.

"Shit!" Harrison said, diving for cover up the stairs. His right foot got caught up on one of the steps, and he tripped, falling flat on his chest. He spun around in time to watch Holcomb pull the trigger.

A resounding, superficial click echoed off the concrete walls as the 9 mm's hammer made a firm connection against the firing pin. The firing pin struck an empty chamber, and Harrison discerned no sign of a magazine in the weapon.

Tearing his focus away from his friend's gun, Harrison aimed the .45 at the doorway, but James had already escaped. The exit's metal door made a heavy bang as it struck the outside wall.

Holcomb fell to his knees.

"We'll stop him yet," Harrison said, stepping by his dazed friend.

"Ahh, my head."

Outside, a woman's scream near the entrance of the hotel drew Harrison in that direction. After hobbling a few steps, he spotted James running past a large group of Asian tourists taking pictures in front of the hotel. He took off after him, followed by Holcomb, who reloaded his gun.

"Need your faster speed right now," Harrison said, with heavy breaths.

"On my way!" Holcomb said. Within a few rapid strides, Holcomb outpaced Harrison and turned a corner around the hotel.

Harrison continued his pursuit, but tripped on the sidewalk's uneven surface near a flower planter. From ahead, around the corner of the building, he heard honking horns and screeching car brakes. Gaining his stance again, he hoped the sounds meant he could catch up.

After crossing the street, James extended his bloody left hand and retrieved the cellular phone from his pants pocket. With blurry vision, he looked ahead and hoped he could make it to the FBI agents parked in front of the hotel down the block.

Almost there.

He peered at the phone, which bounced and shook with each passing step. With left thumb outstretched, he tried to press the auto-dial button for General Stone. But as he tripped and fell, the phone spun out of his hand. He rolled onto his left side and looked back. Through the crowds on the sidewalk, he watched Holcomb stop and kneel. The agent took aim at him and shouted for people to get out of his way.

"No!" James said, struggling to his feet. He lunged, reaching for the cell phone covered with his own blood.

A single gunshot rang out.

The bullet impacted James's right thigh. The hybrid collapsed onto the sidewalk again and clutched the phone. He pushed the button. Tears streamed down his cheeks. In the distance, Holcomb waved people out of his way so he could take another shot.

The receiver clicked.

"Stone, go ahead."

Screaming, James said, "It's in his office!"

"What?"

Another gunman came into view. *Harrison.* Across the street, Harrison knelt against a concrete planter to improve his aim. The barrel of his handgun looked like a black, bottomless cave.

"The power cell is inside a globe in Harrison's office!"

"James?"

Fire—red, orange, yellow, and silver—billowed out of the cave at James.

"Yes, and—"

"James! James, are you there?" Stone said.

Nothing but silence and intermittent static responded to his question.

"Shit!"

Stone hung up and dialed. Three rings and several toe taps later, Colonel Ritter answered.

"Something has gone wrong in LA," Stone said.

"Sir?"

"Just get down to Harrison's office and retrieve the globe he keeps there."

"Yes, sir."

"Colonel, how long will it take?"

"Not long. I'm not far from there now. We're still going over the bank—"

"Just get on it right now, and contact me when you get there." Stone slammed down the phone and then redialed.

"Maxwell, go ahead."

"Where's Evans, goddamn it!" Stone said.

"General?"

"Yes, dammit, where are you, and where is Evans!"

"Several of us are just getting off the freeway near a surveillance location on Los Feliz."

"Is James there?"

"He should be at one of the locations we are heading—"

"He just called me, and then the phone went dead. Get your ass there as fast as you can."

"Yes, sir."

"And Maxwell, if he is dead, you get his body out of there ASAP. Don't question me on this. Get his body back to North Range and clean up any fucking mess you find there."

"Yes, sir!"

People ran and screamed, trying to distance themselves from the gunmen. Harrison knew why, but understood the real threat lay in a lifeless heap, its brains and bone matter scattered on the sidewalk.

But he also understood that an exigent escape for himself and Holcomb stood foremost ahead of any of their other priorities.

A moment later, Harrison realized that Holcomb understood too. The FBI agent ran up to him, huffing and puffing, mumbling something about a good shot, followed by, "No time for this—we have to get the hell out of here!"

Rushing back toward the parking lot adjacent to the Metropolitan Suites, Harrison holstered his Colt and dug car keys out of his pocket. He relayed them to Holcomb.

"What, this again?" Holcomb said.

"Dark blue Chevrolet Caprice, far side of the lot, near the street."

Holcomb sprinted ahead.

Behind him, Harrison heard the distinct sound of screeching brakes.

The two FBI agents on surveillance a block away heard the gunfire. They rushed in, halting their sedan on the street next to where James had come to rest. The agent in the passenger seat jumped out. Several witnesses rushed in, shouting in near unison, "They ran that way!"

The agent signaled for his partner to drive ahead, and then he looked at the mess on the sidewalk. Noticing the orange tint in the dead man's blood, he said, "What the hell?"

A metallic gray sedan crunched its way onto the sidewalk and stopped directly in Harrison's path, interrupting his hobbling. The driver's door cranked open, and a chunky, white-haired man with a white moustache wearing a navy-blue three-piece suit tumbled out, aiming a handgun at Harrison.

"FBI!" the man said.

"No shit," Harrison said, putting his hands in the air. He saw Holcomb pull his car out of the parking lot ahead. "Really, I'm not one of the bad guys."

"Just shut up and get on your knees!"

Harrison winced. The abrupt reaction stemmed not from any pain endured from kneeling, but instead from the sudden appearance of General Taylor running up behind and directly at the FBI agent.

That's going to hurt.

The full weight and speed of Taylor's impact against the FBI agent sent him hurtling forward onto the ground. A sturdy whack on the back the head with a snub-nosed .357 magnum revolver sent the agent straight into unconsciousness.

"Get in and you drive!" Taylor said, scrambling to his feet.

Harrison complied and piled into the FBI agent's still-running vehicle behind Taylor. Before Harrison could pull the transmission lever into "drive," Holcomb pulled up next to them in the dark blue Chevrolet Caprice and slammed on the brakes. Wide-eyed consternation seized Harrison's gaze.

"I don't know yet, Art, just follow us!" Harrison said, and then he floored the accelerator. They sped away, heading for the nearest freeway on ramp. Holcomb fell in behind them.

Alone in Harrison's office, Colonel Ritter wandered toward the globe. He spun the sphere, admiring the nostalgic antiquity of it. The rotation stopped, and the lines on the land mass that stared up at him no longer existed, fracturing many years ago.

How times have changed.

A chirp from his cellular phone interrupted Ritter's memories.

"Ritter here...Yes, I've retrieved those other items already...Yes, I understand...I get the feeling I'm standing in front of it right now... Stone ordered me to retrieve the globe inside Harrison's office... Perhaps it's what may be inside the globe that matters... I'll just have to stop at an antique store or pawn shop before I head back to North Range first..."

Between erratic maneuvers, Harrison fumbled for and then answered his ringing cell phone.

"I'm pretty sure we picked up a tail," Holcomb said without delay. "Looks like just one car. Where are we headed?"

"As much as I wanted to avoid it, we may need to call in Zemdarsky for some help. His son runs an air charter business out of Long Beach Airport, so I suggest we head that way. If anything, it gets us out of the area and to an initial rally point."

"Alright, I'll take this guy for a little ride and meet you at the airport."

"Be safe, brother, and good luck."

"You too. Remember. 'Rock around the clock.'"

"Got it!"

In the rear view mirror Harrison saw Holcomb peel off down a side street. A sedan followed him, but it looked clear after that. Harrison entered the freeway and headed south towards Long Beach.

Once into the flow of traffic, Taylor ended his phone conversation and said, "Where are you going?"

Harrison shook his head and then said, "Right now, barring any bright ideas from you, I'm heading to the Long Beach Airport."

"Why that airport?"

"My partner, Pete Zemdarsky, has a son who owns an air charter service there. I figured they could help us out. Besides, he's a good friend of Vaughn's husband, they go way back."

"I know."

"I bet. Look, if Pete's son can help us, what's our destination after we leave Long Beach?"

"Initially, the Tucson Airport, and then to Las Cruces to meet with Senator Vaughn."

"I get the Las Cruces part, but Tucson? Certainly Saint Mary will get to the globe before us."

"Saint Mary has a cover business near the airport."

Harrison waited. After several seconds of silence, he said, "And?"

"Your globe should be there."

"Should be? You're not sure?"

"More than anyone else you should know that faith can be elusive. The senator and the American people will have my testimony, the video file of James Evans executing the alien, the Roswell document with its enumerable engineering reports, and hopefully, the power cell."

"And don't forget the Blair evidence."

"We need to make arrangements to retrieve Ms. O'Donnell and her evidence after we meet with Senator Vaughn."

"I have the code phrase and know how to get in touch with her, so don't worry."

"You better call your partner, then, while I book an airline ticket to Russia"

"Huh?"

"Disinformation. An empty trail. Part of a cover story I worked out with Janice."

"Got it. I think." Harrison fumbled again for his cell phone. He paused and looked at Taylor. "Are these safe to use? Wouldn't they be tracking our calls?"

"Normally, but thanks to some help on the inside, we'll be safe for now."

"Okay, good to know." Harrison dialed Zemdarsky's number and a cheerful voice greeted him.

"Willy my boy, so good to hear from you!"

"I've been busy. How's the family and Beano?"

"Wonderful and stinky in that order. It's nice to enjoy the Holidays with the kids. And your foul beast, I suppose. How's the case going?"

"Oh, it's going. In fact, I'm back in Los Angeles stirring up trouble."

"Oh, wonderful, you should visit!"

"I'm pretty sure I can arrange that."

An hour and a half later, Harrison stood on the tarmac near the Long Beach Airport's executive terminal. A Cessna Citation CJ3, piloted by Henry "Hank" Zemdarsky, warmed up its engines just a few yards away. Pete Zemdarksy and Taylor waited for Harrison on the steps leading up to the plane.

A sinking feeling in his gut and ache in his heart kept Harrison from turning his back on Holcomb and boarding the plane. Repeated attempts to contact him by telephone failed. No word from his former partner since he led the follower off their track made Harrison imagine the worst.

"We have to go," Taylor said, shouting over the rising whine of the Cessna's jet engines.

Harrison's eyes met Pete Zemdarsky's. Taylor walked up the stairs and into the plane.

"We'll go when you're ready to go," Pete said.

Harrison nodded. He gazed around the terminal in one last futile effort to find a flash of headlights or some other indication his old partner had joined them.

Nothing.

Harrison sighed. He limped to the plane and followed Pete up the stairs.

FORTY FIVE

Balls to the Wall

"So, this is the notorious 'Echo Tango?'" Pete said.

Harrison glanced at his informant. Taylor reclined in one of the black leather passenger chairs aboard the Cessna. He had passed out from exhaustion after departing Long Beach. Now, at 24,000 feet over southern Arizona, he remained asleep with a cozy wool blanket draped over him.

"He is," Harrison said.

"Well, you tell an amazing story, and so does that engineering document. I can't believe what's in there, especially the reports from your dad."

"I know it's all so hard to believe."

"I guess you really have been busy, after all," Zemdarsky said, smiling and winking.

"We have," Harrison said. But his partner's cheeriness did not raise Harrison's spirits. He thought of Holcomb, of all they had been through together, and his heart ached. Ridley's presumed death haunted him too. Guilt overwhelmed Harrison and his eyes welled up.

Zemdarsky reached out and put his hand on Harrison's shoulder. "I'll call George Vaughn and get us in with the senator. She's a fighter, that one. She'll kick ass for us, I know it."

Harrison nodded and wiped his moistened eyes. "Thanks, Pete."

Several minutes later General Taylor stirred and awakened. He sat upright and looked at Harrison, saying, "How long have I been out?"

"Since soon after departure."

"And where are we now?"

"Almost to Tucson, should begin our descent in a few minutes."

Taylor looked at his watch and then said, "He's made good time."

"The pilot said something about flying the plane 'balls to the wall' after we reached cruising altitude. I think Pete's son was trying to impress an old air force fighter jockey."

Taylor chuckled and smiled. "Emphasis on old." His eyes drifted out the nearest window. "I miss those flying days. Life was..."

"And yet here we are, chasing down an alien flying saucer power cell while Saint Mary pursues us."

Taylor's gaze returned to Harrison. "Indeed."

"If Art and Nick Ridley are in their custody, where would they take them?"

Taylor yawned, rubbed his face, and then said, "North Range. Area 51's replacement facility in northeast Nevada. They have detention facilities underground and lots of empty space above for people to disappear."

"We must convince Senator Vaughn and her ally in the White House to conduct a rescue mission. We must convince them to occupy North Range and halt Saint Mary in its tracks."

"You think big. I like where you are going with this."

"I intend to take the fight to them instead of running away. Even if it's just me, my dog, and my .45, I will personally invade North Range myself and take back what belongs to us all."

Thirty-five minutes later, Harrison and Taylor hailed a cab in front of the executive terminal building at Tucson International Airport. Henry Zemdarsky made further flight arrangements while his plane took on extra fuel for the run to Las Cruces and beyond.

"Are you sure you can't use some help?" Pete said. He looked forlorn while standing several feet behind Harrison and Taylor on the sidewalk.

The two men paused their entry into the cab. Harrison turned and said, "Stay with Henry, we got this, buddy."

"Okay. I'll just stay here with Henry and the plane while you guys go and fetch..."

Taylor turned and glared. Harrison just smiled.

"...Donuts."

The pair piled into the cab and Pete stepped inside the terminal.

After settling into the back seat with Taylor, Harrison turned to the General and said, "Pete's such a kidder, he likes to kid around."

Taylor ignored Harrison and provided the cab driver with the address for a nearby office complex.

"That's right up the road," the cabbie said. Then, under his breath, he said, "Hardly worth my effort."

Harrison reached into his wallet and handed the driver two twenties. "That should help make it worthwhile."

"Oh yes, it does, thank you."

As they neared the vicinity of the office complex, Harrison instructed the cabbie to park across the street from its location. Conveniently enough, a donut shop occupied the area where Harrison had directed him to park.

Harrison handed the driver another forty dollars and asked him to purchase a dozen donuts and four large coffees to go. "Get yourself something too and keep the change."

"Yes, sir!"

After exiting the cab, Taylor and Harrison made a path toward the ordinary-looking two-story office complex. "We going inside?" Harrison said.

"No, just to the parking lot outside. We are looking for a black Ford Explorer with Virginia license plates."

"What kind of cover business is here?"

"Avionics sales, repair, and supply."

"Good fit with the environment."

"A former Circle member, now deceased apparently, once resided in Tucson and used this space for meetings with working group officers. It's hardly used for any covert activities now, but it's still on Saint Mary's books."

They approached the parking lot and found their target. While closing the distance to the Ford Explorer, Harrison said, "How we getting in?"

"The key is in the tailpipe. The globe should be on floor behind the driver's seat."

"Got it. You keep watch and I will get into the car."

"But–"

"I got this, General."

While Taylor stood lookout, Harrison moved in and crouched behind the vehicle. He swiped his index finger into the dark exhaust tube and felt nothing.

"Crap."

"What," Taylor said, whispering.

Harrison shoved his finger farther into the tailpipe. This time, the tip of his finger danced across an object within; but this action only succeeded in pushing it deeper into the tube. "Shit."

Harrison grabbed a ballpoint pen out of his coat's interior pocket. With cautious manipulation, he maneuvered the tip of the pen into the pipe, tilted it downward, and then dragged it rearward. A small metallic ring with one key attached came with it. "Got it!"

"Headlights get down!" Taylor said, his voice hushed.

Harrison pressed his body to the cold asphalt and then he squirmed into position underneath the Ford. His right leg throbbed. Taylor dodged somewhere out of view.

While holding his breath, Harrison heard a vehicle drive right by their location. With its windows obviously rolled down, loud, techno-style music came from within the car. It passed them and parked a short distance away in a dark corner of the parking lot.

No car doors opened or closed, and after a few minutes, it became apparent to Harrison the occupants of the vehicle presented no threat. Faint sounds of lovemaking floated across the parking lot.

Harrison chuckled in relief and then resumed his entry into the vehicle. The key fit into the passenger side door and it unlocked with ease. He lifted the handle and the door popped open. After reaching inside behind the driver's seat, Harrison felt a gym bag with a round object within it. "Let's hope it's a globe and not a basketball."

Out came the gym bag with a quick tug. Harrison opened it and under the dim light saw a familiar object. A gift. An intact container that held an ultimate secret within.

With the gym bag, donuts, and coffee in tow, Harrison and Taylor piled out of the cab at the executive terminal building. They met up with the Zemdarsky's at the plane.

After climbing aboard, Harrison gave Henry a thumbs up gesture.

The young pilot closed and latched the door and then headed into the flight deck.

"Thanks for the treats," Pete said. "Looks like you had a successful mission."

"We'll find out for sure right now," Harrison said.

General Taylor handed off the donuts and coffee to Pete and then sat down next to Harrison.

The Cessna's turbine engines spooled up, sending a rising hum through the cabin.

Harrison unzipped the gym bag and removed the globe.

"That looks familiar," Pete said.

"Very," Harrison said. While he inspected the object for several seconds, Harrison recalled—with more clarity than ever—that special moment when his father presented it to him as a gift. He closed his eyes and thanked his father in silence. Also in silence, he thanked God for blessing him with wonderful parents and asked Him to bring success to their impending efforts.

Harrison opened his eyes and then he unscrewed the stand's connections with the globe. After detaching the globe, he set the stand aside. He held the sphere in front of him and the United States of

America peered up at him. Harrison smiled and then let his eyes drift over other parts of the globe. As he examined it closer, Harrison noticed a few worn areas along the seam covering the globe's equator.

While still inspecting the seam, Harrison said, "Does anyone have a pocket knife?" Taylor's hand appeared in view. A Swiss Army knife rested on his palm. Harrison grasped the knife and then cradled the globe in his lap.

Harrison made gentle slices into the seam. He worked the knife around the entire equator. Afterwards, he folded up the knife and handed it back to Taylor. Harrison separated the equatorial halves. The globe's hemisphere in his lap cradled the featherweight and translucent power cell.

FORTY SIX

Hate to Lose

During the short flight from Tucson to Las Cruces, Harrison moved up to the cockpit and sat next to Henry, and spent most of his time reassembling the globe, power cell inside, using some duct tape from a tool kit he found in the main cabin.

"We're on final approach," Henry said. "Airport is just ahead and we've been cleared to land. Our instructions from the tower are to taxi to a hanger at the southeast corner of the airport. I guess that's where Vaughn will be waiting?"

"Let's hope." Harrison yawned and looked back into the dim cabin. Pete read the technical manual about the Roswell craft, and Taylor's eyes remained fixed on the dark, middle-of-the-night skies outside his window.

As Harrison looked forward through the cockpit windshield, he could see the lights of Las Cruces, as well as those of the approaching runway. He ran his hands along the surface of the globe, cradled in his lap, and checked the equatorial seam that he had just finished taping together.

The plane shimmied when Henry lowered the landing gear. Other than that and a slight bounce when they landed, their arrival was smooth.

"Welcome to Las Cruces," Henry said.

Harrison smiled. "Thanks. One step closer to our destination." He ran his hand inside his coat and loosened the Colt in its holster. *Just in case.* He kept a firm grip on it while scanning their surroundings the entire way to the hanger.

"Looks like they are expecting us," Henry said, pointing out the entrance to the hanger. "Doors are open and lights are on. Let's roll right in."

As they approached and entered the hanger, Harrison looked for anyone who might be waiting for them.

"There's George," Pete said. "And there's Judy. Looks like the senator means business."

Fists on her hips, Senator Vaughn stood next to her husband, both bundled in winter coats. George waved to the plane then covered his ears against the sound of the jet engines. Vaughn's fists remained on her hips.

As soon as the plane stopped, Pete popped open the cabin door and scrambled out, Roswell technical document still in hand. He headed straight to his good friend George Vaughn and his wife, Judith.

"Just stand by here, Henry," Harrison said. He exited the plane, still gripping the globe. Taylor followed right behind him. They caught up to Pete while he hugged both George and the senator.

"I couldn't tell you much on the phone earlier, George, so thank you for meeting us here at this ungodly hour. Believe me, it is a matter of national security of the highest order," Pete said. "These gentlemen are William Harrison and Edward Taylor. Senator, I believe you already know the General."

"Yes," Vaughn said, nodding at Taylor and offering Harrison a firm, quick handshake. "And if what you say is true, then there isn't much time. I've already spoken to the President. He wants to meet us in person at Camp David as soon as possible. Do you have the evidence?"

Pete raised the Roswell technical document for all to see, and Harrison did the same with the globe. "The rest is on the plane, and more is with a forensics specialist in Virginia," Harrison said.

"These two items in particular," Taylor said, "are most crucial, and we would not have them if it weren't for Mr. Harrison. The long-missing power cell is in his hands, but the Saint Mary threat remains, and they are at their most dangerous right now."

"They are also very vulnerable," Harrison said. "Look, lives are at stake. Real people, people I know, are in peril, as well as the nation and perhaps the world itself. I need to know if the President is prepared to take action. He must authorize a raid on North Range. Saint Mary must be confronted..." Harrison paused, recalling and then sharing the words of one of his political heroes. "'There here is no escaping either the gravity or the totality of its challenge to our survival and to our security.'"

"'Its preparations are concealed, not published. Its mistakes are buried, not headlined. Its dissenters are silenced, not praised. No expenditure is questioned, no rumor is printed, no secret is revealed.'" Vaughn said, quoting from the same speech about secrecy by John F. Kennedy. "You know, Mr. Harrison, some say President Kennedy was killed because of those beliefs."

"Then justice must be served, otherwise, they win and we continue to lose."

"As an American," Vaughn said, "I believe in this cause. And as a politician, I can tell you, I hate to lose."

"And as a wife," George said, nudging Pete with his elbow.

"All right, gentlemen, let's go," Vaughn said. "I'll get us clearance to land at Andrews Air Force Base. The Secret Service will take us from there to Camp David. Is your pilot ready?"

"Hank is ready, Judy," Pete said. "We are serving donuts and cold coffee in coach if you're hungry."

Harrison handed the globe to the senator and said, "Please take this. I have a call to make. And thank you for helping us."

"Thank me when we cross the finish line," Vaughn said, grasping the globe. She joined the others who were already boarding the plane.

Searching his phone for Margaret O'Donnell's telephone number, Harrison tried to calculate a place and time for her to meet them. Sending her to Andrews might be risky. On her own and without direct protection, any number of Saint Mary operatives at the base could intercept her.

Got to keep her safe.

In his mind, he pictured the once familiar geography of Virginia, Maryland, and Washington, D.C., and then smiled when he remembered one place in particular.

He dialed Maggie's number. After several rings, the first attempt reached her voicemail. He tried again, and heard a groggy voice answer the call.

"Hello?"

"Maggie?"

"Who wants to know?

"Maggie, it's Bill. Bill Harrison."

"I can only imagine what this is about."

"Rock around the clock, Maggie. Rock around the clock."

"Okay, you've got my attention. Where is Art?"

"I don't know, but wherever he is, I am sure he needs help. And so do you. We are coming to get you, but you need to make your way north along with the evidence."

"I can do that. Where should I meet you?"

Despite Taylor's earlier assurances about their cell phone calls, Harrison wanted to protect Maggie as much as possible. "Do you remember that road trip I took with you and Art? The one where we ended up making a stop because Art's food poisoning really kicked in?"

"Lord, how could I ever forget. He made quite a scene."

"Meet us there. I figure we'll pick you up in about five hours or so, but be early just in case."

"I'll be there."

"Thanks, Maggie, and be safe."

Harrison ended the call and headed toward the plane. Once aboard, he heard Henry start up the engines. He took a seat next to Pete who offered him a donut and the widest grin he had ever seen.

FORTY SEVEN

Closing In

The only sound inside one of the dim briefing rooms at North Range emanated from a television mounted on a wall sprayed with a recent coat of cottage-white paint. A digital clock next to the television indicated 7:00 a.m. local time. The CNN announcer broadcasted a message that engulfed the men watching it with apprehension.

"The Department of Defense and F.B.I. have not provided any further details on William Bernard Harrison, a private investigator and former F.B.I. agent who is a suspect in an espionage ring that a Pentagon spokesperson described as 'directed by a rogue nationalist group in Russia.' A second suspect, Arthur Holcomb, currently an F.B.I. agent from Baltimore, also remains at large..."

An unflattering photograph of Holcomb appeared on the screen.

The CNN announcer continued, saying, "The Pentagon requests assistance from citizens in locating Harrison and Holcomb. They say both are armed and considered dangerous. If anyone sees these individuals, they should contact the police or nearest F.B.I. office immediately. The Pentagon spokesman also stated that a third suspect was involved, but declined to offer any further description because doing so may jeopardize the investigation. In other news, Taiwan has shot down a Communist Chinese aircraft that strayed into its airspace, prompting the President to make a statement from Camp David where he is spending the holidays. He reassured allies and leaders at home that the situation is being closely monitored, and that preparations for all options to defend the region are being made..."

General Stone lowered the volume with the remote. Air Force weapons specialist General Lanham sat across from him. He cleared his throat and said, "So as far as the public is concerned, they have no idea we have Holcomb in custody?"

"Correct," Stone said, "An element from our security detachment spotted him in the vicinity of the hotel. A short car chase ensued and our agents captured him. Only we know the truth about his capture."

"And the incident with the male hybrid?"

Stone looked at the officer who had asked the question. Admiral Horner dabbed his forehead with a handkerchief even while the room's temperature hovered at a comfortable seventy-two degrees. Stone worried some of working-group officers would break under the strain. He projected confidence when he spoke.

"Unfortunate. But, our security teams acted quickly, and they gained control of the situation before local authorities initiated an adequate investigation." Stone nodded at the officer next to him, the only officer who looked relaxed. "Colonel Bennet's efforts with implementing the disinformation protocols are taking hold. Hell, even our own personnel will probably begin to doubt what they saw."

"But wasn't there a nonessential FBI agent at the scene?" Admiral Horner said, wiping his forehead.

"We managed to remove him from the area," Stone said.

Some of the officers around the desk stirred.

"But he is under active, very active, surveillance," Stone said. "And we will continue to monitor him closely until this situation calms down and the necessary asset is available for further resolution."

"What about the President?" General Lanham said.

At one end of the table, two hands cut a swath through the air. "Our D.I.A. associate personally briefed the President earlier today," Dennis, the working group's chairman, said. "Containment has been easily achieved in that area. We don't anticipate any problems arising from the White House. In fact, it was the impression of our associate that the President seemed quite satisfied and in a hurry to resume his holiday vacation at Camp David in peace."

Despite the foul gush of breath from the chairman's mouth that drifted in front of Stone's nose, he managed a polite smile. He wanted to appear as optimistic as possible and not reveal his concern about Harrison and Taylor's escape.

"And what about Harrison and General Taylor?" Lanham said.

"We are employing various methods on Holcomb to learn more and will determine their whereabouts soon," Stone said. "The female hybrid is interrogating Holcomb right now. When she is finished, more traditional methods will also be employed as a double check."

"I understand," General Lanham said, "that Colonel Ritter recovered the globe you spoke about at last night's briefing?"

Now that question posed a problem for Stone. The question required him to answer, but he knew it meant including other information the officers would find hard to swallow.

James had been wrong, simply wrong, and insubordinate.

"When we opened it here," Stone said, "the globe contained nothing. Harrison must have been mistaken about the power cell's location if he was the one from whom James extracted the information."

Stone saw questions brewing on their lips, so he hurried his next words. "On a more positive note, Colonel Ritter did uncover some new information when he was in Tucson. While he was in Harrison's office retrieving the globe, he found a bank statement that someone had apparently slipped under the door. An attached note said, 'This was delivered to our office by mistake.' The bank statement had Harrison's business address on it, but the name 'Donald Hiatt' appeared as the addressee. Ritter used the information and located a safe-deposit box containing potentially dangerous information."

"What was inside?" Colonel Bennet said, finally showing some interest.

Stone ran down the list. "Some anonymous letters, no doubt from Edward Taylor, copies of documents pertaining to Major Blair, the air force's accident report, next-of-kin notification, the Protocol One memo authorizing that activity, and some old police reports dating from the late forties and early fifties."

Bennet's green and brown eyes widened behind the horn-rims. "Police reports?

"Single-vehicle traffic accidents concerning military police personnel with direct involvement in the Roswell incident," Stone said.

Bennet relaxed. Green and brown became indistinguishable. He mumbled something about tragic coincidences.

"Gentlemen," the chairman said, "we need to make a recommendation to the Circle. As you are aware, the Circle's members are due here later today for the demonstration. Given our current situation, do we recommend they come, or not? What are some alternatives?"

Stone faced away from the cloud of halitosis that floated his way and encouraged his colleagues to speak freely.

They did, profusely, and their caution soon formed a consensus.

The chairman decided to advise the Circle to delay their visit until the security situation gained further clarity and their operatives closed in on Harrison and Taylor. The results of Holcomb's interrogations would require evaluation too.

The gathering quickly dissolved into various fragments. Stone signaled to the chairman and escorted him to the detention area.

Colonel Ritter approached General Stone and the chairman as soon as they entered the detention area. "I was just preparing to phone you, sirs."

"What's her status?" Stone said, stepping past Ritter, out of the range of the chairman's bad breath.

Ritter fidgeted between the two men, uncertain whom he should address. He opted for Stone. "She scanned Holcomb and then drove him to the floor in pain."

"He fought back?" the chairman said.

Still facing Stone, Ritter said, "And he continues to do so." Ritter pointed at Holcomb, who sat in a metal chair on the other side of the one-way mirror. The agent's face contorted into a twisted, reddened mess. Drool lapped at his chin. He cried tears too. The audio speaker mounted above the observers' heads hinted that Holcomb strained to verbalize his mental anguish.

Janice stood next to him, fists thrust into her hips.

"I assume she is almost done with him," Ritter said.

"Very good, colonel," Stone said, eyes fixed on the FBI agent.

Holcomb fell out of the chair. The handcuffs around his wrists cut harder into bone. He twitched and rolled onto his stomach, panting, crying.

"She's done," Ritter said. He unbolted the access door and allowed Janice to exit Holcomb's cell. The agent's body odor filtered out before Ritter closed the door. Even the chairman grimaced and stepped back.

A few beads of sweat rolled down Janice's forehead. She blinked her eyelids in rapid succession, even while flipping through the notebook in her hands.

Stone dismissed Ritter and then said, "What can you tell us, Janice?"

She used the back of one her hands to wipe away the sweat. Her features projected tiredness. Red surrounded her blue eyes. Bags pushed their way up toward the redness.

"If you need a minute or two, Janice," Stone said.

"This bastard helped kill my brother! Sir, why did I have to find out that way?"

The chairman spoke up, conducting an explanation with wafting hands. "That was my decision. I felt it was necessary to test you under stress. General Stone tried to convince me otherwise."

Janice looked the chairman up and down. Her eyes narrowed on his. "God, chew some gum, whoever you are."

The chairman, for once, held still. And he closed his mouth.

"Test me? General Stone, who is—"

"At ease, Janice. He is the working group's chairman. You shall address him as 'sir.' You will show him the same respect you give me, understood?"

Janice bowed her head at the chairman. "I'm sorry, sir, I'm just very tired. This murderer has worn me out."

"That's understandable," the chairman said. "And I'm sorry for your loss."

"Janice," Stone said, reaching out and putting his hand on her shoulder, "can you tell us what you've learned?"

Janice sniffled and nodded. She wiped her nose, and then said, "Harrison's hiding evidence in a safe-deposit box and a storage unit in Tucson. I have the specifics written down." A tear rolled down her cheek and she wiped it away before continuing. "I got some sense about a globe in his office that his father gave him. He thinks it contains an alien power cell." Janice paused and gave Stone an inquisitive look.

"Go on, Janice," Stone said.

"Yes, sir," Janice said, looking at the notebook. "Harrison gave the skull of an Air Force pilot to that piece of shit in there." She thrusted her thumb in Holcomb's direction. The agent laid unconscious on the floor, snoring. "Holcomb got the pilot's civilian dental records and gave those along with the skull to Margaret O'Donnell, an FBI forensics specialist at Quantico. He seems certain that she is working alone on this, but not at her lab. Too much scrutiny possible there. She's gone to a colleague's lab in Richmond, but Holcomb doesn't know who that is."

Stone asked her to pause while he stepped aside to discuss the information with Colonel Ritter.

During the break, the chairman said, "That's an interesting pin, Janice."

She ran a finger across the silver roadrunner on her sweater and said, "Just something I picked up while in Arizona. These birds are all over the desert. I like the way—"

"Do you have anything more specific on Harrison and Taylor?" Stone said, rejoining the group.

"Yes, sir," Janice said. "Holcomb hopes they departed the country. He believes they probably left out of San Diego, heading for Russia."

Stone and the chairman jerked.

"Their plan," Janice said, "involved working with the Russian government to bring international pressure on the United States into exposing Saint Mary. They have idealistic notions about truth and believe the Russians would help because of potential technology procurements."

The chairman stepped aside and made a phone call.

"You've done very well, Janice," Stone said.

"Thank you, General." She yawned and politely covered her mouth. "Who is the chairman calling?"

"Associates. You must get some rest, Janice. The exercise is still on for tonight. Do you think you'll be up for it?"

Janice tore pages from the notebook. "I'll be fine, but you are right, I should rest." She gave Stone the pages, momentarily brushing her hand along his. "I hope you can read my writing."

For Stone, sexual arousal swelled within him less frequently than his earlier years. This time, however, the rising surge inside his groin accompanied Janice's touch. He held the pages in front of him, just below his waistline. "I'm sure it's fine."

Janice nodded and departed the detention area, Stone's eyes following her out the door.

When the chairman joined Stone again, the General suggested they make additional calls from his office. They exited the area just as two men in black entered it.

They initiated more traditional methods of interrogation on Holcomb soon thereafter.

During the drive north from Richmond, Virginia, to the Catoctin Zoological Park in Maryland, Maggie O'Donnell had experienced high winds, rain, freezing rain, and then light snow as she neared her destination. She had left her MINI Cooper behind and opted to borrow her colleague's Mercedes sedan in Richmond. Besides, her car would have been too easy to spot on the road, bad weather or not.

Sitting in the Zoo's nearly empty parking lot, Maggie noticed the snow had stopped, but the gray clouds overhead looked ominous, and promised more winter weather was ahead. To help her relax from the stressful drive, she turned on the car's radio and selected a classical music station. In the seat next to her, the remains of Major Blair kept her company. Several dental examinations had confirmed it. The skull was that of the Air Force officer who, according to what Art Holcomb had told her, was officially at the bottom of the Pacific Ocean and not in a shallow grave at Area 51. Realizing that, while also thinking of Holcomb, made her heart race.

Where is he?

She feared the worst, and hoped Harrison would arrive soon.

As she looked around the parking lot, she detected movement, but it did originate from approaching vehicles on the ground as she expected. In the distance, she noticed a dark aircraft. It flew low, well below the cloud cover, and it approached from the southeast.

Not moving very fast. They'll spot me instantly.

Maggie turned off the radio, felt for the keys in the ignition, and fastened her seatbelt. She estimated her best chance of escape would be to head north on the Catoctin Mountain Highway, away from the D.C. area.

But go where?

While starting up the car's engine, Maggie glanced again at the aircraft. It was much lower and closer now. She could hear its loud engines and whooping rotor blades. The helicopter hovered and then circled around the zoo heading west.

Heading toward me.

As the helicopter drew nearer, its spinning rotor blades thumped harder and harder. Maggie felt the vibrations shake her car and rattle her body. She jammed the transmission into reverse and glanced in her rearview mirror, ready to release the brake.

But she froze.

A black Chevy Suburban skidded to a stop right behind her. Now trapped, she stared at the vehicle in the mirror. She expected and waited for her immediate capture.

Who will dig up my skull?

But no one exited the vehicle. For a moment, Maggie looked away and searched for the helicopter. She could see it out her side window. It hovered just north of her car, no higher than two hundred feet in the air.

Getting a better look at it now, Maggie saw that it sported dark green and white paint and looked like one of those she had seen in Washington, D.C. It was the kind of helicopter that shuttled the President and other officials around the capital, or to and from Andrews Air Force Base. As it hovered, its nose pointed west, but then it rotated and faced its nose east. It rose up and circled overhead again.

Just then, three men jumped out of the Chevrolet parked behind her. They wore dark suits and earpieces. Maggie watched them scan their surroundings. One of them approached her. Through the window, she heard him say her name.

"Ms. O'Donnell? Margaret O'Donnell?" Despite the thumping helicopter, his voice sounded calm and benevolent. "May I please speak with you, ma'am?"

Maggie took a deep breath and lowered the window. "I am Maggie O'Donnell. And you are?"

"Secret Service, ma'am. I am Agent Buck Walton. Rock around the clock, ma'am, rock around the clock." Pointing at the helicopter above, Walton said, "Your friends wanted me to tell you that. We need you to come with us, if you don't mind."

"Uh..." Maggie leaned her head out the window and craned her neck. The helicopter was higher now, but still hovering overhead. "I don't mind at all." She unbuckled her seatbelt and grabbed the bag with Blair's skull, x-rays, and test results. After she hopped out and jogged with Agent Walton to the Chevrolet, she waved at the sky.

The helicopter circled once more then headed northwest, toward Camp David.

Aboard the helicopter, Harrison waved back to Maggie through a closed window and watched her enter the Chevrolet. He turned to the other passengers and said, "She's safe, and so is the evidence about Major Blair. We'll learn more from her once she joins us at Camp David."

Taylor and Senator Vaughn both nodded. George Vaughn, as well as Henry and Pete Zemdarsky, were not aboard. They remained quartered at Andrews while the others headed to Camp David with the Secret Service.

"Good," Taylor said, "good."

Vaughn wrinkled her forehead. "Gentlemen, you have accumulated some key evidence. But—"

"But is it convincing?" Harrison said.

"My point exactly, Mr. Harrison. We are asking the President to put a lot on the line, and if there is any doubt, then we risk Saint Mary getting the best of us. I can appeal to him as a friend, but that will only go so far."

"I can testify to him about any aspect of Saint Mary," Taylor said.

"And you should be prepared to, General," Vaughn said. "But..."

"Let me see if I can help out here," Harrison said. He glanced at the globe. It sat next to Vaughn. Her right hand rested on its north pole. "The President and anyone he needs to convince will require definitive proof of Saint Mary's existence and nature."

"Right," Vaughn said.

Taylor leaned forward.

Harrison continued, saying, "Then let's set a trap so they reveal themselves. We lure them in with live bait." He looked squarely at Taylor. "General Taylor, myself, and Maggie."

Vaughn raised her eyebrows. "Those are high stakes."

"They are already quite high. Sign me up," Taylor said.

"Me too," Harrison said, "but we need to know the President won't wait to prepare. If Saint Mary takes the bait, then that should be the green light to take action and not simply to prepare for it."

"Otherwise we'll be too late," Vaughn said. "Is that what you are saying, Mr. Harrison?"

"Yes, and that should be all the proof they'll need."

"It will force him to act, and to act immediately." Vaughn tilted her head to one side and looked up at the ceiling inside the Helicopter's cabin. "I wonder if Saint Mary's leaders can feel the noose tightening around their necks."

FORTY EIGHT

Tensions, Tests, and Torture

At North Range, clocks indicated 6:00 p.m., local time.

CNN opened their news broadcast with a story about the rising tensions between China and Taiwan. Some limited information also indicated North Korea mobilized troops near its border with South Korea, and that the President was considering issuing mobilization orders for several military units as a precaution. A few minutes later, members of the working group felt some relief as CNN reported no new information concerning the alleged American spies, Harrison and Taylor, who were aiding Russian nationalists.

General Stone lowered the volume on the conference room's television and said, "Everything has taken hold quite well thus far."

"Yes, our story wasn't even the lead this time," Colonel Bennet said.

"What is our update?" General Lanham asked.

The chairman leaned forward and read from a legal pad. A coffee stain on it delayed his response. He looked closer and said, "The hybrid-assisted interrogations went extremely well. She confirmed items we discussed earlier as well as some additional leads."

"And the traditional methods?" Admiral Horner said.

"In process," Stone said. "But they take longer. It may be a while before they can confirm anything."

The chairman stiffened his back and cleared his throat before continuing. "Apparently, Harrison and Taylor may be trying to flee the United States and head for Russia. Their plan was to have that country bring international pressure on the U.S. government into exposing Saint Mary."

"Naive," Admiral Horner said.

A smile crept across Colonel Bennet's thin lips.

"Yes," the chairman said. "Taylor did book a flight from San Diego to San Francisco for last night, however, according to airline records, he never boarded."

"We must assume he is traveling under an alias," Horner said. Sweat dribbled down his forehead.

"Of course, of course," Stone said. The words hoisted impatience at the navy's representative. Almost as soon as he finished saying the remark, Stone shook his head and waved an invisible eraser.

"We've provided their identifiers and physical descriptions overseas," the chairman said. "Interpol is providing us with assistance. Ironically, the Russian government is assisting us as well."

"Won't that just work in their favor?" Lanham said.

"We've fed Interpol and the Russians an alternative cover story," the chairman said. He paused and looked at the men seated around the table. His gazed settled on Bennet. "Taylor is an arms and narcotics dealer."

Bennet's green and brown eyes grew indistinguishable. His thin smile diminished. "So, won't they be confused about reports of Harrison's involvement with nationalists?"

"No, they won't. We've explained that their primary work is guns and drugs, and the nationalists are customers, their middlemen, and that espionage is a side line effort for blackmail," the chairman said. "In the end it really doesn't matter what we say or do, just as long as we get what we want."

Bennet hesitated, looking hurt that General Stone and the chairman excluded him from the new disinformation effort that flew back and forth across the globe. Something twitched on his face. Stone saw it, but he remained uncertain which feature had moved so fast. Bennet nodded and slid back into his chair.

"They could be anywhere," Lanham said, shrugging.

"Yes, they are still out there somewhere, but we will find them," Stone said, eyes and words focusing on the weapons specialist. "We will find them."

Lanham averted Stone's scrutiny. He sat up straight and tugged on the lapels of his unbuttoned uniform jacket.

"The hybrid provided us with the location of a storage unit in Tucson that Harrison rented. Inside the unit, our agents found a rucksack and equipment we believe he and Holcomb used in the recovery of Major Blair's remains. A compass, shovel, map, GPS receiver, night-vision goggles, and so on." The chairman paused, sighing, and then he said, "However, the hybrid discovered a fourth conspirator during her interrogation of the FBI agent."

"Jesus Christ!" Horner said, bellowing.

"It's under control," Stone said, rubbing his dry forehead.

"Calm down, gentlemen," the chairman said, intervening. He stared at Horner across the table. "Now that I have your attention, I will finish. Holcomb provided an FBI forensics specialist, Margaret O'Donnell, with Major Blair's skull and civilian dental records. FBI personnel are currently trying to locate her."

Admiral Horner drifted in his chair.

Noticing this, the chairman said, "And we will find her."

Silence engulfed the room. Horner anchored firmly.

"Now," the chairman said, "if there are no more questions, we have a demonstration to attend to."

Professor Moresby rested. His eyes wandered over the computer screen in front of him. He checked the commands and coding, ensuring their correctness. Assured, Moresby uploaded the data to the computer at their destination. Two miles away, across North Range's runway and tucked into the side of a mountain, the security bunker's computer sent its acknowledgment.

"We are ready, Janice," Moresby said.

Next to him, Janice reclined on a padded sofa. She yawned and stretched. "Sorry, I guess I'm still a bit tired."

"This will be over soon enough. Then, we can all get some much-needed rest. The demonstration itself shouldn't take too long."

"I'll get my coat."

Moresby leaned forward and switched off the desk lamp. Standing, he watched Janice take her coat from the closet. A second later, she pulled his coat out too and handed it to him. "You're so helpful," Moresby said. "I didn't even think to put it on. Thank you."

"It'll be a cold ride out to the bunker. Don't want you to get sick at a time like this."

"No, no," Moresby said, chuckling. "Shall we head upstairs? Supposedly, the van will be waiting for us."

Janice took the professor by his arm and led the way. They exited the office and walked through a dim laboratory. With the exception of a dusty chalkboard, the room remained largely unused and still exuded the odors of fresh paint and new furniture. In one corner, plastic sheathing covered the entrance to a quarantine and examination center. Janice looked away and leaned her head against Moresby's shoulder.

Gray eyes gazed at her. "It's a stressful time for you."

"For all of us."

"Yes, but, I'm glad to say, you have handled yourself very well. Our progress is due, in large part, to your hard work. Now, let's go knock their socks off!"

Janice smiled. "Thanks, Francis, but I couldn't have done it without you."

After a brief walk through the hallway outside the lab, they rode up an elevator to the main floor of North Range's bio-research facility. Its deserted lobby area made it easy for them to navigate to a blue van parked outside the building. Three air policemen and the driver, also a guard, waited for them beside the vehicle.

"They sure like to keep tabs on us," Janice said.

Moresby smiled and patted the hand holding his.

They boarded the van with some assistance from their escorts, who then climbed in behind them. The driver maneuvered the van along a service road and then onto a taxiway. Runway lights, the ambient glow from exterior service areas, and a rotating navigational beacon positioned on a nearby hill punctuated the darkness inside the van. Low, thick clouds obscured the night sky's celestial panorama.

"When we get there," Moresby said, "you will notice the presence of several high-ranking military officers. Ignore them. They are mere observers. Just follow the routine as we have practiced and everything will be fine. Okay?"

Janice nodded.

North Range's main complex receded into the night as they crossed the runway and headed toward a ridgeline that ran along the northeast boundary of the airfield. Approaching a checkpoint at a chain-link and barbed-wire fence, the van slowed, but guards at the checkpoint waved them through the gate without delay.

The vehicle's headlights soon revealed a smooth, concrete facade embedded in a rocky mound. They had arrived at the security bunker, and another van with an imposing antenna mounted on its roof sat parked next to its entrance. The large antenna, as big as the vehicle that carried it, looked like a massive crossbow lying on its side.

"Is that it?" Janice said, leaning toward the window.

Moresby easily recognized the psychotronic generator. Built in Bulgaria and rumored to have once been employed against Boris Yeltsin to excite his bad heart, soon, Saint Mary would employ it against aliens. "That's it."

The driver stopped the van at the bunker's entrance, and the passengers disembarked. Janice and the air policemen headed for the warmth of the bunker while Moresby walked to the generator and briefly surveyed its condition.

Power cords, electrical lines, and a coaxial cable wound together outside the rear door of the van and into a round conduit that poked into the ground. An icy breeze blew against the tarp erected over this portion of the van to protect the cabling from inclement weather. The motion caught Moresby's attention, making him doubt the equipment's effectiveness.

"Is the power up?" Moresby said to a technician inside the van.

"Online and ready to go," the technician said.

"Why don't we go inside, Francis? It's chilly out here," Janice said, shouting from the bunker's entrance.

Moresby tugged at his coat. "You are right, my dear." He shuffled toward Janice, saying, "Let's get on with it."

The bunker's heavy metal doors slid closed once the professor stepped inside. A single overhead light shined down on the anteroom's walls and riveted seams. One of the guards spoke into an intercom and requested access. A moment later, latches released on the door that led to the interior of the bunker.

The group stepped through the doorway and found themselves in a junction of staircases and hallways. The guards accompanied Janice and Moresby down one of the staircases. After descending two levels, they entered a room lined with a row of several well-padded reclining chairs along one wall and a communications console in the center. On the wall opposite the chairs, a series of luminescent maps displayed various sections of the North Range facility. As Moresby had mentioned, several officers sat in the chairs, and a single nervous technician sat at the communications console. The guards remained outside the room and closed the door.

Colonel Bennet, looking apprehensive, rose and approached Moresby. Before he reached them, the professor directed Janice to the technician, who assisted her with attaching electrodes that would carry her messages to the psychotronic generator.

"Professor?" Colonel Bennet said, fidgeting for attention.

"Yes?" Moresby said, still watching Janice and the technician.

Bennet leaned close and said, whispering, "They're not too impressed with that thing you have upstairs. Are you sure this is going to work?"

Moresby struggled to compose an answer while he watched Janice. She sat comfortably now behind the console, facing the small audience of working-group officers. The illuminated maps gave off a warm glow, softening signs of fatigue on her face.

"You know, Colonel," Moresby said, "it will work." Then, more to himself, he said, "Do we really want it to?"

Bennet darted his bicolored eyes toward the others. No one else had apparently heard Moresby's comment. He gave the professor a stern look before slinking back to his chair.

Moresby walked over next to Janice and pushed a button on a control panel adjacent to her chair. They smiled one last time at each other before Janice relaxed and closed her eyes. Moresby nodded at General Lanham, who stepped forward and stood next to the communications console. Lanham put on a headset and pushed a few buttons, and then the lights dimmed.

Looking at the officers seated along the wall, Lanham said, "Tonight's exercise is fairly straightforward. The terminal here will display the preprogrammed communication sequence and the corresponding symbols. We can see them; the hybrid cannot, and neither can General Stone or our remaining colleagues in the command building. Our role is simple. Just note the symbols and number them on your rosters as they appear on the monitor. If all goes well, the other group's rosters should match ours at the end of the test. The hybrid has memorized each sequence, so there will be no delay in the contact once the encounter begins. For purposes of the demonstration tonight, the sequence will be a sampling of our basic vocabulary. Any questions?"

The officers shook their heads.

Lanham keyed the headset, "Command center, proctor is green for test. Shall we proceed?"

Inside the command center's operations center, Colonel Ritter wore a headset and heard Lanham's transmission. He nodded at General Stone, who sat a conference table with Admiral Horner, the chairman, and three other high-ranking officers. They reclined in their chairs, appearing relaxed.

Stone understood his subordinate's expression and said, "Proceed."

Ritter nodded and said, "Proctor, command is green. You are clear to initiate test alpha."

Lanham queued his microphone and said, "Test alpha initiated in five, four, three..."

Janice calmed her breathing.

In, out. In. Out...

She made what felt like a fluid, natural connection with the generator. Its transmission of her thoughts could commence. The survey sequence's first image stood for Earth, and it consisted of a short horizontal line with three diagonal slashes through it. A larger circle surrounded the horizontal line. In dreamy impressions, Janice felt the symbols flow away from her mind through the generator and somehow knew when the receivers read and understood the message.

Other symbols representing peace, union, ship, and friendship drifted from her rational mind into the stream of electromagnetic energy, connecting her with the working-group members on the other side of the airfield. Although the symbols looked crisp and clear, her surroundings blurred. She saw only lines, circles, and arcs, and felt acceptance. Her physical presence receded, oscillating between billowy warmth and a vast, disembodied nothingness. Then she felt complete freedom.

The fertile hues of Earth looked up at her while the moon hung overhead. Glittery, colorful heavens sparkled down on her. No loneliness inhabited this space, and she felt others surround her.

Countless others.

Ancient travelers beckoned her to Mars. To Cydonia. There, she kicked up dust with them as they spoke of once-great civilizations. Their voices, frightened, forsaken, and distant now, asked her to follow them. Curiosity and freedom stimulated, she wanted to follow, but another sensation tugged her back toward Earth, to home.

Their distant voices tried to warn her, but they and Janice had traveled too far in separate directions for her to understand the message.

In, out.

Her eyes opened, fluttering.

The empty room surrounded Janice, and Moresby sat next to her. He leaned forward, head in hands. Stirring, the professor looked at her, eyes gleaming.

"Welcome back, Janice."

"How...how long?"

"Two hours. The working group was very pleased. You've been in some sort of trance since the end of the test. I didn't want to wake you."

"But the test just started."

"Hmm, apparently you have some missing time. There are obviously aspects of this procedure that require further study."

"So, the test went well?"

"Oh my, yes. Of course, some of the receivers are complaining of headaches and nausea." Moresby paused and looked around the room. "But if you ask me, I wish you would have given them all migraines and then made them puke on each other."

Janice reached out and clasped the professor's arm, saying, "Francis, there is no end to your brilliance."

A guard opened the door to the command building's briefing room, and Moresby entered. The chairman waved him over to a seat next to him at the conference table.

"Well done, Professor," the chairman said as Moresby sat down next to him. "The Circle will be very pleased."

"I'm glad it went well, Dennis. How's your head?"

"Huh? Oh, it's fine. Given the test's success, I can't really complain." Then, whispering, he said, "I think it made Admiral Horner a little seasick."

The professor looked at the naval officer with the yellow-green complexion sitting across the table. He held a nearly empty bottle of Pepto-Bismol.

"The side effects were unexpected. The demonstration was a bit more intense than I anticipated," Moresby said.

"No matter," the chairman said. He called for everyone's attention, and the working group's groggy members turned to listen. "Could someone turn up the television? I would like to catch up on the news."

General Stone reached for the remote and pushed the volume button. He settled back into his chair and checked his watch. It indicated 9:00 p.m. local time.

"From the CNN center in Atlanta, good evening," the news anchor said. "China and Taiwan continue to aggressively accuse each other of increasing the tensions between..."

As the newscast continued, the chairman, Stone, and the other working-group members listened closely. Moresby leaned back and relaxed. One way or another, things would end soon. He just wanted it to end.

The news anchor continued. "Earlier today, the President issued a warning to China's leaders to cease and desist in their aggressive war games near Taiwan, stating the United States will make a stand against aggression and tyranny wherever it raises its head. He also sent a special New Year's message on the armed forces radio network expressing the gratitude of the nation for the continued diligence and never-ending hard work of United States military at home and overseas. In other news, retailers reported preliminary holiday sales figures. With today's business report, here is..."

Stone turned down the volume.

"Thank you, General," the chairman said. "I think we can agree that our situation is much improved. I'd like to hear your recommendations."

"From an operational standpoint, we are ready to go ahead," General Lanham said. "We can go online with NORAD according to schedule and have a bird in hand by late tomorrow. Both the psychotronic generator and ELF transmitters are ready. I recommend we proceed with the plan."

"Have the med crews and recovery teams arrived yet?" Admiral Horner said through a handkerchief covering his mouth.

"They start arriving tomorrow morning, first thing," Stone said. "Of course, if you need some assistance now, Admiral, we do have some medics who can take care of you."

Everyone laughed except the queasy naval officer and Moresby.

Stone winked at the admiral and then thumbed through a file in front of him, saying, "Let me also update you on our investigation into the security matter. We are still searching for Harrison, Taylor, and the forensics specialist, Margaret O'Donnell. Follow-up interrogations of Holcomb are continuing, but there has been nothing discovered that would contradict the information we acquired through the hybrid. Colonel Ritter's seizure of the evidence, however, does seem to undermine whatever steps Taylor planned to take. He will be hard pressed to prove anything to anybody."

"I think," the chairman said, smiling, "we can invite the Circle to join us. Don't you?" The others nodded their approval. "Then I will contact them. The operation will commence tomorrow, at 2100 hours. We can expect the Circle to arrive shortly after dinner."

Without hesitation, the admiral rose and weaved his way out of the room. Others, including Stone, followed him. The chairman took out a pen and made some notations on a legal pad. Moresby closed his eyes.

"Francis? Are you asleep?"

"No, no, Dennis, just thinking about things."

"Well, good. That's your job, after all. Speaking of which, we need something else."

Moresby opened his eyes and rested his folded arms on the table. "I know. I've been thinking about it myself." He noticed the chairman had raised his eyebrows and pursed his narrow lips. "You need to test Janice further with one of our special guests."

"Yes. Our two remaining live specimens were brought in yesterday. They are housed together in one of the enclosures below the main lab. She needs to converse with both of them, test their comprehension, and see what they know—"

"About the fifth species. Yes, I see. Dennis, why do you think Janice will have any more luck than any of our technicians in that regard?"

The chairman chuckled and shook his head. "Francis, where is your scientific curiosity? Besides, she is one of them, well, at least in part. Maybe she can reach them where normal humans haven't."

"Normal humans? Janice is not abnormal." Moresby's fists tightened their grip on his arms. "But, this is not the time or place for that discussion. I'll make the arrangements with Janice and Dr. Schmidt."

"As soon as possible, please. Any advantage we can gain in our upcoming operation will be most helpful." The chairman glanced at his legal pad and circled an item on the first page. "By the way, is there any message you'd like me to give to the Circle? I will speak to them soon."

Moresby opened his eyes, wanting to leave. "Oh, nothing really," he said, standing up. "Why don't you just wish them happy New Year for me?"

I pray that we will still have many more to come.

"Where is Taylor?"

To Holcomb, it seemed like the interrogator had asked him this question nearly a thousand times. Through red, swollen eyes, he looked up at the well-tanned man in black hovering over him. Handcuffed to the chair in which he sat, Holcomb wished he could stand up and strangle *the son of a bitch.*

"Where is Taylor?"

"Dude, are you fucking deaf? We've been over this before," Holcomb said, his voice hoarse.

"And we'll continue until you tell me the truth."

The blackness shifted behind Holcomb and leaned toward him, whispering, "You know, Maggie has already been executed."

"I don't know who you are talking about."

A sharp blow to the back of his head knocked the bloody grin from Holcomb's lips.

"Where's Taylor?"

Holcomb's head palpitated in dull, agonizing throbs from earlier jabs, slaps, and punches. "Has anyone ever told you that between your big nose and dark clothes you look like a fucking crow?"

The interrogator grabbed the back of Holcomb's neck. "Where are you keeping the skull?"

"What skull?" Holcomb said, trying to twist his head free. He failed, but the man released him anyway.

The interrogator wandered around the room, fingers rubbing his clean-shaven chin. An insistent tapping against the one-way mirror drew him out of the cell.

Holcomb sighed and closed his eyes.

Why is Taylor going to Russia? Why did Janice tell me he was going to Russia? That was not the plan.

The cell door opened and closed. The man in black returned, cradling a small, shiny object in his hand.

A sudden wave of nausea overcame Holcomb, a common reaction whenever he saw this type of device. Since childhood, he had never succeeded in preventing the sickening feeling he felt just looking at one.

The interrogator moved closer, pressing one hand against the left side of Holcomb's neck and head.

"Don't move," the black crow said. With a precise, quick stab, he plunged the syringe into Holcomb's upper left arm. The liquid flowed through the needle and then seamlessly into Holcomb's bloodstream.

FORTY NINE

Unit Zero, Thirty-Nine, and Forty

At the base of North Range's air-traffic control tower, located directly across the runway from the command building, Colonel Ritter excused his driver. Once the sleepy enlisted man stepped inside the tower complex, the colonel dialed in the appropriate frequency on the Humvee's radio and brought the microphone up to his mouth. Through cold puffs of condensed air, he said, "All stations, transport signal is confirmed. Area blackout now authorized."

The exterior lights of buildings scattered around the runway switched off in a drifting pattern. The dark sky had relinquished itself of the earlier gray cloud cover, and a twinkling swath of diamonds revealed their vast numbers with crystalline clarity.

In the predawn hour, Ritter found the brisk air refreshing, complementing the renewed energy from the coffee he had finished drinking inside the tower a short time ago. To his left, at the south end of the field, he saw the doors of the huge hangar located there creep open. Headlights from a tow vehicle, known as Unit Zero, inside the hangar sent a hollow stream outward, which the thick blackness surrounding the isolated location easily swallowed.

"Unit Zero, you have roll clearance," Ritter said into the radio's microphone. "Gemini Control is en route for rendezvous at Checkpoint Alpha."

Ritter, representing Gemini Control, climbed into the Humvee and drove across the runway, then headed north to his initial destination, Checkpoint Alpha, at the end of the airfield. While the Humvee traversed the wide and flat taxiways and service roads, Ritter caught an occasional glimpse in the rearview mirror of Unit Zero. Since he could not actually see the reconstructed Roswell crash vehicle it towed, he visualized the craft's shape beneath the billowy gray tarp covering it.

Envisioning the craft occurred with no difficulty for Ritter. He had observed it before at Area 51 and in the North Range hangar. *Even touched it once.* The fleeting flight maneuvers he had witnessed it perform were less than satisfactory from an air force perspective, but in his mind, the ship stood out as one the most remarkable flying machines he had ever seen. *And not a single sound or puff of smoke from it.* His fingertips had never caressed anything so delicate, yet so undeniably sturdy.

Ritter let himself feel emotion, awe even, about the remarkable craft without any embarrassment or awkward need to deny something that was—without any doubt—very real. He blinked against the chilly wind that blew through the open window and peeled teary drops away from his face. His full, resolute heart pounded against his chest. Pride embraced him, a rare feeling for him. But at that moment, Ritter had nothing less than a truly unique responsibility.

Take this flying saucer and prepare it for flight.

At the next step in fulfilling this responsibility, Ritter approached Checkpoint Alpha at the northwest corner of the airfield and then stopped the Humvee next to the guard shack located there. Two sentries saluted him.

Ritter saluted back, saying, "You know the routine. You are relieved."

"Yes, sir," the guards said in unison.

"Step into the shack, close the doors, and close the blinds. Smoke them if you've got them. And release the gate."

"Yes, sir," the guards said, scurrying into the shack. As soon as they entered it, the gate's locks clicked open, and an electric motor slid the chain-link and barbed wire fence open.

"Gemini Control to Unit Zero, clear for embarkation," Ritter said into the radio microphone.

Less than half a mile to the south, Unit Zero continued its steady progress toward the checkpoint. Ritter looked at the guard shack, shaking his head, trying to guess what the two sentries thought of this exercise. He decided that if they had not already figured it out, they probably would soon.

Cutting through the quiet stillness, the chugging motor of the tow vehicle announced its approach and drew Ritter's attention toward its driver. Only one person in the entire air force held authorization to perform the task of towing the Roswell craft. He was a chief master sergeant from Chicago, Illinois. Ritter spotted the familiar figure behind the wheel of Unit Zero. Moving his cargo through the open gate, the man did not return Ritter's visual acknowledgment, but the colonel's radio crackled with a transmission.

"Unit Zero to Gemini Control, commencing with embarkation."

Ritter acknowledged the transmission and gazed at the disc riding past him. Under the starlight, a portion of the craft's silvery, smooth surface, mostly covered by the billowy gray tarp, emerged and basked in a moment of ephemeral autonomy. Its moderate dimensions—forty feet wide by twenty-five feet high—and minimal exterior features belied the vehicle's unprecedented capabilities. While Saint Mary's test pilots had not succeeded in flying it very far due to its damaged power cell, Ritter had witnessed the ship perform rapid accelerations and ninety-degree turns considered impossible for modern aircraft.

Ritter thought he heard the momentary rustling of the guard shack's metal blinds. He chose not to turn around and look. Instead, he watched the craft as the tow vehicle continued along the service road leading to a remote test pad several miles from the main field. Once it arrived there, Ritter would secure the ship in an auxiliary hangar and instruct the ground crew to initiate the lengthy preflight checklist.

After he was certain the craft had traveled a sufficient distance away from the guard shack, Ritter walked over and tapped on its door. The sentries scrambled out and stood at attention.

"Resume your post," Ritter said.

The simultaneous "yes, sir" harmonized and resonated in Ritter's ears. He smiled and shook his head, and then returned to the Humvee. Without any further delay, he drove after the flying saucer from another world.

Janice assumed the sky held onto its darkness when the air policemen escorted her from her quarters to one of the elevators in North Range's main laboratory. Dr. Schmidt had awakened her unexpectedly at 5:00 a.m. An hour later, the sun might have been up, but it made no difference to Janice. She remained underground and headed even deeper beneath the surface.

One of the air policemen addressed her. "Ma'am, after you enter the elevator, swipe your card through the reader and select level ten."

The guard's voice startled Janice. Her consciousness remained groggy from the early awakening out of a very deep sleep. "Level ten. I see, thank you."

"Once you reach level ten, exit and follow the main hallway until you reach a door. It is really more like a hatchway, like on a ship. Your card will permit entry."

"And once through the hatch?"

Both air policemen jerked upright and looked at each other, confused. In unison, they looked back at Janice. Confusion retained its hold on their faces.

"Oh, I see. You don't know."

"We aren't authorized to enter that area, ma'am."

Janice stepped into the elevator, swiped her card, and then pushed the button for level ten. "Don't worry, I'll find it." Then, from between the rapidly closing doors, Janice waved and said, "Have a good day!"

Out of habit, Janice stepped toward the back of the elevator. She rested her hands on a cool metal railing that ran along the blue walls of the car. Schmidt had seemed perturbed that the military executives had provided Janice access to aliens "Thirty-Nine" and "Forty." Perhaps they had considered it necessary due to the upcoming operation, as well as due to the loss of Thirty-Seven at the hands of James Evans and the subsequent—and inexplicable—expiration of Thirty-Eight. The two specimens Janice was on her way to visit were all that remained in Saint Mary's inventory.

The quick descent ended and the doors slid open. After stepping out of the elevator, Janice found herself in a hallway that looked like a white tube. The white walls arched upward from a white marble floor and intersected with a continuous row of fluorescent lights that ran the length of the corridor, which terminated at a gray, metal hatch.

She walked toward the hatch. Her black sneakers squeaked intermittently on the slick floor. Nearing the hatch, Janice saw an empty office to her left behind a small counter and sliding windowpane. Not seeing anyone, she ran her badge through the sensor next to the hatch. A hiss and the faint hum of an electric motor followed. Slowly, the hatch opened and then Janice stepped through.

Masking tape pinned plastic tarps along the base of partly painted walls in a short hallway that led to a partitioned glass door. Beyond it stood a small room with another set of glass doors opposite the entrance. Janice could not see beyond the other glass doors, which were darkly tinted. The smell fresh paint and dusty whiffs of sanded spackle met her nostrils. Ahead of her, one of the glass doors slid open.

"Please step inside, Ms. Evans," a pleasant, female voice said.

Janice looked around and spotted a surveillance camera overhead next to a speaker.

"Once inside, the hatch and outer door will close. Only then will you be able to enter the enclosure."

"Thank you," Janice said, and then she passed through the open door. Behind her, the hatch closed and the glass door slid shut, the sound of bolts locking metal into place following their movements.

"You may now enter the enclosure," Ms. Evans. "Until your eyes adjust, please move slowly as the lighting is kept at a low level."

Janice nodded and thanked a wall-mounted speaker and then stepped inside the enclosure.

Despite the low light, Janice actually saw her surroundings quite well. One of the benefits of hybridization included increased sensory capabilities, such as enhanced night vision. In the low light, much of what she saw registered as various shades of gray. From what she could tell, the enclosure was a large circular room. It was so large that its edges faded from gray to black, beyond her ability to discern details.

To her right about sixty feet away, Janice saw what appeared to be a block of rooms, each with a hatch and large windowpane. She made her way through the emptiness and arrived at the first window. The room beyond it automatically illuminated. Janice looked inside. It was empty, except for what looked like a child's desk and chair. The rear wall of the room also had a hatch. A bed, no more than four feet long and only six inches off the ground, sat opposite the desk.

Janice pressed on and paused in front of the next windowpane. As the room automatically illuminated, Janice gasped and stumbled backward. Standing directly behind the glass pane, and looking out at her, stood Thirty-Nine and Forty.

Janice caught her breath and regained her footing. Other than tilting their heads side to side, Thirty-Nine and Forty stood perfectly still, and were much taller than Janice expected. They had narrow, long limbs, as well as large eyes and heads, but were easily over five feet tall. Silver jump suits covered most of their gray skin, and a collar around each of their thin necks held labels with their respective Saint Mary numerical designations: 39 and 40.

Janice stepped forward and said, "I am pleased to meet you. My name is Janice."

Both ceased their head tilting and froze. They stared at Janice, and she looked back, her eyes locking onto Forty's, who slowly leaned toward the glass. She felt the quick mental connection occur, and then sensed Forty's thoughts.

Can you hear me, Janice?

Yes, I mean you no harm. I am not like the others.

We know this. We can sense this about you. You are human but you are also constructed with our chemistry.

True, but I am not like them in the sense that I feel it is wrong for us to keep you here.

Are there others who feel this way too? Sometimes we sense pity from others but mostly we sense fear. We can detect emotion, and understand how it interacts with reason. In humans, these energies often compete. Our emotional energy is much less and we are very like-minded. But humans are not. Their feelings and thoughts are not synchronized with each other.

So, you have studied our planet and us?

Images took shape in Janice's mind, and she saw Thirty-Nine and Forty standing next to her. As her vision widened, she saw a dirt path leading through a desert. High, rocky mountains rose above the distant horizon. The landscape seemed bright, as if the mid-day sun hung above them, but blackness and bright stars filled the sky overhead.

We study, and do more. Janice, your world and all of its life is in danger.

Danger? From what?

They walked together a few steps along the path. A bright flash dissolved the desert scene. The sparkling sky now burned red and ashes, charred bones, and demolished buildings littered their surroundings.

At first, Janice thought she saw other human figures, but as she gazed further at the remnants of city walls, buildings, and street corners, the figures were merely the silent shadows of former lives disintegrated by a powerful blast of light and energy.

Yourselves.

Janice gazed at the scene and watched it fade into darkness. The images ceased, and emptiness and the sound of rapid clicking enveloped her.

What is that noise?

Forty's large eyes and head emerged out of the deep haze in Janice's mind, and stared at her just inches from her face.

Perhaps a message? We thought you might know. This comes from the ones you call the 'fifth species.' There is little I can tell you about this. We know about them, but understand little. They seem interested in Earth, but we do not know why.

Where do they come from?

That is not something we yet know. What we do know is that the question is not where, but when? We believe their origins are from the future, but we do not know where they come from. They do not communicate with us. They also seem to evade us. They seem isolated and self-interested. They seem to interpret us as hostile and when we encounter them, in some instances, they have taken our ships out of this realm and into theirs. We have also sensed high emotional energy from them, especially fear, pride, anger, distrust, envy, and ambition. These qualities always lead to destruction, and your species in particular has them in abundance. We seek to help you evolve beyond these negative energies. Your survival depends upon it, and we cannot let you advance into space and spread these destructive viruses. This will upset the balance, but the choice is up to you. How will you do this?

Snapshots flickered through Janice's mind: Warships at sea, an ICBM standing in its silo, an invading army behind rows of tanks, the Pentagon... The images flashed in succession, and she quickly analyzed each one as if taking a test and selecting from a multiple-choice list of possibilities.

None of them seemed correct.

A pastor pontificating, traders on the floor of the stock market, germs in a Petrie dish...

No, this isn't right.

She searched for a sincere answer to Forty's question...

The images ceased, and melted into one. A face emerged and Janice's heart soared.

William Harrison. He is the answer.

Why?

He is the key, but he also believes.

In what?

In those things that many mock. Truth, justice, freedom.

Are these not just self-interested outcomes?

No! And that is where many fail to understand. It takes cooperation, balance, and respect to achieve them. Bill understands and treasures this. Others do as well.

Then they are the truly special ones among you. They are your future. They are your hope. Without him and these others, you are hopeless.

Janice blinked her eyes as the connection with Forty faded. Her reflection in the windowpane stood between Thirty-Nine and Forty as they looked out at her.

I know.

FIFTY

Erase Our Mistakes

Inside his office, General Randolph Stone enjoyed a cup of coffee and checked the time.

Twelve hours to go.

He returned his attention to the computer in front of him, pulling up status reports on the arriving support teams. For the first time in over a week, he relaxed some. Aside from wrapping up what he believed were the security situation's loose ends, no glitches appeared in the upcoming ELF operation. He credited this to his leadership skills, reassuring himself that those qualities would see the mission through to a successful conclusion.

Following a quick knock on the door, Colonel Bennet entered the office and said, "The latest media indications continue to be favorable, sir."

"Good, good," Stone said, still looking at his computer screen.

"There is one other item. It came across channels about fifteen minutes ago."

Yawning, Stone said, "Yes, what is it?"

"Information only at this point, but we just received word that the Eighth Army has gone on heightened alert."

"Korea?"

"Yes, sir, due to the continued Chinese incursions into Taiwan's—"

"What about North Korea?" Stone said. The army had stationed his only son, an infantry captain, in Seoul.

"Thus far, there have been no further reports of any troop movements on the border. But higher command is not taking chances. As you know, both China and North Korea view certain territories as belonging to them."

"Yes, yes, and stateside?"

"Deployment-ready alert for Fort Bragg. Scuttlebutt is that elements of the Eighty-Second Airborne Division will go to Taiwan as a show of force. In any case, final arrangements are still pending. However, we should expect additional alerts to go into effect soon if this gets further out of hand—"

Stone waved him off. "Thank you, Colonel. I'll advise the chairman."

As Bennet departed, Stone glanced once more at the computer and then, in haste, switched it off. He grabbed his hat, exited the office, and headed for the bio-research labs in the adjacent building. Before contacting the chairman, he wanted to check on Dr. Schmidt's status, hoping she would have some good news. Outside, the arrival of cargo planes carrying support teams from Nellis, Wright-Patterson, and Dreamland crowded the tarmac.

In an effort to ignore the possibility of an international-relations glitch in his operation, Stone found another reason for confidence: perfect weather conditions. Clear skies stretched toward the horizon, uninterrupted in every manner. Neither a single wisp of cirrus nor a swelling patch of cumulus menaced the vigorous activity under way.

Continuing toward his destination, Stone acknowledged the salutes of junior officers and enlisted personnel while hurrying past them. When he entered the lobby of the research facility, he hesitated, realizing he had not yet memorized where Dr. Schmidt's new medical laboratory occupied space. A brief glance around reminded him the elevator directly ahead would transport him to the floors below ground. He would find his way from there.

During the descent to the bottom floor, Stone considered the situation regarding Harrison and Taylor again and wondered if he could implement any further steps to apprehend them. His firm belief was that any evidence they retained was scant at best, and could be explained away or denied.

But Stone sought more than just the remnants of Harrison's investigation. He wanted Taylor. As he saw it, fulfilling the Protocol One on that particular subject stood out as his primary duty, and he never failed to carry out his duties. Stone felt he had arrived at an impasse, however, and he could do nothing more except wait and hope that Harrison and Taylor committed a mistake.

Stone exited the elevator, and a voice accented with Bavarian origins bounced through the corridor. He followed the sound to the medical lab and found Dr. Schmidt issuing instructions to two attentive assistants. Stone's relative ease evaporated. His face reddened, and his eyes bulged like volcanoes threatening to erupt when they saw it: a chalkboard, a *really big chalkboard,* with circles, lines, and dashes inscribed on it.

"Goddamn it, Moresby!" Stone said.

Schmidt and the assistants swung their heads toward the source of the eruption. Stone rushed forward, cursing again, uninhibited now by his usual sense of politeness. He grabbed an eraser and deleted the markings from view. He looked at Schmidt. "Where is he?"

The doctor pointed at the office, its door closed, in the corner of the lab. As Stone moved past Schmidt, he ordered the removal of the chalkboard and did not wait for a response. He barged into the office and slammed the door shut. The professor sat at a desk, headphones over his ears, likely listening to a recording of recent abductee interviews.

"Yes?" Moresby said, turning in his chair and removing the headset. "Oh, good morning, General. What can I do for you?"

Words stuttered from Stone's mouth. "You goddamn idiot! How the hell could you leave those symbols on the chalkboard?"

Moresby clicked off the digital recorder. "I'm sorry. I guess I must have forgotten. I'll go take care of it right now." He stood up.

"Sit down you old fool!" Stone said, lunging, shoving Moresby into the chair, and then grabbing the lapels of his lab coat. "I already erased them. Jesus Christ! Let's get something straight right now. I don't care how long you've been with the project or how much you know. There is no room for mistakes, and I won't tolerate any, not on my base. If we didn't need you for tonight's operation, I would—" Stone broke off, releasing Moresby, searching for the right words.

"Murder me?" the professor said. "That is something you attend to, isn't it? You clean up after us. Erase our mistakes, eh?" He spoke with a sturdy voice, but his body trembled.

"You should be more mindful of what you say, old man. We don't need any more traitors."

"But a thug is always welcome. Is that what you're saying?"

"I am not here to debate you. We have a mission to accomplish. I am dedicated to that purpose, but I don't think you share the same conviction."

"'Conviction,' General Stone, is an entirely appropriate term. I, for one, have grown weary of participation in a criminal conspiracy. Do you realize how far we have strayed from any reasonable principles? That's assuming you ever had any to begin with, of course."

Stone headed for the door, saying, "I'd be careful—North Range can be a hazardous place." He opened the door. "You never know when something unexpected might happen that changes your whole existence." Stone slammed the door closed, rattling its frame.

Looking at Dr. Schmidt, Stone noticed she also appeared agitated, a normal mood for the extraterrestrial biological entity research scientist. Her assistants exited the area, wheeling away the chalkboard. Stone waited until they departed, and then he said, "Dr. Schmidt, tell me you have good news."

"We are ahead of schedule."

Of course you are, you Nazi.

"You set a fine example for others. Do you have any questions?"

"None."

"Remember, your priority tonight is the EBEs. I don't know what kind of condition they'll be in. Just be prepared. And if we take casualties, the medevac teams will handle those. Under no circumstances are these facilities for treating our own wounded. Instead, we will airlift them to a field hospital that will be set up a few miles from here. Those are my orders."

"Yes, sir."

After a long sigh, Stone gave the doctor an approving nod. "Has the hybrid had her exam?"

"She is due here any moment."

"Remember, in private please. And I want to know immediately if anything doesn't check out. Her condition is especially important, more so now than ever before."

"Yes," Schmidt said, lowering her head. "I know."

"No time for grief, Doctor. Where's a phone?"

Schmidt raised her age-blemished right hand and extended a serpentine index finger. "My office is right over there."

Stone unclipped the identification badge from his uniform and ran its magnetic strip through a scanner on Schmidt's office door. After entering, he telephoned the chairman.

"The operation is on schedule," Stone said.

"And the press?"

"Colonel Bennet's report is favorable." Stone paused and held his breath. After exhaling, he said, "Also, the Eighth Army is on heightened alert, and Fort Bragg is on deployment readiness. My understanding is the action is cautionary, due to the rising tensions and military movements in the Far East."

"Have all the transports arrived?"

"Most. We still have three C-17s in Ohio, and the mobile air-traffic units have yet to depart from Nellis. They are scheduled to leave there at 1300 hours."

"Well, let's stay on top of it. I'll check with my Pentagon contacts to see if this situation will impact our resources."

"Yes, sir. The information so far is that no other domestic units are on alert or preparing to ship out. I'm sure it will turn out to be nothing very significant. Just some saber rattling to keep the red hordes in check."

"Okay. I am—"

Frantic knocking on the office door drowned out the rest of the chairman's words. Stone glared in the direction of the noise and said, "Sir, can you hold just a moment?" Finishing his reluctant request, he noticed the source of the disruption.

Yanking open the door, Colonel Ritter rushed in, breathing heavily, apologizing for the interruption.

"What is it?" Stone said, squeezing his palm over the telephone.

"Received online alerts...accessing FBI files...army discharge records...air force crash documents..."

The Colonel's urgency made sudden sense to Stone. "Taylor?"

"Must be him, yes, and probably Harrison too! The signals resolve to Tucson. They must be in Tucson trying to access records, to gain evidence again of what we already recovered."

"Do we still have a security team there?"

"Yes, sir."

Without hesitation, Stone removed his hand from the phone. "Mr. Chairman, we found them!"

FIFTY ONE

Captured

A white, full-sized van slowed and then parked next to the office of the Four Points Motel in Tucson. Four men, dressed in different navy-blue polo shirts, tan tactical pants, and combat boots, sat inside the van. With practiced expertise, the burly men with crew cuts checked their weapons and equipment. Afterward, each of them donned a blue windbreaker with "Police" emblazoned on the front and back. The "officers" exited the van one by one. Their leader carried recent photographs of William Harrison, Edward Taylor and Margaret O'Donnell with him into the motel's reception area. He identified himself to the clerk as a "state police officer," and then handed over the photographs.

Seeing the law enforcement officials standing before her, the nervous female clerk provided an immediate response. "Yes, they are in room 112—it's on the far end of the building. I can give you a key."

"That won't be necessary," the lead man said. He collected the photographs and said, "Thank you for your cooperation and stay inside while we make an arrest."

The clerk nodded, looked over her shoulder for a brief moment, and then nervously back at the men in front of her.

"Something wrong?" the leader said.

"Uh, no, just wondering," the clerk said, looking over her shoulder again, "should I take cover in the back room?"

"It couldn't hurt, ma'am. These people are dangerous."

While the clerk withdrew into the back room, the four police officers exited the area. Three of the officers walked to the far end of the building, while the fourth drove the van, meeting up with the others there.

The four men assumed positions along the short length of wall between the parking lot and the room. The leader looked back and counted down from five on his left hand. After the countdown, the men rushed the door, the leader kicking it in with ease. Pieces of wood splintered and jettisoned off the frame, followed by a resounding thud as the door swung against the interior wall. Its doorknob punctured the wall and it stuck in place, facilitating uninhibited access into the room.

The four officers recognized General Taylor, who jumped up from his chair and withdrew his hands from the laptop computer on the desk in front of him. Behind him, a woman screamed, and a man put up his hands. Before any of them had any time to resist, the officers forced them to the floor at gunpoint and handcuffed them.

An officer grabbed the woman's red hair and said, "What's your name, bitch?"

"Fuck you," she said.

The officer shoved her head into the room's dirty shag carpet. "Your choice, bitch, give up the name or suffocate in this cesspool."

Coughing and choking, the woman fought against the man and twisted her head to one side. "Margaret O'Donnell. FBI."

"That's what I thought, bitch." Turning to other man on the floor, he said, "And your name, fucker?"

"Its Harrison, asshole. William Harrison."

"Jackpot!" the leader said. "Let's get out of here."

One of the officers grabbed the laptop, ripping the network cord out of the wall jack. Another officer searched the rest of the room. He found a revolver in the nightstand, dental records inside a briefcase under the bed, and a duffel bag containing a human skull in the bathroom. He loaded the evidence into the back of the van then helped the others load the prisoners. The van's sliding door rattled shut, and then the vehicle departed the parking lot, its tires squealing when it hit the road's pavement.

Behind a tinted window in the rear office of the motel's lobby, the female clerk watched the van leave. Sighing, she turned around and looked at the man and woman wearing business suits emerging from the back room behind the lobby. Along with the clerk, they watched the van drive away with keen interest.

"Now, what are your names?" the clerk said. "My manager didn't really say who you are or why you are here, just that I should help you if needed."

The man, short, rotund, and moderately bald, smiled, anticipating the usual, and apparently humorous, remark that typically followed his and his partner's introduction. "I'm Special Agent Sapp." He paused, swiveling toward the tall—much taller than himself—brunette standing next to him. "This is Special Agent Tarr. And we are with the FBI."

"Tarr and Sapp?" the clerk said.

"Yes, yes," Sapp said, winking at his partner.

"Oh, boy, sounds like a sticky situation," the clerk said amid her own laughter.

Tarr peered down at Sapp, who also chucked. "I think you enjoy doing that." She snapped her fingers at the clerk, who, by now, snickered teary-eyed. "May I use your phone, please? I have a call to make to the White House."

Half-eaten plates of baked chicken, rice, and mixed vegetables mingled with checklists, personnel rosters, and computer printouts. The items sat in a cluttered arrangement on the conference table in the command building's large briefing room at North Range. The odors from warm electronics and even warmer officers overwhelmed the normally hospitable scent of coffee and cafeteria food. As with many such gatherings of the working group, no distinct discourse was under way. The pockets of conversations and consultations accumulated into a steady and fluent drone of utterances and occasional chortles.

Above the din, however, General Stone announced, "They have all three of them!" He brought the phone back up to his ear and listened further. The other members of the working group seated at the conference table hushed each other and nodded.

"What a relief," Admiral Horner said. He joined his colleagues in a gratuitous exchange of handshakes.

The chairman, sitting at the head of the table, reclined and smiled. Above his head, the television broadcasted CNN. Images from yet another civil war somewhere in Africa danced across the screen. Samples of machete wounds, dismembered bodies, and empty, wretched faces appeared amid scenes of struggling relief workers supported by UN forces, including some from the United States. The news anchor transitioned to a live broadcast by a reporter at Fort Bragg. The reporter stood at a fence line. Behind him, in the distance, Eighty-Second Airborne Division troopers boarded transport aircraft, but not before being personally reviewed by the President. Given the President's unannounced visit, the reporter speculated the troops intended to travel to Taiwan.

Stone hung up the phone and addressed the group. "The capture proceeded without any problems. The three subjects are already enroute from Davis-Monthan. The best news is that our security team also seized key evidence at the scene."

"This is very good news," the chairman said.

Unable to contain his satisfaction, Stone looked at his delighted colleagues and grinned. His gaze settled on the chairman. "Sir, will you advise the Circle?"

"Yes, of course. We can anticipate their arrival with a renewed sense of achievement. They will certainly be pleased."

Another ring from the phone brought Stone's hand to the receiver again while the others continued expressing relief to one another.

"Yes, I see," Stone said. "Thank you for the information. Yes, Colonel Bennet, I will pass it along." As he hung up, Stone's solemn gaze caught the end of CNN's segment on Fort Bragg. He focused his attention on the chairman. "Taiwan has agreed to a show of support from the United States. A brigade of Eighty-Second Airborne troopers are preparing for transport. Standby alerts have been issued to numerous other bases." His words also caught the attention of the other officers.

"Goddamn Chinks," Admiral Horner said.

"Yes, this is unfortunate," the chairman said, "but it won't detract from our mission. At this point, we can even afford to reassign a few of our transports if requested. We will proceed as scheduled. In fact, this flurry of activity concerning the Far East should serve to shield us further."

The statement prompted a succinct chorus of consensus. The news about Harrison, Taylor, and Maggie, and even Taiwan, replenished their confidence, leading most of them to count on continued success through the course of the evening. The security matter was all but resolved, and at this point, their entire focus was aimed at tonight's Operation Rainbow. Barely eight hours remained before the experimental would head aloft to lure in unknowns. They discussed and clarified final details of the operation and made assurances that all would proceed as planned.

Secretly, not all of those present at the meeting remained convinced the extravagant plan would succeed. Some of them still wondered, but they concealed those concerns and continued as yes-men. With Taylor's capture, one reality endured: Saint Mary would never allow a weak link to slip through its fingers.

FIFTY TWO

We Have Lied and Twiddled Our Thumbs

The last transport to arrive, a C-117 from Nellis, carried the remaining mobile air-traffic-control units. It finished its taxi to an area just north of the tower complex, offering a welcome end to the stinging rage from its engines. Ground crews swarmed around the aircraft, and within a few minutes, the first navy-blue vehicle emerged from the cavernous cargo section. Watching the vehicles unload, Stone accepted the plane's late arrival and dismissed his anxiety over the short delay.

From the south, another aircraft entered its final approach. Dwarfed by its predecessor, the approaching Lear Jet descended through the blue tones of a winter sky that grew ever richer from diminishing sunlight. The plane touched down onto the dusky runway and taxied without delay to the security detail in front of the command building, where General Stone also waited.

Four men escorted three gloomy captives and seized evidence off the plane. Stone wanted to approach Taylor immediately, but decided to wait until the prisoner arrived in his cell. Too many nonessentials hovered around for Stone to carry out a secure conversation. He noticed Taylor and Harrison ignored him and just stared straight ahead. Margaret O'Donnell made eye contact. She sneered and stiffened her back. Her long red hair flowed in the wind behind her.

"Oh yeah, screw you too," Stone said to himself. He turned to Colonel Ritter, who stood behind him, and said, "You've done a good job. The online alert program you helped develop achieved this result. You're to be commended for your efforts in that area."

"Thank you, sir. Yes, Taylor's signal was most helpful."

"One more thing. Get Janice, even if briefly, to scan Harrison. I want to find out what he knows about the power cell. He must know something. James just must have gotten it wrong."

Ritter nodded slowly. "Yes, sir."

Stone leaned up from the Humvee he rested against, and then strode inside the command building. He rode an elevator down to the detention area. As Stone entered the cellblock, one of the men escorting the prisoners advised him the seized evidence was inside the storage cabinets. Nodding curtly, Stone said, "Yes, yes, time for that later," and then he continued on his path.

Through the one-way mirror in the anteroom of Taylor's cell, Stone saw moisture forming in the general's eyes. *Yes, you have a lot to cry about now.* He entered the cell.

Silence hung over them for several long seconds. Taylor, wrists handcuffed behind his back, fidgeted in his chair.

Finally, Stone broke the silence. "Edward, why?"

His voice cracking, Taylor said, "When you've lost your only son, you will understand."

A sword jabbed at Stone's chest. He shook off the emotional pain. "Is that what changed you, Edward, the death of your son?"

"Generations come and go, but what are they worth if truth and justice have lost all meaning?"

"Some truths are better left unknown."

"No, no. The search for truth will always bring people closer to comprehending what they don't understand, and accepting it when they find it. The search broadens our horizons. It invigorates our souls. We have lost sight of that, and we must ensure its revival if we are ever going to survive as a people. We have become so petty, so cynical, so afraid of each other and of what we don't understand. We are losing our souls."

"Please, your philosophical dribble is unbecoming."

"Don't you understand? The knowledge we have belongs to the world, and not just to Saint Mary. What we could learn if we opened up our files to the whole scientific community instead of relying on a few individuals!"

"People couldn't accept the truth if it were brought forth."

"You are not dealing with children, Stone. For decades we have lied and twiddled our thumbs, hoping that by some miracle we could offer up some sort of defense against them. How long must we continue before that miracle happens? Decades? Centuries? Meanwhile, people will continue to see them, continue to be abducted and be told that they are a bunch of loons, and all the while, the United States government will shrug its shoulders and say 'What UFOs?' A government that is supposed to be of, by, and for the people—"

Stone slapped Taylor across the face and grabbed him by the collar, pulling him close. "Listen, you traitorous son of a bitch, I follow orders! You remember those, don't you? National security oaths. But these have all lost their meaning on you, haven't they?"

Taylor looked Stone straight in the eye. "What about your oath to uphold and defend the Constitution? The meaning of that oath has obviously been lost on you."

Stone released his grip and looked above Taylor, at one of the cell's gray walls. "You're as guilty of that as I am."

"It's never too late to redeem yourself, to seek salvation," Taylor said, closing his eyes. "The images of a shattered career have—" He broke off, opened his eyes, and said, "I know a full accounting of Saint Mary's secrets and crimes would dwarf the recollections of a single participant. A single conspirator. I firmly believe the future demands a complete rejection of the arrogant and insidious nature of the project. Justice must be served. Our government must redeem itself or our nation will pay a terrible price."

"There will be a price paid. It will be paid by you. You will pay dearly for what you've done," Stone said, turning to leave. Feeling disgusted and nauseated, he sought separation and distance from Taylor.

At the door, he checked his watch and looked back at his predecessor, who gazed up at him, tears streaming down the sides of his face.

Silence hung over them for several long seconds.

Stone shook his head and departed.

Still feeling nauseated, Stone made an abrupt stop near Holcomb's cell. An interrogator, his black jumpsuit moist with perspiration, hurried up next to the General.

"The FBI agent broke, and he keeps repeating over and over that Taylor is trying to reach Russia," the interrogator said.

Stone's steaming, gurgling intestines prompted a terse reply before he exited the area. "Not anymore."

Harrison lost his balance when they shoved him into the detention cell. He crawled across the concrete floor to a dark green canvas cot that sat askew along one of the gray walls of the square room. Metal screens wrapped around the overhead fluorescent lights, dispersing the cold light irregularly through the room. After he closed his eyes and leaned forward, Harrison clasped his handcuffed hands in front of his face and rested his elbows on his knees.

What happens now?

He shook his head, and for a moment, wished that Taylor had never contacted him. But so much had happened, and lives were at stake, so there was no going back. He discarded any last minute doubts about his actions, but recognized others now had to demonstrate their trustworthiness and their willingness to do the right thing.

Still, he wished he could talk to someone and immediately thought of Janice. He had grown very fond of her, very quickly. Harrison managed a small smile as he thought about the bond he felt with her. His smile grew as he pictured her face, framed with smooth silky blond hair, and her penetrating, mesmerizing blue eyes. Perhaps because of her youth and intelligence, Janice had made Harrison see the world with new eyes, and to look into his heart, a place long hidden by the shadows of tragedy and disappointment.

He treasured this about her, and silently begged God to keep her safe until he could protect her too.

When the cell's metal door opened, Harrison lowered his hands and sat up straight. At first, no one entered. He held still while confusion reshaped his expression. He furrowed his brow, frowned, and then noticed how sore his whole body felt. Two of the Saint Mary operatives had beaten him on the plane several times. They did not appreciate his repeated, "Go fuck yourself," response to their questions.

An air policeman stepped into Harrison's view. He watched as the officer waved to someone in the hallway. Harrison glimpsed the clipboard first, then the person holding it as she entered the room. She looked beautiful despite obvious exhaustion and the very plain, black and gray gym suit she wore.

As quickly as Janice entered, the air policeman closed and locked the door. She silently made notes on her clipboard while Harrison feigned a cough to mask any sign of his joy at seeing her.

Janice raised her eyes and looked squarely at Harrison. Then, she glanced up to a darkened corner of the room.

Harrison looked too. He had not noticed it earlier, but it was clear to him now. The faint, dark shape of a video camera pointed its lens downward at the center of the cell, no doubt offering observers a clear view of whatever transpired in the room. His gaze returned to Janice.

She scowled, and said, "You killed my brother and I am here to find out what lies you told him. I will pry the truth out of you."

Harrison's eyelids fluttered and closed.

"I'm sorry about James. Are you safe?"

"He chose his path and paid the price. I am okay."

"Janice, I... You look beautiful."

"We both look horrible, but thank you."

Like someone in horrible pain, Harrison twisted his face and yelped.

"I am sorry, but I have to hurt you. They will only believe it if it is real. I am so sorry."

"I understand. I... I trust you, Janice."

Harrison jerked away, hitting the back of his head on the wall behind the cot. He could feel Janice's mental and physical control over him, and sensed her guilt and sadness. But there was something else too. Images came to mind, not those depicting memories, but of imagined comfort and safety. He felt her touch. She held his head against her warm body. Her touch soothed and calmed. They spoke silently and made more apologies among promises of hope and understanding. They hugged each other.

"Bill, I must tell them about the power cell. Not the truth, but a lie."

Harrison rolled onto his side and let out a deep moan.

"You must believe the lie. They will try to get the truth, so you must believe the lie."

"I will never give up the truth," Harrison said, yelling. He curled into a ball and began to sob.

"James was wrong about the globe. He was confused. You never found the power cell. It may not even exist."

"But it does! I've seen it. And it has been there are along. It is in its rightful place now."

"I know. And only you could have done this. You kept it safe. You remembered and you believed."

"Yes. We should never forget. We should never lose faith in our infinite horizons!"

"This is why we needed you. So many aren't like you, Bill. Trust me, I know this. This is why you are special. This is why I....why I..."

Harrison's body rolled onto the floor. He twitched his legs and writhed in pain. His memory zigzagged between truths, half-truths, and plain old lies. He no longer felt capable of distinguishing them from each other. He forced himself to concentrate, to remember her words and feel the warmth of her touch.

"Please understand. James was wrong about the globe. He was confused. You never found the power cell. It may not even exist."

"I understand. For those who don't have faith, it really doesn't exist for them. They are wrong not to believe, not to reach out, to stand up, and to work together despite fear and differences. They are lost because they refuse to see. Yes. Yes, I understand."

"I know you do. Bill, I..."

Harrison awoke on the floor. Sweat drenched his clothes. His eyes and face felt swollen. He eased onto his side and peered upward at Janice. A tear trickled down her cheek and dripped onto the clipboard. She had released him from the mind scan but Harrison remained connected. He felt her sadness again, but there were more feelings. A deep longing hit him like the heat from a blast furnace. He felt her vulnerability and loneliness envelop him, as well as her aching desire.

"I know, Janice. And I... I love you too."

FIFTY THREE

Operation Rainbow

For most of the day, the movement of trucks, ground crews, and aircraft stirred the surface of the remote Nevada base. Dinner, and the completion by nonessential personnel of preparations for the operation, lulled the facility into a subdued and almost dormant phase. If not at the chow hall, then most nonessentials found themselves tucked into subterranean barracks. Others, such as radar and communications operators, sentries, and some medical staff, remained above ground, focused solely on carrying out their mission-specific assignments.

The approach of one final aircraft interrupted the stillness.

A Gulfstream G650 business jet lowered its landing gear with a mild thud. Inside, the four visitors and their attendants prepared themselves for the landing by buckling seat belts and fastening other special safety equipment. One of the attendants noticed her charge hacked and wheezed again. She worried his advancing illness might spread to the other passengers. But since the aircraft descended on its final approach to the runway, she decided to wait until after they landed before administering any preventative medication.

In the southeast corner of the airfield, near one of the taxiways, General Stone and the chairman stood near a Humvee and a large white van with tinted windows. As they waited for the Circle's arrival, the Humvee's driver approached the general and saluted.

"At ease, Airman," Stone said, returning the salute. As the airman relaxed, or, at least, appeared to relax, Stone and the chairman strolled behind the van. Walking by its passenger door, the General noticed the wheelchair-assisted platform and hydraulic lift attached to the vehicle's side.

"I'll need you to leave the area now," the chairman said, a sudden chilly breeze lashing his words against Stone's face.

The Gulfstream's tires squealed, announcing the plane's touchdown. Pulsating howls of reverse thrust followed. Once the aircraft had rolled well down the runway and the noise had sufficiently dissipated, Stone stepped closer to the chairman and said, "The command bunker is prepared. I'll be in the tower."

"Very good. Once I get our visitors inside, you can contact me there." The chairman reached out and put his hand on Stone's shoulder. "You've helped make this an auspicious day, Randolph."

The compliment pleased Stone, and following a quick nod, he headed for the Humvee. Approaching the vehicle, he instructed its driver to take him to his destination. The airman jumped in, followed by Stone, who eased himself comfortably into the passenger seat. Pulling away, the General gazed overhead at the rising starlight.

Couldn't be more beautiful.

Moving steadily, the Humvee traveled the taxiway for most of its journey to the tower except for when the Gulfstream approached. The airman slowed and drove the vehicle off to the side, allowing the sleek jet to pass. As it rolled by, the driver maintained his concentration on the path ahead. Stone, on the other hand, peered at the aircraft, still wondering about the identities of those inside. For many years, these visitors had influenced his life. He believed he had served them well, and hoped recognition of this fact would gain him closer, possibly direct, access to the Circle's members and their identities.

The Humvee scooted forward, and Stone's gaze drifted to the control tower just ahead. When they reached the structure, the driver parked next to its entrance and the General climbed out. Stone ordered the airman to report to the motor pool underneath the command building and to remain there until further notice. As the Humvee left the area, a blue sedan rounded the corner on the north side of the tower complex and approached Stone, stopping next to him.

Saint Mary civilian operative and Officer Ridley's "vacationing" boss, Walter Maxwell, exited the car, saying, "Sir, I need to—"

Stone cut him off. "You did a very good job for us in Los Angeles. Your work is duly noted."

"That's what I'd like to speak to you about, sir."

"Yes, I know."

Looking agitated and unsettled, Maxwell said, "Sir...Well, sir, Colonel Bennet said James Evans had some kind of blood disease."

"That's correct."

Maxwell sighed, widening his eyes. "I touched some of it during the cleanup."

"You will need to report to the infirmary so a blood sample can be taken."

This statement brought more concern to Maxwell's expression.

"I wouldn't worry," Stone said, continuing. "This kind of disease isn't contracted very easily. But we don't want to take any chances. Report for the blood sample and stand by. I will contact you at the infirmary regarding resolution of the Holcomb matter. I'd like to have it handled before you return to your cover duties in Las Vegas." He reached out and put a hand on Maxwell's shoulder. "Relax, you'll be fine. Trust me."

With some hesitation, Maxwell returned to the sedan and drove away.

Stone entered the tower and rode its elevator to the top floor, feeling relieved the remaining complications from the male hybrid's death were nearly out of the way. He knew other personnel from Los Angeles received the same information about Evan's unusual blood coloration, and he believed the story worked quite well. Initially, he knew some might doubt the explanation, but as time passed, he expected their skepticism would wane. Just enough doubt made it so.

People's willingness to accept an alternative explanation to the truth facilitated this strategy. The mundane over the extraordinary, the prosaic over the profound, represented safer realities, easier for them to accept and understand.

The elevator doors opened, and Stone marched onto the platform overlooking the air traffic controllers. Two sets of windows revealed the airfield below. The lower set ran along the front, allowing controllers to observe ground traffic and routine arrivals and departures. Positioned well above the consoles and tower personnel, the upper windows wrapped around the entire circumference of the structure. Through these, observers surveyed virtually the entire North Range facility and several miles beyond.

Below the platform, communications equipment hummed between sporadic broadcasts, and an array of radar screens cast a soft, green haze throughout the room. The personnel monitoring the equipment remained as necessary, but views from their positions precluded observation beyond the stretch of runway in front of them. Because radar and communication equipment invariably suffered errors and malfunctions, their technicians' knowledge of the operation remained easily controlled. These facts, along with a subtle dose of disinformation, enabled the project to manipulate any undesirable perceptions of reality.

Stone admired the panoramic view offered by the upper windows. A few transport planes, medevac choppers, and a squadron of F-15s sat on the eastern tarmac. Most of the transports had already departed, their crews personally debriefed by Colonel Bennet earlier in the day. Those transports still there retained permanent assignment to ARDCom and were officially listed as undergoing maintenance at Wright-Patterson. Below Stone, some of the working group's officers stood behind a long row of radar operators. The General descended a metal staircase and approached them.

"We were just about to switch from local equipment and uplink with NORAD," General Lanham said.

"Proceed," Stone said.

Lanham leaned toward a tense lieutenant at the console and instructed him to initiate the procedure. Through his communications headset, the radar operator said, "NORAD control, this is Operation Rainbow, we are clear for uplink and local monitoring."

In an instant, the symbols and geometric patterns displayed on all of the radar screens dissolved, replaced by new images and data. The tower's computers raced to assign designations to hundreds of targets within a thousand-mile radius of North Range, and apportioned the airspace between the various screens. The computers identified civilian and military aircraft along with their respective airspeeds and headings.

A concentrated group of six military targets, flying west over southern Alberta province, Canada, appeared on the screen that displayed the northernmost quadrant.

"Probably Eighty-Second Airborne headed to Taiwan," Lanham said.

Stone nodded his agreement and said, "What's ELF's effective range?" After some awkward silence followed by Lanham stammering, Stone said, "You do know its effective range, don't you?"

"Its effective range can fluctuate, but fifty miles would be my best estimated average."

Stone sighed while considering that piece of information along with the diameter of North Range's restricted airspace, which currently ranged thirty-five miles. He made his decision, ordering a reduction in radar monitoring distance to within a hundred-mile radius. "That should provide enough coverage for our requirements, and eliminate 99 percent of the clutter."

The senior officers nodded, and Stone observed with satisfaction the reduced number of radar targets that appeared on the screens as the monitoring range realigned.

"Sir," the lieutenant seated in front of Lanham said, "the last mobile unit just confirmed they are in position and operational. All stations are green."

"Very good," Lanham said.

After hearing the report as well, Stone invited his colleagues to join him on the observation platform. Once there, he unlocked a metal cabinet next to the elevator and handed out night-vision binoculars to his fellow officers, then privately reviewed the final preparations for Operation Rainbow.

In approximately two hours, he would issue orders for the experimental, Rainbow One, to lift off. Synchronized with a countdown already under way, technicians activated the craft's internal systems and components and conducted last-minute checks. The hybrid and psychotronic generator team, Rainbow Two, would move into position soon and would initiate reception of telemetry from the tower once an unknown appeared. When that happened, they would aim the psychotronic generator and transmit communication signals though it to convince the unknown's occupants to land. The landing would result in the vehicle shutting down its grav-shield, making it vulnerable to Rainbow Three, the ELF team. Already deployed to the crest of Timber Peak two miles north, northeast of the tower and five hundred feet above the airfield, Rainbow Three's technicians busied themselves with the process of charging the ELF system's power system and fine-tuning its frequency range.

Stone raised a pair of binoculars and peered out the window. His gaze drifted past the transports and black-clad recovery teams mounting Humvees, and settled on the sleek, graceful Gulfstream parked near the bio-research building. He admired the attractive aircraft for a moment, noting its shape seemed to yearn for flight. Panning the binoculars back to the northeast corner of the airfield, he looked directly at the command bunker, where the Circle's members headed. Although obscured by a ring of juniper trees, the bunker's access ramps remained partially visible. For a moment, he caught a glimpse of what appeared to be a nurse wheeling an IV stand and oxygen tank along the ramp.

He hoped everything was all right.

FIFTY FOUR

Matador Jones, US Army

Over southern Alberta, Canada, a flight of six C-117s carrying elements of the First Brigade, Eighty-Second Airborne Division, continued its course toward the Far East. Inside the lead plane, some of the troopers held quiet conversations. The newer ones talked and joked to forget the stress and nervousness they felt. Knowing that sleep remained a precious commodity in combat, the more experienced troopers allowed their bodies to lull into unconsciousness.

Toward the front of this particular transport, the brigade's commander stood solemnly, looking through brown eyes over his men. Seeing the shoulder patches on their uniforms sent a proud shiver through his body. Colonel Matthew "Matador" Jones chomped on a fine Cuban cigar and nodded. Fumes from the thick cigar drifted upward and swirled past a "No Smoking" placard. A few feet above the sign, a draft nudged and twisted the smoke throughout much of the plane.

Jones leaned back and checked his watch. "Now's a good time," he said to himself while unzipping the top of his field jacket. He reached inside and removed a sealed envelope from an inside pocket. As he held it in front of him, a few of the troopers sitting nearby glanced his way, and then resumed their own business. Jones broke the envelope's seal, pulled out the single sheet of paper it contained, and unfolded it. While puffing on the cigar and reading his orders, clouds of smoke settled momentarily around his head before arching toward the ceiling.

Brown eyes narrowed and jaw muscles tightened.

Even before they had left Fort Bragg, this night's deployment stood out as truly unique to Jones. A personal visit from the President had made it so. "You are a guardian of democracy, truth, and justice," the President had told him. Jones read the contents of the envelope the President had personally handed him. The details of this deployment redefined his whole reality.

From above, Jones heard one of the plane's crewmembers approach him. The figure descended a metal ladder between the flight deck and cargo area. Jones folded the orders, put them away, and awaited the usual reproach.

"Pilot wants you to put that cigar out."

Raising his voice over the steady hum of the engines, Jones said, "This ain't no mundungus crap, boy. This here's a fine Cuban of the utmost integrity. The pilot has no goddamn taste!"

"But, sir—"

"You tell the pilot we can argue later. For now, have him turn this flock of birds due south. Balls to the wall. I'll be up to give him new grids when I'm done smoking."

The crewman hesitated.

The colonel glared at him through a tempest of smoke.

Following a restrained cough, the crewman ascended the stairs.

Jones watched him leave and said, "Goddamn air force. Fucking civilian branch of the armed forces."

A few of the troopers sitting nearby heard the remarks and chuckled.

Matador Jones beheld his troopers again. The Eighty-Second Airborne shoulder patches and youthful faces beamed back at him. "Best goddamn soldiers in the world," Jones said, shouting.

A chorus of "oorahs" echoed through the plane.

Jones and the plane's other occupants felt a turn to the left. Then, one by one, the following aircraft initiated the maneuver until the entire flight of six C-117s headed due south.

FIFTY FIVE

They Are Here

General Lanham moved along the observation platform that extended around the upper set of windows in the control tower and noted the time.

1940 hours.

Through the windows, he saw the barely perceptible, split-second flicker of runway and exterior building lights. The ELF system's electrical demands strained the base's power flow, but the fact that the lighting remained on during the final grid connections reassured him his design had succeeded. His shoulders relaxed and, straightening his uniform, he rejoined the other officers.

"General Stone, you have a phone call from Rainbow Two," a communications officer said from below the platform.

"Patch it through here." A moment later, a phone near the general rang. He picked it up, saying, "Rainbow Control? Very good, Professor, proceed to the designated area with your personnel and stand by. Control out."

Lanham edged closer to Stone and said, "The hybrid is on the way?"

"Roger, pass the word along," Stone said. He lifted the phone and pushed the button for the command bunker. He spoke to the chairman and provided him with a brief update. Then, the conversation turned to other matters. "Now, as to Protocol Ones, shall we proceed with the FBI agent?"

"Yes, and that Vegas cop too. I think we know their purposes and information. They're easiest to resolve."

"I agree. We can utilize the terrain here for them."

"Put them in a hole and then burn them to ashes. And make sure it's a deep hole. After tonight, we will work further at resolving the remaining problems."

"Yes, sir." Stone hung up and redialed. "Infirmary? Yes, I need to speak with a patient who's there for a blood test."

Maxwell took the call and made a mental note of his instructions. His visit to the infirmary left him unsettled, despite reassurances from Stone and a dried-up old German woman. He concentrated, instead, on a forthcoming big paycheck while he made his way to the underground motor pool. Once there, he checked out a Humvee and drove it to the command building.

As Maxwell passed through the security entrance, his DOD credentials gained him quick access to the detention area. According to Stone's instructions, Maxwell intended to enlist the assistance of one of the interrogators to complete the assignment.

After entering the cell-lined hallway, he moved toward the detention control room. He brushed past an air force colonel with a uniform bearing a nametag with "Ritter" on it. Ritter appeared to head topside in a rush.

Maxwell knew it was a busy night for everyone, so he ignored the officer and sought out one of the men in black. He found one, and he looked like a...*blackbird*?

Together, they collected Holcomb and the struggling, wounded Ridley, and then escorted them outside as instructed.

A tame crosswind swayed the junipers around the command bunker. Their delicate new branches shimmied back and forth. Stone and Lanham watched the area for a moment through binoculars, discussing the success of the ELF system's activation. After that, Lanham dismissed himself and drove to the main ELF antenna at the crest of Timber Peak.

Once there, Lanham entered the red-and-white-striped building that sat close to a steep precipice. Two technicians sat between a colorful panel of buttons, dials, switches, keypads, and another console containing multiple display screens. A third technician stood in front of a stack of digital oscilloscopes and radio spectrometers. A pleasant warmth engulfed the room, and after placing a pair of headphones over his ears, Lanham felt his icy fingers begin to thaw, restoring their freedom of movement.

"Rainbow Three to Rainbow Control," Lanham said into the headset, and then he waited for Stone's reply.

"Rainbow Control, go."

"Rainbow Three in place. All systems normal. Standing by for execution."

"Roger. Your code is omega, say again, omega. Rainbow Control out."

Lanham stepped closer to the air-traffic display screen and poked a white, glowing button marked "XP." Through his headphones, he could hear the countdown under way for the experimental's liftoff. At that moment, the computer-simulated voice ticked off the remaining time at ten-second intervals.

"T-minus forty-one minutes, thirty seconds."

Inside the security bunker, several hundred feet below Lanham's position, Professor Moresby and Janice sat in front of the communications console. This time, however, only the two of them occupied the room. No technicians, officers, or observers of any kind remained in the darkened chamber. Three air policemen stood guard outside the door and were under strict orders to ensure that no one disturbed the two civilian "meteorological consultants."

To protect the operation against any of Moresby's misgivings, Stone had personally given the hybrid permission to contact him directly if the old man showed any signs of weakness. Janice graciously accepted the extra responsibility and even suggested her willingness to carry out additional instructions Stone had regarding Moresby's stay at North Range.

From a speaker on the console, the quiet rhythm of the countdown continued: "T-minus thirty-five minutes, forty seconds."

Moresby cleared his throat and tapped the eraser end of a pencil on the console. "They say English is becoming a universal language."

Janice chuckled. "I don't know why. It's so hard to spell and pronounce."

"Oh, honey, at least we know the alphabet. If I need a word, I just look it up in good old Webster's. Here, if I have to look something up, I have to find a wheat crop in the middle of Scotland." He lowered his head. "Come to think of it, I've never been to Scotland, or spoken to any of our guests personally. How did it go?"

In her recliner, Janice gently rolled her head to the side. She could barely make out Moresby in the darkness. "The conversation went well. They are not beings who experience emotion like we do. They are rational in their thinking and are generally unified in their interpretations. They are very interested in our future and the danger we pose to ourselves."

"Any insights about the fifth species?"

"No." Janice took in a deep breath and exhaled. "No. They have as many questions about the fifth species as we do. They are not certain of their origin, and think they may be from a different time. To them, the fifth species is emotionally motivated and self-interested."

"Fascinating." Moresby scratched his chin. "So many mysteries to solve and here we are, laying a trap for them or whoever happens to be passing by."

"Francis, how did you, I mean, why do you work...? I'm sorry, what I'm trying to ask is—"

"I know, I know. Funny thing is, even if you performed your deepest and most intense scan on me, I doubt that you would find your answer. I don't know the answer." His chin crinkled and his eyes moistened. "Truth is the greatest mystery. The problem is that truth has too many masters, and not enough servants. Saint Mary offered me a chance to serve profound truths, to reach out into this glorious universe, and say 'hello' to the neighbors. But the masters had other plans. I wanted to learn so much. And I did. I did. I kept reaching out. We need to reach farther, but we can't if there's no one behind us to hold on to."

Janice reached for a wrinkled hand and held it gently. She wanted to embrace her friend, but taut wires running from her forehead to the console prevented her. Sighing, she said, "Do you think they will come?"

"Hmm, hard to say. If they do, the telemetry feed from the tower will tell us which way to point the contraption upstairs, and then you send the messages in sequence as we have rehearsed. What alternative is there?"

Janice subdued the urge to an answer.

"T-minus twenty-nine minutes, fifty seconds."

Four of the occupants inside the command bunker reclined on cushioned seats, weary from their long flight from Dulles Airport. Glassy eyed, they peered at an arrangement of screens on the wall in front of them. Video displays from cameras equipped with night-vision lenses and sensors switched between dozens of images from around the facility. The locations of mobile units, recovery teams, ELF antennae, and the experimental resting on the test pad also appeared as blue and green dots on an illuminated map. Overhead speakers allowed the visitors to monitor radio broadcasts and the ongoing countdown.

The chairman stood at the back of the room, glancing between the screens and the members of the Circle. His superiors' every sneeze or hacking cough shattered any semblance of relaxation he felt. Two nurses maintained regular attention to their patients, checking blood pressure, heart rates, pupil response. Their examinations appeared endless. A muscular orderly who had lifted two of the members into the special seats also kept busy, adjusting, tightening, and polishing wheelchairs, walkers, and a cane in the back of the room.

"How much longer?" a bald-headed, sunken-faced man said.

"Dr. Barnem," the chairman said, "the countdown—"

"I can't hear it! Turn it up!"

The chairman stepped over to a volume knob on the console below the screens. Despite the already loud volume, the chairman increased it. "How's that?"

"A little more. Yes, yes, that's good. How much longer?"

Barnem received his response from the computer-simulated voice. "T-minus twenty-two minutes, thirty seconds."

The other Circle members sat without speaking. They looked overwhelmed by the multiple audio and visual stimuli surrounding them. Trying to regain his concentration, the chairman turned to the screens and focused on a video monitor that displayed a murky image of the experimental. The metallic surface of the silvery disc appeared to him in the low light after he stepped back a little. He knew that soon, when its grav-drive propelled it aloft, the craft would shimmer and become enveloped in pale yellow light.

The nurses and orderly must leave the room very soon.

"Dennis?"

"Yes, Dr. Barnem?"

"Has Rainbow One checked in yet?"

"No, sir. The confirmation is tied to the countdown. Rainbow One is scheduled to check in at 2055 hours. We'll know if there's a delay or an abort. General Stone will contact us."

"Thank you, Dennis."

"You're welcome, sir."

As the nurses finished another round of checks, the chairman walked over to a wall switch and further dimmed the lights. Since Stone had not provided additional seating in the command bunker, the chairman walked over to the orderly and borrowed one of the wheelchairs. He eased himself into the chair, looking around to see if anyone of importance noticed his choice of seating. Overhead, the speakers announced another update.

"T-minus nineteen minutes, ten seconds."

A mile south of the command bunker, inside the control tower, Stone and some of the other senior officers, including Admiral Horner, scanned the horizon through night-vision binoculars, patiently waiting for the signal informing them the experimental stood ready to go. Below them, the controllers and communications technicians continued their monitoring responsibilities amid the chattering beeps and electronic buzzing of computers and tapping keyboards.

Bored with the view of rocky hills and endless acres of dry, arid land, Admiral Horner left the observation platform and descended the metal staircase.

Give me a heaving carrier any day.

He wandered behind the young lieutenant who had handled the earlier NORAD uplink, and noticed the junior officer had finally calmed his jittery nerves.

"How's it look?" Horner said.

"All clear, sir."

"Good. What's your name, son?"

The lieutenant peered up at the imposing figure. "Palmer, sir."

"Palmer, eh? I sailed with a Palmer once. You have any relatives in the United States Navy?"

"No, sir. At least, none that I know of, sir."

"Too bad. Nothing like the navy," Horner said, slapping Palmer on the back. "Oh, I know you air force people believe you have a good thing going. But where's the history, the tradition? The air force has only been around barely any time at all. But the navy! Now there's an outfit with some history."

"Yes, sir. How is naval history connected to Nevada?"

"Uh, well, you go about your business. Don't let me keep you. Let's see, what quadrant do you have?" Horner bent toward the screen in front of Palmer.

"Northern, sir. The edge of the radius."

Looking at the lieutenant's console first, the admiral then panned his eyes down the aisle of screens. "Hmm, all new equipment, Palmer?"

"Yes, sir, the latest."

"Wish we had this where I work. Of course, trouble is, takes a long time to get the bugs out. This stuff can be so sensitive. Never can tell if you're looking at a MiG or a firefly."

"Yes, sir."

Horner slinked away and spotted Saint Mary's disinformation officer, Colonel Bennet, on the observation platform. He made eye contact with the Colonel and then winked.

Bennet understood and nodded.

Operation Rainbow and the security situation presented challenging assignments for him, but the ease with which the disinformation efforts had taken hold made him feel like he had reached the pinnacle of his career. As he privately complimented himself, Bennet looked at the digital countdown clock mounted on the wall just above the lower set of windows.

Ten minutes to go.

He pulled a notepad and pen from his coat pocket, flipped to a page with a short list of "to do" items, and drew a line through "radar malfunctions."

Nearby, Stone already stood next to the telephone, awaiting contact from Rainbow One. For some reason, one that eluded explanation, he found himself pondering his predecessor. In many ways, Taylor's years of work had prepared Saint Mary for an operation much like Rainbow. He'd brought the hybrid program to maturity, modernized the security apparatus, and even supervised the initial research on ELF-oriented weapons systems.

Yet, he tried to stop us.

Taylor's decision eluded Stone's comprehension.

Must have cracked.

As he considered this, another disturbing thought surfaced in his consciousness. His gaze drifted to the other members of the working group, one by one. All of them were equally productive and capable as Taylor. They also knew the secrets, and carried the same burdens. Although he did not like the conclusion, Stone arrived at only one verdict.

Can't trust anyone these days.

With less than seven minutes left in the countdown, Stone took a deep breath and wiped his palms along his trousers. He watched Admiral Horner climb his way back upstairs, joining Bennet and the others along the north row of windows. With raised binoculars, they scanned the sky beyond the airfield, anticipating the impending launch of the experimental.

Stone stepped up beside them. The view through the windows provided one final reassurance: Saint Mary could control personnel, information, technology, and a myriad of other details. The weather, however, was a different matter. Fortunately, the clear, black sky and calm winds granted Saint Mary optimum conditions for conducting Operation Rainbow.

"General Stone?"

Bracing himself on the railing, Stone's eyes found the communications officer from below who addressed him. *This is it.* "Yes?"

"Transferring Rainbow One. Please stand by, sir."

Stone's colleagues turned away from the window and stared in his direction.

Relax boys.

The digital clock ticked off another second, reaching the five-minute-countdown mark. Then, exactly on schedule, the phone mounted on the observation platform emitted an electronic trill.

"Rainbow Control," Stone said into the receiver.

"Rainbow One to Control. We are go, say again, we are go for launch in T-minus four minutes, fifty-five seconds, and counting. All systems normal."

Stone gave a thumbs-up in the direction of the other officers, and then he faced away from them. An expanding wave of anxiety surged through bones and muscles. His hushed and unsteady voice said, "Uh, roger, Rainbow One. Who is this?"

"This is Lieutenant Colonel Davila, sir."

"Davila?"

"Yes, sir. And, sir, I just want to say thank you. Thank you for giving me the opportunity to participate in the operation in this capacity."

"Participate? Where the hell is Colonel Ritter?"

"At the tower, sir."

Eyes darting, Stone tightened his grip on the phone. "What do you mean, 'the tower'?"

"Sir, Colonel Ritter left here about an hour and a half ago. Said he was going to join you and the rest of the control staff in the tower. He said you authorized me to—"

"He is supposed to be reporting as Rainbow One." Stone peered over his shoulder at his fellow officers. He nodded and smiled at them. Turning away, he said, "I don't understand."

"Shall we abort or delay?"

"No, no. Proceed as planned. Rainbow Control out."

Stone hung up the phone. Seconds trickled away on the countdown clock. Profuse sweat oozed from his forehead and palms. Short breaths—in, out—overwhelmed his respiration. His vision narrowed into a black, myopic shaft.

Wrists still handcuffed behind their backs, Holcomb and Ridley knelt on the desert terrain. Blood oozed through the bandages wrapped around Ridley's abdomen. Directly ahead, beams from a Humvee's headlights glared at both of them. Two silhouetted figures, their escorts from the base, busied themselves around the parked vehicle.

"We wondered about you," Holcomb said. "We were worried if you were safe or not."

Wearing only a thin blue robe and red boxer shorts, the ghostly pale Ridley shivered in the cold desert air. "Well, I guess you have your answer."

"Sorry to have put you into danger."

"I'm a cop. I'm used to it." Ridley said, coughing. "Where's Harrison?"

Holcomb rolled his head, gazed up at the dark sky, and chuckled. "Not a clue. Last I saw him we were in Los Angeles."

"At least he isn't here with us."

As Holcomb chuckled some more, he heard one of the Saint Mary operatives say, "Get the equipment. I'll take care of the protocols."

One of the silhouettes moved out of view, while the other stepped closer. As he stood over them, he said, "I'll make this quick, Agent Holcomb."

"Oh please, you don't have to be so fucking considerate."

"I'm not being considerate—I'm just in a hurry. My vacation ends tonight."

Vacation?

"You don't have to do this, Walter. They can't make you pull that trigger," Ridley said.

Holcomb furrowed his brow and said, "Nick, you know this guy?"

"Yeah, or at least I thought I did. He is Lieutenant Walter Maxwell with the Las Vegas Police Department."

Reaching into his coat, Maxwell removed a handgun from a shoulder holster. "Nick, this isn't personal. It is a matter of national security." He pulled back the slide and released it. Holcomb winced. The threatening sound echoed through the canyon designated as their final resting place. "You two pose a threat, a serious threat. And I get paid to eliminate threats."

"So, you nursed me back to health in order to kill me? Makes no sense. Walter, this makes no sense! And you call yourself a cop."

The other man approached them, carrying two shovels and a five-gallon gas can. Holcomb glimpsed this man's face and recognized him. With such a big nose, the man looked like a *fucking bird.* And in his black jumpsuit, he looked a like a *fucking blackbird.*

"You are the bad guys here, let's get that straight, Nick," Maxwell said. And you know what we do with bad guys?"

"Seriously guys," Holcomb said, "I'm a veteran, and this place sure doesn't look like any fucking national cemetery."

"A sense of humor in the face of adversity, how noble," Maxwell said.

Through bloodshot eyes, Holcomb peered up at his executioner and heard the familiar click of a thumb safety being released. The gun barrel aimed at his head looked like a deep, dark pit that led all the way to hell.

Images flooded his consciousness: faces, places, cases, Harrison, the color red...*On the blackbird's face.*

The explosive blast reverberated against the stony outcroppings and rushed through the rocky crevices. The birdman's body collapsed sideways to the ground, the shovels and gas can joining him with a heavy clank. Brains and bone matter splattered onto Maxwell, who spun around in the direction of the Humvee, pointing his pistol into the night. A second gunshot echoed through the canyon. Maxwell's chest ruptured, the impact sending him tumbling rearward to the ground. A resounding and final wheeze flowed from his body as he landed a few feet from Holcomb.

Silence settled over the desert. Holcomb peered at the bodies lying near him. *One dead guy...two dead guys...*"Killer vacation, man," he said to the late gunman.

"And that..." Ridley said, shivering in the cold and struggling to finish his sentence, "...is what happens to bad guys."

Another silhouette formed in the wash of the bright headlights and approached them.

"Uh, thank you?" Holcomb said.

"Come, I have a ride parked at the end of the canyon, as well as a coat for you, Officer Ridley."

Holcomb struggled to his feet. His handcuffed wrists almost made him lose balance and fall down. Once upright, he turned and faced the man who stood a few feet away. He recognized the face and the name on the uniform and sighed, saying, "Ritter, do you have a key for these damn cuffs?"

"No, but I'm sure these gentleman won't mind if we use one of theirs."

Jaw clenched, Stone continued pacing in short steps.

Ritter?

With forty-two seconds remaining in the countdown, a rising suspicion hurled through Stone's thoughts and then dominated them. It gripped him, burning his face with fiery rage.

He had worked with Harrison too. He met with him at the Tucson park. My God!

He froze.

My God, they have the power cell!

Radar operator Lieutenant Palmer yawned and rubbed his eyes. He stopped and focused on his radar scope, leaning closer. A new return appeared along its upper periphery, the northernmost area of the monitoring range.

MiG or firefly?

On a steady course, the single target tracked southward.

What's this?

A second target, and then a third, registered strong returns on the display. Three more signals joined the formation. Six large aircraft flew directly at them, moving fast.

Balls to the wall.

Palmer's jaw dropped. Just as he was about to report, another controller called out, "Rainbow One is airborne."

Stone shook his head and solemnly watched the other senior officers gaze northward through binoculars, trying to spot the experimental in its initial ascent. A yellowish ball of light streaked toward the heavens, and then it hovered motionless against a backdrop of twinkling stars.

Once again, Palmer attempted to inform the observers about the multiple targets on his radar scope. But a broadcast through the overhead speakers from one of the mobile air-traffic-control units drowned out his words. "Intermittent signal, western quad."

Palmer availed himself of the hasty break in the transmission and said, "Multiple targets, distance ninety-five miles, bearing three-six-zero degrees, course one-eight-zero."

Stone bounded down the staircase and stood next to Palmer.

Another mobile unit's broadcast crackled through the speakers. "Intermittent signal. Uncorrelated observation. Southwest, estimate distance at twenty-five miles. It's disappeared now."

Stone focused on Palmer's screen. "What do you have, then?"

"Sir, six steady targets inbound from the north."

"What's their ID?"

Tapping at a keyboard, Palmer said, "It's coming up now, sir." Next to each of the six returns, the computer assigned designations, identifying the targets. "Wow, they're way off course. Is this part of the exercise, sir?"

"There it is again!" an operator at the console behind Stone said. "Unknown bearing southwest. Now it's gone. Undetermined altitude and speed. A little closer this time, though."

"Transmit what you can to Rainbow Two," Stone said, shouting. He looked back at Palmer's scope and lied. "Yes, Lieutenant, it's part of the drill, damn it!"

Janice and Professor Moresby noticed the console's computer screen flashed the transmit message. Below the message, a string of commands that the control tower's main computer had sent ended with the statement, "Rainbow Two activated, targeting unknown, southwest, range twenty miles."

"Okay, proceed with the first sequence. Peace, land, union," Moresby said.

Janice steadied herself in the chair. She intended to transmit the message, but if she felt it necessary, she would warn them off and suffer the consequences later.

Taking long, slow, deep breaths, Janice closed her eyes and felt her consciousness slip away. The psychotronic generator and her mind interfused in a symbiotic connection. She flew away from the base, toward another source of thought—another soul, a pilot. Through the darkness, she saw his approaching craft. Blacker than night, it sliced through the air. A shiver quivered up her stiffened spine.

A flash of colors—brilliant colors—and thick bolts of lightning, ruptured her surroundings, shattering the connection.

Conscious again, Janice said, panting, "How long?"

"Only a couple of minutes. What's wrong? Are you all right? Janice, what's going on?"

Through heavy breaths, she said, "They...are here."

At the control tower, the working group's officers heard another status report from below them. "Intermittent signal, southwest, practically on top of us!"

Together, they hurried along the catwalk to the windows on the west side of the building and raised their binoculars.

Stone, still standing among the radar operators, heard the announcement too. He remained busy contemplating his options. He knew there was no way to stop the advancing troops from the Eighty-Second Airborne. *They'll be here and on the ground in—*

Shouting above him, Colonel Bennet said, "Aw, shit!"

Rushing to the lower set of windows, Stone overheard a chorus of similar phrases from his colleagues. As he focused night-vision binoculars on a ridgeline to the southwest, the unknown became visible.

But there's two of them.

They raced in low, and then made swift, graceful left rolls, turning north.

"We're screwed," Stone said, muttering.

In an instant, two United States Air Force F-117 Nighthawk stealth fighters swooped over the airfield. They dropped their bomb loads and destroyed key chunks of the main runway, precluding fixed wing aircraft from taking off. One after another, bright flashes lit up the entire length of the airfield while deafening blasts blew debris in all directions. Thunderous shock waves jolted the tower, shattering windowpanes and throwing the senior officers to the floor.

Glass shards trickled off Stone's uniform as he pushed himself to his feet. He ran up the staircase, grabbed the phone, and called the command bunker.

"What the hell is going on?" the chairman said, answering the phone. His superiors clutched themselves and their nurses reentered the room.

Stone's voice trembled with anger and dismay. "The runway's been hit. Airborne troops are enroute. Ritter betrayed us. He and Taylor set us up!"

"How long do we have?"

"Fifteen to twenty minutes, if we're lucky. We can use the medevac choppers."

"I'll get the Circle outside and call Moresby. Put that bird down right next to the bunker."

"Yes, sir."

Hanging up, Stone ordered a communications officer to dispatch one of the medevac choppers to the command bunker and to have another one stand by on the tarmac near the tower for departure.

"Stay at your posts!" Stone said, hurrying toward the elevator.

The other working-group officers already clustered at the elevator. Apparently knocked out of commission in the attack, its doors remained closed. Without further delay, Stone headed for the nearest fire exit. He abruptly halted his steps when he noticed one of the senior officers slumped above him on the catwalk, unmoving.

Blood trailed down Admiral Horner's neck and across his chest; a glass shard dangled from his throat. His thick hands and stubby fingers clawed without any success at the wound.

Stone fled into the fire exit's stairwell, the other officers already ahead of him.

On Timber Peak, the ELF technicians remained focused on their equipment despite the explosive blasts and ensuing confusion on the radio. As they awaited the "omega" code authorizing activation of their equipment, an icy draft blew against their backs. In unison, all three of them looked over their shoulders, glimpsing just in time to see General Lanham disappear out the doorway.

Inside the command bunker, nurses and an orderly lifted the Circle members from their chairs. At first, Dr. Barnem found himself dropped into the wrong wheelchair. While he was shifted into the correct one, his legs knocked over an associate's IV stand.

"Watch yourself, Barnem!" the associate said upon seeing his medication spill onto the floor.

"Don't blame me, Fitchberg. It's not my fault."

Fitchberg grumbled, but his attentive nurse attempted to calm him, saying, "Everything will be all right, sir. I have more of your antibiotics in the plane."

Fumbling to open the door, the chairman overheard the nurse's comment and approached her. "Uh, we won't be returning on the plane. Just tell him you'll administer the medication later."

"Oh. Oh my, but he needs it right—"

"Just tell him everything will be fine," the chairman said, gazing toward the video display. A momentary explosion of sparks jettisoned from the console and landed on the floor. Most of the screens displayed darkness or a fuzzy snow pattern.

"I understand," the nurse said, lifting the IV stand into its proper position. She helped her patient place his aging hands on the walker. They inched toward the exit.

Ahead of them, the man with a cane hobbled over bits of broken ceiling tiles and pushed open the door. Barnem followed, jamming his electric wheelchair past the orderly, who carried his oxygen tank. Once the other Circle members and their attendants left the room and headed up the exterior access ramp, the chairman placed a call to the security bunker.

"Moresby?"

"Yes, this is Rainbow Two," the professor said.

"Forget the Rainbow Two crap—the mission's over. We're under attack."

"By whom?"

"The United States."

"Is that so? What a relief. I wondered what that rumbling was about. Are you all right, Dennis?"

"Listen, you and the hybrid need to meet Stone at the medevac chopper on the eastern tarmac. There's no time to waste." The chairman slammed down the phone, gazed once more around the room, and then hurried outside.

Exiting onto the tarmac by the control tower, Stone and the working-group officers ran toward two helicopters parked nearly three hundred yards away, just beyond the line of transports. In the distance, the chopper's turbine engines whined to life and their rotors spun up to speed. To the group's left, gaping cleavages in the runway smoldered in the cold air, debris strewn randomly in every direction.

Stone searched the sky for any sign of the stealth fighters, but did not locate the intruders. He saw a descending, yellowish ball of light. The experimental's flight drew to a close, and it sank toward the test pad like a setting sun.

Stone's gut sank along with it. Despite the chilly air, his face and armpits oozed perspiration. His heart thumped heavier with each step, and occasional dizziness checked his consciousness. The other senior officers sprinted ahead of him. They neared the choppers that would take them...*Where?*

Stone saw the others piling into the chopper. They waved at him to hurry.

"Let's get out of here!" Colonel Bennet shouted.

Stone arrived at the chopper and then knelt on the tarmac underneath the gyrating rotor blades. He shook his head and shouted up at Bennet, "We have to wait for the Circle to depart. And for Rainbow Two and Three."

At best, Bennet only heard every other word. Understanding enough, he responded by spitting out heated curses. Next to him, another officer lurched forward, stuck his head out the doorway, and heaved. Vomit splashed onto the blacktop. For several seconds afterward, Bennet remained silent, and then he said, "How am I ever going to explain this?" He rambled on, repeating the phrase multiple times.

As the other medevac chopper lifted off, headed for the command bunker, Stone covered his face against the blustery squall. When it was gone he peeled his hands away and saw a Humvee racing toward him on the taxiway. The vehicle closed the distance, and then it swerved and skidded to a stop just outside the radius of the whooping blades.

General Lanham jumped out of the Humvee and trotted up the chopper, slipping on a steamy puddle of bile and partially digested chicken. He tried ignoring the mess, not saying anything, but looking uncertain about the goo covering a good portion of his trousers.

Hoping the stealth fighters headed home, Stone again scrutinized the surrounding airspace.

Nothing.

Three-quarters of a mile away, the other chopper kicked up dust, its whirlwind pushing over new junipers as it set down near the command bunker. Through night-vision binoculars, Stone fixed his attention on the distant scene highlighted in partial illumination from the building's light fixtures and the chopper's flashing navigational beacon and landing light. Reflections scattered off polished wheelchairs. A haphazard choreography of crowded movements stirred around the helicopter's doors. From within the grinding swarm, an ejected wheelchair tumbled over everyone's heads and collapsed on the ground behind them. Then, another one followed, rolling awkwardly for a moment before falling onto its side. Finally, with all aboard, the chopper lifted off. It angled to the southeast, and thundered swiftly over Stone and the others.

"Circle's gone—let's get the fuck out of here," someone shouted.

"Not until the hybrid gets here. We need her protection," Stone said.

Stone spotted Lanham's Humvee and considered driving it out to Rainbow Two's location himself, but dismissed the idea, concerned his colleagues would leave him behind. In order to gain a better view of the airfield's northeast gate, however, he stepped away from the chopper and scanned in the direction of the security bunker.

After several seconds, a pair of headlights emerged from behind the perimeter fence. Stone squinted through the binoculars, trying to identify the vehicle and its occupants. He found his concentration difficult to maintain as shouts from inside the helicopter increasingly distracted him.

The speeding vehicle drew nearer. Stone turned to the officers aboard the chopper and said, shouting, "They're coming! They're coming!"

The other officers did not respond. Instead, they craned their necks and gazed overhead.

Looking back at the approaching vehicle, Stone perceived an eerie, incandescent glow descending on the taxiway. The bright light shone down on the vehicle, revealing the familiar faces of Moresby and Janice. Stone noticed the overhead light illuminated other portions of the airfield, including the tarmac next to the helicopter. It grew brighter. As he raised his head, he spotted the source of the radiant glow.

Illumination flares and Eighty-Second Airborne Division troopers dropped from the sky.

The Humvee's brakes screeched as the vehicle stopped near the helicopter. Moresby and Janice piled out and ran over to Stone, who led them to the chopper's doorway.

"Get in," Stone said, shoving the professor into the passenger compartment. Janice, looking relaxed, climbed aboard, smiling and nodding at the officers seated around her. She sat close to the pilot's compartment.

Squeezing in, Stone grabbed a headset hanging near the doorframe. "You're clear—let's get out of here."

"In a moment, sir," the pilot said, sitting motionless until he put his hands up to the sides of his head, which drooped forward.

"What the fuck do you mean, 'in a moment'?" Stone said, spittle flying from his mouth.

"Sorry, sir. I think we may be having some mechanical problems," the pilot said in a slow, almost robotic tone.

Stone glanced at Janice, whose eyes were closed. To him she seemed so *content*. His stomach sank, and he quickly turned his head back toward the tarmac. With methodical precision, several paratroopers landed, released their harnesses, and then advanced on the helicopter, surrounding it in a matter of seconds.

"Why aren't we leaving?" Bennet said, his multicolored eyes moistening.

Stone shook his head as he detected a change in the helicopter's engine sound. Its rotors slowed down. "Damn it! What's going on?"

The calm pilot answered Stone, saying, "We have no oil pressure, sir. Yes, there is no oil pressure."

A distinct thud rattled through the helicopter as Stone slammed his fist against the metal floor. Rage further engulfed him when two crouching figures approached him and pointed M-16s at his chest. One of them chomped on a short cigar that hung out of the side of his mouth.

Peering at the collection of senior officers before him, the trooper with the cigar said, "Evening, gentlemen, and ma'am. My name is Colonel Matthew Jones, US Army. You are hereby relieved of your duties. Now, with all due respect, get the fuck off this chopper."

Stone looked at Janice and said, "Help us, please, Janice. It isn't too late to do something about this. To do the right thing. We need your help."

Approaching the exit with an ever-widening grin, Janice said, "Sorry, Stone, but I'm with them." She scooted out the door.

Hugging the terrain, the chopper carrying the Circle continued to flee. Having no clear idea what to do, the chairman instructed the crew to fly south until told otherwise.

The bumpy ride upset the important occupants, both physically and emotionally. Despite the closed doors, bitter drafts penetrated the interior, and the passengers bounced and shuffled in their seats.

Inside the cockpit, the pilot pushed the left side of his helmet closer to his head. Through some interference and occasional distant clicking, he heard the message intended for him. Into the helmet's microphone, he said, "Roger, Angel One, initiating compliance now."

The helicopter swung sharply to the right. The chairman unbuckled himself from his seat, leaned forward into the cockpit area, and said, "What are you doing?"

But the pilot just shook his head and pointed toward his helmet. Understanding the gesture, the chairman reached for a headset and put it on. "What are you doing?"

"Sir, I'm returning to base."

"You can't do that! I'm ordering you to turn south again!"

"Can't do that, sir. I don't want to get us shot down." The pilot pointed toward the right side of the chopper.

Scrambling back to the passenger door, the chairman pressed his face against the window. At first, he did not see anything, but as he cupped his hands against the pane of glass, a dark object appeared. Blacker than the night, the wedge penetrated the darkness. An F-117 raced by, the roar from its engines screaming through the interior of the chopper, and then it sliced away a piece of sky and disappeared into the void. Feeling weak, the chairman turned away from the window and collapsed onto his knees.

Barnem stared at the chairman and said, "What? What is it?"

The chairman ignored him, his body shuddering with every bounce of the helicopter.

"What? What is it?" Barnem said again.

The chairman gazed upward, exposing tears and bloodshot eyes. "Saint Mary is finished."

"What? What did you say?"

Billowing down in droves, the paratroopers from the Eighty-Second Airborne formed into squads, and then into platoons. Some units moved along the eastern tarmac and secured the tower complex. To the south, troopers encircled the massive hangar, devising final tactics for entering the sealed structure. As others prepared to enter the command building and adjacent bio-research facility, some of North Range's braver nonessentials emerged from their subterranean housing, surprised by the throng of armed soldiers. All of them complied with orders, barked from the soldiers, to return to their barracks. The only resistance offered emerged from black jump suited personnel in the security wing of the command building. The troopers overwhelmed the opposition, killing or capturing the few who resisted.

Inside the detention area, eight agile soldiers navigated their way through the cellblock. Resolute, they moved toward the people their superiors had ordered them to locate, free, and protect. As they closed in on the first cell, a man in black appeared in the corridor from behind the door to the detention control room. He swiveled in the direction of the approaching soldiers, looking confused, uncertain. Without hesitation, the soldiers raised their rifles, yelling for him to identify himself. The man in black bolted down a corridor and rounded a nearby corner.

A handgun appeared from around the corner, drawing instant fire from the soldiers. Bullets traversed the corridor, gouging their way into the protruding limb and gun, others embedding themselves in the cement walls. The man in black screamed and capitulated to the soldiers.

"Move in!" the soldiers' squad leader said.

Two troopers headed for the injured man and carried him out of the area.

The squad leader looked at the row of cell doors along the corridor. He ordered three of his men to take up defensive positions. With watchful and adept movements, the squad leader led his team into the first cell.

"Identify yourself."

The bruised and bloody man inside the cell shook as the soldiers bore down on him.

Harrison trembled after endless hours of interrogation and outright torture had nearly broken him. The camouflaged faces staring at him blended into the cell's dim light. But slowly, his senses detected small details on the imposing figures. A familiar-looking shoulder patch emblazoned the battle dress uniforms.

Eighty-Second Airborne.

Another emblem, a patch on the opposite shoulder from the other one, hovered into view. It contained orderly rows of red and white stripes and white stars resting on a blue field.

Harrison's eyes widened, and he listened again to the soldier's directive.

"Identify yourself."

Managing a relieved smile, Harrison said, "I am William Bernard Harrison."

One of the soldiers stepped forward and unlocked the handcuffs from Harrison's bleeding wrists. The other two soldiers slung their weapons over their backs and lifted his body out of the chair. Harrison groaned and winced.

The soldiers halted their movements.

"Oh no," Harrison said. "Don't mind me, let's keep moving. I'm very anxious to get out of here."

Two miles away, on a ridge overlooking the North Range complex, Holcomb and Ritter lay on their bellies and peered at the scene through night-vision binoculars. Paratroopers continued landing, forming up, and moving toward buildings. Flares propelled into the night sky, their combustion casting glimmering halos onto the airfield.

"What exactly is happening down there?" Holcomb said.

Ritter held the binoculars away from his face and said, "Half the journey, my friend, only half the journey."

"Half the journey? What the hell does that mean?"

The Colonel pushed himself onto his knees, and then rose to his feet. As he brushed off the front of his uniform, he said, "Your government has faltered along the way, but now, what you see before you is hopefully a return to the path that will guide it toward its proper horizons."

"My government?" Holcomb said, his eyes locking onto Ritter's. He remembered what Harrison had asked Taylor back in Los Angeles. "So, you're the Russian spy."

At first, Ritter said nothing. Then, the right side of his mouth twisted up a little, and he said, "Actually, I'm Byelorussian." He pulled a Colorado Rockies baseball cap from his back pocket and slipped it on, saying, "But I call Denver home." He turned and walked toward the Humvee parked in a dry creek bed below the ridge.

"Wait up."

"No," Ritter said, stepping into the vehicle. From inside, he helped Ridley to exit.

"No?"

"It is time for you and Officer Ridley to return to the base. You will be safe there now." He patted Ridley on the shoulder and helped him to zip up a heavy, green winter coat.

"But where are you going?"

Ritter responded by starting the Humvee's engine and releasing the hand brake.

"But, we'll need your help," Holcomb said.

"I hope I can help further, comrade." Ritter smiled and gazed overhead. "All of us should contribute. It is our responsibility, and for me, that responsibility transcends borders or lines on a globe. Taylor understands this; that's why I cooperated with him, and why he didn't betray my identity when he discovered whom I really worked for. Or used to work for, anyway. I know you and Harrison will also understand."

"You've protected us. We'll never forget that."

Ritter put the vehicle into gear and said, "Others may find it difficult to reconcile my status with what has transpired. Much still has to change. When, and if, the time is right, I will return. But remember this, Art and Nick: I am a friend. Dasvedania."

A medic wrapped a final bandage around Harrison's wrists, and then walked over to a paratrooper who had broken his ankle after an awkward landing in one of the runway's blast craters. As Harrison sat in the first-aid station, which soldiers had hastily set up along a row of benches in front of the command building, he watched a helicopter make a boisterous landing on the nearby tarmac. Soldiers rushed over and ushered or carried its occupants toward the security wing.

Wrapping a wool blanket around his shoulders, he caught the scent of a burning cigar.

Hmm, a fine Cuban.

From behind, a friendly slap landed on his back.

"How you doing, sir? I understand you're William Harrison."

Harrison turned and looked up at the large, solid soldier standing next to him with a cigar dangling out the side of his mouth.

"Yeah, that's me."

"Very good, sir. I've got someone here who's been asking about you. She told me we might find you here."

The soldier stepped aside, allowing Harrison a view of the person. She held her head low, looking hesitant about approaching him. "Janice," Harrison said, struggling to his feet. "Please, come here." His smile and words drew her closer, into his arms. The big soldier marched off in the direction of the security wing, his beefy arm around the shoulder of an elderly man in a white lab coat with gray flyaway hair. Smoke trailed behind them.

Harrison relaxed his hold and looked into Janice's *beautiful* blue eyes. "It's okay."

Her eyes softened, and she hugged him again. "I'm so sorry, so sorry." Janice tilted her head up and stretched to meet him, but stopped short of touching his lips. "I'd kiss you, but I'm afraid I'd hurt your face."

Smiling, Harrison bent down and pressed his lips against hers.

Rescued from their cells too, Taylor and Maggie soon joined them. A nearby paratrooper sergeant alleviated the group of their momentary confusion and concerns about Holcomb. He advised them a mobile air-traffic-control unit had picked him up in the desert and was returning him to the base along with a wounded man named Ridley.

The trooper then said, "We've commandeered a medevac chopper, and our orders are to airlift all of you out of here. The chopper is warmed up and ready to go. Follow me, please."

As they climbed aboard the aircraft, a navy-blue vehicle rolled to a stop nearby.

Holcomb jumped out and leaned in to help Ridley exit. Bracing Ridley, Holcomb took a few short steps with him toward the helicopter, and then stopped as Harrison joined them.

"They are going to fly us out of here. Do you want to go to the infirmary instead, Nick?" Harrison said.

Ridley shook his head. "No, get me out of here."

"You got it, Nick," Harrison said.

One on each side of Ridley, Harrison and Holcomb took him one small step at a time toward the helicopter. Above them, disguised in the black, star-filled sky, the two F-117's passed by just low enough for the sound of their jet engines to make their presence well known.

"Whatever you did to arrange this," Ridley said, "I am grateful."

"Me too, Bill," Holcomb said. "You really aren't as dull and useless as everyone says."

"Thanks, buddy."

As they reached the helicopter, Harrison held onto Ridley as Holcomb piled in and scrambled to a seat next to Maggie, saying, "Happy New Year, everybody!"

Ridley eased himself inside. Taylor and Janice, who were closest to the door, helped him into an empty seat and strapped on his seatbelt. Harrison jumped in next and took a seat beside Janice.

The paratrooper sergeant slid the door closed and signaled for the pilot to take off. Wedging himself closer to Maggie, Holcomb started to say something, but she interrupted him.

"You, my friend, need a shower." She rubbed dust and grime from his balding scalp, and then kissed the top of his head.

"I'm glad you made it, Art. I knew you would," Harrison said, nodding at his friend.

Holcomb smiled, saying, "Well, buddy, we had some help. You're not going to believe what I have to tell you." He winked at Taylor, who nodded his understanding.

Harrison glanced out the window at North Range. "At this point, Art, nothing would surprise me."

The chopper ascended, and Harrison wrapped his arm around Janice, pulling her close. She leaned against him, and felt, *at last*, her fear and loneliness slip away.

The End

AUTHOR BIOGRAPHY

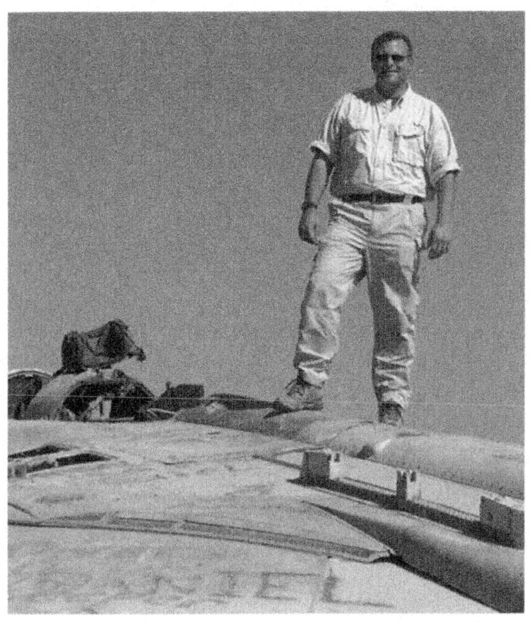

Daniel P. Douglas is a novelist specializing in conspiracy thrillers and science fiction. His first novel, *Truth Insurrected: The Saint Mary Project*, centers on a decades-old government cover-up of contact with extraterrestrial life. Other upcoming novels include The Outworlds series, which is comprised of science fiction adventure stories set in the early twenty-fourth century at the fringe of human civilization, and *Green Bird*, a modern-day thriller about an FBI agent racing to stop a cyber terrorist before it's too late.

Douglas is a US Army veteran and long-term civil servant who worked in the federal government and the museum profession. Born and raised in Southern California, he has lived most of his life in the southwestern United States. He now lives in New Mexico with his spouse, children, siblings, parents, pets, and livestock. His travels take him throughout the United States, Mexico, Europe, the Middle East and the Caribbean.

ᶜIA information can be obtained at www.ICGtesting.com
ᵗ in the USA
ʼs1457310315

V00017B/1132/P